POWERS OF EUNOIA

By: Daze Evander

POWERS OF EUNOIA

The characters and events portrayed in this book are fictitious. Any similarity to real persons, living or dead, is coincidental and not intended by the author.

Copyright © 2023 Daze Evander

First Edition: September 2023

ISBN-13: 979-8-9854845-6-4 (Paperback)

ISBN-13: 979-8-9854845-7-1 (Hardback)

ISBN-13: 979-8-9854845-8-8 (eBook)

Library of Congress Control Number: 2023907805

Published by Faction Realm Press

www.factionrealmpress.com

I've been told it's unhealthy for the mind to stay focused on what you've done that you regret, but instead on what you choose to do after what you have done. I've been told that's what matters.

If you don't control your mind it will control you.

Thank you to absolutely everyone who has supported me and this dream, it has meant more than I can actually put into words.

To my entire family: I will love you all forever.

I will never forget any part of the beautiful journey in creating this story so far and I hope it inspires your mind.

What follows is part three of my series: EUNOIA.

- DAZE EVANDER

"It was actually peaceful and beautiful outside. The sunlight shone through the bushes and trees that created unique and lovely patterns engulfing us with calming ORANGE tones. I let out a deep breath and allowed myself to take in the moment I was living in. This was something I'd neglected to do for a while and knew I needed to slow down and put my mind at ease at the fact that we were all alive and safe... for the time being."

- AMIRA, CHAPTER 1, COE

CONTENTS

LIST OF ACKNOWLEDGEMENTS:

Front and Back Cover: JAMES CHILD

Character Portraits: KEVIN SARDINHA

Planet Map: GAINDDHO

Series Editor: MICHAELA DELANEY
- THE WORDSMITH EDITORIAL

eBook Formatter: SHOAIB SHAHZAD

Music: DUSTIN GILL - DRAWN TO THE SKY

Cover Animator: EIRA STUDIOS

Sending out a never-ending thank you for the extraordinary contributions that you all have made to this project. Thank you so much for helping me bring my vision to life. Your artistic skills, imaginations, and polished insight shine brightly. Your work and creativity is truly out of this world.

You all are so talented and inspiring to work, dream, and create with. Thank you for being so thorough and brilliant in all that you did and collaborated with for this book series. It has truly been an honor to be able to make my dream of EUNOIA a reality with you.

- DAZE EVANDER

PLANET MAP

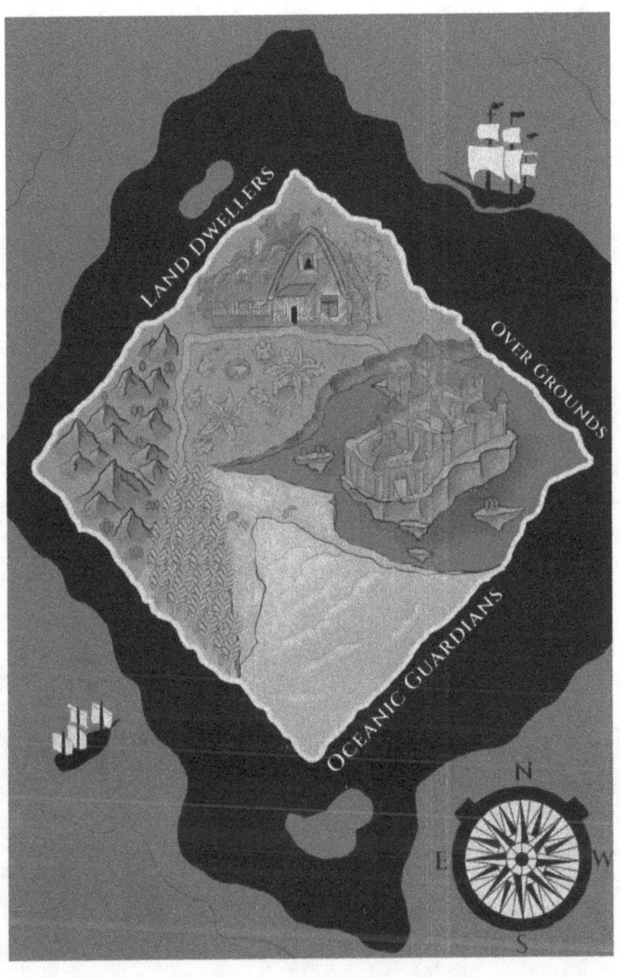

PROLOGUE

A STORM WAS IN FULL MOTION ON PLANET EUNOIA AS
the ocean roared and lightning flashed with rainfall
scattering across the waters. Zayika mustered enough
strength from within to bring both Anon and herself to
safety. The milky clouds watched as she bent over and took
him securely into her arms. Each thigh-high boot was filled
with cold, salty water, and her wet hair fell down far past
her waist. The other four, Amira, Zekiel, Saige, and Omar,
watched anxiously from the shore as he coughed and laid
tiredly over her sturdy arm. She took determined steps in
her sleek white dress when it finally became shallow
enough to stand on her feet in the sand after fighting
against the currents. Each dark magenta colored hair
strand cursed her dreams with a distorted reality. Her mind
still tried desperately to see what was in front of her,
figuratively and literally.

Zayika looked down at Anon as she spoke, "I'm right
here. I've got you. You'll be okay."

He had tears in his eyes as they glistened up at her.
"Z-Zayika?"

"I'm right here," she repeated gently and kept her grip
on him anchored.

"You just saved my life! How could I ever repay you?"

She paused for a moment before answering him in her
thoughts, *please don't ever leave mine.*

CHAPTER ONE: A BEAUTIFUL MISTAKE
Before CARRIERS OF EUNOIA

ONE DAY A CONSCIOUSNESS SPAWNED INTO EXISTENCE in the form of an unusual uninhabited planet with many similarities to Earth. It was divided into three main sections that consisted of the land, water, and sky, with a dwelling space designed for humans at each. The ocean's tides were also controlled by the moon, which possessed a gravitational pull with a power that could not be contained. The leaves of the jungle's trees sparkled and shone brightly in the sunlight during the day and were hardly visible when night fell. The clouds above would sometimes emulate the ocean's waves or become somewhat of a spectator to oversee what was taking place by forming into multiple layers of large, uncanny eyes.

For some time, no one had touched, seen, or even heard of the planet's presence. It was also not aware of itself as each day and night passed, time slowly slipping by in the quiet and peaceful environment. Not a single word had ever been uttered into its pure and blameless atmosphere. The vegetation of each empty faction was thriving and healthy, along with the cluster of unique creatures who inhabited the dangerous ocean. There was stability in the calmness, the untouched, but there was also unknown potential for what the planet could be used for.

One day, this all changed, along with the lives and minds of many. The story begins at a small town's waterfall where what was originally intended as a blessing, created and tailored specifically towards the purpose of strengthening humanity, became something sinister.

"If there is a gateway here… please open up," a person spoke from behind the waterfall with brevity. "Change is needed here… please allow it to happen. Please open up the mind's gateway. Give us another chance." They dropped down to their knees on the wet, rocky foundation and placed a hand onto it. "I need a fresh start, to right my wrongs and to find my purpose."

The woman began to cry softly as she pulled out a bottle from her backpack. The glass was filled with a toxic substance capable of bringing out the worst in those who drank it. It was a bright red color, the same red as her hair.

"I know I'm not the only one who needs my mind renewed." In a desperate attempt to connect to nature and discover inner peace, she let her tears fall as the water in front of her did the same. "Test my strength."

She took off the bottle cap and began crying harder. With hands shaking, she stared at the opening and watched on to see if she was strong enough to leave it alone. "If t-there is a gateway here, please o-open," she said again, completely oblivious to what she was asking for.

As she forced herself off the ground, a single tear fell into the drink. She looked down into her pocket to grab two pills, one white and one pink, that sat there and dropped them inside the bottle. They began to dissolve rapidly. Then the cap was put back on. The shade inside was the exact color hex #BB4B89. Arcadia left the bottle at the falls accompanied by a deep sigh. "I'll finally get rid of these. Maybe this will make room in my mind for peace."

She walked away from the waterfall empty handed and with somehow even more tension and brain fog than before. What she couldn't see was a glistening light shining in the water behind her. The woman wanted to never look back, but unfortunately, that wasn't meant to be due to the frightening string of events that began occurring there. People were going missing around three weeks later. Then murders started being committed, and no one else in the town knew why. She didn't understand why either but knew deep down in her gut she had caused something to go very, very wrong.

Arcadia was a crime scene investigator unable to truly escape her past and kept returning to the one place she always wanted to leave behind. The memory of what she once was became unbearable, and so was living in the reality of an aftermath in which she was reminded of each life she negatively affected because of one decision.

She could've moved away and worked somewhere else but decided not to. Her life's goal became a desperate search for answers in trying to solve the waterfall's mystery and to absolve her mind of the strongest emotion of them all — regret.

One Week Later

Theia, Aadavan, and Lorelai lived in the very same small town as Arcadia and managed to get themselves into exceptionally unbelievable situations. Each around ten years older than her, all in their early thirties, were risk takers who willingly chose to visit the waterfall as much as possible. The three were constantly searching for a greater meaning in all that was said and done in the world, seeking out inspiration and hidden meanings within life; fueled by a strong sense of urgency everywhere they went. This led them to throw caution to the wind often. Aadavan was the self-elected leader of the trio who always kept them on their toes as they never knew what he would say next. Lorelai tried to keep the other two grounded and safe, almost always in a constant state of worry. She couldn't hide her concern even if she tried her best to. They made plans to meet at the captivating falls again which eventually became the usual spot to discuss their dreams.

On one particularly eerie day, their typical conversation became far more interesting than normal. Lorelai was recalling one of her dreams to Theia as Aadavan wandered off. He also listened as she went into detail about how vivid it was to her, that it almost seemed tangible. Something was caught in Aadavan's peripheral vision near the flowing waters. He moved his luscious black curls out of the way to get a better view of what he found as Lorelai continued detailing what she remembered from the night before.

Aadavan soon interrupted her as he excitedly grabbed and brought over a beautiful, handcrafted glass bottle that contained a mysterious red substance. Something about it was instantaneously captivating to the three, especially to Aadavan, who curiously gripped it in his hand. They'd never found anything at the waterfall before, but believed one day they would come across a piece of tangible proof which would help them discover part, if not all, of their true destiny. That day had finally arrived.

Aadavan was the most thrilled to discover what was inside. The other two were more cautious at first, both suspicious at how enticed he was to tamper with it. His eyes couldn't stop staring at the liquid as it sloshed around. It was as if the glass had some sort of drug laced on its surface, seeping into his fingertips past each layer of skin and casting a spell directly into his bloodstream. He expressed wanting to take a sip of it to see what would happen.

"One day your luck might run out, Aadavan," Lorelai initially tried to warn him. "Be careful where you choose to disperse what of it you have left."

"Are you kidding?" He put a hand up to his chest. "This find is one of the most interesting things we've come across in the last few weeks! I would most certainly take the risk to find out what it can do. Of all places to discover this, there must be a reason why it's here!" He swiftly twisted the cap off and put the bottle up to his lips, taking a swig without thinking longer about potential consequences. It seemed that his actions weren't completely his own.

"That's gross." Lorelai stated with disgust — something she would forget once the bottle eventually landed in her own hands.

"How do you feel? What did it taste like?" Theia felt a desire to try it too, as usual following Aadavan's suit. She enjoyed the adrenaline rush of experimenting to test the limits of their bond and trust with one another. "May I get a closer look?"

He handed her the bottle. A borderline haunting grin spread across her face as the colorful glass touched her skin. She couldn't resist taking a sip too.

"What do you think?" Aadavan asked after wiping the glowing liquid off of his lips. "This must've been left behind recently."

"I'm not sure." Theia paused before trying more of it.

"You both shouldn't be drinking this." Lorelai's hands were shaking.

My intuition isn't ringing any alarm bells, Theia thought to herself. *Everything should be fine. I've followed my instincts up until now and look at how far we've come.*

It was freezing cold outside as the three ended up sitting in a circle in front of the tall and spectacular rushing waterfall. They lived in a town with several small and narrow roads that were inhabited by an ever-smaller number of people, with what they felt seemed to be even narrower minds than the roads they hardly traveled on.

They felt led to one another by a greater force, something that couldn't be seen or directly spoken to. Time they spent together felt surreal because it didn't seem to exist when their conversations were overflowing with visions and dreams for a future they couldn't completely comprehend.

"It's okay Lorelai. Take your time," Theia reassured her. "These types of choices can take some time to make, more than most allow themselves before making hasty decisions."

Aadavan let out an impatient sigh. "Why waste time? This is a simple choice!" Each word flew out of his mouth before he thought of them at all.

They both looked at Lorelai, who anxiously shivered against the wind. Countless trees towered over them as a light rain fell down.

I love the rain, Theia thought as she put her hands out in front of her and felt the little droplets hit her steady palms. *I love how it feels when it touches my skin.* It made her feel powerful, something about observing the sky; everything about it. Throughout her entire life, she always felt connected to the cotton clouds above, creating lively shapes, and the refreshing rain which routinely healed the aftermath of droughts.

"The thing is... I can drink it too." Lorelai's short platinum blonde hair was getting wetter with each passing second. "But this choice cannot be undone. You know?"

Theia was still holding the bottle. "Can you imagine a world in which each one of us truly tries to pursue our purpose? What would that be like? If we actually faced and shaped our own destiny? What would it be like if we didn't ever regret any of our past mistakes?"

Lorelai shifted back and forth uncomfortably. "What if we get sick?"

"Do you know how productive society would be? If we became truly aware of the power our minds' possess?"

"What if this drink kills us?"

"What if we are all much more powerful than we realize?"

A loud crack of lightning filled the air, the waterfall becoming deafeningly loud at the same moment. Theia's heart pounded in sync with the booming thunder.

"What if that was a sign?" she asked. "From the universe?"

"I think it was a sign for you both to stop having separate conversations at the same time." Aadavan got up from the ground hurriedly and yanked the bottle out of Theia's hold. "I'm going to speed this along."

"But, Aadavan, you…" Lorelai stopped herself from speaking further, noticing his expression had changed from excitement to irritation mid-sentence.

"I'll show you how it's done." He started to chug the drink as they watched in awe at how easily he was downing it.

"It's so bitter." Theia said. "I wonder what it will do?"

Aadavan smiled. "What's the worst that could happen? Something in life could change?" He handed the bottle to Lorelai, who mistakenly took it into her grasp without thinking twice. The spell immediately entered her bloodstream.

"Change isn't always a good thing, but at least we'd all be trying it together, I guess," and she drank from the bottle too.

Soon, they each became gravely ill. They held onto their stomachs and groaned in unbearable pain. It was abnormally cold outside as they grew sicker. Raindrops raced each other to reach the Earth's surface as the wind blew so roughly that leaves were being torn off of the tree branches. Aadavan felt the worst as he'd had the most to drink. He was desperate to make the sinking feeling in his stomach go away and began cupping his hands under the flow of the waterfall.

"No, Aadavan, don't drink that either!" Lorelai groaned. "What if it also has harmful effects?"

"Like I care?" he responded. "We were supposed to drink what we did. You felt led to partake in it as well. Lorelai, why try to make it seem now like we don't have good judgment?" Aadavan became defensive.

"Do you both see that person over there?" She suddenly looked worried and tried to hide behind a large nearby boulder.

"What?" Theia spun to see who she was talking about.

No one else was at the falls—Lorelai was beginning to hallucinate. She rubbed her eyes in disbelief.

"I just saw someone! Right over there!"

"What did they look like?"

"There was a woman with silver and purple hair."

Flashforward to CHP. 3 of ECHOES OF EUNOIA

Zayika and Anon were brought to one another, feet apart on the starting hills in a state of confusion as to where they had been taken. Anon woke up first and looked over his hands, legs, and body. He pinched at his skin to see if he was still dreaming or not.

"Where am I?" He took in the sights of countless hills as he stepped across the one he was on. "Who is over there?"

He noticed a woman sleeping and went over to where she was lying. She had straight silver hair at the top of her head that gradually became wavy and faded into a memorable shade of purple. She opened her eyes slowly and saw Anon's face staring at her as they focused on his features.

"Hey." His heart fluttered with excitement. "I'm Anon." He reached his hand out to help her off of the ground.

"Um… hello?" she replied in a bewildered tone and refused his help, instead standing on her own. "Who are you?"

"I wanted to ask you the same thing." He grinned apprehensively. "I'm not sure what we are doing here."

"Me either." She shuddered.

"Are you okay?"

"Yeah. My head just… I have a headache." Zayika put her hands on either side of her head, her white nail polish glistening in the sunlight.

"Nice nails. I hope your head feels better soon," he told her kindly.

"Thank you."

"I was actually just dreaming before I woke up here. Pretty painfully."

She lost interest in his words and instead took in the scenery. "This place is beautiful."

She stood up past Anon, and he noticed that she was taller than him as she straightened out her posture. "It's nice to meet you," he told her and started biting on his lip.

"Guess I should ask what's wrong with you?"

He didn't think she would take notice of his rising anxiety. "What?"

She pointed to his lips and looked at them intently. "You're stressing out. Chewing your lips."

"Yeah." Anon looked at the grass to avoid eye contact with her. "I do that sometimes, and I'm kind of trying to keep it cool right now. How are you staying so calm?"

Zayika didn't know why she was so at ease, but the headache forming in her head was too distracting for her to worry about much else.

"Intuition, I guess." She inhaled sharply through her teeth. "My head hurts, like, really bad."

"Let's try to find some other people and figure out how to get back home."

Her eyes darted over to meet his as he looked up at her, his black hair falling near his brown eyes. "What is your name?"

"Anon," he replied. "You?"

"Zayika," she stated confidently. "My name is Zayika."

"It's nice to meet you."

"Likewise."

A small spark of electricity ignited between them as they shook hands. They stepped away from the other.

"That was odd." He waved his hand around from the shock.

"Well, wherever we are, at least we found each other." Zayika's voice was comforting as she spoke, "We can figure out where we are and get some help."

"Definitely."

Their attention was caught next by two other people making their way towards them from a different set of hills off to the right. One was a man with blonde hair and the other a shorter woman who walked next to him with black hair, both swaying at shoulder-length.

Anon started waving at them. "Let's go see who they are. Maybe they know what's going on here and can help us."

Zayika gave him an alarming smile, her eyes threatening. "Are you going to let them down, too?"

He felt his chest tighten as a sinking feeling hit his gut. "What?" He was freaked out by her sudden change in expression.

"You know what I'm talking about." She got up in his face as it flushed red. "Are you going to screw them over, too? Like you do to everyone?"

"What are you t-talking about? I don't even know you!" he stuttered.

Zayika put her pointer finger up to Anon's face and tenderly dragged it along his cheek. He shivered at her touch. Her white nail polish turned into wet paint that left a trail on him. "You will have to suffer the consequences of your actions. It's such a shame how much wasted potential there is in you."

Every ounce of him went into fight or flight mode. "Excuse me?"

"You almost have it all… but don't have what it takes."

He felt the urge to run away from Zayika. "How about you leave me alone?"

"Go ahead and try to run, Anon. The great thing about regret is that it will always catch up to you, no matter how far and long you run. Go ahead. I'll see you later."

Anon suddenly woke up in a cold sweat next to Amira. "Are you okay?" she asked as he sprang forward, promptly waking her up.

"I-I'm fine. Just had a bad dream."

"You're okay, Anon, we aren't on that planet anymore." She wrapped her arm around him and pulled their blankets in tighter. "What was your dream about?"

"Zayika; she was in it."

Amira could feel his heart racing as she laid partly on top of him. She tapped her fingers on his chest lightly. "Really? Zayika? Why?"

"That's a great question." He sighed deeply. "It's like I can't get her out of my mind. Even when I'm not thinking about her, it's like I am subconsciously."

He felt Amira pull away as she got off of him and flipped around in the bed. "Alright then."

"What's wrong?" he asked. "I was the one who had a nightmare."

"Didn't seem like one."

"What?"

"Doesn't matter." Amira faced the other side of the room instead of facing him. "You just keep bringing her up."

"I mean, can you blame me after what happened?" Anon was distraught. "Why are you getting upset like this?"

"Just forget it. I'm going back to sleep." Amira huffed as she grew envious. "Why don't you say hi to Zayika in your dreams for me?"

"Really?" his voice broke. "I-it's not like that, alright?"

Tension grew thick in the air as he sat up and kept his attention focused closely on her. She was withdrawn for a few moments, and he waited in suspense, frustrated at how he had been misunderstood. He fought off seeing flashes of his dreams that Zayika continuously invaded, desperate to convey to Amira how real they felt.

"Then what is it?" she asked defensively.

"She's haunting me." He glanced out the window and noticed what seemed to be a pink outline glowing in a soft blur around the moon. "Do you see that outside?"

Anon lept off their bed and tugged to completely pull the curtains open. He pointed at the second circle and his finger nervously hit the glass.

Amira sat up to see what he was referring to. "What are you talking about?"

"Look! Don't you see that there? Around the moon? It looks like…" *Her hair color.* The thought sent pins and needles along his skin. *Zayika's everywhere, isn't she? Is she somehow back here on Earth? Is she going to force me back to Eunoia?*

"You don't see how concerning this is, Anon?" Amira got out of bed with an exaggerated sigh to walk over to the bathroom. "Why are you thinking and talking about her so much? You decided to leave her behind. Why don't you actually do that then?"

"Amira, please listen to me! My intuition is telling me that something is not right, it's not okay, her words were a curs—"

"Your intuition also told you to leave her! Maybe your judgment really is so awful, Anon! Maybe you really cannot make decisions under any pressure at all!" she cut him off and immediately paused in her steps towards the doorway. Amira looked down at the ground and shakily held onto herself with both arms. "I'm sorry for speaking to you that way, it's just th—"

He rashly chose to hurt her with disingenuous words in the same way hers got under his skin, "Maybe I should have picked Zayika instead of you."

She left the room with tear-filled eyes and slammed the door behind her. Anon briefly thought about his parents and how many times he'd heard the door slam with pent up emotion as he grew up—feeling and seeing a poisonous wedge being driven between the genuine love they once shared deeply for one another. Each year as he got older, the wedge widened and eventually split the bond he innocently believed as a child could never truly be broken.

Their marriage was ultimately destroyed by miscommunication and unhealed trauma that Anon watched unfold as his mind developed, observing and learning what love looked like between the two people who gave him life.

He went to close the door, his hand hovering over the handle as he almost spoke. The words were stuck in his thoughts. Anon fearfully kept them to himself.

Amira, I'm so sorry for how this seems. I think I'm cursed. I didn't mean what I said. I'm just scared, but that doesn't mean I don't love you.

I love you.

Theia

Present

"You're hallucinating?" I asked Lorelai, who was swaying back and forth. I went over to check on her while fighting off the feeling of vertigo slowly creeping up on me.

"All will be okay. Just stay calm." Aadavan jumped in as he attempted to stay still. "Where did that woman go?

The one you saw, Lorelai? The one with the colorful hair? Who could she be?"

"I don't know!" Lorelai panicked. "She just disappeared!"

We three stumbled around, stepping on dirty rocks and snapping stacks of small tree branches as we restlessly tried to get comfortable. There was a great deal of unease brewing inside of me. I felt that something was taking a hold of my consciousness and draining all of my energy to replace it with something else. I dizzily darted my eyes between the swaying trees, Aadavan's were planted on the waterfall itself, and Lorelai was worriedly watching the small figures of other people in their cars driving past the parking lot with crossed fingers, presumably wishing no one else would come across us in our inebriated state.

"We will be alright." Aadavan breathed heavily.

I could sense that he was deciding to let go of his fear. Whatever we drank was providing him with the courage to carry himself with the utmost confidence and curiosity to find what the unknown held for us. Reality slowed as I faltered in my steps. I walked over to him, tripping on myself before he caught me in his strong arms. His words were reassuring and his presence mesmerizing as he held onto me. I began to fall deeper into the spell.

A new type of energy was breathing life into me. The clouds traveled gracefully in the sky, and I could see various colors flicking within them, greenish purple mixed with a dominating orange lighting up above us. I couldn't resist making and maintaining eye contact with Aadavan. His long, curly hair fell onto my shoulders as our arms wrapped around the others' in a beautiful embrace.

"I feel powerful," he whispered in my ear.

"You are powerful," I quietly told him something I'd always known.

The two of us watched Lorelai in silence as she paced around and looked over her shoulder. "What if we aren't alone? What if that woman reappears?"

"You need to relax," Aadavan told her, his voice stern. I felt him tense up behind me. "You're stressing me out, Lorelai, and I would like to enjoy whatever this feeling is."

She spun in a circle and placed a hand to her mouth, motioning for us to stay quiet as she crept closer to some of the trees. "I just saw someone."

"Let me guess, it was that woman with the dyed hair again? Silver and pur—"

"Red. Her hair is red." Her eyes anxiously followed a mysterious figure sidestepping in the shadows.

Is she hallucinating? Or is someone else really here? Are they watching us?

The clouds seemed to have stopped moving in the sky before falling downwards. Some sort of rare anomaly was happening right in front of us, as if part of the sky was breaking open into something else.

"What's happening?" I asked the other two, Aadavan stepping away from me to investigate the clouds.

We watched as a grouping of them came together at eye level and began spinning around in a circle. Oranges, greens, and a hot pink vibrancy merged together to create a gorgeous medley of colors. It seemed that a piece of the sky was opening through some sort of portal which invited us to step in. The hole that widened from within revealed an unfamiliar place on the other side of it.

"It's some sort of gateway!" I could hear in Aadavan's voice how joyful he was.

He always said we were meant for something greater than this life on Earth. This may be it, the opportunity we always dreamed about. Is this some sort of sign? A chance worth taki —

He interrupted my thoughts as he shared his own out loud, "There are no such things as coincidences."

"I'm not sure exactly what we're looking at," Lorelai stated.

"Maybe we should find out where it leads?" I suggested. "What's the worst that could happen?"

CHAPTER TWO: GHOULISH

Aadavan

Present

A phenomenal portal began opening right before our very eyes as the ground rocked beneath our feet. A habitual visit at the falls on a stormy day had turned into a once in a lifetime opportunity to travel directly into a dream come true. I stood in wonder at what was before me. We all had to cover our ears as a giant hole seemed to form out of the clouds and eventually merged downwards with the waterfall. The sound was overwhelming in the best way possible. Swirling stars and droplets of water were in a mesmerizing mix which led to an opening that grew large enough to step into. From where we stood, we began to see an ocean through the other side. Wind blew harshly against the heavy rainfall. The risk worth taking was fleeting. Temptation to cross through whatever was in front of us became irresistible.

"What is this?" Lorelai asked timidly.

I glanced over my shoulders to make sure no one else was watching from afar. Thankfully, we seemed to be the only ones there.

We have to keep this a secret.

I was fascinated at the thought of jumping into whatever was in front of us, risking our lives and potentially completely changing our future.

"We should go in," I told them.

"No." Lorelai put her arm out to try to push us away from the portal.

"What are you doing?" I snapped. "Don't touch me!"

"Aadavan, relax! Don't speak to her that way." Theia gave me a disappointed stare.

"I can defend myself." Lorelai crossed her arms.

The entrance to whatever unknown world was on the other side of us looked like it was starting to shrink in on itself.

No! It's closing! We need to go inside before it closes completely! What if we can't open it again?

My thoughts raced faster than the rain drenching the three of us.

"I'm going in!" I started to step forward.

Lorelai grabbed my shoulders and frantically yanked me backwards. Both of us slid and fell painfully onto the muddy ground and bumpy rocks that covered it.

"No!" she shouted at me over the sound of the waterfall and mystifying gateway.

"We are running out of time!" I promptly wrestled myself away from her.

"I don't care! We could die if we go in there!"

"She is right!" Theia stepped in between us. "This could be a terrible idea!"

My frustration with Lorelai—and with Theia for not siding with me—was growing by the second.

I'll just do this myself, alone, like everything else in life. Even when they are right beside me it's as if they are not by my side.

I tightened my fists and clenched my teeth to try and refrain from saying something that would hurt either of their feelings, but it felt impossible. Too many times in life had I missed out on taking chances because I was fearful of what others would think. I needed to uncover the unknown on my own accord.

"The two of you are useless without me!" I maintained eye contact with them. "I don't need either of you! I never have, honestly, and I can discover for myself what's on the other side of that portal!"

"What? You don't mean that." Theia replied.

"Of course, I do!" *I don't, but I'll say anything to be left alone! Push them away!* "I've always been the strongest, wisest, and most deserving of greatness! Neither of you have anything to offer; all you do is worry about the most pointless things! Lorelai, you are too scared to actually live, you're pretty much a complete waste of life! Theia, you constantly run your mouth and manage to say nothing at all! You talk so much that neither of us get to ever share what we think! You stand in my way and create walls that keep us from succeeding! Well today my words are my hammer and the wall you made to hide behind is getting knocked down! Get out of my way!"

Lorelai looked away from me and instead at Theia as her eyes filled with tears.

Theia walked over to comfort her, her piercing brown eyes fixed on me. "Are you sure this isn't a rash decision?"

"What you call a 'rash decision' I call undiscovered destiny!" I laughed. "You both can't see things how I can. You just don't understand! I'm going in! If we are meant to cross paths again, then we will!"

I can't believe Lorelai is crying. My head, and heart, ached as I stomped away. *I've never made her cry before.* I clenched my teeth. *What if I don't come back? I should at least apologize.* My attention was focused on the portal again and how its passageway was slowly growing smaller. I kept my eyes on it, though I could hear them talking behind me.

"He said we are 'useless'!"

"It's okay." Theia was holding back tears too, I could tell by how shaky her voice was. "I don't think he really meant what he said."

I felt consumed by an unfamiliar fire from within and swung around to face them as my skin stung with rushing blood, shaking with rage. "Yes I did! You both only waste my time and squander opportunities!"

Suddenly, a strong current of energy ran through me and down into the ground. Everything nearby started uncontrollably shaking.

"What's happening?" I kept myself from falling over by steadying my hands on both knees.

"You're doing something, Aadavan! Look at your feet!" Lorelai pointed at my shoes as the patterned lines blurrily vibrated.

"You started an earthquake!" Theia couldn't hide her excitement as her attention shifted over to the portal. "It stopped closing... Aadavan... like it's..."

"Waiting for us to go inside," I responded peacefully.

My mood just flipped as fast as a light switch. Why? I didn't feel like my usual self as I extended my arms outward.

"Why are you motioning to us?" Lorelai looked fearful next to Theia as she shivered in the cold rain.

"Because it's time for us to go where we belong. It's time to finally start our story, the one we deserve, whatever that means for each of us."

Theia showed intrigue, Lorelai was visibly afraid, and I was downright euphoric.

"Maybe we should go." Theia was also drawn to the entrance.

"Really? Am I the only one thinking clearly here?" Lorelai started to back away.

"Yes," I spoke softly. "You are the only one thinking and you should stop. Stop thinking and instead start seeing what could be on the other side of your own thoughts."

Theia nodded as if my words had cast an irresistible trance on her. "I want to go with you Aadavan." She stepped over to me and took my hand in hers, my other one still empty as we simultaneously shifted our gaze to Lorelai.

"Ugh..." She anxiously tapped her foot against the swampy dirt so hard it caused mud to splash up into the air. "Just, why? How do we manage to get ourselves into these types of situations? Continuously?"

"You're doing it again." I told her.

"Doing what?"

"Thinking."

Theia chimed in, "Let's stop thinking."

"Fine." Lorelai's eyes widened as she let out a deep breath, evidently trying to relax, which was a rarity for her. "Let's stop thinking."

For a minute, the only sound was the rain hitting the ground, all three of us rapidly exchanging glances with one another. I felt like she was fighting the urge to come with us, barely able to hide that she wanted to join.

"You can go without me." She tried to act uninterested. "I'll stay and wait for you to come back. I'll just wait and then you can tell me about whatever it is you find."

"Please don't test my patience," I told her and felt Theia's grip tighten slightly. "I-I mean, it's up to you and we will—"

"Respect whatever decision you make," Theia thankfully finished my sentence. "You have every right to decide, and we'll support you either way Lorelai."

She bit her lip and chewed on it for a couple seconds. "Okay. Goodbye. I'll miss you, and I hope you'll be safe."

"We'll miss you too." Theia motioned at me to start walking ahead.

"Bye," I said coldly.

She should be coming with us! I just know that she's supposed to come along too! Theia ruined this!

My thoughts ran rampant as we walked towards the ocean through the spinning portal ahead of us. The unthinkable happened after stepping inside with Theia. We entered into the purest form of and state of true consciousness. I could feel how mutual it was in the air. We became extremely aware of our existence and fueled with the drive to seek out, reveal, and subsequently pursue life's true purpose. We could hear the portal closing as our feet hit the warm, untouched sand of an entirely new and undiscovered planet.

Then, a somehow even more unthinkable event happened. Lorelai placed her hands on both of our shoulders right as we stepped off of Earth together. She had finally stopped thinking so that we could finally start doing just that.

Three Weeks Later

The three had unknowingly signed into a lifelong agreement to become the representatives, morphed beings with extraordinary capabilities far beyond their wildest dreams and nightmares. They were in awe of what was around them. After exploring the ocean shore, they made their way to what they found to be a field of wheat. The dry stalks were taller than they'd ever seen, and feeling like needles dropped into a giant hay bale, they were cautious and careful to keep track of where they'd already stepped to not get lost. They eventually came across another area filled with seemingly never-ending green hills which varied in height and width; the grass covering them was thick and well-watered.

The reality of how much their lives had changed became apparent once their initial shock wore off. The realization that they were unsure of what to do sunk in; *how could they use the magical abilities they had been given? Would they ever be able to return to their previous lives again?* They felt it was natural to divide everything into three sections, each getting their own, and name their newly made factions. Aadavan became the representative for the Land Dweller faction, Theia took on the Over Ground faction, and Lorelai was left with overseeing the Oceanic Guardian faction.

A large structure was erected in the jungle. It was covered in overgrown plants and had several rooms inside. Aadavan thought about how he could be a leader to his own group. The urge he felt within him to discover his true purpose in life had grown substantially since the waterfall.

He examined every inch of his new terrain, making mental notes of the specific types of plants he found along the way. He had an insanely sharp photographic memory which allowed him to truly take in his surroundings with a heightened level of attention to detail and accurate memories.

Aadavan spent a great deal of time at the pond close to the edge. He studied the murky water, rocks, and whatever seemed to be growing on them. Specifically, he noticed how special they seemed to be, especially the large stone slabs in many of the indoor rooms.

A human body would fit on this nicely; what would happen if someone were to lay on it? These must be tested. I can sense purpose here, he thought.

He noted almost every detail about the area around him, but he almost missed one very important thing, and it wasn't until he paid closer attention to the tangled moss at the farthest end that he noticed something shining within it. He gently moved it away to uncover a small baby crocodile with purple eyes. It looked as though it had been born not too long ago and was already malnourished.

"What are you doing here?" Aadavan spoke to it. He was very surprised and thrilled to find a creature living in his faction. "We need to feed you something, don't we?" The crocodile allowed himself to be picked up and was taken into the jungle's main headquarters. Aadavan was excited to show Lorelai and Theia and see their reactions.

"Look what I found!" he shouted out, his steps moving quicker on the grass.

The two were surprised by how worried he seemed to look as he approached.

"What's wrong?" Lorelai dropped the wood she was shaping to meet with him faster as Theia trailed behind curiously.

"I found something! Look!" He pulled a hand away to reveal the fragile crocodile tightly held in his other one. "Look at his eyes! Aren't they magical? What a lovely color."

"That's so strange." She was taken aback by light beaming out from its face.

"In such a fantastic way, right?" Aadavan glanced at Theia. "What do you think we should name him?"

"I don't think we should at all," Lorelai responded again.

"It wasn't you that I was asking," he said as politely as he could. "I was asking Theia. So?"

"I agree with Lorelai. We should be careful. Make sure he doesn't bite you. The poor thing looks like he's starving."

"What does naming him have to do with nursing him back to health?" he asked.

"Don't get too attached. That's all." Theia lightly brushed her fingers over its head. "Just in case he doesn't survive."

"Well, he will. We just have to feed him." *Maybe he'll like some of our food that we've found. The castle and tree house may have more resources we've yet to discover.*

"This crocodile must've been born recently." Lorelai stared closely at it.

"I'm not sure what he will eat. There doesn't seem to be a whole lot else living here besides us." Aadavan stated loudly.

"We'll figure something out. I'm sure there's even sea life in that massive ocean that we will eventually learn much more about in time." Theia responded.

"But will it be safe? What if something bad happens? Like after we drank the liquid? What if we get sick aga—"

"Lorelai…" Aadavan spoke slowly.

"What?"

"It would be nice if we could enjoy a moment without resorting to worrying, you know?"

"I'll work on that."

"I hope you do."

Theia stepped aside and spoke, "I think we need to shift our attention to more important matters. Like bringing other people here to inhabit this space with us."

Lorelai grew confused. "'Inhabit'? Do you want others to live here with us? Like creating a community?"

"Yes."

"No." Aadavan cautiously placed the crocodile on one of the stone tables in the middle of the room. "I don't think that's a good idea."

"For once I really agree with Aadavan," Lorelai responded.

He smiled. "We need to bring people here to compete in a game of life or death."

"Oh, there it is. Never mind. Theia, your judgment is better, as usual."

"Wait, Aadavan, why did you say that?" Theia couldn't help but ask for more information from Aadavan, someone who was bold enough to challenge her own ideas.

"I feel as though the planet has been speaking to me lately," he started to explain.

"Let's hope it doesn't have a mind of its own," Lorelai grimaced.

"Of course, it doesn't." He threw a hand up into the air and continued, "A game where the mind's power is tested. Those who survive will go back to Earth. Society will be improved. We could appoint others and help them find the path to their destiny."

"You said 'death'… I don't want to kill other people." Theia leaned her back against the closest dusty wall.

"When did I ever say that we would?" Aadavan smirked. "They would be killing each other."

Lorelai crossed her legs uncomfortably. "You can't make a game out of life."

"Life already is one back on Earth, and death is promised either way there too. We need to begin bringing others here. It's time."

The three eventually started to interact with any of the plants and objects they could find, searching for a way to call other people who were back on Earth over to the waterfall portal. Almost everything they tried did nothing but create exhausting confusion and frustration as the days drew on.

"I need to step outside for a moment," Theia said, exiting her faction's castle.

She looked over the floating platform's edge and ignored the vertigo that hit her as she watched the patterns that the waves created in the greenish blue ocean below. The air was fresh and flowing in rushing gusts of wind, filling her lungs as her mind started to feel empty. She closed her eyes and steadied herself on both feet planted firmly on the layered rows of grey cobblestones.

Theia felt peaceful, thoughtless in that moment as a shining light started to glow from the tip of her pointer finger. Though she didn't see what was happening outwardly, she felt inside that something was changing. Another type of energy was entering the environment.

Her eyes flew open at the sensation, the light already extinguished as she caught sight of a man standing in front of her. He had dark hair, full lips, and a chiseled jawline. Slightly taller than her, he looked down at her perplexed expression.

"Where am I?" he asked.

Theia was shocked to suddenly see another person speaking to her face. "You... this is a new planet."

He rubbed his eyes and walked in a circle to look around, taking in every bright color. "What?"

Her finger stung as she placed her hand into her pocket. "You aren't on Earth anymore. You have a new purpose now."

He was hardly given a chance to react or speak before Theia stepped closer to him without warning, and without consent, she placed her hand on his chest, directly over his heart.

"Please don't touch m—" he began to say, but his words were cut off by a bolt of electricity that flashed through her hand and into his back.

"You will assist me," she told him.

Flashforward to CHP. 4 of ECHOES OF EUNOIA

Amira was fast asleep next to Anon, back on Earth together. He would frequently battle between trying to get some rest and keeping nightmares of Zayika at bay. He woke up with sweat all over his face and a heaving chest, her voice taunting him like it did at least once every single night.

The two of them struggled with feeling like it was only just them, that somehow in an unnatural way Zayika was there too… and she was always dissatisfied and on the brink of releasing all her pent-up frustration and sadness she had buried inside. Falling asleep was like entering a minefield for Anon, as he never knew what each night's nightmares would bring.

Amira laid next to him as the hours and panic attacks came and passed too fast for them to count. Thoughts concerning Anon's wellbeing and safety would weigh down on her mind often in a way she wasn't familiar experiencing with anyone else besides him.

Her empathetic side was deep and ran into her core as she closely meditated on and tried to understand the meanings and motives behind most of what he'd say or do. She felt how his energy would shift throughout the day, feeling especially upset for him if something stressful or unfair happened.

I'm glad we left Zayika behind — it's where she belongs, she thought to herself. *I just wish he would stop thinking about her so much, I mean… really? She only causes trouble, and I knew it since the moment I met her.* Amira tossed and turned in their bed as moonlight crept through the curtains. *Just as the moon controls the waves. She's no different.*

She kicked the blankets off as her body temperature rose. *She threatened to kill me.* Her heart began pounding. *She said she would kill me. Is she going to?* Amira clenched her teeth. *What she said on the canoe…* Her hand flew to the other side of the mattress, and it was met with cold fabric. Anon was gone. *Was it somehow true?*

A strong current wrapped around her body while she was still in bed. The dark room around her flipped upside down in her dreams and began filling with water. She was rapidly consumed by the ocean deep as she took a breath to hold in. *What is happening?*

She held in a scream as the bed she was on suddenly plummeted downwards, frantically holding onto the wooden beams and clawing her nails into it to grip tighter. The moonlight from above was becoming blurry in the distance as she felt the weight of water crashing around her and items from the room swirled past her quickly. She kicked her legs in a panic as everything began sinking, as if a giant sinkhole had appeared beneath her.

Everything shook and rattled as Amira was yanked further into the deep with everything else like she was entering a pressurized vortex. *Anon!* She thought she was having a night terror. *Anon! Where are you?* Her own thoughts were screams in her mind as she came to the stark realization that she was awake, not drowning, but returning to her morphed state and to the one place she never desired to see again.

Planet Eunoia.

I cannot believe this! Anon was right! Amira felt a regretful lump form in her throat as she realized the truth behind his vague and eerily unforgettable words about Zayika. To her unfortunate astonishment, his worries concerning a curse-like hold she possessed were true and taking a complete toll on their reality. *Please tell me he is safe! I shouldn't have doubted him! What was it he really saw around the moon?*

Her orange tail covered her legs, eating away at each layer of skin as they were soon replaced with countless scales. She shuddered at the feeling of her body changing against her will again and at the cold abyss' presence and unseen depths that engulfed her. *Try to stay calm!* Amira could hardly fight against the current that kept pulling her down like there was a massive drainpipe in the ocean's floor. *Please! Anon, someone, help me!*

Her hands were out in front of her, pointed upwards as brightness started to come into view, like a strong beam from a massive lighthouse. The light was a bright white with what she instantly recognized was a tint of a distinct greenish-blue. Her brown eyes widened. *Hippo?*

Within seconds, the very tips of the anglerfish's teeth sprawled out into different directions, surrounding Amira. She let out the breath she was holding as her companion dove down to get her, pulling her away from the nightmarish undercurrent of the sinking ocean. Hippo swam quickly to bring her out of harm's way and into what normally would be the safer parts of the waters, but in this case safety was very, very far away.

As they rose out from the waters together, her on top of the fish, she could hear a familiar shrieking voice call out to her distastefully, "Amira?"

Zayika had her fists clenched as a loving smile spread across Anon's face beside her, venturing towards them at the shore.

"What's going on?" Amira asked. "How am I back here?" *Anon?* She coughed up some water from her anxious lungs as her stomach tightened. *Oh no… Zayika?*

Anon stood up and waved his arms to get her attention as he yelled, "Amira!"

"I might as well have fun with this." Zayika was clearly blindsided and unsure of what to say in the moment, her previous excitement now challenged by the startling oceanside entrance by her former foe.

"Anon! I'm not dreaming, am I?"

"Unfortunately, we aren't," he responded. "I'm right here. Sta—"

But Amira could hardly hear what Anon said as he held her in his arms and intrusive questions seeped into her mind.

Will Anon forgive me for how I've treated him? What are we going to do to survive? How was Zayika able to bring us back here?

Aadavan

Present

"Let me try to get this straight." I paced back and forth at the Over Ground's courtyard with Lorelai, Theia, and by some miracle another person from Earth. "You're telling me that you are able to make others appear here with just your finger?"

"I suppose so," Theia responded too calmly for my liking.

"I-I mean, the man over there is proof enough. The man that none of us know! How in the world did you accomplish this? Who is he?"

"I don't know how I brought him here. I just meditated."

This is incredible. It's no longer just us three. Soon, there will be many more people here. We will create a game unlike any other.

"Ahem," the stranger cleared his throat. "You don't have to talk about me as if I'm not right here."

"No, Theia, I don't think it was simply meditation." I ignored him briefly. "It was man—"

"Manifestation," Lorelai and Theia finished my sentence at the same time.

"Well then," he interrupted our conversation again, "may you please manifest me back to where I came from?"

"Of course not." I wasted no time in letting him know where his place would be. "You're here for a reason, and you aren't going back to Earth until it's fulfilled."

"We don't even know if we can go back to Earth." Lorelai started tapping her fingers against one another nervously.

"You can't keep me captive," he tried to tell me.

"Yes, I can."

He squared his shoulders and stood taller, the yellow speckles scattered in his eyes catching the light. "Send me back right now."

"We don't know how to do that." Theia went to step closer to him.

"Don't come near me." He started to back away. "Don't touch me! I don't want to be kept here. I don't know any of you!"

I was astonished, and somewhat startled, at how steady his voice was despite the recent turn of events.

"Or what?" I couldn't hide my grin. *If I have to use force to get my way, then I will.*

"Do you really want to try me?" he asked aggressively.

"Take that energy and put it towards bringing others here."

"You mean kidnap them? Yeah, I'm not doing that for you."

"You do not have a choice in this matter," I informed him politely. "What is your name?"

"Cloudburst."

I laughed. "You don't have to go by a fake name here."

"It isn't fake." He moved towards me to whisper, "But the importance you seem to think you have is. You should drop the tough guy act because it won't get you far. Now send me back home."

For a moment, I was too stunned to speak. *Excuse me? Who does he think he is?*

"Let's make a deal. Can we compromise?" Theia's expression lit up.

"What?" Cloudburst spun to face her.

"If you can successfully bring back someone else from Earth… then we will let you go back to your life there."

He furrowed his eyebrows as he thought.

Absolutely not. What a terrible idea. There's no way we will ever possibly let him go if he can accomplish that for us. Even if she can bring more herself, we need him to stay. What if the others he brings back don't have the ability to do so themselves? He has to stay.

"Fine," he agreed with a frown.

"Lorelai, why don't you keep Cloudburst company for just a little while? Try to not stress him out too much, you know?" I swiftly grabbed a firm hold of Theia's hand and pulled her off to the side with me. "We need to talk."

"Without Lorelai?"

"Yes, because she doesn't need to hear this, I'm just—"

"Going to scold me."

"'Scold' you?" *Is that what she thinks my advice is? Scolding? I don't mean it that way.* "No, I'm just really worried about the promise you made to Cloudburst."

"Why? It was a compromise, not a promise." She patted my shoulder with affection. "We can break a deal."

As more time eventually passed, we tried to complete two tasks simultaneously. One of them was trying to get the reptile to eat something; attempting to catch any small fish seemed nearly impossible in the ocean, and it was as if he simply wouldn't eat anything at all. I was very concerned about saving his life, knowing that he must have some sort of purpose that maybe we weren't fully aware of yet.

The other task was trying to strengthen the people who were brought to the planet. Cloudburst was able to bring them to us, which was fantastic, but in trying to reduce their panic and distress, we attempted to morph them right away in our respective faction's grounds.

I would take them to my stone beds and have them lay down, and Theia would put them into cylindrical chambers made of glass, where they were nearly suffocated by the air in it before they became one with it. I wasn't entirely sure of how the morphing process worked in Lorelai's faction, but I assumed that it was probably the least pleasant of the three.

I looked over at the pile of dead bodies from those who didn't survive the harrowing ordeal. A grim feeling sat in the air as misty clouds covered the sky, a strikingly and otherworldly shade of green. Cloudburst clapped meekly at my side.

"Look how your decision turned out," he spoke vapidly. "How many people have died now? And for no reason at all? Not like there is a good reason for someone to die anyway."

"I believe in the death penalty," I told him, not taking my eyes off of who we had lost.

"Who would say such a twisted thing in this situation?" His arms were crossed as he started to step around me, trying to make me feel bad about my judgment. "Has anyone ever told you three how psychopathic you all are?"

"I think that sometimes nature decides who lives or dies, survival of the fittest." My eyes followed him as he marched around in a fixed path. "Our decisions can result in consequences like the death penalty."

"These people never agreed to come here!" He was getting angry. "They were forced! They would still be alive if you hadn't forced me to go get them! So, can you explain that to me? Huh? What's your name again? Aaron? Andrew?"

"Aadavan."

"Okay then, Aadavan, how about you explain why you think they deserved to die. How does your messed up mind justify it?"

"They were either guilty by association, at the wrong place at the wrong time, or it was part of their fate."

"Forget this. I'm out." His voice deepened, "I did what you asked of me, and it didn't work out, but now you have to keep your word and send me back."

"Not until you bring someone who can survive here," Theia added.

"That was never a part of the deal!" Cloudburst shouted back. "You can't start making up rules now!"

Suddenly, a faint crunching noise came from our left.

"Where is the reptile?" Theia asked, and my thoughts started racing.

Where is he? He can't be far! I just had him nearby! I started to look around when, to our horror and astonishment, the crocodile had run over to the deceased and started feasting on pieces of their flesh. It was almost as if he was getting bigger and stronger before our very eyes with each bite he took.

"So…" Lorelai spoke first. "What if the crocodile only eats humans? We've tried everything else."

"It's as if the planet has spawned its own living graveyard." I shook my head. "How are we going to keep this monster fed?"

CHAPTER THREE: SEA DEVIL

Lorelai

Present

As Aadavan and Theia discussed the next steps to take with the crocodile and man from Earth, I decided to explore the ocean. I left the Land Dweller faction and took my shoes off to walk over the sand. *This is beautiful… but I'm a bit disappointed that I have the least amount of land.* I spotted a canoe out on the waters but not much else. There was no castle on the shore, unlike Theia and Aadavan's dwelling places. *Unless…* Unsure how it hadn't crossed my mind before, I questioned if there was something in the depths below that was concealed from the naked eye. *There has to be a lot down in the water. It must be unsafe to venture down there though, right?*

The waves rose and fell soothingly as my breath fell in unison with them. It took a leap of faith for me to decide to explore whatever was lurking underneath the water.

I truly had to push myself further out of my comfort zone than I'd ever been before, but I found the strength to journey forward. *Find out what lies below.* I walked close to the water's edge. *Aadavan and Theia don't need to know that I'm going in.* I chuckled. *They may not believe me when I tell them that I did. I bet they think I'd never make a decision like this on my own. The joke is on them.*

As I treaded lightly into the ocean, I felt a nipping at my toes and heels. Bubbles burst around my feet as I went in further. *Are those sand crabs?* Scales started growing on my skin, stinging my pores. I scratched at them, trying to tear each one off as they appeared. *Get off of me!*

I felt sick to my stomach as the second half of my body went numb, and I hit my head hard as I fell onto the sand. My legs were changing into something else right in front of me. *No, make this stop! What is going on?* A particularly large wave swallowed me up and pulled me into the ocean. I screamed and scratched at the shore desperately as if a giant had me in its strong grip.

"Theia! Aadavan!" I called out desperately. "Help!"

My blood curdling screams rang out as their figures approached in the distance. They threw their arms in the air and started shouting, but I couldn't hear what they said as I was pulled into the waves. My head was completely engulfed while I let out one last muffled scream, the bubbles from it spewing out in front of me. I kept getting dragged deeper down like an anchor was wrapped around my waist.

I was taken down to the ocean floor, where it was pitch black. *Someone please save me! I'm going to die here!* I'd held my breath for far longer than normal, and it felt like my lungs were about to collapse. *I'm going to die!* I was down so far it felt almost impossible to try to swim upwards. *Please, not like this...* I couldn't move my legs. In fact, they were no longer there, replaced by a large tail that felt like heavy rubber. *What's happened to me? Why? Someone save me, please, please fix this!*

I felt the water vibrating around me, getting closer and closer. *I'm not alone.* I felt lightheaded as I sensed a creature's presence directly come up to me. A massive aquatic monster that was most likely mutated similarly to the crocodile that Aadavan found. *It's going to swallow me alive if I don't do something!* Almost instinctually, I started to move the currents of the water, gradually pushing whatever was lurking nearby further from me as I became more determined to survive. It started to make a jarring clicking sound from its massive mouth, but it was so hard to see anything that I had no idea what type of sea beast was trying to attack.

"Go away," I managed to say out loud in the water, even though it seemed to be filling my lungs.

As it swam away, a new one appeared, lighting up the way. She was a tiny anglerfish, her green scales slightly translucent, with a small shining orb that stemmed out from the middle of her face. She had several little pointy teeth and fluttering fins on either side of her. I gently put out my hands to touch the fish's head. She backed away slowly with a surprising growl which produced a high-pitched beeping sound. The bulb in front of her glowed brightly as she kept squealing.

"Hey, there," I spoke to her softly as her big, glossy, marble eyes stared at me curiously. *She's so cute in an odd way. I wonder how big she will grow to be? Maybe she will stay this size.* "You're okay. I'm not going to hurt you. Why are you here?" I asked her, in awe of finding such a unique and rarely seen creature in our new planet's ocean. Though, to my misfortune, the anglerfish wouldn't stop squeaking and swimming backwards. *I don't want to draw any other creatures here with all of this noise!* I pulled my hand away, hoping that would calm her down, but instead she got even more upset with me.

"What's wrong?" I asked as she kept panicking. Her growl became ear-piercing. "Please stop!"

The miniature anglerfish suddenly sprang forwards with its jaw extended. Before I could fully process what had happened, I saw a cloud of my own blood in the water, illuminated by the fish's light. My arm stung, a chunk of flesh torn off. Each of her teeth left marks deep enough to scar my flesh permanently.

I should've just left her alone!

I put my hand on the wound and pressed down as hard as I could.

I have to get back to the castle and take care of this.

After my blood had spread through the water, her appetite grew, and she started feasting on the other creatures in the ocean, somehow able to catch up with and even eat those that were bigger than her. With every single kill, she grew exponentially in size, even right in front of me. I could hear her attacking, then eating her prey while I stayed in the castle. She hunted the most during the hours of the night, which made it difficult for me to get proper rest. The anglerfish kept growing and growing, and as it grew, so did the intensity of its radiant bulb.

Flashforward to CHP 1. of CARRIERS OF EUNOIA
SPEAKER: Anon

"Let's meet halfway then." I was so excited to find another new person as I traveled with the four I'd met and tried my best to lead the way. We began approaching someone off in the distance by the green hills. Stars shone above us as I saw her for the very first time. "Who are you?" I yelled into the night.

"I'm not here to hurt you! I'm lost and looking for safety," she replied with her hands up. "Can any of you help me?"

I was in awe of her as she walked towards us. *Say something.*

"I'm Anon. It's honestly very nice to meet someone else." *It's very nice to meet you.* I caught Zayika staring at me in my peripheral vision. *What does she want?* "I heard you're also looking for help? I have with me Saige, Zekiel, Omar, and Zayika who I met earlier. We all ran into one another and have been traveling as a group, wandering aimlessly for what has felt like forever. What's your name?"

"I'm Amira. It's nice to meet you too." She shook my hand and looked at the others. "I'm glad to meet you all as well."

Maybe she knows something that we don't. "Do you have any idea where we are or what's going on?"

"Unfortunately, I don't. I was going to ask if any of you did."

"We're just as clueless as you seem to be, sorry." *Ugh, why did I just call her 'clueless'?* "We've been trying to get our hands on some weapons along with shelter, food, and water."

"How long have you been walking exactly?"

"We've lost track of the hours now. We woke up on these hills and have been without a clue ever since. I'm not sure where we are; I don't even think we are on Earth."

"You don't know that for sure," Omar interrupted.

Please shut up, Omar. I thought to myself. *She's not talking to you.*

"My intuition is telling me otherwise." I couldn't keep myself from biting my lip as I looked at Amira's body. I'd never seen a woman as beautiful as her before.

Zayika rolled her eyes.

"You don't have any weapons, do you?" I changed the topic before Zayika opened her mouth to say something embarrassing.

"No, I don't. Why?" Amira was worried by my words.

I pointed to the jungle. "We've heard some fighting, people yelling at one another, specifically in that direction. I feel like we need to be able to protect ourselves in case anything bad happens." I couldn't hide my interest in her as I continued speaking, "Do you want to join us?"

Please say yes.

"Sure, it's better to travel as a growing group than to do it alone, right?"

Present

The planet didn't want those brought to it to work together. It wanted them to face their own destinies, shaped and determined by the choices they made, by themselves. It was given the most energy through Aadavan's existence when the three representatives were morphed because of how much he had drunk, which meant it took on his most dominant trait of stubbornness.

It also paid attention to the words he would use in his mind to justify his choices and make change happen, specifically the ones he thought were best no matter what it took. It began thinking for itself, questioning all who inhabited it and how to get its way. After it spawned, it needed a host who could be a catalyst for uncovering a greater purpose and carrying out fate, and through the very specific color hue she dyed her hair, Zayika was cursed under its command even before she woke up on the soft, grassy hills.

There was a sequence of letters and numbers carefully carved into the bottom of a stone that it formed by itself. One day, it was pushed upwards through the ground in the Land Dweller's faction so that plants would eventually grow around and cover it, similarly to a skull protecting a brain.

It didn't want the representatives to know of its decisions and truths, but it was unable to activate itself if they weren't exposed on its surface. It chose its name—EUNOIA—and those who it brought to the hills; the final six to eventually compete in the second and final game. For the six individuals, there were six letters. For their five abilities, there were five vowels. Similarly to the ridges of a brain, there were words engraved on the stone that outlined the planet's truth.

It wasn't pleased. Rage was born and growing at what the representatives were doing to its land. Frustration was created out of their morbid curiosities and experimental approach to life. It thought about the lives that were also brought by their choosing, not its own.

The term Wish Carriers was coined by the stone as it developed, shaped to describe those who could supersede the rules and torture that Theia, Aadavan, and Lorelai created. Those with the ultimate gift carried a wish of unfathomable power to decide what would happen in their life. They would be able to create their reality, ultimately dreaming and manifesting what would unfold next.

#BB4B89 was written on the bottom of what resembled a cemetery headstone. The color hex began to weave its way into all life forms and energy sources. It infiltrated its forces of nature. It seeped into corrupting the original intended purpose of the space. Just as the waterfall's substance took over the three representatives, the color-coded curse entered the planet's mind, unable to win against its corrupted influence.

CHAPTER FOUR: GREEN HILLS

Cloudburst

Present

The representatives didn't, as they say, "morph" me… not entirely at least. Theia talked Aadavan out of torturing me like the others. He wasn't easy to forget. He was constantly trying to tell the rest of us what to do. I was held captive by three monsters in an unknown place that they'd claim was an entirely new planet. They were doing some type of twisted experiments on other human beings. I was brought to one of them out of nowhere and against my will. I'm not sure what Theia did to my body when she touched it afterwards, but it had never been the same since.

They forced me to go back to the waterfall on Earth where I was taken from and kidnap others to bring to them. Now I know what you're probably thinking… you might be wondering why I didn't try to escape while I was on Earth and the representatives were still on their planet. What a bright idea, which was of course also too good to be true. They… shocked me when I tried to run away. Some sort of invisible collar had been placed inside my neck. I couldn't escape their command, no matter what I did or didn't do.

I followed their original orders and started forcing others to the place I wanted to leave so desperately. They were all tortured and killed, their corpses devoured by a reptile. Every single life weighed on my mind, the weight of regret quite unbearable to carry. I tried to think of new ways to escape every single day, but most of them required me to step far out of my own moral boundaries.

Only Theia can send me home, but even if she felt led to, I doubt the others would let her. She gives them too much power over her emotions. I have no chance.

So many people died on the jungle's stone slabs, the castle's glass boxes, and who knows how many more down in the treacherous waters below. Aadavan, being how he was, just couldn't stop despite how awful their experiments were. Thankfully, they didn't try to morph me as they did to the others. I was only afforded this stroke of luck because Theia had appointed me to be her right-hand man. I was sent out to Earth to retrieve the people that Lorelai claimed to see in visions, which I personally believe were hallucinations from whatever drugs the representatives were using and becoming increasingly dependent on. Since I was important to them, risking my life in order to steal others', they didn't want to accidentally kill me too.

People kept dying on the rocks over and over again in dreadful and unimaginably barbaric ways until one day things started to change.

The representatives asked me to go out and get someone for them, a tall man that Lorelai said she kept seeing in the messy snake-like vines of the jungle. I had no choice but to agree to this request, and Theia transported me back to the landmark site in a split second with her fingertip. It was nighttime when I arrived, and the air was bone chillingly cold.

I can't believe I'm doing this. I have to find a way out of their grasp.

Trees swayed in what seemed to be slow motion. I wished that the representatives weren't watching my every move, that I could get away and have my freedom back, but they were speaking too many words without any actions to support their claims. They lied about sending me back to Earth after bringing more victims here. I should've seen that coming. It felt as though any time I confided or had trust in someone else, I ended up regretting it.

No more regret, not any longer. Whoever I'm bringing from here tonight needs to join forces with me. If I can convince someone else to work with me, we may be able to escape.

Who I ended up stumbling across in the neighboring woods of the waterfall was a man bundled up in what seemed to be several layers of jackets with big, dirty boots on. I watched him from afar for a little while as I tried to figure out what he was doing there so late in the night.

Why is he walking back and forth between those two trees over there like that? It sounds like he's talking to himself too. What could he be saying? Why do I have to do this at all?

I maneuvered my feet carefully over the dirt and fallen branches to get closer and hear what he was saying better.

"I swear the storms have been so bad lately," he grunted. "When will it ever stop? The rain, the thunder, the chaos. I hope I don't get struck by lightning one of these days."

How am I going to convince him to keep his mouth shut and help me when we are back on the planet? Maybe if I try to discreetly explain to him what's happening to me he may listen. He could assist me in finally escaping... Or he'll think I'm insane.

I looked up at the sky and somehow felt the representatives watching what I was doing.

They can see me, but I don't think they can hear me. I guess I'm going to find that out.

I breathed into my palms and rubbed them together.

Please, please don't hear me.

I knew that taking a chance by telling the other man what was going on was my best bet at getting rescued, but I had to play along with the others' plan for a little while longer. I knew that if I tried to simply escape to the parking lot, alone or with anyone else, they would take matters into their own hands, which I'm sure they'd use to kill each one of us. I had to play my cards carefully. One wrong move meant unimaginable consequences.

"Hey you!" I called out after the man.

He stopped in his tracks and stiffened his stance. "Yes?"

"We need to speak. It's urgent."

He waved for me to walk over to him. "Why are you out here? This place isn't safe for the public."

"I'm in danger. I was kidnapped," I spoke quickly and made sure to not act in any way that would draw suspicion. "You need to go along with what I say. Please help now and ask questions later. My name is Cloudburst. I'm sorry, but that's all I can tell you."

He nodded.

"I'm sorry for anything I do that may be uncomfortable." I tried to forewarn him for what was coming next. "There's somewhere I have to take you or else I will die, we both will, but once we get there, we can devise a way back to our freedom. Just go along with whatever I say when we get where we're going. We don't have much time, and I cannot answer any questions as we are both currently being watched."

"What do you mean?"

I grabbed him by the wrists and yanked his arms up towards the sky as a worried feeling built up in my stomach. "I got him!" I yelled.

Theia began teleporting us back, a bright light engulfing our bodies from the ground up.

"You lied to me!" the man shouted as we started to teleport. "What's wrong with you? How dare you trap me! Get away from me! You lied!"

"No, I didn't!"

"Yes, you did!"

Ugh, he doesn't understand! Hopefully he will hear me out later. If not? I may have really made a mess of things.

We were brought to the planet in an instant.

"What is the meaning of this? Where have you taken me?" he asked from beside me.

Theia was making her way towards us, slowly approaching over a particularly large hill.

She teleported us close to Aadavan's faction. The stranger distanced himself from me immediately with rushed steps.

"Just trust me, okay? I'm the only one here that you can trust," I tried to tell him.

"You're mistaken! I trust no one. I'm very selective if I do."

"That's a good thing, and if you have any will to live, you need to listen to me before she gets here. We are not safe. There are three leaders here who are trying to control us."

He sharpened his defenses. "How do I know you are not lying to me?"

I sighed. "I wish I could show you the shock collar they forced in my neck so you could believe me. I don't know what faction they will put you in, they each have one, and they'll attempt to mutate you. They're forcing people to fight here. We need to escape."

"I'm not sure I can believe you."

How can I convince him?

"Well, who is it that we have here?" Theia's voice drew nearer. "I see you are speaking to our newcomer, Cloudburst. I'm sure you are sharing words of welcome, but that is not needed. We must retreat to the castle at once. Not another word may be uttered by you."

I looked down at the ground and felt the stranger's stare on me.

"What is this?" he asked her with a hollow expression. "What is going on?"

"I'll answer your questions soon. If you try to get any information, or try in any way to escape, I'll make sure my assistant here electrocutes you to make sure you behave."

He saw how serious she was, his body going rigid with fear.

The two of us were commanded to the platform that brought us up to her headquarters. We were eventually forced to start traveling on foot towards it. Theia walked behind us dominantly, her pointer finger slightly outward with what looked to be a small light bulb inside of it, shining through her skin. Our trip was short lived, though, as Aadavan interrupted us not long into it. Before he approached, I tried to mentally brace myself for what was coming next.

I'm going to be forced to bring others. When am I going to get the chance to speak with him or anyone else that can help me?

I had no other choice but to follow the representatives' strict orders. I tried my best to not learn or remember the names of those I took from the waterfall. Even back at the faction grounds, I tried to speak as little as possible to everyone. I didn't want to get my feelings involved, and knowing their names made it that much harder to live with myself.

Lorelai, Aadavan, and Theia had been discussing some type of "game" that they wanted the victims to play. I knew they were trying to keep me from hearing their conversations about it, but with how high their emotions typically ran, it was nearly impossible to not eavesdrop with them speaking so loudly to one another.

They were plotting something that would end up causing trouble, forcing others to partake in an unethical competition. I needed to get as far away from them as possible and figure out a plan with the new arrival, I just had to get a chance to further explain my motives to him. Since I first heard the three speaking quietly in strained voices about "showing people their true destiny," I felt something horrific draw ever nearer.

We have to outsmart them in some way. There has to be something we can do to get back to Earth. I really hope he will listen to me. I have to explain myself, this all looks so wrong.

As I got closer to the castle with Theia and the stranger, knowing I soon had to set out on another waterfall abduction yet again, Aadavan stomped over us, fuming with what seemed to be uncontrollable rage.

"Do you know what's going on?" he asked loudly after the rising platform landed on the ground in front of the gates.

"What are you talking about?" Theia responded, turning her attention away from the platform.

"At the hills!" He threw his arms up. "People are waking up on them!"

"What are you talking about?"

He kept his voice raised, "Exactly what I just said! Random people are spawning on the hills, the green ones. You know what I'm talking about, don't you?"

"Aadavan, please calm down."

"You need to come look for yourself at what's going on because I'm pretty sure you didn't cause it."

"Okay." Theia looked at me. "We'll take Cloudburst and our newest member with us, and we four can see what's going on. Lorelai is down in the ocean, I presume?"

"Of course she is," Aadavan replied matter-of-factly. "Where else would she be?"

I'd be really irritated trying to put up with this guys' attitude as much as Theia does.

We left the Over Ground's faction as they spoke to one another. The unnamed man remained extremely quiet, timid, and withdrawn. *How is he staying so silent? Why does he seem calm?*

"It's as if something in the air changed," Aadavan stated.

"I feel the same way too. Isn't that odd?" Theia asked while looking up intently at the sky. "Do you also sense that we're being watched?"

"Since yesterday? All the time."

A shiver ran down my spine.

"Something is different."

I chimed in, "Maybe because of the people you've cursed by bringing here."

Aadavan shot me a dirty look. "Don't speak about what you don't understand."

"Don't try to silence me." I met his energy.

"Both of you, please don't fight with one another." Theia redirected our attention to moving forwards. "We have greater matters to worry about."

"Yes, we do, like taking care of this new fighter right here." Aadavan put a hand on his shoulder. "He will be in my group. Let's find out if he will take to this place before we get to the hills. Those who've arrived won't be going anywhere. I have no idea how they'd go back to where they came from."

We ventured over in the opposite direction, retracing our steps across the divided terrain and past the vegetation of the land group. Aadavan took the stranger into his treehouse and did a number of things to him in there, I'm sure it was torture, but he called it 'morphing'.

I heard his screams echo from the open windows, even though I was a fair distance away outside. It was so awful that I had to cover my ears, trying to muffle his screams for help.

I hate feeling so powerless.

They left him on one of the rocks to rest. He'd apparently survived whatever Aadavan did to him and was trusted enough to be left alone there. I looked forward to crossing paths with him again so that we could try to strategize a way out of the mess we were in. I expected to see him soon, but until then, I had to go along with whatever the representatives said they needed help with next. I had to keep my mouth shut long enough to stay out of more trouble.

It was especially difficult to not say anything when we approached the group of people who were still half-asleep on the grass-covered hills. They were spread out and calling out at each other, trying to figure out where they had been taken. There was a bigger overarching question, though, that was silently asked by Theia and Aadavan's reactions—how exactly had they gotten there? Because she nor I had anything to do with it and most certainly neither did Aadavan.

"I really hope something beyond our control isn't happening." Aaadavan frantically tapped a foot on the ground.

We stood far enough away from the strangers so that they didn't notice us watching them.

"Too late for that." Theia crossed her arms. "I didn't bring them here."

"Maybe it was somehow Lorelai," Aadavan suggested.

"I doubt it. She didn't seem to be given the ability to teleport people."

It was obvious how Aadavan couldn't help but be slightly annoyed with others who made a valid point which refuted his own.

"Well, whatever." He crossed his arms the same way she did.

"Let's just try to look at this as a good thing. We needed more people, right? Well, we got them. It will speed along the process for pursuing our…" Theia glanced at me nervously for a second, "…our plans." Her voice lowered as she turned towards Aadavan.

"Alright, but something feels suspicious. Like another energy is trying to prove a point." He shook his head.

"Maybe I'm overthinking things. Hmm. Lorelai might be rubbing off on me too much."

The two let out what sounded like forced laughter.

"Speaking of her, after we start getting the people out here situated, we need to inform her of what's going on."

"Of course."

They looked at me and spoke in unison, "Go get more people while we handle things here."

Then Theia lifted her finger.

I was back at the waterfall in the blink of an eye and in desperate need of a plan or miracle. I followed the instructions I was given with no missteps. I figured that I would be let free sooner if I played along with their mind games.

I won't be stuck in this dreamworld forever. I have to believe I can get out of it one day. If I lose hope, it will be over for me.

I spotted the next victim out of the corner of my eye.

I have to do what has to be done no matter what.

Flashforward to CHP. 1 of CARRIERS OF EUNOIA

"I don't understand. Where are we?" Saige woke up near Zekiel on the starting hills. "What happened?"

He suddenly sat upright, "What?"

"Look, Zeek, how did we get here?"

The only thing she could see was hills on either side of them with what seemed to be nothing else nearby. For a bit of time, she felt like they were the only two people in existence. *Is this a dream?* Saige grabbed at her skin. *But Zekiel is here?* He ran his hands over his shirt as she kept her attention on him. *I have to be dreaming; we're just in another dream together.*

He stood up and noticed two people to their right; Anon wearing entirely black clothes and Zayika with her silver purple hair standing out against everything else.

"There are other people here, wherever we are," he told her sheepishly as the haze of his tiredness was just barely beginning to taper off. *I feel miserable. Where is Jasmine?* His chest tightened as he remembered and looked at his friend with worry. *Why is Saige in this dream with me? She shouldn't be here... I do not understand what's going on.*

"Zekiel, are you okay?" Saige helped him stand.

"I'm alright." *I never am.* "How are you though?"

He looked over her head and body, softly checking over her shoulders and legs. *Nothing can happen to Saige, nothing bad.* Zekiel didn't want the attention on himself and redirected it whenever he could to his closest friend.

She smiled at him tenderly as he looked after her. *I have to make sure he is okay.*

"I'm doing alright, too. Feeling a bit... off," she told him. "I had an unnerving dream."

"What happened in it?" He waited intently for her answer as she took a drawn-out pause.

"It was painful." Saige always told him anything he wanted to know.

"In what way?"

"Physically." She put her hands on her face and couldn't keep them from shaking.

Zekiel placed his over hers to steady them. "Stay relaxed, okay? We're going to be alright. I think I saw some other people that way."

It wasn't until he pointed to Zayika and Anon that Saige realized they were there. *Maybe they can help us.* She nodded hopefully and held onto him. *But they better not try anything because I'm not taking any chances.*

Zekiel maintained a serious expression as he thought to himself, *I'll do whatever is needed to protect Saige. Without her around I don't stand much of a fighting chance. I need her reassurance.* "I'll look after you, okay?" *I need support.*

"I'll be honest, Zeek." Her heart raced faster with each word. "I'm sorry for bringing this up if it bothers you."

He waited anxiously to hear what she was going to tell him.

"But when Jasmine asked me to make that promise, to take care of you, I quietly promised her that I would."

His feelings plummeted as Saige said her name out loud. *Please don't bring her up. Please do not speak about her, Saige, please.*

She could practically read his thoughts because of how much emotion his eyes carried. *I need to ease off.* Saige kicked at the grass nervously.

Zekiel held his emotions in with a quivering lip, as he usually did, and used few words to convey his thoughts and feelings. "Alright then." He held back tears. "That's very nice of you to care."

"Zekiel." She used his full name when she wanted his undivided attention. "I will always care about you and that will never ever go away." With both hands on each of his arms, she held him and looked up at his solemn expression. "Please don't ever forget how much you mean to me. I have love for you, I-I love you, a-as friends, you know?"

Unsure of how to accept her love, he created distance between them with withdrawn steps away from her. *Why would I mean so much to her anyways? How am I deserving of this life? Does she love having me around or the idea of me?* Zekiel put his attention on the clouds above them. *What did I do to deserve losing Jasmine? Can she hear me right now? Can she see me in some way?* He thought one of them looked to have an eye inside of it. *Am I dreaming right now? Is she watching?*

"Zekiel, did you hear me?"

He looked back at Saige, her big doe eyes staring at him intently. "I love you too." *Not myself, though.* "And I always will." *That will never change, but I cannot live life without you. Please, Saige, don't leave me too.*

"Let's go talk to those people and find our way back home. Maybe they have some sort of idea on what is happening."

They headed over to the other two as they were introducing themselves to each other.

"My name is Anon. I wanted to ask you the same thing."

"I'm Zayika."

"My name is Saige and this is—"

"Zekiel."

Zayika took it upon herself to direct them all to where to go next with a growing interest in discovering her purpose. "Let's try to figure out where we are and get out of here."

Cloudburst

Present

"Where are you taking us?" one of the women from the falls asked. "Please don't do this! Please!"

I grimaced and covered her mouth with my hand. "No more talking, no more."

I didn't make eye contact with her as Theia surrounded us with light. Exhausted and emotionally drained from an entire day of kidnapping, unbeknownst to me, everything was about to change within the next few hours.

When I arrived with the newest prisoner at the green hills, losing count of all the others by that point, a trumpet rang out with a pitch and cadence I'd never heard anywhere else before. The woman immediately began screaming and ran far and fast away from me. I could see the representatives together on top of one of the hills.

"Everyone else is already over by the ocean, Cloudburst. We have to move quickly for Lorelai. Meet us there," Theia spoke informatively.

What's going on?

"Hey, you!" Aadavan called out to the screaming woman, as she was heading in the wrong direction. "Get over here!"

All he seemed to really be able to do was make the ground shake. Theia used teleportation often, and I was unsure about Lorelai, whose time was mainly spent down in the ocean after becoming a mermaid. As the newest prisoner ran for her life, a different one who was already morphed appeared behind the representatives. She put a palm out in front of her and started wrapping up the woman's limbs in seaweed from afar.

They changed everyone else while I was gone, didn't they? They're being tortured in increments. Let me guess… the woman I just brought was the final prisoner they needed for whatever game we're going to be forced to play.

My throat became dry, and my stomach turned.

Oh no… they're going to make us fight soon, aren't they? Kill each other? How many of us are going to die?

I felt my anxiety growing every second, dreading what was to come.

Do I have to be a part of this? Am I going to die soon?

Ten Hours Later

The representatives each remained at their own faction when the fight was occuring. They stayed locked away in each of their rooms to spectate and listen to the fighters outside attacking or pleading for their lives to one another.

Aadavan had given his group the most advice out of the three and was involved alongside training them each in their abilities. He tried to intervene the most with those who were susceptible to listening to him out of desperation, fear, or a combination of both. The crocodile was much larger, resting in the pond.

Theia's fighters were reluctant to leave the castle for a little while, intimidated by the opponents from Aadavan's faction. Only a handful of them were able to face and defeat them. The men and women had to work together strategically in order to support their strengths and weaknesses productively in the face of their fear.

The sound of them fighting was the hardest for Lorelai to hear, as the darkness of the ocean felt consuming more often than not. Unknown dangers lurked in the depths and were ready at any moment to strike an unsuspecting passerby. The anglerfish had grown substantially past its original size and was larger than most of the other fish in the planet's entire sea. It continued to feed on a daily basis but took no interest in those who fought in the water with the Oceanic Guardians.

One fighter in particular named Isaac stood at the shore with a pitchfork in his hand as he came across an entire group of those under Lorelai's orders. Aadavan was hopeful he would make it far and encouraged him before it started to not waste any time at all.

Someone from my faction needs to win, Aadavan told himself, *I will have the most respect if my group is feared.*

"You have to pursue the thoughts you have," Aadavan had told him. "Your ability to craft weapons is outstanding. Up until now you've been able to make anything, right? What weapon have you thought of that you haven't been able to spawn at your fingertips?"

"None so far."

"Wow." Aadavan clapped. *Theia doesn't have anyone this strong. I may have a chance at winning if my people are consistently this powerful.*

Isaac was watched extra carefully compared to the others.

"I'm nervous," Isaac said quietly.

"Don't show the others that. They won't be able to tell that you're nervous. You need to guide them, Isaac."

"But I don't want to."

"You have to. You were clearly given this much capability for a reason. Why would you want to waste it?"

"I just want to go back home. Please let me go back to my family."

Aadavan threw a hand into the air. "You said you wanted advice from me, so that's why I've granted you this time. It's a gift. If you want to waste it, then you can go outside and beg elsewhere. You will not be sent home without fighting for it."

"What you said earlier..." Isaac's shoulders dropped. "What did you mean about 'pursuing my thoughts'?"

"Don't hesitate for any reason. Simply do what you have to do."

This fighter in particular tended to take advice literally. He took note of Aadavan's attention and, in an attempt to win, challenged himself on the most extreme level he could possibly think of. *I need to show him I deserve to be sent back. I have to get out of here, I have to… take out more than one life in one fell swoop. Two birds, one stone.* Only one hour into the fight, he was the first to break away from the Land Dweller's faction to walk along an opposing team's terrain.

The others watched in shock as he left them in the early morning, trying to maintain his composure long enough while they observed his stance and admired his bravery. He created a pitchfork to hold tightly as he waved goodbye and mentally attempted to brace himself for whatever was coming next.

I'll be back soon. I'm getting out of here and taking you all with me.

Aadavan clapped and cheered for Isaac from inside his room, his anticipation for the round's outcome becoming unbearable.

"You have to pursue the thoughts you have," he spoke to himself out loud as he tried to bravely approach the ocean.

I know they're down there, the mermaids. Just come out and fight me. Let's get this over with.

His palm was clammy with sweat.

I can make anything. I can do anything. I have to pursue the thoughts I have, Aadavan's words were in his head as he became lightheaded.

Four heads appeared in the waves in front of him. They didn't rise far enough out of the water to reveal their entire faces, only until right below their eyes. He hardly saw them through the morning mist, colored a light pink in the sunrise that was just barely creeping up against the blue sky and soft white clouds. He kept his spine straightened as his face twitched with great fear. His feet were firmly planted in the sand.

Four? It's fine. I can do this. Just throw this — wait no, throw this at the one on the right! The one that went — oh no, they're under the water now!

Isaac panicked as they disappeared in an instant.

Where are they?

Sand crabs ran up his shoes and onto his pants.

Several moments of pure silence passed as he watched the waters calmly sway back and forth. The guardians left together and made him wait idly by. He turned to look behind him and in an instant felt the small prickle of crab legs crawling on his pants suddenly turn into the slithering salty feeling of seaweed wrapping up and along all of his limbs. Isaac felt a tingling sensation in his arms and legs at the force of the grip. He was pulled quickly to the ground and plummeted forwards, both hands behind him, unable to block the impact of his face hitting the sand.

"Pull!" he heard one of them yell as he skidded along the shore with stinging skin, forced into the ocean.

He was unable to break free from the seaweed as he was pulled down deeper and deeper. Without a proper breath of air before he plunged in, his lungs felt as though they would burst. Isaac began creating a small, sharpened knife out from his palms, bubbles clouding his vision. The chilling waters were an ombre greenish-blue that faded richly into black as the four dragged him further into it. He could hear the rumbling echoes of whale calls below him, making his toes curl.

No! I can't die here!

He rolled his wrist in an attempt to cut the vines that had them in a bind. His heart pounded harder with every failed attempt at cutting the seaweed. Isaac was running out of air, his eyes focused on the guardians surrounding him.

"Let's make this as humane as possible," one of the mermen suggested. "It would be wrong to not let him drown."

"Just keep him tied." The woman next to him swam up to Isaac and placed her hands on his shoulders, pushing him slightly downwards. "It will be over soon. Everything will fade to black."

A third mermaid tried to sympathize with him, "Sorry, but we have to go home."

Just as he was running out of air, an unsuspected horror arose from the depths. A wide open mouth belonging to a barnacle-covered whale appeared from beneath them and engulfed Isaac as three of the mermaids were pushed away by the current it created, the other also swallowed alive. Lorelai was close enough to hear their terrified screams and felt the ocean rumbling around her; several victims were eaten by the enormous fish. She felt chills crawl over her skin, her heart cold. As she watched from the castle, she briefly experienced a dissociative numbness, an unpleasant question seeping into her mind.

What are we really doing here?

CHAPTER FIVE: TIME TRAVEL
Present

The fighters eventually resorted to following the representative's orders. They could only hide for so long until they were involuntarily included in, or becoming a victim of, the bloodshed. The other side disagreed with the notion of hiding, finding it best to face their destiny, whether that meant escaping or losing their lives on a planet they didn't even know the name of. Several of them struggled in their self-defense as their minds wrestled and battled with the regret of every choice they made that led them to where they stood.

Aadavan attempted to influence the minds of those under his control. He would give them unsolicited advice and twisted pep talks on the best strategic ways to hunt down and get the upper hand against the enemy members. His words were said with careful emphasis on the importance of manipulating other's emotions in whatever way they could or outnumbering unsuspecting rivals.

Regret was all Thomas could feel after he was pinned down by Land Dwellers who began making a handcrafted saw. He had lost track of his path and accidentally wandered too closely to the opposing faction while looking for others on his own. Unable to wrestle them off, he tried crying out for help, but no one from the Over Grounds faction came to assist. He was unsure if any were close enough to see what was happening. His yells were carried aimlessly by the wind.

"Get away from me!" he screamed at them as they laughed.

A woman grabbed a hold of his right wing. "You should've known better than to run off on your own like this!"

"Aadavan told us that Theia's fighters would be weak minded," one entirely covered in tattoos chuckled as he stepped forward. "Didn't realize his words would be so true. He told us we'd go home. Not everyone gets to win here."

Nathaniel was the only eyewitness to the brutality in the jungle as they proceeded to saw off both of Thomas' light grey wings. He screamed in ear-splitting distress as his blood gushed all over the dwellers and trees around them. Almost every shiny leaf nearby was covered in blood splatter.

Thomas' life flashed before his eyes. He let out his last breath painfully, his chest rattling and his thoughts fading into darkness. He'd lost his life at such a young age, in his early twenties, defenseless as no one was there to help or look out for him. The Land Dwellers were in shock but morbidly surprised at what they'd done. The removal of his wings had broken into some part of the atmosphere in a way that no one there could have seen coming.

Nathaniel was shaken to his core at what he'd just seen and heard, which developed into further tenseness as a literal hole began tearing through the air, opening up into some sort of entrance to what seemed to be a part of the galaxy. It looked like a black canvas that had been splattered with many layers of multicolored paint, fizzling and burning in glimmering waves as the others looked at it in pure wonder.

"W-what is that?" a dweller asked the others.

"I'm not sure." Another stepped towards it with a smile, Thomas bleeding out next to him. "It looks a lot like the portal Aadavan told us about. You know, the one that he, Lorelai, and Theia found? He said going into it was the best decision he's ever made."

"Maybe we shouldn't go in. We aren't sure what it is."

"We were told that if we murder a member of another faction then we can get sent home, right? Well, we just took someone's life."

"This must be the passageway we have to enter to go back to Earth!" one proclaimed.

Nathaniel watched each of them be suddenly pulled into the void, mid-conversation, because as they got closer, the portal emitted a whirlpool of air that drew them in, catching each off guard and without any way of fighting the current. He stumbled backwards and scrambled to race away before he was pulled in too.

What was that? Where did they just go? Did they die? I shouldn't mention this to anyone, should I? What if that was something I was not supposed to see? Certain knowledge could put me in danger.

Throughout most of the brutal challenge, he utilized the magical luxury of rendering himself unseen to everyone else. The only other fighter he tended to speak to was Cloudburst, since he knew for a fact what his intentions were and he also found it incredibly overwhelming to socialize with those in his own faction. The opposing fighters intimidated him greatly.

Nathaniel reminded himself though that he may have to put up a fight at the end of the killing sprees. *I will do what has to be done in the shadows. I cannot allow the representatives to have anything else to hold against me. If I have to kill another…* he took a deep breath … *I will do so to survive.*

The all-consuming void that swallowed up his fellow fighters left a scar in his thoughts. Nathaniel trudged along the dweller grounds alone after that. He knew it was better to not mention anything about what he saw to Aadavan, and most certainly not Theia or Lorelai.

The other groups don't need more of an upper hand. His footsteps on the soil were too soft to be heard by anyone else. *The Over Grounds definitely don't need to know about what happened. The retaliation against us remaining dwellers for what ours did to one of their own would be catastrophic.*

Nathaniel planned to stay hidden in the sidelines for as long as possible until enough deaths brought the remaining few closer to the ending. He thought of developing a plan, which included trying whatever it took to convince Theia to let him and Cloudburst go back to Earth. He hoped to see some sort of sign or shooting star that could reaffirm that he was making the right decision in surviving alone nomadically until he and his friend crossed paths.

It wasn't until the number of fighters started to dwindle that he saw him again. Unfortunately, nothing was pleasant or peaceful about their reunion. Blood could be seen almost everywhere. The ocean was many shades of red, chunks of wheat stems were missing, and the Over Grounds' blue castle looked to be splattered with brown dried blood even from a faraway distance.

Cloudburst was hiding behind one of Theia's faction doors as three Land Dweller's stomped inside with too many weapons in their hands to count. He tried to keep his breaths steady, his heart thumping in sync with each loud step they took. The sounds on the dirty floors bounced off the walls.

"We outnumber you!" one of them shouted. "Whoever is in here is better off making themselves known!"

Another put on a hardened exterior as well, "Why don't you just put up a fight so we can get this over with?"

There's no way everyone in the ocean is dead, right? He stood completely still while the other fighters shook the foundation as they trudged deeper into the castle. Dust fell from the ceiling's beams and hit his eyes and nose. *Don't sneeze, don't sneeze.* But he couldn't hold it in.

"Did you hear that? Over there!"

He heard their voices drawing nearer as he glanced at his shaking hands. *I may need to fight. I have to calm down!* As he let out a strained breath, he heard the unsuspecting footsteps of another ground member. She had long, thick, black hair that partly swept over her face and was wearing what seemed to be a red jumpsuit and shiny black tap shoes that made it very clear where she was headed. She passed by Cloudburst, who was huddled in the shadows, in order to face Aadavan's remaining victims.

"Psst!" he whispered as she passed, "Why the shoes? Shouldn't we be quiet?"

"Stop hiding. This game is almost over, so let's go out fighting at least!" she told him, not holding back any volume.

I can't believe out of all the clothes to pick from she chose those!

"There she is!" A dweller threw a spear in her direction as she sprang out from the dining hall.

Theia listened to the confrontation behind her bedroom door. *One of my fighters will win. I just know it. Cherry can do it. If she and Cloudburst work together? Unstoppable.*

Their aim wasn't precise enough as they missed her, instead hitting one of the wooden tables past her right thigh. She rolled her shoulders and closed her eyes. Within seconds, she summoned a large, strong shield around herself. All attempts from the others to hit her failed. Inside the light green protection bubble, she lit her hands up with weaponized power. The planet had granted her gifts of healing and bulletproof self-defense. Aadavan's fighters thought quickly, and two quietly communicated in looks between each other to split up and flank the Over Ground member. One dropped all of their spears and went invisible. Her shield was beginning to crack, as she was only able to have it activated for a limited amount of time.

"Where did they go?" she questioned out loud.

"Now, why would we tell you that?" The group snickered.

A woman in the opposing group was visibly more distressed than the rest. "I-I don't want to fight here like this! You said it was going to be strictly long-range attacks! I can't f-fight up close!"

"Do you not remember what Aadavan told you? Control your thoughts! Shut up and fig—" As the man turned to confront her, he was struck in the back by a burst of light out of Cherry's palm. He screamed and fell to his knees, the burning hole exposing his damaged insides.

Cherry felt a surge of adrenaline as she fixed her posture. *Stay numb inside. I can feel emotions later.* She refused to look at the man she'd just killed but found it too difficult to continue attacking the rest. *Come on, I'm so close to getting out of here. I've made it this far. Finish the rest!* But soon she was unable to hear own thoughts anymore and could only listen to the sounds of the man groaning in agony. In a split second, she began running instead of casting her safety bubble to deflect their attacks, trying to reason with them somehow.

"I'm sorry for what I did, okay?" She had her hands in the air and was bewildered by the fact that the other four no longer had their weapons pointed towards her. *This may work. They might listen to me. Maybe this doesn't have to be a fight to the death.* "How about we discuss what we can do instead of murdering one another? Let's talk this through. All of our lives have meaning, right?"

Within seconds, she noticed how their eyes moved to someone who had just leapt onto a table directly behind her.

"What are you looking at?" She turned around on the balls of her feet and yelled in terror as the fifth dweller from their crew jumped down and killed her with a takedown attack.

Oh no… Cloudburst watched on at everything that had unfolded. *I can't take on these four people, I just can't!* He decided to head towards the bedroom window and climb out of it, falling roughly onto the pebbles outside and sprinting off towards the platform. Right as he stepped onto it, the other faction spotted him from out of the open front doors.

"There he is! The last one! Go get him!" the fighter from the table shouted.

The platform began lowering as they ran towards him. One dweller was so desperate to win that they sprang forwards off the ledge, trying to land next to where Cloudburst stood, but narrowly missed the platform. He plummeted to the ground, every bone breaking on impact, before being crushed as the platform landed on top of him.

Nathaniel watched in terror as Cloudburst sprinted towards the jungle to get away before the platform raised up and brought down the last three enemies. Nathaniel was silent as he left his faction, invisible as he went to meet his friend halfway. *He cannot come over here! Aadavan can't see him!* Nathaniel ran quickly to steer him away and over to the wheat field instead. *Why would he decide to run into the enemy's territory? Come on Cloudburst, you're smarter than this, aren't you?*

Cloudburst's hair swung around frantically, hitting against his neck and face as it came loose from his ponytail. As he ran, he was struck and stunned by an unseen force. He felt panicked hands grab at his left arm, but he knew exactly who it was.

"Keep running!" Nathaniel's voice commanded him. "Into the field! Now! You'll be like a needle in a haystack!"

He followed his friend's advice, and the two ran in between the huge grouping of prickly brown stems. The approaching dwellers caught onto his plan and went in after him, though unaware of their fellow fighter's presence.

"We know you're in here!"

"Come out where we can see you!"

Cloudburst spoke in barely a whisper to Nathaniel, "I seriously cannot kill anyone."

He heard him breath heavily before responding, "You don't have to."

"What? How?"

"Just run towards the ocean. Distract them." Nathaniel crafted a long sword from his arms and scrap metal from his pockets. The top of the weapon was made to resemble the shape of a tree that faded down into the stump, which seemed to be made with his bloody bone shards. He partly appeared, holding it steadily. "Just run! I'll protect you."

"A-are you sure?"

"Why wouldn't I be?"

"But they are your own people."

Nathaniel stared at his injured arm as he thoughtfully replied, "Cloudburst… don't deny yourself of recognizing your true reality and what you deserve. You've been enslaved on this planet. So wrongfully controlled and forced to live out a reality of torment and unfairness. I refuse to stand with those who I know nothing about, who have shown me no hospitality, and most importantly, those who have shown me no honesty. I will protect you. You will win this game and go back to Earth."

"What about you?"

"Just run. They're coming closer." Nathaniel and his sword promptly disappeared again. "I'll figure out the rest after we both survive this bloodbath. Go lead them to the water and I'll follow suit."

"What if they strike me?"

"You might as well die trying to survive if death is imminent either way."

Cloudburst ran with his hands extended outwards on either side, making more noise as he rustled the stems against each other. "I'm over here!" he yelled.

The three dwellers chased after him with bloodthirsty stares. They ran behind him in a line, one in front of the other, completely unsuspecting that Nathaniel was creeping up behind them in a determined run of his own separate intentions. He caught up to the one farthest from the others and tripped them from the sidelines. They fell into the wheat, left behind by the remaining two who stayed focused on their pursuit of Cloudburst.

Nathaniel flipped over the man's body and drove his sharp blade across his neck. He gurgled on his blood as he recognized the face that came into view above him. His fellow faction member tried to stop the bleeding as his life left him. He then followed after the next one, taking her down the same exact way, unsuspected and ruthlessly with even more precision than the time just before that.

Soon, only one remained of his faction. They had just escaped the wheat field, following Cloudburst with their axe aimed in his direction. The cliff sides were right next to them as the ocean came into view.

"Don't do this, okay?" Cloudburst tried to stall, watching Nathaniel stealthily come up behind his opponent.

The stranger began to reply, "You must be crazy to think I won't take this opportuni—" Before he could finish, Nathaniel shoved his blade through him again and again.

Cloudburst was covered in blood as the trumpets rang. Nathaniel and his clothes were spotless as he held onto the massive sword impaled through their opponents' chest. The representatives started to make their way over to assess who survived. Nathaniel remained invisible as he spoke hastily.

"Take the weapon!" he spoke urgently under his breath. "I don't want them to know I'm here! It has to look like you did this!"

Cloudburst thought for a moment, *I have to, right? What else can I do?*

"We are not of the same faction," Nathaniel reminded him. "You know that they will want us to kill one another, and I'm not letting that happen."

"Really?"

"Yes. I'm going into hiding, just take the weapon! They will be here soon!"

A light escaped from the dead man's skin and enveloped Nathaniel. *What could this be?* he thought as he felt a surge of energy fly through him.

"They're going to think that I won?" Cloudburst was in disbelief.

"Yes, and that's fine with me. Out of the two of us you deserve to go home the most. I'm not letting them have us fight to the death."

"If they grant me the ability to do anything, I can have you return to Earth with me," Cloudburst spoke to the air in front of him.

"You can choose whatever you feel led to." Nathaniel remained unseen and left to go into hiding after he passed the sword to Cloudburst.

"Who is our lucky winner?" They heard Aadavan's voice nearby.

"We don't have any more time. I will see you later. I refuse for us to fight and kill one another. I'll be hiding in the bunker."

With those words, Nathaniel was gone.

"Cloudburst? You won?" Theia was overwhelmed with pride and joy. "You won!"

Aadavan was struck with jealousy. "What? Really?" He looked down, catching sight of the deceased Land Dweller who had bled out on the ground, and knelt by his side. "Not Michael..."

"I have to get back to the water soon." Lorelai kept looking at her legs.

Theia stepped forward. "Well, Cloudburst, it seems that you get to wish for anything you w—"

"That's not entirely true." Aadavan pulled her aside and whispered, "We can't give him this power, this choice. He is going to ruin everything."

"What do you mean?" she asked.

"We need him, Theia. You and I both know this."

"Do I get to be a part of this conversation?" Lorelai asked. "Seems like you're rushing to a conclusion here."

"Just get back in the water. We will figure out the rest from here." Aadavan dismissed her and turned back to Theia. "He has proven to have incredible capabilities, and even though I'd have preferred it to be one of my own fighters, I'll at least admit that we still need to keep him around. He can bring the appointed to us from the falls. He literally spawned out of thin air in front of your eyes and that hasn't happened with anyone else before!"

"H-hello?" Blood dripped from Cloudburst's face as he waited impatiently to find out his fate. "What are you both discussing?"

Lorelai left to the ocean as the other representatives quietly tried to figure out who would be breaking the devastating news to their first perceived victor.

"You're staying here," Theia broke the ice. "You need to stay."

Cloudburst felt his entire world turn upside down all over again as he dropped Nathaniel's sword. "W-what? You didn't say those were the rules! You can't do this to me! You can't say one thing and then do something completely dif—you can't! You just can't!"

"You are staying." Aadavan walked up to him. "You cannot leave. You are far too valuable to us. I'm sure Lorelai would also agree."

"You can't do this to me!" he exclaimed.

"I'm fairly certain that we can." Theia stood beside Aadavan.

Cloudburst's head was spinning. *If only I could go back in time and free myself from ever getting involved in this mess. How can I possibly escape? Why treat someone else with so much… injustice?*

Flashforward to CHP. 1 of CARRIERS OF EUNOIA

"Well, I'm moving onwards. Anyone who wants to follow has the option to," Amira said in a shaky voice.

Discomfort filled the air shortly after Zekiel punched Anon in the face. Four from the group followed Amira, but Anon held back and distanced himself for a little while. He ran his fingers over the sensitive skin on his cheek and inhaled loudly, making it clear that he was still in a lot of pain as he traced his cheekbone in disbelief at what just happened. He took wary steps forwards behind the rest. The jungle was up ahead, coming into view for the six travelers who were confused and uncomfortably angry at the dire turn of events.

"Why did you do that?" Amira asked Zekiel who was close to her left, just barely out of hearing range from Saige.

"Excuse me?" He turned to meet her concerned stare.

"To Anon. You know what I'm referring to. Why did you do that to him? He didn't deserve to be punched."

She has absolutely no idea. Zekiel was completely quiet for a few steps as he pondered what to say to her. *I don't need to explain myself to anyone, though, especially not someone I just met.* "You don't remember what he said to me? He's ignorant and has no business saying those types of things to other people. Very careless and shockingly insensitive."

Amira held her tongue for a second and replayed Anon's words in her mind before she responded. *Nothing he said was that rude, he was just trying to regroup our thoughts.* A small shock of pain hit her heart as she kept her eyes on Zekiel. *Unless him talking about a 'suicide mission' trigged something?* "He said we shouldn't lose hope. That's not a bad thing."

"Let's just drop it." Zekiel looked down at the ground and sensed that Saige was walking near them.

"I'm here for you if you ever need to talk about anything." She sensed grief within him, a misery he didn't know how to navigate.

"If you want to talk about a plan to get out of here then fine. Other than that? I have nothing else to say." He began to withdraw his energy from their conversation as she made one last thing clear to him.

"Don't ever hurt him again," Amira spoke strongly.

Zekiel's head shot upwards. "What?" *She cannot tell me how to treat others.*

"Anon," she clarified and then repeated, "Don't ever hurt him again."

There was silence for a few moments as Anon eventually caught up to rejoin the group. "Just for the record, I think tha–"

Zekiel turned around to face him with a look full of distaste. "Anon, contrary to what you seem to believe, none of us care what you think."

Amira tugged on Zekiel's shirt to stop his verbal attacks as she thought to herself, *I will defend Anon, no matter what it takes. He won't get hurt again.*

Present

"We have to think of a plan to get out of here," Nathaniel told Cloudburst as they stood in front of each other near the bunker. "That terrible, wretched string of violence is finally over. We cannot celebrate our freedom yet until it's real. We have to get out of here. Follow me." He guided him down the steps and motioned for him to close the door. "It's so hard to not think about all of the lives that have been tortured and lost here."

"You sure the representatives can't hear us?" Cloudburst asked.

"You always feel like you're being watched and listened to, don't you?" He turned one of the lights on and pointed to a chair in the corner of the room for him to take a seat in. "You carry around a lot of unease. Major trust issues."

"What makes you say that?" he inquired with caution.

"Takes one to know one." Nathaniel frowned and sat across from him.

"I suppose that could be true. Sorry to hear that you struggle with the same."

"Do you want something to drink?"

"No, thanks. I'm okay right now. Been hard for me to eat, drink, or sleep since… everything."

"I don't think the reps can hear us. We should be fine down here," Nathaniel reassured him.

"We need to get Theia to finally send us back home." Cloudburst got straight to the point. "There's no other way we will survive and escape as far as I know. I've been the closest to her, I know her routines and capabilities. She sends me to the falls all the time."

"Does she have any other abilities that you're aware of? Even potentially?" Nathaniel tapped on the arm of his chair impatiently.

"No, not that I know of." Cloudburst put his elbows on his knees, face in both palms as his hair fell downwards. "I'm not even entirely sure what the two others can do. To my knowledge, even Aadavan can't do what Theia can. It's all on her. She's the one who would have to help us."

Nathaniel nodded and took a swig of his bitter drink. "Do you think we could convince her?"

"I'm not sure. She seems to think more for herself when Aadavan isn't around. He greatly sways her opinions and attitudes towards others. This has been evident since I first met them."

"Well, I wonder if what you said is true."

"Oh, it is, trust me. She's almost a different person when he isn't around — more independent and relaxed."

"...alright then," Nathaniel responded. "I was referring to what you said before that. I wonder if Theia really is the only true key to surviving here. It seems like that would be too simple. There has to be something else missing, I can sense it. I think there are other forces at play here beyond anything we can see."

"Even the reps themselves say and think that at times, actually." Cloudburst stood up to stretch. "But even if there are other ways out of here for good, how do we even figure that out? What if we don't get to decide?"

"What do you mean?"

Thunder struck outside before he answered.

"How is there already another storm? It's as if this planet is trying to put us in a specific place, like it's holding us here, you know? Similar to our magical abilities, this place has mood swings and shows them through elements in nature. There's no denying it," Nathaniel said.

A chill crawled over his friend's skin. "Yeah. I can see the picture."

"No really. Think about it."

Cloudburst agreed, "What if it's not even the representatives creating any of what exists at this point?"

"At what 'point' are you referring to?" Aadavan's voice grimly traveled down the staircase.

Nathaniel tightened his grip on the chair as he started to go invisible. "I thought I told you to close the door!" he mouthed silently.

"I thought I did!" Cloudburst panicked back. "How much of that did you hear?" he raised his voice, asking

Aadavan who had just appeared at the bottom of the rusted stairs.

"Just enough. Seems oddly suspicious that you're talking to yourself down here." Aadavan spat out. "We couldn't hear you, by the way, when you captured Nathaniel."

Cloudburst felt what was left of his hope plummet. *Oh no, he's bringing that up… I don't want them to find out about him still alive here. I don't want them to listen in on me when I try to strategize with others.*

"We'll make sure your future hunts aren't… muted… so you don't try to betray us again." He shoved him against the wall. "Why are you even in this bunker anyway?"

"Just keep it a secret, please. I need my own space," he told him, expecting a harsh, angry response.

"It would make me claustrophobic, staying here," Aadavan replied, taking some time to look around. "As long as you follow our rules and stay in your own lane, I really don't care where you choose to sleep at night."

"You're okay with me keeping this bunker?"

"It doesn't really matter," he replied, heading back to the stairs again. "Besides, as I said before, I will take it away if you don't follow the rules. We don't have much time to stand around and chat anyways. It's almost time for you to retrieve more fighters from the falls. Are you ready? Theia sent me to come find you."

"Of course I'm ready," he replied dryly, making the shape of a gun with his fingers pointed at his head.

"She will see you soon then." Aadavan began to storm out of the bunker, and right as his foot stepped onto the final stair, he added, "Don't hurt yourself."

Cloudburst double checked that Aadavan had indeed left and then spoke confidently, "Your insane representative is gone. You can come out now."

Nathaniel let out the sigh he had been holding in, reappearing. "Alright then. It's evident that I don't have much time to talk this over with you, do I?"

"Yeah, our escape plan, so where were we?"

"Discussing how the planet's control is quite unfathomable. In our case… Theia might be the only one true key to escaping."

CHAPTER SIX: WISHFUL THINKING

Theia

Present

I wasn't sure what went so wrong in one of Cloudburst's hunts until Aadavan told me after the first game. *What did I miss?* My fighters tried the best they could to survive, which was ultimately evident in the final results. The special power I shared with Cloudburst was proven to be effective, as he won in the end. I knew he had a fire within that was ready to be unleashed. He was practically overflowing with potential. I tried my best to convince the other two that he didn't win based on luck or certain unrelated circumstances — he won because of his mental fortitude.

He has some reasonable judgment. I'm glad he works for me.

Aadavan and I had private plans to speak. I planned to relay the most important takeaways from my discussion with him to Lorelai.

She'll thank me later for condensing what Aadavan was about to tell me.

"So, what do you feel we need to talk about regarding the previous captures? I thought they went shockingly well. Almost all of them went off without a hitch." I pulled out one of my chairs for Aadavan to sit on as he joined me at the castle.

"Anything that seems too good to be true always is," he told me. "I didn't bring your attention to what happened between Nathaniel and Cloudburst when he was retrieved for us because I didn't want you to worry. We both know Lorelai would have had a full-blown panic if she found out I kept the information from you. Keep that in mind."

"So what happened exactly?"

"Did you not notice when we were watching him that his mouth was moving? That he was speaking to the man named Nathaniel?"

"Well, of course he was." I sat down beside him at the empty table. "Doesn't he normally exchange a few words with the captives? That's to be expected, no?"

Aadavan let out an airy laugh. "You're missing what I'm alluding to. He had a certain expression on his face—one of worry. Worry that we might catch on to how he was being untruthful at the falls. I could see it written all over his face that he was sharing things with Nathaniel that he should not have been. He made it too obvious that he was taking advantage of us not knowing exactly what he was saying."

"I didn't notice anything to that degree in particular." *Aadavan can be more observant than me, that's for sure.* "So what do we do then? We don't want him oversharing with any of the fighters before they even arrive. He can't be corrupting their thoughts before they even meet us!"

"That's exactly why I'm so concerned." Aadavan stood up, unable to sit still as he walked in circles around me.

Seeing him pace around made me feel even more anxious. "What do we do? We're able to see him, but how do we find a way to hear him?"

"I'm not sure that's something we can even do at all. But we can use intimidation."

"Have you already spoken to him about this?"

"Of course I have."

"Without consulting me first?"

Aadavan rolled his eyes and stopped pacing to reassure me. "Don't worry about it, I hardly said anything to him. I lied and said we'd somehow change the second captures. He is well aware that he cannot talk behind our backs without there being consequences."

"Let's hope instilling fear in him will work." I took a caring hold of one of Aadavan's hands as he passed close to me. "He won't try to cross us again like that, at least with your quick thinking you've made sure of that. There's nothing he can say to them that can alter our vision and purpose here. He isn't that powerful."

"Thank you for reminding me that what we are doing is beyond even us three." With his free hand, he pushed his glasses up snugly on the bridge of his nose.

I smiled up at him. "Of course it is. Those who make it back to Earth will be even stronger because of what they will survive through."

He finally dropped his tense shoulders and responded thoughtfully, "We got lucky that the first match ended so cleanly. I can't imagine what it would have been like if there was a more monumental decision at stake with who lived or died. Thank goodness that Nathaniel disappeared. He must've also been swallowed by some sort of giant whale like several of Lorelai's fighters and opponents."

"Why do you say it that way?" I searched for clarification.

"That we 'got lucky'?"

"No, that there could have been a 'monumental decision at stake'?"

Aadavan sighed. "Just imagine what it would've been like if Cloudburst and Nathaniel were the last two standing there in front of the other. It would have been a travesty for it to end with the complication of such deep feelings of care involved. Who would be able to make such a decision, or sacrifice, like that? Sounds like the recipe for a perfect storm if you ask me."

Flashforward to CHP. 12 of CARRIERS OF EUNOIA
SPEAKER: Theia

Creating the game turned out to be the worst idea that Aadavan, Lorelai, and I ever thought of. We never could have foreseen the sheer amount of panic and death that resulted as a consequence of our decisions. Our lives were at stake too. I would never have thought that someone would leave one of their own behind after getting to the end.

Why is Anon doing this to Zayika?

As Anon and Amira told me what their winning wishes would be, I stood in disbelief at where their priorities were.

"You're not going to pick Amira over me, right Anon? It's not like you'd waste your wish on her," Zayika said.

I've never seen a contestant get this far and have to make such a tough decision. Anon can bring them both back... but I shouldn't say anything, right? Let him decide for himself. People should get to decide the rules for themselves—not be told them. I'll ask Amira to pick first. Maybe she will change the course of all of this.

"What is it you are choosing, Amira?" I asked her. "You might want to make your decision quickly, we don't want you to return to your morphed state while you're not near the water." *It always makes me nervous when Lorelai loses track of her time.*

Amira held onto Anon's hand in an unmistakably loving way as she responded to me, "I want the waterfall destroyed."

My stomach dropped. What? We cannot do that... What would happen? No one has ever asked for this before! Why does she know the waterfall is so interconnected with this? When she was captured, she wasn't paying that much attention to the falls, right? Will she really destroy the landmark? Why did we not foresee this happening? "How do you know about the waterfall? Yo-you're not supposed to know about that." I instantly regretted what I said. *Don't reveal anything to her that she doesn't know already. Cloudburst was told to capture her there... Theia... this doesn't mean that she understands anything about the portal. Pick your words more carefully.* "I mean, what are you talking about? Where is this waterfall located?" *What a terrible save.*

"You know what I'm talking about. You know it's tied to this planet, Eunoia, along with the string of incidents and lost lives that take place around it. I want it gone without a trace of its existence left over, that is my wish."

Wait... "How do you know the planet's name?" I asked her. *We've never told them that before. We've made sure to leave that out. How observant is she?*

"I'm not sure I'm required to tell you that." Amira looked proud of herself.

I tried to convince her to change her mind, but deep down, I already knew that it wasn't going to change, that I couldn't, and shouldn't, try to force her to since she had followed the rules up until then fairly. "You should wish for something else, truly. You could wish for anything under the sun. Please reconsider this decision."

I hope they didn't catch what I just said. Aadavan caught my wording and shook his head exasperatedly. *I'm never going to hear the end of this from him. I hope he isn't too upset with me.*

"Amira—please change your wish," he told her. I knew he was restraining himself from being controlling. I was shocked that he even used the word 'please'.

"No."

Aadavan resorted to begging. "Please—"

"No."

It was easy to see what Anon saw so clearly in Amira; her confidence was admirable, to say the least. He watched her face with fondness as she spoke that one simple and very powerful word to us without a crack in her composure. I made eye contact with Lorelai and Aadavan as we silently told one another to group together to discuss granting her wish. I stepped off to the side with them, having an extremely difficult time not looking down at my shoes in order to avoid confronting what I knew would be a very strong difference in opinions.

"What is wrong with you, Theia?" Aadavan lashed out as soon as we were out of hearing range from the other three.

"I'm doing the best I can," I told him the truth. "I'm not sure how this unfolded the way it did."

"Well, I can tell you how, Theia, I can tell you!" He raised a finger at my face. "Lorelai and I took too much of your uncalculated advice! We were hardly involved this time around! You constantly decided to sit back and never, ever, intervene! Why did the last one end so well, can you tell me why?"

I stood in silence.

"You're not making this any better, Aadavan," Lorelai tried to tell him.

"It went so well because I took charge!"

"Then you get to decide what happens here if Lorelai doesn't object," I shrugged, and she quickly nodded in agreement.

"You have made a mess of things, Theia," he spoke hastily.

"We have made people teleport to and from this planet and appointed others to go and get more individuals by force. We've already taken away enough of their freedom. Let's try to not silence their voices completely while we are at it. I think we've already caused enough damage as it—"

"Just let her destroy the waterfall," Aadavan interrupted harshly.

I stepped back over to Amira, Zayika, and Anon and tried to ignore the giant weight on my chest as I spoke, "Upon careful thought and reflection, we have come to the consensus that Amira's wish... will be granted. We will keep our promise of granting any wish, whatever it may be, even though we strongly... we strongly... advise you against choosing this, Amira."

"I stand by what I asked for." She nodded.

As I looked over to Anon, I noticed out of the corner of my eye how worried Zayika was becoming. *This poor woman hasn't been given a chance this entire time, has she? Not a chance to truly shine in her own way; what a shame.* She looked lost and hopeless. I felt a piece of myself hurting for her as I intuitively sensed what he was going to say next. *Anon doesn't see things the same way Zayika does. He doesn't understand her curse. This man is going to absolutely break her heart.*

"It's time for a decision, Anon. What will your wish be?"

He looked at both of the women as he thought to himself longer than he usually seemed to before speaking. "My wish..." Zayika looked down at how their hands were interlocked and kicked the dirt with what looked to be raving jealousy as Anon bit his lip.

"Go on." *Please, Anon, let's get this over with.* I was fearful of what Zayika's reaction would be, understanding on a level that no one else did about the power and influence she was under. "Please, Anon, time is being wasted."

"I wish for Amira's life to be spared on this planet, resulting in her being allowed to return home despite being from another faction."

That's his wish... that's what he chooses to say? He will regret this, and one day when he realizes what he's done... I hope he will be able to live with himself.

Zayika fell down to her knees in devastation. "Anon..."

"What?" he asked.

You don't understand what you've just done.

"You... you're leaving me behind?" Her hope crumbled.

"I can't take both of you."

Yes, you can.

"We're from the same faction. How could you do this to me?" Zayika's usually deep, warm voice grew into a sharp yell. "Do you know how many times I've saved your pathetic life?"

She doesn't really think he's 'pathetic', she's speaking out of hurt. I know this all too well. I looked over at Aadavan. *She's trying to make Anon question his reality because she cannot accept her own. The painful cycle continues.*

Amira tucked her arm completely under Anon's. "He made his choice, Zayika. Not everyone gets what they want."

"You can't leave me here! I'm going to lose my mind, my identity, and my future. What am I supposed to do?"

I felt desperate to comfort her in some way.

"You will wait for the other humans who will be brought here. You will wait until each faction becomes whole again with ten members."

"When will that be?" She was on the verge of tears.

"Their calling can't be predicted. When it's destined to be, they will arrive."

"Will they be Wish Carriers?"

"We don't know. It's rare that as many of them appeared in your group during this time." It was extremely rare, actually, and all very much meant to happen.

"So you're telling me that I can be stuck here for years? Even if after waiting for others to arrive, I may be killed regardless? Or miss out on getting a wish again?" I was shocked at how much Zayika was able to comprehend what unfolded. Her mind was strong, but it was being tested every second by the color-coded curse in her hair.

"Yes, you're correct." She was devastated, and I had to look away from her. "Congratulations Amira and Anon. You're going to make it home."

Zayika was desperate. "Amira, wait, please give me a chance. Give me a ticket home, I'm begging you. Use your wish on me like Anon did for you. I promise that I will find a way to repay you."

Her true heart is showing through. Zayika, please do not lose it. I thought to the planet, *please don't take it all from her.*

"No. I already made my choice." Amira kept her word.

The sinister side in Zayika immediately took over at her opponent's response, the planet wanting to get its way. "Well, if I kill you right now then I will get your wish."

Her words caused Anon to step in between them, and he spoke insecurely, "I won't let you."

He's not sure of his own words. If he really had to save Amira's life, he would of course want to try to, but would he actually be able to?

"You will regret this Anon. I will never forget you. I promise that I will find a way to make you regret this," Zayika said.

A handful of asperatis clouds in the sky watched intently as she spoke into existence what their fate would be.

Anon faced Amira instead of her. "It's time for us to go back."

"Yes, it's time."

They didn't even wish for their abilities to be taken away. This is a tragic mess. Lorelai and Aadavan looked at me with what felt to be utter disappointment. *I want to go back to Earth too. Maybe I'm not meant to be here either.* I was tempted to lift my fingers and escape too… even from one of my best friends and the love of my life… but I agreed to stay with them. *What about my own wish? I don't think I should have ever stepped into this realm. There's no way I could leave my own behind here.*

I put my arm into the air, silently keeping myself from wishing that I was sending myself back home, and sent the other two back to where they came from. Zayika and I made extraordinarily uncomfortable eye contact once they disappeared. I had no idea what to say. Her eyes were challenging to not look into, like green mosaic windows to her soul, and it was screaming for help. The weather was melancholic as a new type of storm had officially begun. I knew instinctively that the worst was to come when the sky turned the same color as her hair. *The curse...* More cloudy eyes appeared above to watch her.

"What's going on?" she asked me.

"I'm not sure." *I am sure, but I can't say what's happening to her. This is a battle she is going to have to face on her own.*

Lightning struck down, and the sound of the thunder unfortunately wasn't loud enough to drown out Zayika's frightened and pain-filled voice. "Take me to Earth too. I'm right here and ready to go!"

"I can't do that."

"What do you mean? Don't tell me that you're as awful as Amira and Anon. I know that you can help me, you're just refusing to."

"It's not that." *I can't send her back to Earth with this curse, but I also cannot tell her about it. I have to leave her behind.*

"Then what is it?" her voice caused an electric chill up my spine.

"You would never understand." I was horrified by what the curse was going to bring. *I don't want her to hurt me.* I looked at Lorelai and Aadavan with a raised hand. "We have to go."

"Where?" Zayika stomped forwards at me, and my heart rate spiked more with each step she angrily took. "Take me with yo—"

Then for the first, and only time ever, as the color-coded curse came into full effect, I was able to make the three of us disappear and teleport to safety.

I think the planet, through Zayika, is going to kill us... if she doesn't kill herself first.

Present

Aadavan straightened out his clothes and dusted off the extra dirt that had accumulated on his pants from meticulously combing through his grounds. "We must not lose sight of what we are doing. We can't allow it to get messy between the fighters here on a personal level."

Theia felt inclined to challenge his perspective. "I do think that we should try a hands-off approach with the next chosen participants."

"Really? Seriously?"

"Our purpose here is to strengthen their minds through survival, right?"

"Obviously."

"So why hinder and hold back the amount of effort they will use to think for themselves? Survival of the mentally fittest."

"Don't get offended, but I led a lot of our first events here, particularly with my fighters of course, and it went better than we thought it would. What may have been the strongest contender won. Is that not the point to a certain degree?"

"I think you're misunderstanding what I'm saying," Theia replied patiently.

"I don't really care what you think right now, with all due respect." Aadavan, on the contrary, grew impatient. "Why change anything? Why not try to train these people? Why try to change something that is not broken?"

"Are you really going to speak to me like that?" Theia stood up too. "Do you really not even feel the slightest bit sorry for disrespecting me?"

"Speak like what? With honesty? I won't apologize for speaking my truth—especially with logical reasoning. Theia, I am not trying to hurt your feelings. But tell me this... are we not representatives? We need to guide, direct, and influence those who are appointed underneath the umbrella of our factions."

"I disagree. I don't see what we are doing as leading, contrary to that I'm seeing it as controlling."

Footsteps approached through the main corridor, and Cloudburst entered the room. "I agree with Theia."

"Knock before you come in!" Aadavan demanded. "You shouldn't be hearing any of these confidential matters!"

"Has anyone ever told you to lighten up before?" He stood next to Theia and turned to face only her while continuing, "I-I'm ready to begin bringing others for the second test." *I better watch my wording, I don't want them to think that I'm up to anything.*

Did I just hear what he is thinking? Theia was shocked to hear Cloudburst's thoughts in her own mind. *I shouldn't tell Aadavan this. Keep this between the two of us. There has to be a reason why I have this ability. It must be that I hear him when he is close enough to me. A one-sided mental walkie talkie.*

"If you're ready then we must get moving. Aadavan, why don't you let off some steam back at your own place? Cloudburst, you remain on standby and stay with me to await the next command. We will check in with Lorelai soon enough to see if she has had any new visions. We can remain in the castle while we wait for who, and what, is to come next."

"You're really going to send me away?" Aadavan asked, offended.

"Everyone needs space from time to time. You should go get some," Theia responded.

As Aadavan hastily went through the castle doors, he stopped in his tracks at the sight of the sky. "It looks different out here. The sky seems to be entirely purple."

"It must be the sunset. It is around evening time, after all," Theia told him from the dining hall, not bothering to go see what he was referring to.

"It's never looked this way before." He tried to shake off the feeling that made his skin crawl as he closed the doors behind him.

The unusual color was beginning to fade back into greenish blues as he thought to himself, *we may have bit off far more than we can chew. Something very wrong is fast approaching.*

CHAPTER SEVEN: EUNOIAQUAKE

Aadavan

Present

The energy in the atmosphere was off, and it wasn't because of the first game that took place. Despite the struggle, strife, and bloodshed of the first round of survival, something else was lingering in the air. There was a type of presence or force that was threatening to destroy everything that the other representatives and I had created. I just knew it. I needed to locate the source of this disorder. I found it incredibly difficult to get any rest at night. Impending doom started to attack the peace and confidence I thoughtfully built up around becoming the strongest leader of the three factions. After speaking with Theia, I saw something peculiar outside—the sky was entirely a very distinct shade of purple, particularly close to a shade of dark magenta. Since seeing it, I was unable to slow down my thoughts.

Unable to get proper rest later into the beginning of the night, I ventured around the vegetation, as I usually did. I kicked at the dirt beneath my feet and pondered how to fix whatever was unfolding. *Why do I feel this way?* A force of nature was coming after me. *What is this feeling? Regret?* I truthfully felt bad about what had happened with Theia, as we weren't seeing eye to eye, but I knew that I couldn't hold onto that guilt if I wanted to be a strong representative who was capable of overseeing the strongest fighters. *I can't expect those beneath me to have sharpened minds if I don't keep mine in check.* The competitive challenges that arose between her and I were what inspired me the most to wake up in the morning and discover what each day would bring. I knew that we had found our truest purpose through the waterfall portal.

We found where we were meant to be.

Of all the things that perplexed and intrigued me about the planet, I wanted almost nothing more than to understand why people began waking up on the hills. One by one, it was bringing people to it without us intervening, which was a very bad sign as order was falling out of our control and somehow being designated to a higher and more prominent unseen figure than us. *We have to keep in control here; it's the one thing we cannot afford to lose.* I was looking forward to the next game, but I couldn't shake the feeling that what was happening around us was inauthentic, tarnished and poisoned by something else that intruded past our defenses.

Cloudburst, through Theia's power, was thankfully ready to begin bringing the next batch of fighters to be morphed and dispersed fairly amongst our factions. He was being compliant, which I knew would be temporary. Even though he won before, we decided to keep him here. He was someone we couldn't lose as his help was beyond our wildest imaginations. The lines between our original vision and some sort of dark, twisted fantasy started to blur as we got knee-deep into what was beginning to feel like a tangled mess. Since drinking the bottled liquid in our hometown, Lorelai experienced hallucinations. I truly believed that those she saw were of great importance. They were chosen for a higher calling.

Theia had already made it clear to me that the next person to arrive would be placed in her faction to see if they were the right fit. *She's already acting greedy this time around, forgetting what went smoother because of my input and direction.*

I gritted my teeth.

The first to fight this time around should be appointed to me. It makes more sense that way. I need one of my fighters to win this time around; in fact, I have no idea how none of my own did before. Why did it have to be Cloudburst of all people? Why him?

I was unable to hold my tongue when it came to her desire for an imbalance of powers and numbers between us. It was unfair how her words and decisions concerning them had a greater pull compared to mine. It hadn't been long since we last talked, but I had to tell her what was on my mind and hoped it would bring me at least an ounce of peace, or somehow, greater understanding.

I followed the path directly to her. *Hopefully she provides those she gets with adequate advice, just as long as it isn't better than what I tell my own. I don't need the competition to be too strong.*

"Have a minute to speak with me?" I asked her, leaning against a doorframe while she prepped the glass cages.

"Yes, I can talk for a bit. What is it?" she asked in a patient tone.

"I'll cut right to the chase." I cleared my throat. *Let's hope this doesn't put her in a bad mood.* "I think it's unfair how you expect to be the first to receive the new fighters and leave Lorelai and I with less options from the beginning. You even tried to do so in our first go of things."

"Really?" She had the nerve to laugh in my face.

"What's funny?"

"That you are acting this way over human lives."

"Well…" I waited for a moment before replying, "You're greedy with them."

"Aadavan, Cloudburst brought them to me."

"And? Of course he did."

"Why do you say it like that?"

"Like what?"

"Like there is some type of inappropriate reason why Cloudburst brings them to me instead of either of you." She shrugged. "Lorelai is understandably never around and sometimes… neither are you."

What? "Excuse me?" I put my hand on my chest. "What do you mean? I'm always around. We're always talk—"

"Let's be honest. We both know our energy has shifted and never returned to what it once was after we got into that disagreement at the waterfall."

"Please don't talk about that."

"Why?" She challenged me. "So we just have to accept your treatment and pretend it never happened? Why is it that you are allowed to call me 'greedy', but I am not able to bring to light your own behavior that has caused tension, divide, and cause for concern then as well?"

Swallow my pride and tell her I didn't mean it. I tried to make myself reply, to say the words I was able to think privately out loud instead, but for some reason, knowing I should be saying them made it even harder to speak.

"Really? Now you're quiet? You sure have a lot to say when you want to put someone else in check, but you can't handle even a word of it ever thrown back at you." She started walking away from me and back to her testing room. "I will speak to you later once you're ready to have a two-sided conversation."

I looked like a deer in headlights as guilt panged at my insides. *I should've never insulted either of them that way, especially not Theia, who has never once spoken to me with such ill intent.*

Theia walked past the door and stopped to speak to me again once more before closing it. "They're my fighters, Aadavan. And you know what? I think that yet again one of mine will be the next to win."

There has to be an explanation for all of this. While I wait for my next fighters to arrive, I will get to the bottom of what's wrong and fix it before it makes things even worse somehow. Her words ignited what felt like fury inside of me as I stormed out of her castle. I took the floating platform back to the ground to look around and try to find what had changed in my faction.

I ventured behind my headquarters and closer towards the pond where I originally found the crocodile. At first, everything seemed just as it typically did, until an unfamiliar object stood out to me. *Was that there before?* There was a tall stone standing upright in the middle of a particularly thick cluster of trees and hanging vines. *When did that get here?* I noticed that vines were already starting to grab and grow along the base of it. *There are words written on it...* As I approached it, the planet's core started to shake. *What's happening?* It grew so strong that I fell to my knees. *It's like something is trying to keep me from going to it!*

I got up and ran, stumbling side to side as everything writhed beneath me. *That stone shouldn't be here, I just know it!* My instincts spoke to me often and almost always they were correct. Something was coming after me, Theia, everyone. There turned out to be words scribbled onto one side of the stone that spoke of rules about who could go back to Earth and who wouldn't. Based on what I was able to read, it did not accurately reflect the decisions, purpose, and vision that the three of us had formulated. *I don't want fighters reading misleading information! What if this is what's causing these horrendous earthquakes? Creating the feeling of despair in the air? Did the planet make this? How can I get rid of it?*

I focused my energy on the stone with the intent of damaging it.

There is nothing else I can do besides try!

For some reason, what I did angered the cloudy eyes above that were watching me, their pupils dilated. The sight of them made my blood run cold. *What is happening?* I tried my hardest to break the foundation of the stone, but instead a gigantic navy-blue lightning bolt shot down from the sky, landing just far enough from me that I wasn't killed. Shock from the wave made contact with my skin, and I hissed in pain.

Fire stung down into my bones as I screamed out in agony. It felt as if all my power, energy, and abilities were completely stripped from me at the source of my heart. I was in so much pain that I couldn't see straight and laid hopelessly on the ground for what felt like hours. I could hardly lift my head up to see if anyone was nearby who would be able to help me. *Theia… Lorelai…* I strained my eyes to see the stone which was broken in half and saw how the cloud's eyes kept staring down eerily. Somehow, they were bloodshot. On the verge of tears, just like I was.

"What do you want?" I shouted despite the stabbing sensation in my rib cage. "What do you really want? What are you? What are you trying to do? Stop trying to interfere! Leave us alone, will you? Stop!"

I was answered by the ocean booming at me, light coming from it off in the distance, and suddenly the tide changed and rose high enough for me to see it from where I was laying. *It's going to swallow me alive!* I thought in distress as the massive wave was headed right towards my direction.

Flashforward to CHP. 1 of CARRIERS OF EUNOIA

Desperate for answers and safety, the group of six was trying to survive and find a way to escape their warped sense of reality during their first day on Eunoia. After waking up on the starting hills, they ventured together in search of hope, uncovering small parts of the planet with each step along with the deepest fears buried within their subconscious.

Zayika saved Anon's life from the ocean's waters as he sought out to discover where a shining bright light was coming from. She carried him in her arms as water dripped and fell from their quivering limbs. The other five were anxious as they got to the shore. Amira immediately felt compelled to take care of Anon, similarly to Zayika, and took his face in her steady hands with extra caution once they reached the sand.

"Speak to us. Are you okay? Don't pass out. Are you hurt anywhere? I don't see blood."

Zayika rolled her eyes several times as Amira took him from her arms into her own and sat with him laid out in her lap. *Oh please, like he needs you to watch over him. Give me a break. You didn't do anything at all, Amira. I saved him — not you.*

"I think it was the lip of the creature that got a hold of me! It was slippery, cold, and felt like bumpy rubber trying to grip onto my leg. I didn't feel any teeth thankfully. I'm alright. Just not the best swimmer," Anon replied, exhausted.

"Clearly," Omar stated.

"No one asked for your input, Omar."

"Well, no one asked you to take on the role of being the hero here."

Amira broke up the fight before it got any further, and they all tried to maintain their composure despite what had just happened. The conversation eventually ended with Zayika defensively trying to silence Anon in the midst of her frustration. The six kept traveling onwards together away from the ocean. Everyone walked in very awkward silence for some time, only the droplets of water falling off of Anon and Zayika and the squelching of their shoes making any sound.

Zekiel got closer to Amira and spoke under his breath, "This is all pretty frightening, but you seem to be staying calm enough."

I must be pretending pretty well then. "I'm a crime scene investigator. Well, I was back on Earth. New to the field… but also new to whatever we are dealing with now."

He looked over his shoulder to see that Saige and Omar had begun talking. *What does she have to say to him?* Zayika and Anon purposefully avoided walking near each other as Zekiel continued talking to Amira.

"Tell me a little more about that. Your profession."

"Why?"

"I have a lot I need to get my mind off of," he replied. *I'd rather hear about your life than reveal anything about mine.*

The two led the way for the others. Amira proceeded to tell Zekiel about her work to the best of her ability, finding it helpful to get her mind off of more pressing matters as she recalled some of her encounters in great detail. Omar was trying to keep his envy from growing too thickly at Anon for getting a hold of everyone's attention at the ocean. He crossed his arms and looked over at Saige who was walking on her own and not directly right by her best friend for once. He took the window of opportunity to try to get to know her.

"Hey. That was all pretty crazy back there, huh?"

"Definitely." Her eyes met his. "I'm sure those two are freezing cold. I wish we had a blanket or some towels for them."

"Yeah…" Omar was unsure of what to say at first. "Why do you think we're here? Wherever it is that we are?"

"Maybe we're supposed to learn something." She tried to remain positive. "Maybe this is all a dream."

They both laughed and looked up at the greenish stars scattered in the royally blue sky. "Are you doing okay?"

"A bit frightened, but keeping it together," she responded. "Glad we've been able to come across others in the same boat looking for a way back home. You?"

"Same. Trying to keep in mind the most important things to focus on. I think doing outrageous stuff for attention is so stupid. Not sure why Anon was so desperate to be talked about."

"It was alarming how he went into the waters like that," Saige agreed. "Also how fast Zayika went out there to save him. She can't keep her eyes off of him."

"Like you and that Zekiel guy?"

Saige's mouth opened slightly. "Ah, well he and I are close. I would save him too if something happened."

Omar felt a small pain in his chest. *What would it be like to have someone who'd do that for me?* "Well, I'm sure he'd save you too."

"Yeah." She looked doubtful. *Would he?* "I'm sure he would."

Present

Part of the ocean came after Aadavan and the stone. He was soaking wet and gasping for air as the waters sprang forward with enough vigor to reach and tower over him. The planet was making its boundaries clear by sending out a message to those attempting to operate by their own rules. He found himself searching for answers as the ocean swept one half of the stone entirely out to sea and narrowly missed bludgeoning him in the head as it passed. Theia and Cloudburst in the airborne castle watched from afar at the raging storm, naively thinking they were out of reach from harm.

"No!" Aadavan yelled helplessly as he struggled to lift himself off the ground.

I never saw the other side, I can't believe this, what did it say? What did it say?

"What is even happening out here?" he heard a man's familiar voice reach him from a distance.

"Stay away!" Aadavan's voice shot through the air with a similar rage to the planet's. "Just stay away!" He gripped onto the weeds and rocks tightly.

Nathaniel covered his mouth in horror as he realized what he'd just done.

"Nathaniel? I recognize your voice! Wait! Was that you? Nathaniel! Get over here at once! Did you have something to do with this? You're still alive?"

Nathaniel immediately went invisible and sprinted towards the back of the Land Dweller's faction near the pond as Aadavan continued questioning him from afar. *No… he cannot know I'm here! How stupid of me to have opened my mouth!* He mentally scolded himself. *I can't try to save him; this man ruined my life, why should I value his? I can never open my mouth like that again! No matter the consequences! I swear, my words will get me killed one of these days!*

"Get back over here!" Aadavan was on his feet, his eyes darting back and forth between observing the jungle up ahead and over to the ocean behind him. He watched the stormy clouds as they flickered with warm purple hues. "What do you want?" he screamed at the raindrops that had just begun to fall.

Thunder boomed in the distance, and spider-web like patterns of white lightning filled the sky. His clothes were dripping water onto the soil as he went to see what was left of the ominous stone. Only half of it was left partially standing. Brokenly incomplete. He read, reread, and soon memorized the words that were still legible.

DON'T DESTROY YOUR MIND'S FREEDOM KEY
IT IS IN THE DARKNESS THAT OUR
DESTINY'S SUBCONSCIOUS REALITY IS REVEALED

What does this mean? He studied the curvature of the ingrained letters with his bloody, bruised, wet fingertips. *Theia, Lorelai, and I decide who arrives and gets their minds tested here. If some other force is trying to control what takes place, they will regret it. This land, water, everything is ours.* Raindrops fell gently onto the rock and dissolved quickly as the storm outside began to subside, but the storm within Aadavan had just started. He wasted no time at all stomping towards Theia's faction yet again, soon coming across her having another conversation with Cloudburst.

"We have been keeping our distance for safety in the castle," Theia stated as the two of them stepped off the platform. "Actually, we were on our way to see how you were doing. I've never seen a storm like that here. Are you okay, Aadavan?" She stepped near him and grabbed lovingly onto his muscular arms.

"I'm not." He was shaking from the cold and looked over at the thick jacket Cloudburst was wearing.

"Not a chance." Cloudburst shook his head. "How about you take hers?"

Theia took her long and tattered blue coat off and put it around Aadavan without question. "What happened down there? The ocean, the sky, it seemed…"

"Angry, and so am I."

"What's going on?"

"The planet made some sort of stone and decided to place it directly in my headquarters!" He wrung out a fistful of his pants and proceeded to take off and empty each shoe of salty water.

"Since when?" Theia's interest grew stronger. "Why didn't you mention this to me earlier?"

"I found it not too long ago before I had the chance to speak with you." Aadavan's eyes uncomfortably shifted towards Cloudburst as he lowered his voice. "Something is happening here, beyond our vision, superseding our hopes, Theia. This is not a joke. Doom is truly impending."

"What do you think it is?"

Aadavan began tying his dripping curls back into a low bun. "That storm was some sort of message. I just know it."

"What kind of 'message'?" Cloudburst chimed in.

"Get out of here! Seriously! This has nothing to do with you!" He kept his gaze on Theia. "Why is he even here with you right now anyways? He doesn't need to be near us all the time!"

"We have to keep an eye on him. You know that, Aadavan."

"I simply don't care! Cloud-whatever, go do something else! Go bother someone else! Seriously!" Aadavan huffed loudly.

"Hardly anyone else is here, remember?" Cloudburst tried to keep them off track as he began to leave. *They can't know about Nathaniel in hiding,* he thought once he was too far away for Theia to hear what was in his head.

Aadavan decided to not mention the sound of Nathaniel's voice. *If that really was him… I may have to take matters into my own hands by disposing of him to the crocodile. I don't need Cloudburst thinking he has a friend to create an escape plan with. I also don't need Theia to put her hand in matters that she doesn't need to. I'll have to look for him later.* "Well, that will not be for long! Soon you will be retrieving new fighters from the falls! Make sure you are ready. Lorelai better have some new visions soon."

"I still think that we shouldn't intervene much in the next round," Theia continued their conversation as it was only the two of them.

"Oh, come on!" he put a hand up to his scratched forehead. "Don't give me a headache on top of everything else. I just told you that the planet gave us a sign of pure insanity. Lighting shooting down from the sky! One blue bolt in particular was much larger than the others! It cracked the rock! It was as if we were tilted over to one side, Theia! The ocean halfway emptied itself to cover part of this land. Did you not see how much water spilled over? Look around at this! Even the hills are soaking, the wheat field; we are dealing with something far beyond what we may be able to comprehend! We have to be involved now more than ever before!"

"Just relax."

"Don't you dare tell me to relax!" He pointed a finger at her face, which she gently pushed aside.

"Aadavan… what did that stone have on it? Words? Symbols?"

He sent his fist up at the sky with an intimidating glare. "Words were written on it, but I didn't get to check the entire thing before it was partly obliterated!"

"What did it say? Why don't you lead me over to where you found it?"

"Certainly."

The two began walking side by side as he tried to calm down. *The water better not have destroyed our living space! The stone slabs need to stay intact! The crocodile better be safe, too!*

"I'm sure that you showing me this will not make whatever is watching us happy." Theia tried to hold in a small chuckle, unsure of how to carry herself in the midst of his distress while confronting the haunting happenings taking place.

"Oh, it won't! But that doesn't matter. This planet can try to come after us." Aadavan turned to her with a smile. "We will fight back."

Lorelai was finishing up a worrisome conversation with Theia and Aadavan at the shore. They told her their perspectives of the messy storm and recalled what happened to both of them. She recounted how most of the miscellaneous junk and other items in the underwater castle were lost after the storm. Some of the fish were washed up and dead on the sand. Lorelai held on for dear life on one of the structural beams as the ocean floor seemingly tipped to one side, a huge portion of the water spilling across the land. The remaining sea creatures anxiously tried their best to swim with substantially less water for a small amount of time before it began refilling at the planet's doing.

"That anglerfish, the basking shark, all those creatures almost died! Was that some sort of earthquake you caused, Aadavan? What in the world happened?" She was lying on her stomach, elbows dug deeply into the sand as small waves greeted her silver tail every now and again. "I thought I was going to die!"

"I didn't do anything wrong! How dare you assume I created such a terrible problem? I found something in my vines and investigated it," Aadavan said.

"It wasn't him." Theia knelt down closer to her friend. "It was the planet."

"Why?"

Aadavan placed a hand down onto Theia's shoulder and hers met his quickly. "We need to tell you about the stone. It may be something you can find down in the waters, the piece that was dragged out to sea. It almost hit me in the head and killed me. I'm glad I'm still standing here to tell you about it. It's clearly your duty to go after what was lost. You will have to go find it and tell us what it says."

"Seriously?" Lorelai genuinely laughed for a moment and looked at Theia then back at Aadavan. "Oh, you aren't kidding?

"There are not many details to discuss yet. But yes, seriously. This is a mission that only you can be sent on. We have to know what was put in my yard and what that missing half of the stone says. It may destroy all we've already decided and built. It could derail our destiny before we're able to reach our potential… I mean… before society can reach their potential."

"Nice slip up." Lorelai faked a smile. "I'm sorry to hear that you almost died, Aadavan, that must have been terrifying. I've had quite a few near-death experiences myself."

"That's fascinating." He paid no attention to what she was sharing. "But we can't spend time talking about anything less important than you retrieving that stone. Go down at once."

Theia held her tongue as she looked at him and, against her better judgment, Lorelai took orders from the other two and traveled the deepest she'd ever been in the ocean. She kept each breath under the water steady, still unsettled by the feeling of it entering through her nervous windpipe. Two small groupings of partially translucent fish swam past her as she descended further. It was beginning to be too dark to see. She navigated carefully past venomous groupings of flickering light pink jellyfish.

I can't believe I want this, but I hope that anglerfish makes an appearance. I just need it to not be hostile towards me. How else am I supposed to find this blasted stone? I can hardly see anything through the colors of the water.

To her luck, the large fish eventually made its way to her and swam close enough to light a path, enabling her to look around. She made sure to not swim past the boundary it liked others to remain away from. It was so large that it pushed a significant amount of water with it as it went along near the ocean floor. Most other life forms would stay in hiding or head in the opposite direction when she came nearby.

I need to find something down here. I just can't come up empty handed. I have to prove to Theia and Aadavan that I can contribute too.

Several minutes passed as the weight of deep water increased around Lorelai's goosebump-covered body. For a bit of time, she only came across random pieces of metal, moss-covered statues, and bones from deceased fighters of the first game. She spent around half an hour searching, although there was nothing to be found. She was just about to give up and return to her headquarters when a stone shard caught her eye. The fish's light was bright enough for her to make out what it said.

#BB4B89

It's a color hex… Her fingers brushed against the engravings, and she felt an immediate shocking pain behind both her eyes. With her eyelids closed in discomfort, all she could see was purple. Lorelai experienced what felt like severe brain freeze for almost an entire minute, like her brain was growing in her skull without enough room to expand any further. *What is happening? Why am I in so much pain?* Her thoughts soon refocused. *Something is behind me! Something is watching me! It's going to come after me!* She sensed unknown life forms in the deep around her.

With that thought, she felt the ocean floor vibrating below her, not realizing that the shard was resting on top of a monstrous whale's head. It opened its sizable eyes and through them the same glowing color she saw from the darkness filled up the ocean as the creature woke up. *Just like Aadavan's crocodile!*

Her stomach turned at the sight of the color as anxiety slowly creeped up on her. The hairs on the back of her neck stood up as a familiar feeling reintroduced itself. She held both of her water wrinkled hands together, gripping so hard that the blood flow was being cut off. The anglerfish swam away as worry tightened at her throat. She swallowed painfully. The darkness, loneliness, vulnerability, and insecurity that she felt was all consuming.

Flashforward to CHP. 3 of ECHOES OF EUNOIA

Anon was exhausted as he walked into Amira's bedroom with a restless expression. She sat in the corner occupied with her phone, trying to catch up with all of the unread messages that were left by her family and friends. It was quiet as each of them pondered what they were going to do next. Despite how big his wings were, Anon tried to forget they were there, which he could do only for so long before being reminded again. He caught his reflection in a mirror that was leaning against her wall, which brought on another bout of anxiety.

"Seriously?" he grunted. "Why is this still facing this way?"

Anon grabbed the mirror and swung it backwards, loudly dropping it against the wall in a panic.

"I'm sorry, I forgot to turn it around." Amira locked and set her new phone face down, overwhelmed by the amount of red badge notification icons on her screen. "It's going to be okay, Anon."

"You don't know that," he snapped back. "It's also easy for you to say that since you don't have… you don't have wings, Amira! I'm a freak! You don't understand! This isn't the same for you! You can actually control your own—ugh, just forget about it!"

His lip was trembling as he slowly turned to see her. Even though the bedroom lights were dim, the blinds were still open and let the moonlight in, leaving him unable to hide his facial expressions. He had never felt more vulnerable and exposed before that moment. A single tear escaped his eye as he looked down at his arms.

"It's alright Anon…"

"No, it's not! It's not fair! This isn't right! I think we really messed up!"

"I messed up too?" she asked, surprised by his choice in words.

"No, me, whatever! I messed up! I think I really made a mistake with my wish."

She felt a shock of pain in her heart. "You wished for me. How was that a mistake?"

"Seriously? Don't say it that way." He wiped the tear off his cheek, and his voice cracked, "I'm just so tired of crying in front of you."

She noticed how he was biting on his lips again, pacing around, and running quivering fingers through his hair. Amira was very concerned about his mental state as it seemed to be crumbling before her eyes on a daily basis ever since they made their wishes to go home.

"It's alright to cry Anon. There's no need to be embarrassed." She stood up to wrap her arms around him.

"Please don't touch me right now." He looked everywhere but her eyes and put his hand into the air to keep distance between them.

Her feelings were becoming hurt. "This is hard for me too, okay?"

"Don't make this about yourself, Amira, please. You don't understand. I was sort of given a great set of cards compared to most of the others on that planet, and I may have played them awfully."

"You chose for us to come back here together."

"I-I'm not saying that was a mistake, okay? It's not what I wished for that's wrong... it's what I didn't wish for."

"You mean Zayika?" Amira chose to sit back down. "Do you have any feelings for her?"

"Oh, come on. Don't tell me you're jealous or think that I like her in some type of way."

"What?"

"It's not like that. I just… maybe, I shouldn't have just… left her there? I don't know! I do care about her."

"Why do you think I'm jealous?"

"It's obvious that you are… that you get jealous. I mean, you did when I mentioned Estrella."

"Your ex-girlfriend? Oh, come on, Anon, I was being playful. I wasn't actually jealous."

"I'm not too sure about that." He stopped pacing to give her his undivided attention.

"What? You care about Zayika that much?"

"No…"

It started to rain outside in the calm neighborhood, and the repeating rhythm of raindrops tapped softly on the window.

Amira's brown eyes were momentarily defenseless, showing a piece of her inner struggle with embracing her confidence. "How much do you care about me?"

"A lot." Anon's face was flushed. "Like, a lot."

"In what way?"

The two stared at each other as he shied away from the full truth.

"Like how I care about everyone. I care about all of you on the planet, and I feel bad that Zayika is just there alone. Have we screwed up her life?"

"Maybe you should try to not think about her."

"I'm not sure how to. It's like she placed a curse on my mind."

"Let's lie down together." Amira took his hand in hers and led him over to her bed.

Anon slowly, and carefully, fell onto the mattress on his wings and back with Amira's help. After dimming the room's lights, she went to lie down next to him on her side. Her face rested on the palm of her hand, her heart racing.

"I don't think I've ever felt so, I don't know, alive before?" His eyes met hers.

"Same." She smiled.

"I'm glad you are happy." He moved closer to her. "I feel happy too at times, rare moments, but I feel guilty when I am."

"It's not good to focus on what you regret. We have to keep moving forward. Don't feel bad about what you chose to do. We will never have to see Zayika again."

"I hope that's true."

But that came to be untrue, as she was always at the forefront of Anon's mind, becoming plagued with nightmares of her. He couldn't sleep well at night with her in his thoughts. There was seemingly no escape, as there was no way to predict what he would think of next while he slept.

Most of the time he experienced various degrees of sleep paralysis—quite literally trapped under Zayika's control when he was vulnerable, cold, and trying his best to finally get some rest.

One nightmare in particular was not like the others. Anon was back on the treacherous survival grounds again with Zayika, as he normally was, but something was inexplicably different this time. The nightmare felt real… too real to him. In this one, he found himself seeking her out. He walked and eventually ran everywhere he could, trying to see where she was. "Anon, I'm over here!" echoed around him as he tried to figure out if he was getting any nearer to her voice. It wasn't until he reached the Oceanic Guardian's faction that he found her.

"Zayika?" Anon asked. "Is that… you?"

She was sitting down on her knees and facing the ocean as he approached. It was unlike her to be so mute. He touched her back lightly with his pointer finger, accidentally shocking her, and she flipped around in a split second. Her purple hair flowed with every gust of strong wind. Her eyes were bloodshot, a mix of red and green, and looked far larger than normal. Anon was startled and lost his footing while stepping backwards to create space between them.

"What is wrong with you?"

Zayika's steps were sluggish and heavy, like she was walking through quicksand or was too far into a bottle of alcohol. She lost her balance, tipping over while trying to get closer to him.

"Help me, p-please," she begged in what was hardly even a whisper, clutching onto her stomach in a great deal of agony. "This isn't m—"

"What?" He was unsure of what to do when she stopped in her tracks.

"Anon…" Zayika began to cry. "I think it's my — m-my, it's making me sick, I'm s-so sick."

He could see in her eyes that something was very wrong and caught a glimpse of the part of Zayika's consciousness that was trapped, controlled, and desperate to be set free. She started to pull roughly on her silver and purple hair, like she was trying to tear it out of her scalp. Lightning bolts, the color of neon purple, which he had never seen before, cracked down and the raindrops were colder than ever before.

"I-I don't know what it did."

"What?"

"This planet, Anon." Her head fell downwards.

"I'm sorry I left you behind here." He walked over and bent down to look at her at eye level.

"It's okay," she said brokenly with her deep voice, keeping her face hidden from his view again.

"It is?"

She leapt forwards with a high-pitched scream, "Of course it's not, you ruined every single thing!"

Before he could blink, she had her hand around his throat and began lifting him up into the air. Anon clawed desperately at her skin, trying to burn her, but he was unable to create any lightning. He looked at her face as it contorted from displaying vulnerable suffering to an intimidating glare. Her eyes were yearning for self-destruction and escape from whatever substance was drowning the real her under the guise of the planet.

"Please put me down!" he shouted.

"I promise that I will make you regret what you di—"

"Why are you doing this to me?"

"I will never forget you."

"I'm sorry I left you behind, okay?"

"I will make you regret what you did."

"Z-Zayika..." he could hardly speak as her grip tightened.

"I will never forget you."

"Please forget me, forget and let it go, I'm begging you!"

"It's time for you to face the consequences."

Then... he woke up in a cold sweat.

Anon wasn't in bed with Amira anymore.

He was falling from the sky and down into the depths of Eunoia again. Consumed by a sinking feeling, and forced against his will, he was pulled away from Earth. His eyes flew open as he realized this was reality and not just a nightmare. Zayika was over on the cliff sides near the ocean watching him fall.

Her hair was changing colors, closely resembling a swarm of bugs crawling through it as it did so, from the bottom to the top eating invasively into where it was silver. It became fully purple from a radiant curse taking control of her from within. The planet had a hold on her soul and wasn't going to let go without a fight.

The left and right sides of her brain were being operated under the magenta colored spell. She took its orders and commanded Anon to be sent back to Eunoia for a deathly round of hide and seek.

Lorelai

Present

I found myself in another underwater life or death situation, attempting to retrieve information from some sort of stone for Theia and Aadavan. *Why am I pushing myself like this for them? Do they have any idea about the dangers that lurk in these waters?* Then a very important thought crossed my mind: *would they do the same for me?* I began to doubt the loyalty between the three of us, noticing a very distinguished imbalance of treatment. I was beginning to feel left out. Severely misunderstood. Neglected. *Who cares what this random stone says anyways? Is it really worth risking my life down here? I can only see a few shards engraved with random letters and numbers. All this has done is make my head hurt.*

Another creature lurked near me, and the darkness was infiltrating my peace of mind. I started to swim upwards and towards, what I best guessed, the direction of my residing ruins. My hands were empty, but I used them to blindly create underwater currents below, pushing back whatever had its huge eyes hungrily watching. Fatigue was overwhelming as I used my improving core strength to push upwards. My muscles were sore, stripped of all strength so that I may be able to become stronger. I recognized a distinct hue in the depths that felt unnerving to see again. A color that would also appear from time to time in the sunsets and what also seemed to be seasonally disastrous mood swings.

I escaped whatever unknown was going to swallow me whole and returned to my usual thinking place as soon as I could get there. It took a while for my heart rate to return to its usual pace. Residing in the corner felt the safest to me. It wasn't until I fell into a deep meditative state that I began to have visions of who was to be brought next.

I'll make sure to tell Theia I didn't see any large stone piece, only a small shard. I can't just make it sound like I gave up. The mission they sent me on was impossible without some sort of guidance.

I ran my fingers softly over the scar on my arm left by the anglerfish and kept my eyes closed.

Maybe the next fighters can keep me better company than the fish or even the other two do. They hardly come to see me. Sometimes Theia does. It can't be that no one is on my side. It can't be this lonely and dangerous here. If so, why did I ever step into that portal in the first place?

Within the next few dark hours, I saw who was to arrive from the falls. My visions were never completely silent, as the sounds of various whale calls always accompanied them; high and low pitches fading in and out on a loop for hours. They sounded like tubas; violins but with broken strings. A mutant underwater orchestra.

I was thankful for the visions returning to me as it meant we could meet new people and recruit the minds of others who were intended for a greater purpose than what Earth had to offer.

Was Earth really so bad, though? I asked myself. My mind felt like it was changing. My memories, thoughts, and feelings weren't being soberly navigated anymore. *I don't recall feeling this alone there. Or unsafe.*

Theia met with me at the shore again, accompanied by her assistant Cloudburst. He always kept his words with me to a minimum, like everyone else, as she took charge in leading our discussions. *I'll tell her about the color hex I found later. Cloudburst doesn't need to hear about matters that don't concern him.* I only told them that I did not find an entire stone, a partial lie, and was thankful I didn't have to face Aadavan's reaction at my disappointing news.

"He won't want to hear this. We really need more pieces of the puzzle that the planet has left behind for us to decipher." Theia told me what I already knew. "Please tell me that you're at least having vi—"

"Visions." I finished her sentence. "Yes, of course."

"What terrible news for the next thirty unsuspecting souls," Cloudburst muttered to himself, intentionally loud enough for us to hear.

"Well, let's not waste any time." Theia ignored him. "Let's get the next fight started."

I held back a nervous laugh. "Want to know something interesting? I already know one of their names."

"How?" Theia's excitement was cut short as she looked over at Cloudburst with an odd look on her face, as if she was able to hear his thoughts.

"He was wearing a name tag in my vision, doing some sort of research on the rocks there." I paused for a moment. "The man's name is Gebu."

CHAPTER NINE: THE LOBBY

Cloudburst

Present

I had good news and bad news. Thanks to Nathaniel giving me all of the credit for surviving the last ordeal, it seemed that I won the representative's terrible test. He and I made it with the use of instinctual decisiveness and pure adrenaline. The strongest mental hurdle of it all was trying to keep my eyes off of the faces of the people I took against their will in order to survive. I was at first given an unfair disadvantage because everyone else was morphed in a way that I wasn't—not that I was complaining. I think someone would have to be wildly insecure to be upset about not being morphed. Though the game was an extreme challenge at first with trying to accept the ways in which I was vastly different… I didn't give up.

I had to push through how mentally taxing it was to feel helpless in the face of inequity. Because I remained so patient and determined, Theia secretly rewarded me with what you could call a boost. I was given stronger abilities, able to shoot a yellow bolt of electricity from my arms, a painful but necessary upgrade if I wanted a fair chance of winning whatever the planet chose to give me.

So that was the good news. We were told that the winner would be granted a wish at the very end when we got to return home. I don't think the representatives foresaw me winning; they seemed… regretful for making me even compete at all. I could tell by their expressions when it was over that they were disappointed that I survived. By a rare stroke of luck, they didn't find out about Nathaniel, who was hiding in the jungle bunker, thanks to his sheer amount of stealth.

It was almost as if they wanted nothing to do with me specifically but that they ironically wouldn't be able to do anything without me. I felt they grew dependent on my involvement after all the chores and dirty work I did for them.

They better grant me a wish like they said they would. They can no longer string me along like this. They tell me one thing and then do or say something the complete opposite. I refuse to be played like this over and over again!

The bad news… I was still trapped, and I didn't know how I would find a way out. I was commanded by all three of them—but let's be entirely honest, mainly bossed around by Aadavan—to kidnap more people to get set up for a second cruel competition.

They told me that I wouldn't have to fight in the upcoming one, but that if I was supposed to live, then I had to help somehow. The type of help they asked for I would classify as manipulation, but they never challenged their own views enough to see it that way. Truthfully, only Theia seemed to sometimes.

In what felt like the blink of an eye, time passed from the end of the first killings to the beginning of the next getting planned. They tried to decide what they wanted to do differently this time around. I was eventually demanded to go back to the waterfall over and over again to get more people. The representatives decided that they wanted ten prisoners assigned to each of them. Thirty people fighting in total; three groups set against one another and destroyed for their entertainment.

Bringing the next set of people back from the waterfall happened as it usually did. Most of them died while getting morphed shortly after arriving, the representatives would fight about it, and then the crocodile would eat the corpse after they tossed it into his mouth. Every time that thing ate more human bodies it grew abnormally, yet somehow it was magically still able to fit in the pond at the edge. It was seldom awake and would sleep for long periods of time when waiting to be gruesomely fed.

This must be why they're making us start another game so soon; they feel some type of responsibility for this place and these monsters that inhabit it. How is the anglerfish going to sustain itself? There must be other fish it eats down there. I never want to touch that ocean. If I go in, I know I'd never get out.

My thoughts wandered aimlessly just as I did right after getting transported back to the small town. The man that Lorelai saw in her vision was there, apparently doing some sort of research with the rocks. I could already sense timidness from him. He seemed like a loner who stood out in a clean, white coat, taking notes of everything nearby. Clear goggles covered the majority of his face, comically too big for him. He had tan skin and short, curly hair. Everything about him fit the description I was given, although he was a bit taller than I imagined.

I really hate this.

Even though I was given special abilities, I tried to never use them for evil or with the intent of harming someone else. Some days, though, there were grey areas in which I couldn't see a way a problem could be resolved without using some of the power I had. It was hard to restrain myself sometimes, and I wasn't proud of it.

"Is there anyone else here with you?" I asked, stepping out from behind one side of the waterfall and over to the stranger.

"What? Who are you?" he asked me, his voice high-pitched and fearful.

"Please answer my question," I said. "No one else can see this."

"I don't have to answer you."

He dropped a petri dish while trying to dodge my arms as I leapt forward. "You're coming with me!"

"This study isn't illegal, it's—" He attempted to turn away.

I grabbed onto his shoulder and sent a sunny shockwave through one half of his body that temporarily paralyzed him. I held his hands together behind his back as he stared at me silently. His work name tag was in capital lettering, GEBU M.

"Well G-Gebu…" I wasn't sure what to say at first or how to pronounce his name correctly. "You could've at least tried to put up a fight. You'll want to learn how to do that where we are going, and if you don't, you won't be coming back. Let's go."

I brought him to the representatives, and Theia wasted no time in torturing him, no time at all in fact, and was shocked at what the results were when he managed to survive, unlike her other victims. They seemed regretful of how he turned out, wondering what went wrong and if they'd rushed too quickly through the morphing process. He wasn't given as many abilities as the previous fighters before him. Theia had established him as a faction fighter under her direction and was trying to hold in her disappointment as they looked at Gebu, who was in one of the containers.

"Why are his wings different? Why didn't you wait until the paralysis wore off first?" Aadavan asked. "I almost couldn't even tell that he had been morphed at all."

"No wonder he survived, barely anything happened," Lorelai said. "I guess that's a good thing?"

"Not really. He's fighting for my faction. No offense." Theia sighed.

"It's fine! I just want to get out of here! My back really hurts," he responded, both hands resting in front of him.

The representatives all gave me a serious look as Aadavan spoke, "You'll need to hunt more, Cloudburst. Remember, we each need ten members. Hopefully most will come from your captures and not from the green hills."

A little while later, I brought the next victim who survived morphing—though it wasn't pretty. After some wrestling, he put up a true fight just as I would in his place. I was able to apprehend him and he got assigned into Theia's faction too. He had a difficult time handling his hostility with the rest of us, and the entire situation really… which was understandable.

His name ended up being revealed as Nero, and he tried to keep a brave face when being morphed. Medium-sized white wings sprouted from his back and looked incredibly similar to many of the men who I once fought alongside. Blood dripped down his skin as he convulsed in pain.

"Why did you freaks do this to me?!" he shouted at the representatives from one of the cages with knotted fists.

"Let me talk to him, please! I need company!" I heard Gebu say from a room down the hall.

"Shut up!" Aadavan yelled back and slammed the door, leaving him and Theia standing across from me near the newcomer. Lorelai was already back in the ocean.

I tapped on some of the glass next to me. "You should let him out of there… it's unpleasant to be trapped." I kept my eyes planted on Aadavan. *Can you comprehend that?*

"Well, Theia, are you going to do the honors?"

Nero's eyes exuded revenge as he dripped sweat onto the metal flooring. "Get me out of here! What have you all done to me?"

"Hey, don't drag me into this!" I interjected.

He flipped me off through the glass. "You are the one who, literally, dragged me into this!"

"Ugh, that was against my will—"

"Stop talking!" Aadavan interrupted. "Theia, we need to see what he can do."

"Don't rush the process." Theia squared both shoulders clad in her tattered clothes.

"The process is already over." Aadavan retorted.

Nero punched the door in front of him. "It's about to be all over for you the second you let me out of here!"

Aadavan turned to face Theia, speaking within earshot of me but not their newest victim, "So now we are getting death threats. What is our backup plan for if, and when, certain fighters really do attempt to kill us?"

She held back an entertained chuckle even though she looked afraid. "We didn't think that far, did we Aadavan?"

"This is in no way funny." He looked back at Nero for a quick second. "Yeah, not funny in any type of way. He really might kill us!"

"Get me out of here!"

I walked over to the door and our eyes met. "Give them hell," I said, unlocking it for him.

Flashforward to CHP. 6 of CARRIERS OF EUNOIA

Zayika, Omar, and Anon were all chosen to fight in the Over Grounds faction and taken by Mae, commanded by the representative Theia, to the morphing chambers. The only one who hadn't been changed was Omar, to his surprise and… disappointment.

"Why did I not get morphed too?" He couldn't keep himself from staring enviously at the other two.

"You just simply weren't chosen," Mae replied and left the room.

"I'm going to excuse myself," Zayika stated as she felt lightheaded, needing a fresh perspective and air.

Omar's heart was conflicted and ached tenderly as it endured a never-ending battle of selfish jealousy versus genuinely caring for others. "Make sure you stay safe," he told her as he went into his room alongside Anon. "How am I going to survive what's coming next?"

Anon turned on a lamp near his bedside as his friend followed him. The atmosphere was tense as they looked at each other curiously—the main focus being Anon's changes. He'd painfully survived being morphed and couldn't stop looking back at his new wings that went right up above his head. The feathers were jet black, unlike his arms that had a neon blue pulsing through them.

"What did they do to you?" Omar asked.

"No idea, but I feel awful. I need to lay down." Anon sat as well as he could on his thin bed and hunched over. "My back hurts so bad. Why can't this thing have any padding, like at all? This hurts so bad." Sweat dripped from his face. "I need to get this shirt off, it's so hot in here. Is it hot to you? Can you help me get this off?"

"I wonder why my body didn't change?"

"You're lucky it didn't," Anon groaned.

Omar crossed his arms tightly. "Just seems odd that I didn't have an outward change. Maybe it's just an unseen effect. Maybe I have mental abilities that you don't have."

Anon groaned again and clutched onto his stomach. "I feel like I'm dying. I need to be put out of this misery."

"I don't understand why I am still the same but you and Za—"

"Omar, no one else will tell you this but I will," Anon stood up slightly from the bed. "You need to stop talking sometimes. You have a tendency to, a-ah that's a sharp pain, ugh—a tendency to make things about y-yourself."

"What?" Omar kept a guarded stance.

"It's pretty t-terrible. I'm in so much pain right now."

Omar's head started spinning. *No one's ever told me that before. Is it true? What? Am I not allowed to have feelings? Am I not allowed to want to be included?*

Anon caught Mae walking past their door out of his peripheral vision and desperately shuffled over to call after her, "Hey! Please come over here! Mae!"

She excitedly stopped whatever she was doing to come back around and see what he wanted. "Yes?"

"What can you do? I'm assuming you're morphed too, right?"

Omar walked up behind Anon to hear their conversation better.

"Um… I'm actually a healer." She blushed at his sudden interest in discovering her ability.

Anon breathed in deeply through his teeth at the pain running deep in his bones. "That's great. P-please help me, I need this to hurt way less. I'm having a hard time adjusting. I tried to keep a brave face back there, but I can't keep up appearances any longer."

"You look pretty good to me." She winked at him again.

Anon started blushing too. "Uh, t-thanks."

Omar rolled his eyes and went back to the room to look out of the window. "Ugh, whatever." *I doubt she can even heal him, she's just flirting. It's ridiculous how he needs validation and attention from women to feel good about himself.*

She stood taller. "Yes, I can help with the pain."

"It's so hot, I need to get my shirt off." Anon started to take it off.

"I can help with that too." She smiled, giggling, and helped him pull off the fabric as much as possible. "I may have to give you a custom shirt to fit around these wings."

"That's fine." He smiled back through the pain as he tore away his shirt.

Mae started to put a hand out to him as they stood in the hallway. "Is it okay if I touch you?"

"Of course, anything that will help me feel better," he replied enthusiastically.

The two caught Kason's eye as he went to step out into the courtyard. "Shirt off now? Well, well, well. What's going on over here?"

"Just helping one of the newcomers get accustomed to the new space."

"I'm Anon."

He gave a teasing grin. "Oh, you are the one she was just telling me abou—"

"Not the time or place to talk, Kason." Her face grew redder. "How about you head outside like you were going to do?" He laughed as he walked outside, and she refocused her attention on Anon. "Sorry about that."

"No worries." He felt her cold touch his chest as light gracefully escaped her fingertips, and within seconds, his pain went away completely.

"How did you do that? I feel so much better now."

"Magic touch." She bit her lip to keep from smiling more at him. "I may have provided you with a little something extra."

"What could that be?"

"I may have… sped up a few things for you."

"You know how to do that? In what way?"

"With your abilities. Let's just say you may not have too difficult of a time learning to fly."

Anon smiled as the daredevil within him took an interest in her words. "There's someone I need to go talk to. Now is as good a time as any to pursue what we want, right?"

Her interested eyes widened. "Yes."

"I'm going to go see Amira down by the water."

Her smile fell. "Oh, okay then. Have a good time."

"I really hope those of us the representatives are trying to keep separate don't have to turn against one another," he stated while turning to leave. "Thank you, by the way, for helping me."

"Anytime for you, just let me know." Mae gave a half-hearted wave as he left.

Anon quickly took on flying around outside and tested his abilities out near Zayika, who wore signs of jealousy on her sleeve. Mae had given him a helpful boost and advantage of inner strength that he soon discovered would greatly come in handy. With no time to waste, and hardly any pain left at all from being morphed, he headed towards Amira who swam out from the ocean to speak with him again. He felt Zayika's eyes on his back, but her pressure wasn't enough to hinder the connection he felt between who he was told was supposed to be his enemy. Anon got as comfortable as he could in the sand as Amira was laid out in front of him, her bottom half covered by the water.

"Hey, you." He couldn't hold back his beaming grin.

"Hey. Why are you so happy?" Amira asked curiously. "I'm shocked you were flying up there! How are you so good already? Are you in pain at all? I have to tell you that I am also, as the others down there say, morphed."

"I'm actually doing okay. So are Omar and Zayika. We're getting as accustomed as we can to all of this. You wouldn't believe what some people look like up in that castle! There were these huge glass containers they locked us in. Wind blew all around me, and I was stuck within a small storm that changed my arms! Look at them! I create a type of lightning! There are other men with wings too! A guy even has three clouds that, like, follow him around! It's crazy!"

"How are you so… excited? Is that the right word?"

Anon kept smiling. "I have no idea. Don't get me wrong, I am worried, but someone from the group I'm in placed some sort of magical spell on me, I think. Really helped calm my nerves. I hope this feeling doesn't wear off, though. Either way… I'm happy to see you."

"Likewise."

He tried to not blush at her response as he continued, "I have to be honest. Ever since you were taken down, I couldn't stop thinking about you. I've kept this from the others, they probably would have teased me, but I needed to know for myself if you were okay. Even after hearing about some sort of 'faction' underwater, people in mine told me you were probably still alive, but seeing you face to face is something else. I'm so glad you're okay, Amira. Please tell me about what happened to you down there."

"There's not much for me to recall, actually. Some woman who I think is named Enya took me down to a broken castle with a bubble in front of my mouth so I didn't drown."

"That must have been terrifying."

"It was. So was the giant anglerfish that I've found is assigned to fight with me in whatever game we're in."

Anon thought she was joking at first. "Did you just say 'anglerfish'?"

"You think that's shocking?" Amira asked and pulled herself fully out from the water. "Look at this." She showed Anon her shiny, wet, orange tail.

"Oh my goodness." He couldn't take his eyes off of her as Omar began calling out for him from the Over Grounds castle. "W-we have so much to talk about."

"In the meantime, you may want to go see what Omar needs. We can meet again."

"Okay." He slowly stood up and forced out a small laugh. "I'll be back. Don't forget about me, alright?"

"How could I?" Amira asked jokingly, accompanied by a flirtatious wink that sent Anon stumbling as he walked.

"Whatever is happening here, whatever is coming next Amira…" he said from his heart, "I want you by my side."

Present

Cloudburst let Nero out of his cage, and he immediately bolted over to Aadavan. "You scumbag!" He grabbed him by his buttoned shirt and lifted him up.

"You need to put him down!" Theia interjected. "Don't you dare hurt him!"

"Let me go!" Nero looked at her with a threatening stance and didn't loosen his hold on Aadavan.

"W-we will work out a deal, okay?" She tried to talk him out of doing something rash.

"What sort of deal?"

"Just set him down, and we can discuss this."

Nero's teeth chattered as he threw Aadavan to the ground. He tried to catch his breath as Theia hurried over to check on him and make sure he wasn't hurt. They both embraced each other, and Cloudburst felt their attention eventually fall onto him.

"You can never do anything like that again," Aadavan told him.

"Oh really, what will happen if I do?"

"We will put you to work if you're unable to stay out of trouble during your downtime." Theia spitefully lifted her pointer finger. *No one hurts Aadavan. Cloudburst cannot help this man try to take him down. I need to make his anger more manageable to deal with.*

Without hesitation, or forewarning, she quickly sent Cloudburst back to the waterfall to retrieve three people; Mae, Kason, and Lyra. The three were on a hiking excursion at the falls when he arrived.

So, Lorelai told Theia about these people from another vision? How many has she been getting? Do they increase over time? He saw his foggy breath in the air in front of him as he inhaled sharply. *It's always so chilly here.* He rubbed his hands together to create some warmth, catching sight of the group climbing down the rocks near the gated entrance.

Looks like they're done with their hike and going to the parking lot. He grew confused as he counted how many there were. *Six? How do I know which three to take? I can't recall their descriptions right now, did they even tell me? I swear they rushed me here.*

It was with that thought that one of the most invasively uncomfortable things happened to him. The representative, Theia, somehow replied to him in his head; *I will cast a light around those you need to collect.*

He shivered at the sound of her voice. *Did she just speak to me?* He saw that the sky was normal, everything seemed just as it did before he heard her, but there were indeed now three glowing lights circling three of the strangers up ahead, and somehow they didn't see the brightness encompassing them. *T-they can hear my thoughts?*

Only me, she responded. *Only when you are within a certain distance from me or at the falls.*

A chill sparked up his spine as he carried out Theia's orders, feeling violated as he no longer had anything in life to himself. He crouched and knelt in the trees, waiting for the right moment to stun and grab the unsuspecting victims one by one. He tried to keep his thoughts to a complete minimum. When all three were restrained, Theia promptly brought them back to the castle for dispersion to the factions.

They waited in their cages with the doors locked shut. The room was very brightly lit as extra light poured in from the open window, highlighting their terrified expressions.

"What's going to happen to us?" Mae asked, pounding on the rounded shatterproof glass in front of her. "Please don't hurt us! Just let us go! Why are you doing this? Please!"

It was around the same time that something out of the ordinary happened again. More fighters continued to wake up on the planet's hills. Only two unsuspecting people were selected, and their names were Draydon and Saylor. They began talking right after they woke up and quickly became friends as they offered encouragement and support to one another.

Aadavan soon found both of them while searching for Nathaniel as they were lost in the wheat field. *I deserve more fighters in my group. The other two will understand when they find out later.* He tried to justify his actions to himself in his mind. *Besides, Theia has an advantage with her fighter winning last time. It wouldn't hurt her to be a bit humbled and see someone from my faction overtake her own. I know one will have the strength within them.*

He took Draydon and Saylor to his faction through the use of lies and manipulation and had them morphed on the stone slabs without telling Lorelai or Theia.

"Who are you?" Saylor asked Aadavan as he approached them, faking a limp.

"I'm someone who can help," he replied. "I also woke up here. I created a safe shelter for us to stay in while we wait to be rescued and taken back home. You both will have to follow me."

Draydon was more hesitant compared to Saylor. "Really? What is your name? Why is your leg hurt?"

"My name is Aadavan. It's sore from all the running around on these hills and stumbling through that field over there." He pointed to distract them.

"How many people are already at your shelter?" Saylor asked, naively buying his lies.

"Around five others are safe there. You both need to come with me at once, we can't risk being out in the open like this in an unknown place."

"Alright then," Draydon said as the two strangers decided to follow him, unsure of what other options there were to take.

Once they reached the jungle, he led them to the tree house. The air was foggy, and a light mist creeped through all of the vines they pushed out of their way to get to their destination. Aadavan walked in front of the two, unable to stop smiling as he led them deeper into his trap.

"How did your glasses break?" Draydon broke the silence as they got close to his courtyard.

"Oh, you noticed that?" Aadavan was caught slightly off guard. "Um… I tripped while exploring out here."

"Interesting."

Saylor gently nudged him and whispered, "Maybe we shouldn't be asking so many questions."

"I'll ask as many as I want to," Draydon told her quietly.

Aadavan still heard their words. *I need to secure them in this faction.* "You both must be a bit tired from all of this walking. Please follow me, I'll take you somewhere you can rest."

They took his words as truth and made the mistake of following his faulty instruction.

"Where are the others that you told us about?" Saylor asked as she went to sit on the first stone slab that came into view.

"Do they even exist at all?" Draydon asked, trying to cover up his skepticism with a joke.

"Of course, they do." Aadavan tried to not roll his eyes as he went to step out of the door. "Please just take a seat. I will bring them in from the backyard."

Right as Draydon and Saylor sat on the rocks, their skin began burning. They jumped off once they were able to, screaming out for help, but he ignored them.

"What is going on?" Saylor yelled first. "This hurts so badly!"

Draydon tore off his extra layers of clothing as his skin felt like it was melting and becoming one with the fuzzy fabric.

Saylor started sprinting down the halls and into each room, looking for water to douse herself with. "We need water! We need him to help. Aadavan! Where are you? Come back! Something is in here! We are burning!"

"Who is to say that he didn't cause this?" Draydon yelled at her, practically naked by that point.

She yanked her jacket off and waved her hands all around herself, desperate to cool down. "I have no idea! Where is everyone else?"

"Come back, Aadavan!" Draydon called out. They watched in horror as he walked calmly towards what seemed to be a toxic-looking pond.

Aadavan smiled at the sounds of their screams as he kept walking forward.

"Why is he not coming back?" Saylor tried to catch her breath.

Draydon and Saylor looked down at their skin and saw that it was changing before their eyes. Rough tree bark, sprouts of green little leaves, and mushroom-like growths began to grow out of their skin.

Everything is going according to plan, Aadavan thought as he went to check on his crocodile. *They will adjust to their new home. They will fight for me.*

"Hope you aren't too hungry because I have bad news for you," he told the crocodile, who was just barely peeking out of the dirty water. "They morphed successfully."

Its huge purple eyes dimmed slightly in anger.

"At least that is good news for me." Aadavan pressed his lips together happily, not noticing one particularly haunting eye staring at him from the sky behind his back.

The iris was the exact hex color #BB4B89.

CHAPTER TEN: CAST PROTECTION
Present

Nero needed to burn off some steam after being morphed. Theia told him to take a walk outside. *How dare they do this to me? To any of us?* He was fuming. *What have they done?* His back was in excruciating pain as he peered over the edge at what they called their 'faction grounds'. He was held captive, forced into a glass container in a floating castle, and none of his questions were being answered. *What the actual hell?* His head, his feet, everything was sore as he ventured around and eventually met a few others... Gebu, Mae, Kason, and Lyra. He was the second person to arrive and survive being morphed from his group. Wings branched out of his back, like out of some sort of twisted fairytale.

He had so much hatred for Theia since she tricked him into the cage and left him feeling powerless. After it happened, she mentioned that he may also have been given more powers which he had yet to discover. This was proven to be true as Nero later discovered the control and effects he could have on the wind. *This has to be a nightmare, this cannot possibly be happening.* He kept trying to talk himself out of his own reality. *This isn't real, it just isn't!* He would tug at his back and try to tear out whatever he could get a hold of, always ending up with a handful of white, bloody feathers and utterly disgusted at how he felt. He was too nervous to fly and didn't trust whatever it was they put into his body to create what he believed were fake wings.

"Try them out. Let's see you fly," Theia told him when they were outside near the gated entrance. "Jump from the edge."

He was shocked at her demand. "Are you serious? No way am I doing that! You go first, you crazy bit—"

"Nero," she interrupted. "Let's refrain from being rude here."

"I'll push you off the edge if I have to! I'm not kidding!" he shouted, walking towards her.

Aadavan put his hand out to stop him. "If you try to harm her, we will have to kill you!"

"Oh really?" Nero gave him his best glare. "How are you going to do that? You're going to what? Make the ground quiver a little bit? I've heard that's all you can even do! You're pathetic!"

"You don't want to ever have to meet the crocodile, Nero," Theia spoke calmly.

"What are you even talking about?" *Crocodile?*

Aadavan added, "He's hungry for another feeding."

"You know you're both crazy, right?" Nero ran both hands through his black hair as his chest tightened. "Change me back to how I was and let me go! You can't run experiments on me! Let me go!"

He wished he could go back in time and turn down the plans he'd made with his friends.

Going to the waterfall was such a terrible mistake. This has to be a nightmare. All because Taya threw my phone over a small joke? Stupid bitch.

Nero was told to 'take a hike', so he went off on his own away from the two representatives and, who he perceived to be, his clingy roommate who always had something to say—Gebu.

Only tolerable person here is the blonde in the ocean because I never have to see her.

Nero felt as though his body wasn't completely his own anymore in an infuriating way. He tightened both fists and sauntered throughout the jungle.

There's no way I'm flying; I'm not doing anything they tell me to. They aren't even telling me the real truth here! Screw all of them!

He was starving for answers.

Why did she throw my phone? Seriously! Screw Cloudburst too, what an absolute coward for taking their psychopathic orders instead of kicking their asses and getting out of this place!

He kicked the dirt and pulled on some vines that were in his way, feeling suffocated and powerless.

Karma will come after each and every one of them!

"Seriously! Screw all of them!" Nero couldn't contain his rage and could no longer silence his voice at all. His thoughts had to be let out, loud enough for everyone else to hear.

"Can you please keep it down?"

"Screw you too!"

"What did I do?"

A man from the Land Dwellers faction had come into view from the sidelines, wearing blue overalls and holding metal tools in his hands. He had a mop of messy brown hair on his head that fell over most of his friendly face. His pale skin was covered in dirt as he stepped out from the peculiar shadows.

"You and everyone else here deserves to die!"

"Calm down, man, seriously." He shoved the tools in his hands into several deep pockets and didn't take his eyes off Nero. "Do you want to talk at all?"

"No. I jus—" His voice broke as it trailed off. *I don't know how I'm going to survive this. How am I going to protect myself? How have I already failed in protecting myself this badly to have ended up here?*

"Hey… relax. You know we are in the same boat here, right? I was lied to as well."

"W-what do you mean?" *Seriously, keep it together. Don't cry in front of this random stranger.*

Nero reminded himself of what his mom always told him; "Don't be weak, Nero," she would say with a stale expression, "Don't be weak."

"I'm not your enemy. I am also a victim, okay? I woke up on those hills over there, forced from my dreams and ripped into this unknown place."

"No, you weren't 'forced'! You weren't b-beaten and attacked at a waterfall!" Nero's eyebrows furrowed, his eyes slightly illuminated by the sun creeping through the trees. "You woke up on comfy grass! Our story is not the same! You don't understand what I lived through to even be here right now, to be standing in front of you."

"That's not what I'm—"

"You can't stand there and tell me that you know how I feel in any way. Oh, they gave you some metal tools to play with? How cute. Me on the other hand? I'm utterly screwed. Look at my back! Why don't you look at it?" There was subtle shuffling in the trees nearby as Nero spun around.

The other man sighed. "Why are you turning at all? I can already see them from—"

"Because you clearly don't get it!" he yelled. "We are not in the same boat! You will never understand how I feel! You cannot, you just can't!" He knelt down to the ground, overcome with emotion.

"It's going to be alright." The stranger walked to his side and went to put his hand on Nero's shoulder.

"I don't need to be comforted!" Nero sprung up and pushed him away. "Do not touch me! Ever!"

"I'm sorry, I wasn't trying to make you uncomfortable. My name is Draydon, by the way. Would you like to shake my hand?"

"No."

He nodded and crossed his arms. "That's okay, but can I offer you some unsolicited advice?"

"Absolutely not." Nero turned to head in the opposite direction.

"You need to get your thoughts together. Your head isn't in the right place."

"Excuse me?" He stopped dead in his tracks. *What does this poser even know about me? I'm not going to let him speak to me like that!*

"You are angry, which is understandable, but if you don't get it under control... your thoughts... you will probably die here."

"What do you know about this 'fight'?"

"Do you not know much about it yet?"

"Does it seem like I do?" he replied in irritation and muttered under his breath, "Idiot."

"I'm going to ignore that."

Does this guy have super hearing or something?

"What do you know about the… fight? We aren't really fighting each other, right?" There was forced laughter.

"Yes we are," he said nervously. "Aadavan told me."

"What? Seriously? And I get, what, these wings? Moving air around? What in the world? What can everyone else do? Where are the guns?" *How am I going to protect myself?* "When is this fight?"

"Apparently, it starts when enough people arrive and successfully get morphed. They're going to sound a trumpet for some type of ceremony. Aadavan told me they will go into more detail during it."

"Forget this! I'm getting out of here!"

"I don't think that's possible. It's a, you know, fight until death sort of thing. Last one standing," Draydon told him.

What type of cult have I been forced into? "Absolutely not! How much time do we have before this even starts?"

"Um. We don't know for sure."

"What? This can't actually be happening!"

"I would really suggest calming down. Aadavan told me to not be confused by our physical changes. They're apparently more of a reflection of our personalities, strengths, and weaknesses than anything else."

"Yeah right."

"No, seriously. Wanna know what power we truly will be using to fight? Our minds."

"What?"

"Your thoughts are your ammunition."

Draydon's words awakened a realization in Nero. *I have to do whatever it takes to survive. I may have to take the life of someone else. It's kill or be killed, and I will definitely kill whoever I have to.*

"My thoughts? Alright then." His breathing became steadier as he lowered his voice.

"Yes, and I'll give you something else that could be proven very useful in time."

Draydon went to a large nearby boulder and pulled out the scraps he was saving. He laid them out in front of him meaningfully. He set off a light in his palms and began creating absolute magic at his fingertips. His skin seemed to melt off, his bones exposed and his falling flesh somehow on fire.

What am I looking at?

"How are they metal? Your bones?" Nero winced. "Are you in pain? Does that hurt? What are you doing?"

He was focused intently on whatever it was he started crafting. "I'm not in pain. They will be made soon. Give me a moment please."

There was another rustling in the bushes.

"Did you hear that?" *I better not be losing my mind.*

"Must have been the wind." He laughed. "Do you know what game I'm talking abou—"

"Nice reference. Not the time for joking, though." Nero rolled his eyes. "What is it you're making down there anyways?"

He was molding something in front of himself on the rocks. Nero could hear hammering and sawing as Draydon tinkered with whatever it was he was making. *These jungle people have no chance winni* – Draydon eventually turned around with a handful of handmade throwing knives.

"These are for you. Use them wisely."

He hesitantly reached out to grab them. "Why are you helping me?"

"Because I believe greatly in karma. Please, take them."

"You don't have to tell me twice." Nero followed his instruction and couldn't resist his smile from spreading at how they felt to hold. *Time to practice.*

"Feel free to use some of our tree stumps for aiming practice! We've painted a few of them already over there." Draydon pointed somewhere else, but Nero couldn't take his eyes off the knives. "Saylor is probably over there right now and, to be honest, she is the one who painted those, so I can't take all the credit. She has a steadier hand compared to me anyways so it's better she did it. Would've been a bit lopsided if I tried."

"You said your name was Draydon right? I'm Nero."

"Yes. It's been nice meeting you. I hope the next time we cross paths that it's in better circumstances. I should go see what Saylor is up to now. I'm not sure if you've met her yet. She's sort of incredible. Stay safe out there."

Nero stared down at the knives in awe and disbelief. *I'll be able to protect myself.* "Alright then. Tell your friend that I say hello. Maybe I'll meet her soon," he said, although his attention was more focused on the knives in front of him.

Draydon practically skipped off, content with himself for helping. "I'll tell her."

With that, they parted ways. Nero thought he was alone in the jungle after Draydon wandered off, but quite the opposite was true. He stayed there a little while longer because of how quiet it was, wanting to keep his distance from the representatives, Aadavan and Theia, who mainly spent time in the castle together talking.

He looked over and played with his knives, feeling more confident with them by the second. He noticed the solid craftsmanship of the weapons, the improved accuracy created by the knives' chiseled feathered tips, and brought his attention to how useful they'd be with his windborne ability.

These are just what I needed to survive here. I have to practice my aim. If this all is real, if we really have to hunt each other, there's no way I'm going down without a fight. Anyone who crosses me will regret it. I'll make sure of that.

Flashforward to CHP. 11 of CARRIERS OF EUNOIA

Shortly after Amira was turned into a mermaid in the ocean's underwater structure, she was brought to her fighting companion, the large, intimidating anglerfish she named Hippo. She felt protected while swimming with her, those in the same faction keeping their distance from the two, as the fish seldomly refrained from being hostile with others. Amira was able to navigate the planet's deep waters while following the bright light emitted from her orb; it would sway side to side slowly as it glowed and lit the way for them and whoever else was close enough in the distance to be led too.

Many hours were spent aimlessly swimming in circles as Hippo kept Amira from venturing too closely to the other aquatic danger lurking from within the shadows or deteriorating coral reefs. *This ocean…* Amira thought to herself as she looked around… *it seems unwell.* She took note of how the seaweed withered lifelessly, schools of fish seemed to have rotting scales, and many broken pieces of scrap metal and fractured statues cut the bellies or fins of fish as they swam by, accidentally dragging against them uncomfortably. *I don't want to fight anyone down here. Us mermaids aren't turning against one another, are we?* She looked up at Hippo who was staying idly beside her. *Why does Enya not have an entire tail too? Is there something special about her?*

Her attention shifted once a stone caught her eye near what somehow looked to be a ship wreckage. *What if I find something down here that may help? Maybe this rock can direct me towards a clue. What if there's some sort of map on it?* She pointed down, and the anglerfish moved slightly towards it, illuminating what she needed to see.

THE WISH CARRIERS
ONLY THOSE DESTINED

HOLD FREEDOM'S KEY
THOSE WHO FEEL IT IN THEIR DREAMS
DON'T WASTE YOUR LIFE
ON PLANET EUNOIA

After Amira read the words, she was in disbelief and wonder. She was the first person to ever discover the name of the planet. Text describing and calling attention to the Wish Carriers was before her, and so was the unveiling of the title of the place that they all inhabited. *Those who feel it in their dreams?*

The wording on the rock reminded her of a particular dream she had prior to working on a crime scene with Arcadia on Earth before being taken to the starting hills. The night before that case, she dreamt of resting in her room in complete darkness. She was completely alone and experienced sleep paralysis, unable to do anything once the sounds of wind and rushing water filled her ears. A weight was on her chest as each breath became harder to take. Amira grabbed at her bed sheets, but she couldn't open her eyes. There was some sort of force fighting against her. She tried calling out for help, but she was unable to say anything at all. Only the thoughts in her mind kept her grounded in her own existence as fear began to fill her head and lungs. It wasn't until footsteps entered her room that the dream came to an end, becoming the worst night terror she'd ever experienced. Amira felt someone step onto her mattress and jam some sort of pointed weapon through her heart. She woke up sweating, panicked and traumatized. *What was that? Why did that just happen while I was sleeping?* Pain lingered in her heart as she got out of bed and checked to make sure she was okay in her bathroom mirror.

In the ocean, she felt anticipation rise in her chest as she breathed unsteadily in the water. She read each word out thoughtfully to her pet companion. *Our dreams? They determine if we are carriers of wishes?* Her heart beat faster as she had her hand over it. *Am I one?* She glanced down at her glimmering tail. Deep down she already understood that nightmare in particular was foreshadowing a specific type of calling. It wasn't until then that she realized the importance she truly held.

Amira thought about the conversation the others were having in the bunker when the six of them first joined together near the ocean. *Saige, Anon…* it was made known to her that at least half of them carried power beyond any understanding. She felt the need to immediately swim up to the surface as fast as possible to go speak with Anon about what she'd just discovered. *Is he a Wish Carrier too?* A smile sprang across her face at the surprising discovery. *Are we both going to go home? We're going to find a way out of here.*

Present

"Shh," a noise came from someone in the shadows. "Remain calm. I'm just passing by."

"Who's there?" Nero didn't see anyone.

"You have tenacity in you along with a twisted desire to get your way."

"Who is talking?"

"You remind me a lot of someone else you have recently met. You two men are a lot alike."

What are they talking about? Who? Draydon? Kason? Hopefully they're not referring to Aadavan.

"Show yourself!" he demanded.

"That's not possible right now," a booming voice told him. "I'm here to give you the other half of Draydon's brilliant advice. If you want to live, you will listen."

"Of course I want to live, who doesn't?"

"There are others who don't… trust me. You may meet someone here who doesn't. Be there for them if you do." He sighed. "It's very disheartening what others suffer through when hope is lost. There's really not much left but the support from others who genuinely care."

"Why are you talking to me?" Nero looked up at the sky.

"Because I only give my advice to two types of people. The people who don't want to live, I can sense it, I want to offer them some guidance and hope."

"Wh—"

"And the people who want to live because I want to help them fight."

"You sort of have everyone covered with those two extremes," Nero replied.

"That's not true because it doesn't cover everyone. There are some who fall in the middle of that spectrum. They want a life but don't at the same time. They want their life, but they will not fight for change to save and maintain it."

"What is this advice you're supposedly giving me? Right now, it's sounding a lot like those cultish tall tales Aadavan and Theia debate about."

"You cannot lose your wings. Don't ever allow anyone else to touch them," the voice rattled with a sense of despair that shook the trees. "I can't unsee the events that took place on this planet or unhear the screams of torture as his life was pried out of his own grasp."

His body went cold. "W-what are you talking about?"

"Others from my group in the past, they tortured a specific fighter from the Over Grounds faction. Similarly to Draydon, as you've now seen, they were able to craft weapons with their hands and…"

"What? They did what?" Nero's heart was pounding.

"The man they cornered had wings like you, all the men received them."

"I know this!" *Get to the point.* The suspense was killing him.

"They ganged up on him. He was outnumbered as they crafted a large and very sharp saw and tied him down to the base of a fallen tree here in the jungle."

No…

"He couldn't move. They took turns sawing away at the base of his wings at his back."

Nero clenched his teeth at the horrific mental image. *What if that happens to me? I'm going to puke.* "So he died? He bled out and died?"

"No, somehow something even worse than that happened."

"What could possibly be worse?"

"He was pulled into a giant portal where his consciousness may likely be forever trapped."

"Like… a void?"

"Exactly."

"What happened to him?"

"I never found out, and I haven't seen him since he disappeared into it. No one has. He was completely swallowed whole like it was a ravenous monster. Not even the representatives know what happens when both wings are removed."

"So…" Nero spoke into the darkness.

"So value your life and protect your wings," the strange voice instructed him.

Then, yet again, his mother's words repeated in his mind. *Don't be weak, Nero.*

CHAPTER ELEVEN: CLOUDY VISION

Theia

Present

For most of the morning, there were only clouds covering the entire sky. I was thankful to see many potential great fighters already and slowly, but surely, beginning to train and understand their emotional abilities in preparation for the second game. Aadavan was hesitant to trust the approach I was advocating for from a leadership standpoint. I was thankful that one of my own fighters and greatest helpers, Cloudburst to be specific, won the first challenge. The boost I gave him was proven to be effective. I had a great advantage and amount of respect given to me from the others for such an extraordinary win so soon into what we were creating. I already felt a large amount of care for the lives of those morphed. The thought of almost all of them dying ate away at me with each passing minute.

There has to be a way to avoid more lives getting lost, though, I reflected. *I'm sure the outcome of this next game will be better if we step back. We need to allow the fighters to think for themselves to a degree – just as we are able to. What about fairness?*

After the stone appeared in Aadavan's jungle, we met together to discuss what was going on. Some sort of rare anomaly unlike we'd ever seen before had occurred, and it had brought along a list of surprises… guests of the planet's own choosing. This meant that we needed more help than ever to continue achieving our goals and crafting a stronger society through putting those from Lorelai's visions to the ultimate test. She went down deeper than ever before into the ocean to search for the missing stone piece, but unfortunately, she didn't have anything to report to me when I last saw her. Regardless of that, her visions were helping us greatly, and I wanted to keep encouraging her to venture further into that realm for us.

I knew that Cloudburst was our best bet at carrying out Lorelai's visions and helping us get ready for the next fight. *He doesn't know how valuable he is.* I had been able to hear what he was thinking ever since I granted him more strength, and I was able to communicate to him via his own thoughts. The closer we were, the clearer I could hear him, able to hear him while he was at the falls too. To my knowledge, he wasn't able to hear mine, which was a relief. I hadn't told Aadavan about the rare ability that seemed to only be tethered between Cloudburst and me. In a way, I knew it would make him uncomfortable and probably envious, although he'd never admit it.

On the contrary, I was admittedly nervous as we gathered to announce the news to Cloudburst that he had to stay. I was unsure of what his reaction would be, hoping that he would not retaliate with a physical attack or unbridled anger. He was the only person left from the past events. The one body we never found was Nathaniel's. *He may have been burned alive. Not even ashes can be found. An entire existence swept away in the wind. What an awful way to die.* I sensed that a friendship had formed between him and Cloudburst before his passing. *It must be hard on him to have lost the one person he seemed to be able to talk to. I never, ever want to lose Aadavan. I'm not sure I could survive the heartbreak.*

I needed to regroup with the representatives, so the three of us gathered to meet with Cloudburst close to the wheat field. *This will be fast, like ripping off a bandage. Don't draw out the suspense. Cloudburst has to know his place here. We cannot afford to lose him.*

Aadavan was thrilled as we came together. He took me into his arms for a long, caring hug. "I missed you."

I laughed a bit. "Oh, come on, we haven't been apart for that long! Don't be dramatic," I gently teased.

"Where is he?" Lorelai approached and cut right to the chase.

"He'll be here any moment," I told them. "He successfully brought another three people here to us. Their names are Mae, Kason, and Lyra."

"They took to the morphing process well, I presume?" Aadavan asked.

"Yes. All of them did." *I'm surprised he is in such a good mood. Normally, he gets upset when I've taken fighters before he could. Is Aadavan hiding something from me?* "No one has spawned on the hills since the last ones, right?"

Lorelai shrugged, and Aadavan was quick to answer. "Of course not! If so, I would've told you! There is no one on the hills. Just silence. There is certainly no need to worry."

I was uncertain of his assurance, seeing right through him, but Lorelai seemed to not pick up on his mischievous enthusiasm. *Why question him further? Even if he's lying and took some new individuals for himself before asking us, I don't really mind. He deserves more support anyways. Leave it be. We have more valuable things to discuss. I'm glad he is in a good mood.*

Cloudburst came into view past some of the wheat stems as I continued talking, "One of my own is showing great promise."

"Who?" Lorelai asked curiously. "I'm hoping I will feel the same way with mine."

"Nero."

Aadavan rolled his eyes and adjusted his glasses. "I've seen him train. He's alright. He's ridiculous, though, for trying to kill us when he was first brought here."

"Can you blame him, though?" I responded.

The two looked at me with blank expressions.

"If the roles were reversed and we were in his shoes, try to tell me that you honestly wouldn't be as angry or upset in the same way?"

"The roles would never be reversed," Aadavan replied defensively.

"You sure about that?" Lorelai stared at the cracks in his glasses. "We've seemed to be put in our place."

He threw his hands in the air. "How dare you even say such a thing, Lorelai? Why don't you go back down into the ocean and speak your nonsense to the fish instead!"

She retreated from the conversation right as Cloudburst joined. "What's going on? Is there someone new I have to go after? Why do you all need to talk with me?"

Present

The representatives had no idea where Nathaniel was. For the first time ever, since setting foot on the planet, he felt an ounce of privacy to himself, which was overwhelmingly refreshing. He was able to survive off of the resources in the bunker and got his exercise and fresh air throughout the day, remaining invisible to the others—especially Aadavan. He was able to find some escapism, privacy, and even the smallest ounce of peace at times. The same couldn't have been said for Cloudburst. *That poor man can't get a break from their constant demands and lies*, his ally thought. The energy surrounding all of them was turning foul after a recent phenomenon occurred, best described as an earthquake. Everyone was even more on edge. Eunoia shook everything. A message had been sent to the representatives to back down.

Nathaniel had overheard the rest arguing about some sort of stone that appeared in the Land Dweller's jungle, but he wasn't sure where it was exactly. They were debating what certain phrases on it meant and why it was there in the first place. He kept quiet and used his ability to become entirely invisible, sneaking his way through and around tough situations. He seized the perfect time and rare opportunity while Aadavan was distracted to find the remaining stone piece and figure out what it said. They were near the wheat field when he heard the unsettling things they were sharing with his teammate while he was on his way to it.

"Your appointment... we decided that it will be permanent." Theia stared at the ground as if she was ashamed of her own choice in words.

"What? What do you mean?" Cloudburst asked, dumbfounded.

Aadavan stood tall with a stiffened back. "You are staying here."

"We need you," Theia continued, "I know we are going back on our word—but you need to understand."

"'Understand' what?!" he shouted. "You three are liars! You told me that if I worked long and hard enough that I could go home! You either ignore me completely or work me to death! There is no in between with you extremists!"

"Watch what you say to us." Aadavan got up in his face. "You should be more careful with your words, they'll only get you so far, and you may not like the direction they take you in."

Lorelai stayed silent and tried to warm herself with her hands, legs shaking. She needed to return to the rushing waters soon before her tail reappeared.

"Just stay. We need you, okay?" Theia and Cloudburst maintained eye contact.

"I won't ever forgive you for this," he told her.

"Okay. I don't care," she said brokenly, like she was lying to him and to herself.

Nathaniel listened close by and thought, *I need to leave now. I can't stay here any longer if I want any chance of privately visiting and seeing the stone for myself. Soon, they will all go back to their grounds. I have to move quickly. Time is of the utmost essence.* It was with that thought that he went off into the jungle, lit up by the ethereal moonlight. He blended right in with the leaves and vines. He breathed quietly and made sure to step lightly in case Aadavan was close by. *I have no idea how much longer they will be. I have to keep moving.* His heart raced, the thrill of getting caught making him feel alive.

When he eventually came across and saw the stone in person, he was taken aback by how remarkably big it was compared to what he had pictured. He started to pull off some of the plants that were growing on it, the roots of them tightly secured. He tugged as hard as he possibly could and was shocked at Aadavan's negligence in uncovering the entirety of what still remained. *With how uptight that man is, I'm surprised he didn't do a better job at examining this. Although, if I was almost killed for getting this close, I would be hesitant too.* The words along the side of it were clear as day, but to his astonishment... *half of it is missing?*

THE VOID WILL CONSUME THOSE
WHOSE WINGS ARE REMOVED

THE VOID WILL RELEASE THOSE IN ITS HOLD
FROM THE TELEPORTATION COMMAND'S REVERSAL
THE FATE OF ONLY THOSE CHOSEN TO SURVIVE
THE COMMONERS WITH NO DREAMS AT ALL
THE UNMORPHED
THE WISH CARRIERS

It was jaggedly cut in half. *I won't be able to read everything that it says.* He curiously looked around. *If this half is here, where is the other?* Smaller shards of it were also nowhere to be found. He peered over his shoulder at the ocean and saw just how far the tide came in during the storm. *Aadavan most certainly had something to do with this. His stubborn temper almost always makes things blow out of proportion. How will I know what the other half says?*

Nathaniel wasn't a glass half-full type of person. In fact, it infuriated him that he only had his halfway filled. He took what he could get and read the cryptic text laid out on full display. *Is this some sort of cheat code on how to get out of here?*

It was then that he learned just how untruthful the representatives were to the fighters. *Did they know what this stone said before the first challenge started? Did it appear before or after the murders? How will it change the trajectory of the upcoming one?* He looked around to make sure Aadavan wasn't nearby as he memorized the words and did his best to cover up his tracks in the leaves and vines around him. *Have to make sure Aadavan doesn't see all of this.*

There was something called a Wish Carrier; one of the only ways someone could get back to where they were supposed to be. *We didn't hear anything about this. Is this all rigged? I wouldn't be surprised. Is Cloudburst working with them in some way? When we met... was he trying to trick or confuse me? Doesn't seem in his nature.* He also learned that ordinary people who do not get morphed at all are also special and chosen to hold the power of wishing for anything they want. The commoners.

Nathaniel realized he needed to do a better job of looking after himself as he tried to uncover more about the dangerous situation he was in. He yearned for solitude and privacy, it was in his nature, and because of that he felt very drawn to and trusting of others who were the same way.

Flashforward to CHP. 8 of CARRIERS OF EUNOIA

Nathaniel wanted to find someone to help in the grand scheme of things. He was hopeful that if he put some support out into his faction that he would be rewarded with good karma. While more members were eventually assigned to the Land Dwellers for the second game, he took it upon himself to go to the courtyard and speak to one of them about the stone's information when Aadavan made it clear he would be locked away with no involvement in his room as a result of Theia's input. He was exhausted from hiding in the bunker day after day, but he had been there so long that he hardly felt as though there was any way truly out of it—that he had a fate waiting for him which surpassed the confinement of the metal walls around him.

He had completely lost hope that Theia and the other representatives would ever let him go back to Earth.

He kept a close eye on all of the new fighters who were assigned under Aadavan's watch just as he was in the past. They were also morphed on the stone beds. He heard their screams from miles away, even from down underneath the ground's surface, in his hidden space.

I wonder if any of them have the same ability as me? Turning invisible is one of the most useful ones.

As the leaders were reaching the amount of people they needed for their upcoming plans, there were only a few remaining slots to be filled before the intimidating trumpets would sound again.

Cloudburst brought one of the last six to the representatives who was eventually taken by one of Lorelai's people, Enya. Nathaniel never saw him again after that capture. The other five were dispersed too, the rest awoke on the hills, and two of them ended up becoming Land Dwellers.

That particular group invaded his bunker before they were finally split up by the harshness of the representative trio. He overheard their conversation which revealed interesting truths—such as some of them stating they had dreams that awoke something completely brand new in them. *I cannot believe it… they are Wish Carriers!* he thought from his bedroom.

One of them was named Saige. For some reason, he was compelled to intervene in her friendship with Zekiel, the man who he felt had great potential as a result of even greater suffering. *I want these two to make it back.* He was rooting for them and felt ecstatic that he was able to share knowledge that was worth more than gold.

He also figured out that their group had a commoner in it: Omar. The one with no powers at all was one of the most powerful of the six. *This man is more special than he thinks he is. What a shame. Hopefully he is able to see himself for what he really is.*

One evening he ventured from his bunker into the jungle, and to his fortune, Aadavan was either in his room or away at the castle with Theia. *I'm glad they choose to spend so much time there instead of here. I would go insane if I could never feel the sun on my skin.* He went up to the front of the treehouse that he was so familiar with and felt his heart thump with anticipation in his chest at what their reaction would be to his overwhelmingly great news.

The vine-covered rusty gates opened. Zekiel walked out from the building first, highly suspicious of the unknown man coming their way. He told Saige to stay inside while they spoke to protect her from any potential danger.

"We don't know who you are, sir. Why should we even trust what you have to say?" Zekiel asked.

Skeptical of others like me, good man. "My name is Nathaniel. I'm a Land Dweller. I'm fifty-four years old and have lived on this planet for over twenty, so I think I might be able to offer you some advice." *Keep exaggerating, I can't tell him the full truth. I can't get myself killed.* "I even know of a valuable stone on this planet that you probably haven't even seen before."

"That doesn't make any sense. We previously had our complete ten, but unfortunately are at six casualties now," Fabian stated. "How could you be one of us? We have never seen you before."

I must have been hiding pretty well if Fabian doesn't recognize me. Good to know. I'm glad that Over Grounds member didn't tell them about me.

"I'm from a previous battle that took place many years ago. The representatives neglected to inform you of the true past and current history of this planet. I listened in on that pathetic excuse of a presentation. I survived through hiding. There is a bunker that I've inhabited, and to my luck, it hasn't been taken away from me so far."

I'm going to tell him the truth. I'm going to let him know of the Wish Carriers, and if he listens closely, he and anyone else he wants to take with him will survive. As long as no one is eavesdropping nearby, everything should work out. The representatives can't hear anything I'm about to say, they can't even know I'm right here.

Present

Nathaniel figured it was best to keep what he found to himself for the time being so that only he and the representatives knew of the stone's proclamation. He was unsure if they told Cloudburst or not, but assumed they didn't. *I doubt they would provide him with that much honesty. I absolutely cannot give them that much credit or expect that much humanity within any of their hearts.* He could hardly calm down after that particular discovery. A new thought presented itself with each step he took.

This type of information cannot be shared lightly. If the wrong people overheard the truth about the Wish Carriers, ugh, there would be many lives lost. Maybe this would be beneficial to share later. I'll wait until someone worthy enough comes along. Too many people act rashly on their emotions.

He reminded himself that words could never be unspoken, so it was best to wait to open his mouth until he was sure enough that he wouldn't regret doing so. He activated his ability and returned to the shallow bunker, always closing the door behind him with a very intentionally steady hand. He went down the steps and to the shelves to get something to drink, his thoughts running wilder than ever before.

CHAPTER TWELVE: THE WOOD CHIPPER

Aadavan

Present

We were unable to find any type of distinct purpose for the crocodile in my faction when it came to those under our commands. Upon discovering its hunger for humans, we kept it fed with each failed attempt at morphing. With every person we lost, some type of feeling kept growing in me. I'm not sure what to call what I was experiencing… but I'd imagine the most accurate word to describe it would be regret. Regret was one thing I always feared the most. Trying to stop the cycle of it was almost always impossible once it got started.

Lorelai shared about an anglerfish in the ocean deep; similarly to the reptile, it had been growing at an unrealistic rate each time it fed on other fish in the waters. Also, they both refused to fight with any of the members or show any interest in participating in anything we were doing. *He must only be a cemetery. And the fish? I quite honestly have no idea why she is out there and swimming in circles.*

I asked Theia if she would come down from her castle to see the crocodile with me. It had been inside of the pond far longer than normal, and I was becoming worried about its health. *I don't want to lose it. It's here for a reason.* She thankfully agreed to come see how he was doing with me and to find out if we could lure him out of the water in any way.

I couldn't accept that the creature was only there to eat the dead; such a morbid existence. I wanted to believe it was with us to be helpful and fight alongside someone from my faction, not to just be stagnant. *It could substantially raise my odds at having someone from my group win. Why can't it just do something else other than lie around?*

"You can see the tops of his eyes right there." I pointed to where they were peeking out from the murky water.

"Oh, I see. I thought those were boulders." Theia laughed and dug her chilly hands into her pockets as she took a closer look. "He's grown so much already."

"Yes, but he's growing hungrier by the hour. I'm sure he's starving now, and I'm not sure how long he will live without another feeding soon."

"I have no idea either," she responded. "Hopefully he will be okay. We can try to interact with him a bit and see what may be done."

I felt an urge to check in on how she felt as I watched her observe the ill reptile. "Thank you for stopping by. I know you have a lot to look after in the castle. Your presence means a lot to me."

She focused on me. "Yours to me, too, Aadavan."

"How do you feel about how our conversation went with Cloudburst? About his appointment?"

She looked sad. "It went better than I thought it would, I guess. What did you think?"

"Same." I crossed my arms and moved to stand by her side, looking ahead at the pond's still, muddy waters.

A thick fog surrounded us, and the air became solemn.

"Do you feel bad at all about what we're doing to him?" she asked me.

Don't bring those types of emotions into this, please. I cannot live with them. "What makes you ask me this? Don't tell me the planet has something to do with making you second guess yourself?"

Theia took some of her lovely hair into her hands to play with. "I don't know if that is what's causing this feeling, but it might be."

"What feeling? How would you best describe it?" *Please don't say regret, Theia, we've come so far. There is loss and heartache — but there is also beauty in the unknown. Lost and suffering lives can be sacrificed for a greater good that may not be fully revealed to us for a long time. That time will come, though, soon enough.*

"Aadavan... I feel conviction."

She looked up at me, tears just barely showing in her eyes, as I knew she'd never opened up in that way with anyone else besides me. *She better not tell Cloudburst any of this.* I took her hand in mine and led her closer to the wet moss.

"Well, you shouldn't. We came across that drink for a reason. That portal opened before us; we were the chosen ones. Don't lose sight of the bigger picture over fleeting and insignificant emotions."

There was rumbling in the sky at my words.

"Are you sure?" She searched my face for validation.

"I'm sure." With my free hand, I gestured up ahead. "Why don't you see if the crocodile may be able to provide any type of a sign? Maybe, perhaps, you both can offer one another comfort?"

Theia trusted me and took small steps near the edge of the pond, occasionally turning to see my expression. "Has anyone ever gotten this close to him before since he's grown? You sure he won't lunge at me?"

"I doubt he will. Everyone here keeps a healthy distance from him. He's never tried to attack me before, just given me some warnings."

"Glad to know your creature has a similar temperament to you."

"Nice one."

"He must be hungry." She knelt down to take a closer look.

Theia's shoe suddenly slipped on the mud underneath her, and she fell into the dirty water, yelling out with her hand reaching up to me. "Aadavan! Pull me out! Aadavan!" she yelled as her head came up out of the swampy mess.

"It's okay!" I went into a panic. My heart had never hurt so badly before seeing her in so much danger and distress. "It's okay! Take my hand! You'll be alright!"

"These waters, t-the mud is like quicksand!" She thrashed around in the water and had fallen partly in the front of the crocodile as it started opening its mouth. The dirt in front of her that she clawed at broke away from the edge and fell down in front of her as she tried to get to me. I could hardly lean over far enough to rescue her without falling in myself. "It's going to eat me! Please, Aadavan, help!"

Flashforward to CHP. 5 of CARRIERS OF EUNOIA

Saige and Zekiel witnessed Nero brutally slicing open Saylor's throat at the Land Dweller faction, and they ran for their lives in the opposite direction. Saige went invisible and was able to hide Zekiel from view too with the touch of her fingertips. Without hesitation, she used all of her energy and willpower to keep the both of them safe.

I guess I can make others go invisible too. We need to get out of here, I have to make sure we aren't seen!

They held hands as they ran frantically, trying not to trip in the foggy and gloomy jungle.

"Where did you both go? Get back here!" Nero screamed after them as his blood rushed out from the gaping wound where one of his wings had previously been. He spun in a circle to take in the devastating mess in front of him as he went into a full-blown panic. *What have I just done? What have I just done?* He dropped the knife as he felt himself on the verge of breaking down. He looked at Saylor who was dead, her empty eyes planted on the colorful sky. *What have*

I done? Why did I do this? What have I done? What have I just done?

Saige tried her best to keep Zekiel from tripping on the wet vines. "Are you okay?" she asked him as they got farther away from Nero.

"Keep your voice down!" he told her sternly.

"I'm sorry, I just want to know if you're okay or not."

Zekiel pulled away from her grasp and returned to normal as they came into view again. "I'm fine. You know I always am! It's you I need to be worried about. Did you get hurt?"

"No, Zekiel, I'm okay."

He stepped away from her and ran his hands through his long hair. "Why did you not help me when Nero blew my flames out?"

"What?" She tried to catch her breath.

"When I tried to save Saylor, you got in the way!"

"How did I get in the way? I tried to warn her!" Saige raised her voice.

"Don't yell at me," Zekiel told her.

"I'm not yelling at you! I'm just saying that I did warn her! Do you not remember what I said?"

"Whatever," he replied sourly as he remembered. "Just forget it, she's just, she's dead now! I could've stopped him! I almost did!"

"It wasn't your fault she died, Zeek!" *I know this is what he needs to hear right now.* But she kept half of her thoughts to herself — as she usually did with him. *You don't have to blame me. It wasn't my fault either. Please don't take your hurt out on me again. Stop pushing me away.*

"I know it wasn't my fault. What are you trying to say?" he replied defensively.

"Just forget I said anything. It's all okay."

"I need to step away! I really can't deal with this right now!" He trudged off away from Saige as his shock was on the brink of wearing off. The two were covered in warm blood. *No more death, please, no more of this. No more fighting and judgment. Why did Saige have to also be brought here? More importantly, why can't she just leave me alone? Just leave me alone!*

Present

Saylor and Draydon sat in a circular resting area near where Aadavan had prepared for them to train in. He had a handful of trees cut down and put together targets with painted wood for sharpening their aim, precision, and dexterity for the coming challenges. Many who were morphed didn't survive the process, and several that did remained in the dwelling house until the opening ceremony. They waited uncomfortably until their fate would be revealed to them, worried to see what would be taking place next.

"I hate those stone slabs," Saylor said. "How are we supposed to sleep on the same thing that tortured us when we got here? I feel phantom pains every time I try to lie on it. I just sleep on the ground now."

Draydon scoffed. "I wouldn't say that the rocks are what 'tortured' us. It's that Aadavan guy. I mean, he is the reason we sat on them in the first place."

"But he didn't bring us here. We woke up on those hills. Remember he said that he is looking out for us, that whatever this planet is planning, he will equip us to defend ourselves."

"You really believe all of that talk? Seems naive to do so. I swear you're under a spell that's completely controlling your mind. He literally lied to us. I don't know what sort of things these people here tamper around with, but I believe the source of it all is corruption."

"Aadavan, Lorelai, and the other woman he's always telling us abou-"

"Theia," Draydon reminded her.

"Yes, Theia, they are humans too just like us. They have their own fears about what's happening as well. How can you not feel bad for them at all?"

"Because we have no idea how they got here in the first place and how they are in charge of all of this."

Saylor rocked back and forth, sitting on her hands as her feet fretfully kicked up dirt. "I'm just trying to stay human. You know, practice some sympathy?"

Admirable, but her kindness might backfire. "Alright then."

"I'm sure we will return to Earth, all of us, and also return to our normal selves. We have to work together and be mindful about what's happening to us. Aadavan said to harness our thoughts and practice broadening our perspectives."

"Just be careful what notions and beliefs you take from him. Not all advice is good advice."

"Let's keep a positive mindset. It's the least we can do." She turned her head quickly. "Did you hear that?"

"Hear what?"

"It sounds lik—"

Theia's screams rang through the air, each louder than the last.

"It's coming from the pond. We need to find out what's going on!" They both raced towards the frightening sounds.

Aadavan used both shaky hands to get a firm hold on Theia. Muddy water splattered up onto his face as she tried to get a grip on him. Draydon and Saylor came into view from the sidelines. Each had their mouths wide open as they frantically looked at one another, shocked beyond belief at what was before them.

"Oh my goodness! We have to get in there!" Saylor spoke first, leading the way as Draydon followed behind. "What happened?"

"I fell in!" Theia had tears in her eyes as she tried to not let go of Aadavan's slippery hand.

The crocodile fully opened its mouth and almost pulled her in between his teeth alongside the rushing pond water falling from the top of his face.

"Don't let go!" Aadavan told her. "Just, hold on! Some of my people will help!"

The crocodile's mouth began to close. *She's not going to make it!*

Draydon used the newly crafted harpoon gun he was holding onto and sent out a solid shot at the crocodile, which pierced into its calloused side. It let out a loud growl, and Theia was able to pull herself forwards with

Aadavan's hand as it was distracted. Saylor formed a jagged spear, sprinting with it in her hand.

Wow, they are actually using their abilities in a real fight already. One of them might actually win for me! Aadavan thought selfishly.

Are they really saving my life right now? Theia couldn't believe her eyes. *They're actually coming to help, despite all we've done to them.*

Saylor launched herself into the air and aimed the metal tip at the crocodile's left eye. It dodged her attack with a full-blown death roll off to its right, almost entirely falling off of the face of the planet.

"Move out of the way!" Draydon yelled as it got ready to roll, tumbling and pulling heaps of water with it as it went.

Everyone ran for their lives, headed in opposite directions. Theia was covered in wet moss and dripping with dirt as they hurriedly ran towards the jungle and away from the two dwellers. "So much for trusting you, Aadavan! Seriously? I thought you told me he's never lunged like that before? I almost died!"

"I'll make it up to you! I'm just glad you are alive," he told her as regret truly began eating at his emotions. "I'm so sorry! I promise that I will make it up to you!"

CHAPTER THIRTEEN: JINXED
Present

As the representatives circled around Cloudburst, telling him of yet another new vision, the waterfall was packed with many visitors. He tried to hide his anxiety from them as he kept his eyes on the windows, observing the other fighters conversing nervously together out in the courtyard. *We need some sort of miracle to happen for us to get out of this trap.* He tuned out what they were saying to him by focusing on his inner monologue. *I don't want to fight again, I really cannot do this.* The memories of everything that had already been lost resurfaced. *How many people have to die before they wake up and realize what they're doing here is wrong?* He shook his head. *Is death the only escape?*

"Are you even listening to her?" Aadavan towered over Cloudburst on the tips of his toes. "It's impolite to not pay attention."

"I was thinking about something else."

"Well, you shouldn't be. Your attention has to be on this conversation," he continued. "Do you know at all how catastrophically terrible it would be if you brought the wrong person? You have to pay attention to the details of Lorelai's descriptions!"

"Has anyone ever told you that you need to ease off and get a life?" he fired back. "If you had your own then maybe you wouldn't be so inclined to try to control everyone else's."

Lorelai spoke up, "The man you need to bring us is currently at the waterfall with his family. His mom, dad, and brother named Yestin. The one you are going to retrieve is named Var—"

"I don't want to hear it!" Cloudburst stood from his chair abruptly.

"Excuse me?"

"Don't tell me their names, please! We've been over this already! I don't want to know!"

"Why is that?"

"Because I humanize them, unlike you three! You don't treat others like they are people!"

"That's not true," Theia joined in.

"Yes, it is! You treat us like we are just accessories to your twisted fantasies! Like we don't have thoughts, feelings, or anything!"

"You're speaking out of incessant ignorance." Aadavan pointed at him. "Stop running your mouth before it gets you killed. You will only paint a target on your back if you allow your emotions to run high. But then again, why give you advice anyways? I don't need to build you up against my own fighters."

"I won't tear them down," Cloudburst said confidently. "I won't kill anyone."

"You won't survive if you don't defend yourself," Aadavan threatened, "And you most certainly will not survive if you don't follow orders. Don't get caught up in weak-minded thinking."

Lorelai jumped in, "Go get Varid at the falls. He is supposed to fight for his destiny here too. He is of average height, wearing a neon graffiti jacket, and he has greyish-white dyed hair. His fingernails are painted and match the yellow in his clothes."

"So he stands out quite a bit."

"Yes."

"Good to know."

Lorelai remained soft spoken despite the circumstances. "He is keeping close to his brother, who is the one wearing all black with long black hair in a bun. He's quite the opposite to Varid visually."

"Alright then." Cloudburst's guilty gaze shifted to Theia. "Shall you transport me over to ruin this guy's life now or later?"

"Time cannot be wasted." Theia raised her hand and sighed calmly. "It's of the utmost essence."

Garbage. He began dissolving as the light from her fingertip formed around him and faded back to the place he knew too well. *Their beliefs are such garbage. I'm so sorry Varid. I'm so irritated I even know your name.*

Cloudburst was there in a blink of an eye and had no trouble spotting the next victim he was sent after in the crowd. It was a very stormy evening as all the visitors congregated near the parking lot. Almost every inch of the sky was covered in grey clouds, packed so closely that they seemed to create one large cloud together. The wind was too loud for him to hear everything that they were saying. He caught sight of the family he was going to break apart as the two men Lorelai described strayed off from their parents in a visible confrontation with each other.

"Okay, then you could have said that to my face," the older one said.

"What would have been the point?" Varid asked. "Not like you listen to me anyways."

"Seriously? Stop talking back. Why are you always in a bad mood?"

"What?"

"You heard me. I'm tired of being around it." Yestin shoved Varid backwards.

"Don't touch me! Come on, why'd you have to ruin the day?"

"Can you two stop arguing please?" their mother asked.

"Seriously, Yestin, what's your problem?" Varid dug his hands into his pockets. "What did I do?"

"You're constantly unhappy and making everything about yourself. You cower away and run from your real problems. No one is able to read your mind." Yestin scolded him. "Please stay home on the next trip."

Cloudburst listened in the shadows to the strained responses, tension lingering in the air as the siblings stepped away from each other.

"I'll leave you alone then." Varid spoke his secrets quietly to himself, "If only I could be accepted for who I am. I doubt my family would love the real me. They won't."

This will be my only window of opportunity. Cloudburst crouched and crept closer to Varid. He snuck up behind him as he was resting near a barbed wire fence and put his hand up over his mouth, muffling his immediate screams.

"I'm sorry I'm doing this, but you have to come with me."

He tried to scratch at his hands and break free, but was unable to, captured against his will and brought back to Eunoia.

Varid was promptly placed into the Over Grounds, designated enthusiastically by Theia who was looking forward to seeing what abilities he would be given. She sent Cloudburst to get Mae and have her assist at the glass cages, on standby as a healer ready to help if a situation turned dire, which reduced the number of deaths. Kason and Lyra watched alongside him as another person was designated to join them.

"This isn't right," Lyra said to the other two, looking through the window.

Cloudburst rolled his uncomfortably tense shoulders. "It's out of our control. All of this, everything, even our lives are out of our control now. It's certainly not right."

"What's he like?" Kason asked.

"I don't want to talk about it." Cloudburst began to turn away, wanting to go outside, as Mae forced Varid past the doorway and secured him into the glass chamber.

"Cloudburst, we know you don't like talking to other people much and that's okay, but it's also okay for you to still be a person. We all are still people here, and we need each other now more than ever."

"We understand what's happening to you, man, alright?" Kason said. "We know that you didn't force us here by your own choice. We know you're on the same side as us."

"Then please exercise some sympathy and leave me alone. I don't even know what to say about this."

"Our individuality still matters. What is he like?"

"You'll meet Varid soon enough."

"But from your perspective," Lyra clarified. "What would you say about him?"

"He seems like a good guy. He's hurting in more ways than physically," Cloudburst talked over Varid's screams in the background. "Conflict with his brother. Just such a shame when ties are cut before resolution is established, you know? I hate unresolved conflicts between people at war with each other when they shouldn't be. Especially in families when someone feels like they don't belong."

"I'm an only child so I wouldn't know much about that," Lyra said.

"Lucky you. I'm one of seven. Thankfully, we get along well, though." Kason looked at Cloudburst. "We will all fight together to get out of here, then when we get back home? We can clean up whatever mess we left behind."

Suddenly, Varid burst through the door and fell onto the ground at their feet, gasping for air and holding onto his chest. "What'd you just do to me? Why?"

Mae followed after him and offered a hand to help him up. "You don't need to be afraid of any of us here now. You remember the three leaders, right? The ones you met when you first arrived?"

He took her hand and brushed himself off gently, hissing at how painful his skin was to the touch. "Yes, um, the two women and that man… Are they in charge?"

"I'll help with the pain." Once he agreed with a desperate nod, she placed her hands on his shoulders and took his pain away with her power. "I'm a healer here. There is a battle coming our way that we need to prepare for so we can escape the control of those three representatives. They are trying to push every boundary they can. We have to resist them."

"You said you're a 'healer'?" Varid's posture relaxed as relief flooded his body. "Does your ability also get rid of emotional pain too?"

Everyone was silent as he laughed.

"What? It was a joke."

"You're… joking?" Lyra cracked a half-hearted smile. "Didn't even think that was possible with how seriously grim everything is around here."

"Just trying to make the best out of an awful situation." He shrugged. "I'm trying."

"That's all we can do." Mae's tone changed, "You must have an ability too now. We are all typically given at least one if we are of the chosen. Aside from your wings, there may be something else."

"Can I ever get rid of these?" Varid asked, referring to his yellow feathered wings. "Please tell me I don't have to fly, and please tell me I don't have to keep these."

"We can't answer all of your questions." Kason started to clarify. "We also have many and are figuring this out as we go along."

"How do I know if I can do anything else? Will it hurt?" Varid looked at everyone fearfully.

"We can't really say." Cloudburst began to walk out of the room. *I can't become friends with anyone here, not if I will just lose them. I can't stomach this.* "Let's just hope whatever you uncover will be useful and that it won't make you too uncomfortable."

Varid's confusion grew. "How would it make me uncomfor—"

"Questions later," Mae interrupted. "For now, let's just live in the moment."

"And try to make ourselves stronger," Kason interjected. "Let's go outside and see what you can do, Varid."

Lyra motioned for him to follow them down a different pathway. "I have a feeling there's more to you than initially meets the eye."

As they stepped outside, the stormy sky came into view.

"It's gorgeous out here," Varid said as he glanced at them. "Wouldn't you say so? Wherever we are, this place has some amazing views. I can at least say that."

"I can tell you're trying to distract yourself," Lyra responded.

"Close your eyes and take a deep breath. Concentrate on the present moment. It's what we've heard from the others, what Aadavan instructs them to do in order to ascend into the furthest level of thinking they're able to. Harness the present, let go of the past, then you can conquer the future."

Varid followed his teammate's instruction. As he inhaled deeply and his chest fell with the long breath, he temporarily took his mind off of the unnerving realization of what his, and the rest of the fighters', reality had become. The wind was picking up, slight condensation in the air as the gloomy weather created a melancholic atmosphere. *I hope it rains soon.* With that thought, he heard everyone in front of him gasping in shock.

"What?" His eyes shot open. "W-what is it? What's wrong?"

He noticed their confused expressions and followed his gaze to see what they were staring at. Above his head were three miniature floating clouds. One cloud was greenish blue, one a purple and pink mixture, and the last a golden orange.

"You've activated a new ability!" Lyra told him.

"I wonder if they follow you?" Kason showed intrigue as he went over to observe them. "I wonder what they do?"

Varid took a few steps back to test if they would indeed keep hovering close by to him. "They are following me! Look!" He closed his fists in excitement and nervousness at his next thought, *but how are they going to help me fight?*

Flashforward to CHP. 3 of CARRIERS OF EUNOIA

Amira had been taken down to the Oceanic Guardian faction and morphed. After she swam with Hippo for a short amount of time, she went back to the castle to meet and try to get information from the others who had taken control of her life after she arrived.

I wonder how the other five are doing, she thought. *They must think that I've died down here. I need to tell them what's going on. It'll be hard for them to believe me at first, I hardly believe that any of this is really happening right now. I wonder if Anon is safe? I hope I can speak with him again soon.*

When she returned to the structure, she came across the same three people she quickly met before becoming morphed. Orson, Enya, and Marcellus were passing time talking to one another as she approached cautiously. They all became silent once they noticed her swimming to them from big portions of seaweed greenery.

"Why did you bring me down here?" She looked directly at Enya. "What have you done to me?"

"It wasn't by my own choice. I'm playing along so that I don't die," she informed her.

"Speaking of not dying, what do you think of that fish? Did it try to hurt you? We watched as you were pulled off into the currents by it, but we couldn't do anything to stop it. No way would we risk our lives like that. No offense. I don't think any of us would be able to survive confronting that beast." Orson was curious and leaned forward anxiously to hear her response.

"Our representative, Lorelai, has told us a bit about it. That sea devil has a very bad temper and hunger to feast on whomever comes close to it," Marcellus added. "I'm sure you'll be meeting her soon. You can see the scar her bite wound left behind before we arrived if you don't believe me."

"I believe you," Amira finally said. "It didn't hurt me, though. It seemed completely calm with having me around. Though I don't feel necessarily calm around any of you. Please tell me what is really going on. How are we speaking right now? How have our bodies been changed in this way?" Her tail was bright orange with big, sparkly scales.

"I'd rather delegate your concerns to our leader," Enya jumped back into the conversation.

"Why?"

"Because she can answer them far better than we can. There's a lot that we don't know either. She told us that we have a special calling here, that nothing is a mistake. Though it seems as if she is trying to convince herself of that far more than attempting to convince us."

"We're able to walk around out of the water for a short amount of time," Kason told her. "We've already tested it. Enya really has no issues with that, but the rest of us? We've fully transformed into mermaids and mermen, as you've already discovered. Make sure you stay close by. There are a host of things swimming around constantly, and we have no idea what they'll do to us. We have to make sure we stay together and prepare for whatever is coming next. Your fish will come in handy."

"When do we get back to Earth?" Amira asked. "How do we return home?"

"Not everyone will get to," Enya answered. "Which is a shame because I think that all of us, even the representatives deep down, truly want to return to where we came from."

Amira excused herself from the conversation and ventured back out to the more open part of the waters. She had no interest in speaking to Lorelai at that moment but instead got closer to the shore and remained near the shallow parts of the water to see if anyone from her group of the original six would stop by to see her. Specifically, Anon, who she could hardly stop thinking about.

Present

At the Oceanic Guardian faction, Lorelai continued to experience vivid, chilling visions of the falls. Next in line were Fabian, Zavier, and Elena. She had seen them all in the same vision together and was excited to receive some support and validation from the other two on her progress in collecting the information that they needed. They were at the falls late at night, unable to start their hike earlier in the day. Lorelai decided that they were to be taken away to the planet right before they got into their cars to leave the parking lot.

I hope Theia and Aadavan are happy. Cloudburst will bring the next person destined to join us here.

The visions she had didn't last very long, just enough so that she could accurately provide their description, at least a simple sketch drafted in words of what they looked like so that they were correctly selected.

I'm glad the retrieval process has gone this smoothly so far. It's helpful that Theia is able to guide Cloudburst effectively in carrying out what he has to do. I wonder if he will ever leave back to Earth? Would they let him? It's almost as if I have no say in any matters here.

As the booming roars of creatures echoed around her, she let one thought come to the forefront of her attention, even though she tried to suppress it, *will we ever get to go and stay back on Earth? Theia? Aadavan? Me?*

She thought of herself last, and it was then that she felt for the very first time the overwhelming emotion of mental claustrophobia.

Will I ever be able to... escape?

CHAPTER FOURTEEN: THE APPOINTED
Cloudburst

Present

I was back at the waterfall to get more victims for the representatives. It took longer than normal as the people I was waiting for arrived far later than the others I'd captured before. This time around I had already been warned by Theia that I would have to use my recently given abilities to subdue the next three in line. *Please don't blame me for what's coming next.* I grimaced at the thought of what was to come for the unsuspecting few. *I have no control over what I say or do.* Three people were speaking to each other as they made their way closer to the waterfall through the trees past the parking lot. I hid in the shadows and plotted how to bring them back with me without making them freak out or getting myself hurt.

"Yeah, no, it was really nice meeting you too!" one said to the others. "My name is Elena." She shook their hands. "What were yours again? Forgive me for asking."

"I'm Fabian."

"Zavier."

I could practically feel the representative's eyes on me as they observed the exchange taking place. Even though the clouds above didn't have eyes back on Earth, it was as though I could still see them looking at me just as they did back on the planet. I inserted myself into the end of their interaction as soon as I could, tired of carrying out the representatives' sick commands.

"And I am Cloudburst." I made my presence known.

"Where did you come from?" Fabian asked.

I'm not going to waste any time. I know they won't listen to me, and this isn't going to be easy without a fight.

"All your questions will be answered soon," I told them.

Zavier began to walk towards me, "What are you talking ab—"

In an instant, I spewed out multiple yellow lassos that wrapped around each of their arms and legs, yanking them to the floor, and I commanded them to knot together so they could be tethered. My own thoughts controlled the magical strings, making them do what I wanted them to.

"This stings! Get it off!" Elena screamed out.

"Save your energy." I wiped sweat off my brow as I felt my own depleting yet again. "Trust me."

"What are you doing to us?" Zavier asked me.

"Take these off at once!" Fabian demanded.

I said nothing else as light began swirling around each of us. Just like that, within an entire minute we were teleported back, and each representative was right there hovering and debating who would take which person to their faction. Theia had specifically brought us to the ocean since Lorelai required more fighters.

"I want two." Lorelai was halfway out of the water and more comfortable in the conversation than usual since we were in her terrain.

"Fine then." Aadavan looked at Theia. "One left. He should join me in the jungle. I can already sense he will be a great weapon crafter."

"My group," Theia said and gestured for Fabian to join her. "We will go up to the castle to begin changing you as soon as possible."

"Actually…" Fabian spoke up. "I'd like to join the group in the jungle instead."

"Really?" Aadavan was ecstatic. "Is that so? Could you tell Theia that again?"

She started to roll her eyes playfully. "He's all yours."

"It's time to be morphed," he told all three of them. "Lorelai, if they don't survive, just let me know. The crocodile has been starving."

Before the strangers could begin asking any of their questions, sudden yells could be heard from the direction of the hills.

"Where are we?" a woman asked. "What is going on?"

Aadavan was also on the brink of raising his voice. "Why are more people waking up on the hills?"

Lorelai forced Zavier and Elena into the waters, using the currents they tried to fight against before almost all the air was knocked out of their lungs. Aadavan took Fabian with him to the treehouse, and Theia made eye contact with me.

"We have to retrieve the people on the hills and sort each into factions too. Let's go find out how many have awoken."

Flashforward to CHP. 5 of ECHOES OF EUNOIA

Thunder rumbled as a storm unlike any other soon approached. Rain clouds filled the sky. Anon and Amira escaped Zayika's grasp in hiding as they navigated the taunting playground. She was left with Jameson as they fled from her presence, and the rising feeling of destruction steadily filled her mind with the curse's influence. *Hunt them down and put an end to this, Zayika. Tell Jameson exactly how it is.*

"They're so blinded by their own interests that they don't stop to think about the interests of others, even those who have sacrificed for them. It would be a stupid choice for them to repeat the past, but unfortunately I wouldn't expect them to be smarter than that. I can't give them too much credit."

I won't give Anon and Amira any credit for anything good. They've ruined everything. The weakest get away with everything because they resort to screwing over others.

"But Zayika... you know that if they kill me and get another wish then they could not only ask to go home but... ask for you to die?" Jameson's thoughts were overwhelming him.

He saw a glimpse of the fragile sense of self she tried to keep hidden away which reminded him very closely of himself. He stood in awe of her as he couldn't stay focused on just one thing to admire. *I want to help out here, I really do, but I have no idea what to say or where to start. Can I trust her? What about Anon, Amira, and Zekiel? Who is truly in the right here?*

She kept her words to herself in that moment while figuring out what to say next, shocked at how quickly the rug of stability could be tugged out from underneath her power. *I never thought about that; what if that's what they do? What if they kill me? I don't know how to ask for help.* Zayika kicked at the colorful weeds at her feet with scratched up boots, each hand on her hips while avoiding his gaze.

"Thank you for bringing that to my attention." *I wish you hadn't.* "Make sure they don't kill you, okay?"

She continued on with the best response she could muster, despite the thumping pain in her head and the tears she kept from filling her eyes. Jameson could feel her conflicted energy in the air as she withheld completely revealing her truest self to him.

"I'm pretty sure you were already planning on not letting that happen. I'm going after them. If you join my side in this, I will keep you healed in battle. I won't let you die." *I'm telling him the truth.* "If you go your own way, then your outcome completely falls on you. Remember, Jameson, that you have potential."

So does she. He gave her a small smile at her reassuring words.

"With your wish, you are worth more than you realize."
So are you, Zayika, and I wish you could see it.

"I don't have a problem with you unless you try to help them with it. I have to go."

Jameson knew she was cutting the conversation short and she didn't really have somewhere else she needed to go; she was just looking for an excuse to run away. He wrestled with his thoughts as he tried to come to a conclusion on what path would be best to take. He was freezing cold as he stood alone and watched her maroon stars guiding her away from him, sprinting fast as the day was drawing to a devastating close. *What is going on with her head?* Zayika pulled strongly on his heartstrings, every aspect of her captivated his undivided attention, but he was too unsure of where her heart was to pursue the unknown.

Present

"Orson."

"Marcellus."

"Enya, my name is Enya."

Each stood in a line in front of Theia and Cloudburst as they pondered what to do next. Many hills surrounded the group as they observed each other closely. *We should probably appoint all three of them to the Oceanic Guardians; Lorelai needs them more than me or Aadavan do,* Theia thought to herself. *We'll have to force them to the waters, there's no way they'll go down willingly.* She looked over at Cloudburst, who was standing attentively by her right side.

His eyes met hers, and he felt a rising panic at her dramatic expression. *Oh no,* he tapped his foot on the ground, *what is she about to tell me to do?*

You'll see soon enough, she mentally responded.

"Remain calm, please. Do not panic." She kept her words simple and spoke clearly. "All of your questions will be answered soon, I can promise you that."

"We need answers now!" Orson was the most furious. "Who brought us here?"

Marcellus joined in with the questions, "I just woke up. What is going on?"

"As I said, you will get answers, but the most important thing for you to do right now is to not lose control of your emotions."

Orson raised his voice, "Don't try to tell me what to do!"

Theia turned to Cloudburst suddenly and took his arm in her hand without question. She led him a handful of steps away from the strangers in a hurry as their confusion came pouring in.

"I'm going to need your help here, okay?"

He rolled his shoulders. "Mhm, of course you will. When do you not need something from me?"

"Good point." She nodded at the others. "Those three will be sent to Lorelai. You need to use your ability to restrain and bring them to the ocean. She'll understand why they've been sent down and will morph them. She can handle it, I trust her to not rely on constant explanations."

He inhaled deeply. "Are you serious? That's unlike anything you've asked of me before. No way."

"Do not move! Stay right there!" She quickly commanded the two who were trying to disperse amongst the grass and turned back to Cloudburst. "As I was saying, you need to tie them up and bring them down into the water. Lorelai can take it from there to get them to the castle and prepare them."

"So you are serious?"

"Well, how else would we get them there?"

"You could just tell them that they have to go. Like you do to me every single day. I can shoot the ground near their feet a little to freak them out if I'm forced to, but you don't have to be so needlessly aggressive in your ways," Cloudburst said.

Threats are effective too. I can't forget that. She nodded and thought about his idea. *We need to make the morphing process smoother, with less conflict and hostility. We need to earn trust and respect from our fighters much faster. He makes a good point here. I don't want to be seen as 'aggressive'.*

"Alright then." She checked her composure as her thoughts slowed down.

"So?"

"We will try it your way."

Theia stepped back over to them, and they were forced to walk towards the ocean. Cloudburst was also commanded to remain behind them as they traveled from the grassy hills, past the towering field, and eventually to the shore.

Theia's stern words and Cloudburst demonstrating his electric abilities sent them into survival mode. Reality hit the victims as a foul feeling filled the air. None of them spoke to one another as they traveled on foot, uncomfortably being pushed onwards by the two strangers who also acted unnaturally towards each other.

As they got closer to their destination, Theia began to speak to them in increments, being vague and concerning in her choice of words. It wasn't until then that the feeling of fear truly filled the hearts of those held captive. They knew something was about to happen to them that they could never undo, and they were unable to run away.

Wait, it sounds like... Marcellus only watched the ground. *They are going to torture us. Please, whatever we've done wrong to be put in this place, may we please have another chance?* He and the rest felt absolutely powerless as they kept their heads low and steps in line with how fast Theia told them to walk.

"They can join Zavier and Elena!" Theia called out to Lorelai as her head peeked out from the waves, slightly surprised to see her waiting, her two new members morphed already. "Do you know where Aadavan is?"

"He's morphing Fabian right now."

"Splendid." She smiled and pointed to the newest three.

"Will you all please step into the waters for me?" Lorelai asked. "Walk until it reaches your waist, and I will do the rest. Hold your breath."

Cloudburst couldn't believe what was happening. *What makes the representatives think they can do this to people? No part of this is okay. I can't keep being an accessory to this, I can't stand by any longer without doing more to fight back.* He stared at Theia with determined eyes as he continued thinking, *I need less attention on me. I need a plan to get off of this planet.*

Did you forget I can hear you? she replied mindfully to him but didn't turn to see his expression.

He looked back over to everyone else and saw how Lorelai was controlling the waves to grab Enya, Marcellus, and Orson. They cried out for help while being pulled into the chilling ocean, horrified expressions on their faces as they each went under at once.

The castle was surrounded by tall coral stems and covered in moss. Schools of small fish swam by as they approached. Lorelai pulled them under as far as she needed, bubbles streaming out of their mouths. *I just hope you all survive,* she thought.

The anglerfish wasn't too far when she made it down to her faction, and with the ability to command any sea creature, she attempted to call her closer to them. For once, the fish followed. *It never listens to me. Why is it helping right now? Must be following because it wants to.* Light from its orb illuminated the path in front of her as the three were forced to go in through the front doors.

It was mostly barren inside with some metal scraps and what seemed to be parts of a shipwreck in the corners of most rooms. There were a few statues surrounding the castle. Similar to Aadavan, Lorelai had large, rocky tables for her morphing process.

To her surprise, all three of them survived the painful ordeal. Orson and Marcellus became merman, each with their own specific weapons. Orson received a heavy hammer with several engravings of intricate waves along either side of it. Marcellus was given a bow and cluster of arrows to use. Enya didn't have a complete tail like the rest of the Oceanic Guardians, but instead fin-like legs that were layered in scales.

Cloudburst thought to himself as he watched the peaceful waves steadily rock back and forth, *I'll play nice for as long as I have to, but there is absolutely no way I will work for the representatives much longer. I don't know how to control my thoughts, how to keep certain information to myself. How am I supp —*

Just work for us, Theia replied. *Stop thinking so much, Cloudburst, and do what you're told.*

"I need to get some fresh air by myself," he said nervously.

"You want to get away from me, right? To go think by yourself about how much you hate us and want to get out of here?" Theia asked.

"Just allow me to still have some space for myself. Be as human as you're able to be, if that's even possible."

"We don't have time to overthink. There are more people to appoint." Theia started to walk towards her faction. "Let's head back now. I don't trust you alone. We'll need you to bring more people here soon. You should get some rest."

"There's no way that will be possible," Cloudburst muttered back as he traveled behind her with tired footsteps to the platform.

Theia and Cloudburst spoke no words to one another as they rode up into the air. He made as much effort as he could to keep his thoughts at bay while they were side by side, trying to pay attention to the scenery around them as much as possible to distract himself from giving away personal thoughts and feelings to her. Their ride up on the platform felt longer than normal after she caught on to what he was telling himself. The only thing he was easily able to do was strengthen his balance. Everything else was still challenging to navigate. They immediately parted ways once they reached the top and entered through the gateway. Some of the other Over Grounds members caught Cloudburst's eye, huddled and crouched next to one of the castle walls away from Theia's view as she walked swiftly inside, muttering to herself about what was to be taken care of next. Each frantically motioned for him to come over and speak with them. *I'm not trying to make friends here. I can't get close to anyone else, not if they're going to get torn apart, not if I will just lose them. Avoid conversations,* Cloudburst told himself and tried to look away and walk inside, but he couldn't help but notice the sheer desperation in each of their eyes. A drawn-out sigh escaped him as he went over to where they stood.

"What is it?"

"Glad to see you again, Cloudburst." Varid jumped in first with a smile. "We were just talking about you."

Nero shook his head. "I wouldn't put it so simply."

"Really? What is there to discuss about me when I'm not here?"

"Not in a bad way, just, we are making some plans. We need you to help."

Mae supported his plea, "The other members up here aren't being so cooperative. You have a unique advantage that none of us do."

"They'd rather wallow, retreat into solitary, and hide alone instead of working together. It's like they don't hear anything. They have no idea what is to come." Nero clenched his jaw. "These lunatics, have you heard them lately?"

"Which 'lunatics'?" Cloudburst laughed. "Please be more specific."

Nero pointed in the directions of each faction. "These representative cultists! They're about to thrust us head first into the beginning of the end. We can kiss our sweet lives on Earth goodbye if we don't find a way to get the hell out of here."

"You're referring to the second challenge, aren't you?"

There was silence amongst the entire group.

"This isn't the first one?" Lyra spoke up from the back.

"Wait, I'm confused, how did you survive the first one?" Varid asked. "What happened? How many people died? What about these wings, these powers, will they go away? Why are you still here? Are you secretly helping them? Like, you are actually on their side?"

"Please don't overwhelm me with an interrogation right now." Cloudburst turned around from the rest for a moment to gather his thoughts.

"For the record, I don't think you are on their side." Kason looked at Varid.

"I-I didn't either! It was just a question! I have so many things to ask!" His clouds were waiting idly by.

"I can't answer much, I'm afraid." A gust of wind whistled past Cloudburst's ears that reminded him of the softness of an up-close whisper. It was as if Theia's lips grazed up against his earlobe. *Remember that I can hear your thoughts. Did you forget? Stay in line. I can't afford for you to falter.* He turned around in a circle multiple times, anxiously looking at the sky and over to the castle's windows. "I wonder how close she is? She must not be far."

Nero's concern grew. "Dude, what are you talking about? You seriously look like you've just seen a ghost."

"So why are you all out here having an entire get together without me?" Gebu appeared from around the corner, floating slowly with his arms crossed in a bothered manner.

"What have you even been doing?" Nero asked. "I told you to meet us out here like fifteen minutes ago."

"I was talking to some of the others, you know, the ones here that you all continuously forget about? They are important too. They also have names."

"Well, I'm not bothering to learn them if they'll be dead within seconds of the first few minutes of combat."

Multiple groans from the group rang out.

"Bad taste, Nero." Kason facepalmed.

"What? Am I really so wrong?" He threw his hands up. "They don't even train, let alone try out their basic abilities! If you could even call them that!"

Gebu patted his shoulder. "Read the room."

"First... don't touch me." Nero shoved his hand off. "Second... we aren't and won't ever be friends here."

"What is it you all want to ask me? Let's get on with this. With all due respect, I don't have the energy for all of this right now," Cloudburst said.

Lyra stepped forwards to take the lead, "Why don't you tell us how you won?"

"Well, I, the thing about that. There is a lot to say. Where can I really begin to explain all of that?" Cloudburst quickly thought, *Nathan-no, no, I can't speak about this. I can't replay this memory, I don't need her seeing. She shouldn't know, no. Stop! Think of anything else!* His eyes shot up to the castle windows again. *I wonder how big the crocodile will get?* "That creature in the pond should be avoided."

"Seriously?" Nero snickered. "This guy is just staring at the windows and spouting meaningless information. Don't tell me you're making anything up? Are you lying? I've learned more here already from Gebu, and that's saying something."

"No offense taken." Gebu smiled.

"I didn't say no offense."

"Cloudburst might be giving us fake advice," Kason tried to say quietly.

"He might be working for the representatives." Varid looked at him over his shoulder. "I was just asking earlier, but now… I'm a bit unsure."

What are you trying to not think about? Theia's voice filled his head.

"Stop!" Cloudburst yelled out as he tried to distract himself. "The waterf-fall. I have been there many times!"

"Alright, I'm out." Nero went back towards the courtyard. "Let me know when this guy starts acting like a normal person enough for us to actually talk."

"What are you going to do?" Mae asked.

"I'll be throwing knives. Lots of them." He trailed off into the shadows.

Flashforward to CHP. 12 of CARRIERS OF EUNOIA

The day was drawing to the end for those remaining in the second round. The weather would drastically change in the blink of an eye, and often, it would also provide great sources of inspiration and escapism for those who had an artistic perspective. Many lives were already lost, with very few remaining, and those still alive were trying to cling to the methods of survival that had worked for them long enough thus far.

Omar was laying out painting supplies he took from Nathaniel's bunker as Zayika counted her items on one of the chairs.

"Anon is so irritating," she said out of nowhere. "He took so much stuff from the bunker for himself. He can be so selfish."

Omar shrugged. "I thought it ended up getting split pretty evenly. Just seems like something unnecessary to complain about. Do you think it really matters? I mean, come on, look at what's happening to us. How is that important?"

"Well, that's interesting because I'm pretty sure I didn't just ask for your opinion," she retorted in his direction.

"Are you alright, Zayika?" He stopped pulling paint brushes out of his bag to face her. "What's wrong?"

"Excuse me?" She drank some water and tried to pretend nothing was bothering her. "Just a headache. Not sure why I have one, but it's been getting worse ever since I went to a salon with my friend back at home."

"Do you realize how you get when you talk about Anon?"

She closed the plastic cap aggressively. "How do I 'get'? What does that even mean?"

"How you act. You change when you talk about him, like, a lot."

"Omar, what makes you think you are in any position to talk about me? To assess me?" Zayika looked at her own reflection in the dresser's mirror, her two-toned hair standing out. "I don't even know what you're talking about."

"It's like you're hiding something." Omar fiddled with his fingers, mildly afraid of what Zayika would think of his words.

"Speak for yourself. Don't project your issues onto me," she responded. "I'm not hiding anything. I just have a headache and it's not going away." She hit the side of her head sporadically. "So irritating!"

"Alright t-then…" Omar stuttered. "If you ever need to talk about something I'm here for you. I care."

She gave him a sarcastic thumbs up and went to drink more water. "That's very cool."

He grabbed the bottles of the colors he was going to paint with next. "I'm being serious, Zayika. It seems like you're stressed about something."

"I'm fine now, but I will become stressed if you don't stop prying for information that isn't your business. If I had something I wanted to share with you then I would. I've never asked for, or need, your input."

Omar changed the subject, "What made you choose to dye your hair those two colors?" Zayika sat up on the dresser in front of the mirror while he stepped over to take a closer look at it.

"Because I like them."

He pointed to the wavy purple tips. "Can I touch it?"

"Sure, I don't care."

Omar's skin was zapped immediately when he made contact with her hair. "Ow!" he shouted out and backed away.

"What happened?"

"I don't know. It just shocked me, like static electricity."

"That's odd." She grabbed a piece of it and swirled it around her fingers. "It doesn't do that to me."

"Well, that's good. I've never felt something like that before." He blew on his skin and created more distance between them.

"What colors are you picking for your painting?" she asked with a mischievous smile.

"Um… a few different ones." *Just not anything close to the color of your hair…* he thought to himself and grabbed his supplies. "I'm going to paint outside so I can watch the ocean. The sun will be setting soon, and I'd like to capture it."

"If you see Anon out there wasting more valuable time with Amira, why don't you tell him I say hi?"

"Why don't you tell him yourself, Zayika?" Omar gave a half-smile as he stepped outside, his big curls bouncing around in the warm wind. "Tell him yourself," he said softly as he exited the room.

Why don't you go figure out the reason why you're even here, Omar? Doubt your life has a purpose at all, she thought. *Ugh, I didn't mean it like that.* Zayika wrestled against her thoughts on a constant basis. Exhausted and becoming desperate for relief, she tiredly looked at her hair in the mirror. *What is it with these intrusive thoughts? Will they ever go away?*

Present

As Nero left the others to go train, Gebu invited himself to join. "I'm going to go with him in case he needs a spotter or some company. Let us know if you need anything or if something important happens, okay?"

"Alright, Gebu." Kason waved him away and focused his attention on Mae, Varid, and Lyra. "Do any of you have a clue of what we should try out here? I'm at a loss for ideas.

I don't know much of what these leaders are actually capable of."

Cloudburst gave them all a serious look. "I'll cut this discussion short. Unless one of you is left still standing at the end, there is no way to return to Earth. The representatives won't be keen on your ideas or persuasion attempts. There isn't much that can be tried. I've been here longer than all of you and have said every possible thing to them that can be thought of. Words don't work. They don't care about our emotions or where we are coming from. Sometimes there seems to be a glimpse of hope, but it tends to be shut down not too long after it's shown."

"Well... that's disappointing," Lyra responded. "With how much time you spend with Theia, well, we figured there must be something you know that we'd not be able to decipher on our own."

Kason nodded in agreement. "I was really hoping you had some sort of unique way of helping us."

"I'm sorry I don't have better news," he replied. "If there were more options, I would have explored them by now. I wouldn't still be here if there was some sort of magical way of escaping, and if there is? I haven't been lucky enough to find it."

"That's alright. I guess we have to face whatever our fate is meant to be." Varid said defeatedly.

Lyra's eyes showed intrigue. "Not true. We don't have to be a doormat to those three. Cloudburst, you seem to have abilities too. In your arms, right? You weren't fully altered, but we can all see that you also have powers. You've even used them at the falls."

"I can produce bolts of electricity, but I don't really tend to use them. I don't want to harm anyone else with it."

"Well, you should. As terrible as that sounds." Lyra cleared her throat as everyone stared at her choice of words. "All of us should team together and take down the three ourselves. We have the power to do it, so why wouldn't we?"

Everyone stood quietly and exchanged worried glances.

"If we kill them…" Mae paused. "Then how would we get back to Earth? It would be impossible. Why trap ourselves here with no way at all of ever returning? Seems ignorantly counterintuitive."

"Instead of resorting to killing, like they do, why don't we just threaten them? Get them in a tight situation where they're unable to give us any answer besides yes," Kason suggested. "We'll have to devise a plan to get them all cornered, and then all of us, including Nero and maybe Gebu, can come together and refuse to take part in their plan. We won't accept no for an answer. The fear of dying should make them agree."

"And we'll make sure they change us back to our normal selves," Lyra agreed.

"Not a bad idea. We need to figure out how to pull this off before this opening ceremony begins." Mae nodded her head in agreement with the rest. "Cloudburst, what do you think? Are you on board with helping us?"

He took a while to think before he responded. *I can't go along with this. I refuse to threaten them, why would I? Our threats will mean nothing. We're disposable to them. They'll just feed us to the crocodile or the monstrous waters. There's no way any of this will actually work. But if this helps them feel better at all, even if it's false hope, I'll try to carry my role out the best way I can. Maybe a miracle will happen somehow.* "I think we know what to do next."

"Where should we start? You know their routines and personalities better than we do." Lyra replied.

"The first step is to tell Nero, Gebu, and whoever else wants to help. Once it's nightfall, we can meet here again when we know they're most likely asleep. The less aware they are of us meeting up, the better," Mae suggested.

"There's something you all need to keep in mind, though," Cloudburst jumped in once more. "It's not about taking down all representatives. Only one. Theia. Only she can teleport people to and from Earth."

Everyone in the group came to a general agreement on which direction to take in order to put an escape plan in motion. Most dispersed back into the castle to rest until it got darker, aside from Varid, who was unable to get comfortable at all with his new wings... or the thoughts and feelings that were surfacing in his mind due to what was going on. Instead of heading to bed, he decided to see how training was going for Gebu and Nero, who were also outside but on the opposite side of the castle. As he approached, he saw Gebu sitting on the sidelines, encouraging Nero as he threw knives at a hanging slab of wood. Over and over again, he hit the bullseyes.

"Wow," Varid said after he walked around the corner, his three tiny clouds following him over his shoulder. "You have really good aim."

Nero didn't take his eyes off the painted circles in front of him. "Yeah. I know."

He threw a knife.

Bullseye.

He threw another knife.

Bullseye again.

Varid took a seat next to Gebu to watch their teammate polish his skills.

"These clouds aren't going to hurt me, right?" Gebu asked him loud enough over the sounds of each sharp blade meeting the freshly cut wood. "Why are they different colors?"

"I'm not sure. They've never hurt me before, so you should be okay." Varid answered.

The sounds of knives suddenly stopped, and the two refocused their attention on Nero.

"What did you just say?" Nero stopped training for the first time in a while to look over at them. "Did you just say that you have no idea what those clouds even do?"

Varid watched as they floated near his head. "Umm. Pretty much."

"Well, you should try to figure that out before we get attacked out on the grounds once everything is flipped upside down." Nero shook his head. "Have you even tried activating them? Seeing at all in any way what your true fighting ability may be?"

"No, I haven't," Varied replied truthfully.

"Nero, why don't you help him discover what it could be?" Gebu suggested.

"I might as well since you just volunteered me." Nero delicately placed his weapons into one of his pockets.

Varid stood up and walked over to him. Each cloud trailed behind as the orange took the lead with the green and then pink one behind it. "So what can you do?" he asked.

"I can move the wind around. Fly, like you. I have the knives you've already seen," Nero told him bluntly.

Varid's interest in discovering his own power began to manifest. "Where did you get them?"

"A guy in the jungle made them for him. Super nice, right? One of those dweller people," Gebu jumped in.

"Nice? Sure. Naive? Definitely." Nero let out a snicker. "To my advantage? Undeniably. I wouldn't turn down such a helpful offer, so I took them. I have six on me."

"How do you activate your wind ability?" Varid looked over Nero's arms, their pores wider and more visible than normal, as if they were under a magnifying glass. "Extra air flows through your skin?"

"Yeah, that's what it feels like. I never feel like I have to take a deep breath. I also have a more challenging time holding it. It's odd."

"Interesting." Varid let out a deep breath he didn't realize he'd been holding in while listening.

"Yeah, and to control the wind?" Nero smiled confidently. "At first it wasn't a conscious effort I made, to be honest. I had to find my mental footing. Once I got a hold of my thoughts and put more effort into sharpening my thought patterns like I sharpen my knives, well… the rest is history."

Varid felt a rise of inspiration. "So similar to mediation?"

Nero nodded as Gebu jumped back into the conversation, "I've heard others say that's what worked for them too."

With that response, Varid closed his eyes and inhaled deeply. Everything was quiet for a few moments as the two other men waited patiently to see if anything was going to happen. Wind blew around softly, and he breathed in time with the sounds of rising and crashing waves off in the distance. The sun was setting and created a calming glowing orange hue that shone warmly all around them. As he opened his eyes, the first thing he chose to look at was the orange cloud since it was closest to him.

I want to know why I'm here, he thought to himself. *I wish I could have better insight and see what I need to do to defend myself.* With that, the tiny cloud, for the first time ever, flew away from him and behind the area of the courtyard he had been looking at — the vine covered archway. To his surprise, he was able to see what the cloud saw for at least a full fifteen seconds.

"It's showing me something!" Varid exclaimed to Nero and Gebu. "I can see the plants over there as if I'm standing in front of them!"

"Really?" Nero's head turned to where the compact cloud was. "Are you serious? It's like a drone?"

"Wow." Gebu was extremely excited as he suggested, "Let's see what the other two can do!"

"Okay," Varid responded once his attention was redirected to Gebu. He closed his eyes again and inhaled sharply. *I wonder if there are any other abilities that Gebu has that he doesn't know of? Is there anything that can be revealed to him?* His eyelids sprang open and focused on his teammate.

"Why are you looking at me?" Gebu got nervous.

Nero watched closely as the little pink cloud immediately flew over Gebu's head and let out a small flickering bolt of yellow lightning.

"What's happening?" he asked, and right as he went to put his hand up to his head, his curious tone changed to frustration. "Why is any of this even happening in the first place? Everything here, this place, these people... so irritating!"

Varid and Nero looked at each other and shrugged as his mood flipped all of a sudden.

"You just did that?" Nero asked him.

Varid shrugged again. "Guess so."

"What are you two even talking about?" Gebu raised his voice at them as Mae stepped outside, the sudden rise in noise catching her attention. "Agh! My head hurts so bad!"

Almost ten seconds had passed.

"I can help with that," Mae told Gebu as she lightly laid her hands on his shoulders and led him away from the courtyard and inside to calm down. "You don't need to yell, Gebu, you'll be alright."

Nero started clapping and gave a sarcastic bow towards Varid as they stood across from one another. "Nice job. Never seen Gebu angry before. That was a first."

"Really?"

"Yeah, he's usually a calm guy. He gets overly anxious, confused, or annoying… but never angry. How were you able to command the cloud like that?"

Varid watched as the orange and pink clouds returned to him. "I don't know. I thought about him for a moment and asked some vague open-ended questions in my mind."

"Let's find out what the third one does, that green one." Nero pointed at it as it seemed to shy away the most, hiding itself near Varid's neck.

Varid closed his eyes for a third time, sighing and releasing the extra tension in his shoulders as he tried his best to relax for a moment.

Nero waited patiently in silence. *I can't distract him.* he thought. *His powers will be really useful. Let him get better. Encourage him to strengthen them. I wonder if his abilities will last longer if he trains with them? Fifteen seconds seems to be their initial duration. Not bad.*

"Not much is happening." Varid, his eyes still closed, broke the growing silence.

"Why don't you think about something close to you? Like, something someone close to you says? For instance…" Nero looked around to make sure no one else was listening to them. "My mom always told me to not be weak when I was growing up… she even tells me that now as an adult."

Varid smiled as he listened.

"Don't be weak, Nero," he said just as she did in her heavy accent. "Don't be weak, Nero."

The wind began blowing faster.

Who should I think about? Varid tried to activate his powerful thoughts again. *My family?* A chill ran up his spine. *Myself? Who I am, or who they want me to be?*

Soft rain fell. Both of their wings got wet, their feathers heavy as they waited to see what would happen next. The greenish cloud traveled slowly up above Varid's dyed grey-white hair. It started to gather up the courage to release a bolt above him — hesitant and unsure, waiting for a thought that evoked a feeling strong enough from within him to command it down.

Varid made nervous, tight fists with both hands. The nail polish on his fingers matched his wings almost perfectly. In an uncomfortable instant, all taunting and berating insults anyone had ever told him had flooded his mind, drowning all peace from it. Their judgemental looks and hurtful words. Nero noticed how his facial expression changed.

Do I deserve to be treated the way I am? Varid lowered his head, his wet hair dripping rain down onto his face as it twitched with painful insecurity. *Did my family truly care that I disappeared at the falls? Do they really care about me? Do I care about myself? Do I... accept my own self?*

With that thought, the cloud gained enough emotional energy to strike down its yellow bolt. It was in that second of sudden shock that Varid looked all around him. Worriedly running his hands over his cut-up, graffiti covered jacket, he looked from Nero, over to the cloud trio hanging out at his side, and then at the planet, which he had no recollection of.

"What is going on? Who are you?" Varid asked loudly. "Where am I? What is this place?"

Nero blinked twice. "Um…"

"Who are you? Answer me!" he said hastily. "Who am… I?"

The cloud causes amnesia. Nero understood right away what was happening around ten seconds in. *Should only last fifteen seconds.*

"Tell me what's going on right now!" Varid continued.

Nero began counting down, "Five."

"What is going on?" his voice lowered and slowed.

"Four."

Varid stopped talking.

"Three."

He watched the clouds move steadily in the sky.

"Two."

Rain fell on his face.

"One."

Varid let out the deepest breath he ever had.

"How do you feel?" Nero asked him as his awareness came back to the surface.

"What just happened?" Varid couldn't hold back a peaceful smile.

"You just left everything for a little while. That cloud, the green one, made you forget everything," Nero informed him. "I just watched it all unfold."

"Wow. That was amazing."

"You enjoyed it? You seemed worried."

Varid shook his head. "Yes, it was great. I've always wanted that. To forget everything. To fully escape all my painful thoughts, my memories, to be free."

Nero almost laughed, but quickly realized how serious he was. *The color codes are extremely important. Better to not make fun of this guy and instead see this as a coaching opportunity.* "Varid." He wanted his full, undivided attention.

"Yes?"

"Use those clouds to our advantage."

CHAPTER SIXTEEN: THE MOST BEAUTIFUL PART
Present

Aadavan had a hard time leaving the pond and reliving how Theia almost tragically lost her life because of his idea. *How can I make it up to her?* He sat near the waters and looked at the silent crocodile, waiting to eat again. For a brief moment, he thought about those who had died and were fed to him. *What will everyone back home think? What if I was back on Earth and lost Theia to the unknown?* The cold air gave him goosebumps as he felt certain effects of the potent substance that began at the falls starting to gradually wear off. *I wish I had more of that liquid to drink. It made me feel invincible. Like I can do anything I put my mind to. The stronger the influence of whatever it was, the stronger I am.*

He couldn't stop thinking about how the crocodile attacked Theia when she accidentally slipped in. *Theia almost lost her life under my supervision. I failed to look out for her. This reality is practically unbearable to face. What truly could have happened? How would I have ever slept again after such a catastrophe? Could I even live with myself? The regret?*

He felt the overwhelming need to find more time for them to speak. Each time she sent Cloudburst to the falls, he noticed something near the outskirts of the planet. Aadavan wanted to show her, a bit hesitant because of where exactly it was located, but thought to himself, *I'm sure enough that she can see the beauty in the danger and the complexity in the unpredictable circumstances. Deep down, I believe she still trusts me. I've given her some time to calm down. Perhaps she will hear me out despite my mistakes.* He went to see her against the piece of his mind telling him that maybe he shouldn't—that he should leave her alone and punish himself some more for the wrong he'd done. *She deserves better than me. I've messed up far too many times to count. Perhaps my efforts now can nullify the past.*

"Theia." Aadavan knocked on her door softly, ignoring the spiteful side-eye looks from the grounds members who were passing by. "I'm sorry about what happened, please believe me. We need to speak."

"How about you leave her alone for once?" Nero said as he passed by, with Gebu not too far behind him. "Maybe she doesn't want to talk to you. Can you get that through your head? We heard about the trap you had her walk into. Do everyone a favor and jump in there yourself, would you? How sad that you can't even be loyal and fair to the only person here who puts up with you."

Aadavan didn't respond. *I won't give him the attention he so desperately needs. What would he possibly know about me or my matters with Theia? He's lucky I don't throw him into the croc's mouth for his hostility and cruel comments.* The two men went outside. *I hope he doesn't train too hard, I don't need him to be more prepared than my own.*

"Theia, please." He knocked again.

She opened the door slightly and stared at her feet. He felt worried as he could just barely see her. "What is it? I'm not sure I'd like to talk right now. I have a lot on my mind that I'm trying to process. Space would be nice."

"I have something I want to show you. Please trust me. You know I'm very sorry for what happened. I couldn't predict what that reptile was going to do. You have to understand."

Theia looked him up and down, taking in a breath of frustration while admiring his appearance. "I know you didn't want that to happen, Aadavan. I shouldn't have stepped so close. You wouldn't want me in harm's way."

"I'm glad you know that. Don't listen to what others are saying about me — they have no idea who I really am. You know that." *For that, I'll always be thankful. Despite their judgment, she knows and believes the truth.*

"What is it you want to show me?" Theia asked. "Is everything okay?"

"All is well. It's a surprise. Something that you will never forget. I want to experience it with you as I know you will appreciate it more than everyone else."

Theia opened the door some more. "Better be a safer surprise than the previous one."

Flashforward to CHP. 9 of ECHOES OF EUNOIA

For a brief amount of time, Anon and Amira were able to get away from Zayika as she hunted them down. They were separated on the planet and searching for one another. The color-coded curse had completely eaten into Eunoia's sky, ocean, almost everything, and most unfortunately — Zayika's vulnerable brain.

Amira ran into and stayed close to Zekiel and Jameson while looking for Anon and began devising a plan to dismantle Zayika's efforts to destroy them. She found it difficult to not hold her breath and remain calm as she waited to find out what happened to the man she loved, running as fast as he could from confronting the wrath that his former friend had coming for him.

"Regret will always catch up to you, Anon," he heard her words echo through the air as he looked everywhere to see where she was talking from. "No matter how far and wide you run."

"Please, just stop! Just leave me alone!" he yelled out loud and tried to catch his breath. Sweat fell from his face as he leaned on the nearest tree that he was able to land on. "I said I was sorry! I didn't want to leave you behind! I messed up under pressure! What else do you want from me? Zayika, please! Why can you not accept an honest apology?"

Anon's tired eyes studied the purple sky as he felt lost in a nightmarish daydream, running from the greatest fears of his subconscious. He thought he saw her out of the corner of his eye sprinting through the trees. *I need to get back to Amira!* he told himself and began traveling forwards again.

He could see Zayika in between each tree venturing onwards in unison with his steps. Her white dress showed throughout the dark brown trees along with her hair that collected the majority of raindrops that fell. He kept turning to look at her in between watching where he was stepping. Anon almost tripped over the vines and the feeling the look on her face gave him. He could sense that there was more to her antagonizing nature, built on something much sadder, a twisted combination of a root meaning to her actions. His words were making no difference in how determined she was after him. *Am I hallucinating? Is that even her?* Anon decided to stop moving, and she suddenly disappeared. It wasn't until he went and hid near cover that he saw someone else again, unsure of where Zayika truly was. The next person who approached him was Amira. The peace that overcame him at the sight of her was life-changing.

"Hey!" she said to him, and he replied the same back as they embraced and held onto one another, sharing a kiss that they each wanted to last for a lifetime.

Anon never wanted to let Amira go.

Present

Theia let Aadavan into her room, which was as cozy as she was able to make it. The walls were dark blue, and she had decorated each corner with different types of plants that Aadavan had collected for her on his various scavenges. He noticed that she kept them well watered as she nervously touched them, checking their soil, while he lingered near the door.

"What are you doing later tonight?" Aadavan asked.

"Planning for tomorrow. Why?"

"I would like you to join me on an outing for the surprise."

Here he goes again trying to sound mysterious. "When?"

"Nightfall."

"Will Lorelai be joining us?"

"No, just us two."

Even though Theia cared about Lorelai dearly, she was thrilled when her and Aadavan had their alone time together away from everyone else, when it was peaceful enough to do so. She hoped that was what he had planned—a means of escaping the stress and terrors the planet itself presented them with. Theia was nervous for the upcoming events, worried about what their results would end up being, and even more nervous to hopefully one day explain to Aadavan that she secretly wanted to leave it all behind and go back to Earth.

I don't think he will understand. I also don't want him to feel that he has to give up this dream because of me. He would expect Lorelai to leave and back down from the plans we've made together… but not me. He's depending on me. But I want to escape with him. I want us to have a life together back on Earth. Just the two of us.

"Are you in?" He noticed she was falling into a sea of thoughts again.

"Yes." Theia cleared her throat. "I am."

He snapped his fingers. "Great."

"There's actually something I think I should tell you…" she began to say, fiddling with the leaves of another plant as she avoided eye contact.

"What is it?"

Just wait. I don't know how he'll feel about the news with Cloudburst. Tell him later. He's in a good mood right now. No need to spoil it. She talked herself out of telling him. "I'll share it with you after whatever it is you have planned for us."

He acknowledged her hesitancy with a curt nod. "I'll circle back around here when the moon is the brightest light. Please make sure you don't overthink whatever may be on your mind. You've been using a lot of brain power lately. I look forward to seeing you later, Theia."

Her heart beat faster as he promptly started to leave the room. She felt timid about their conversation being cut short and was unsure if it was because of how much she was holding back. "What is it we're doing? Why later tonight, why not right now? What are you going to show me?"

"The planet." Aadavan stopped walking and faced her once more. "The most beautiful part."

Flashforward to CHP. 11 of ECHOES OF EUNOIA

Everything had fallen apart at the ocean's shore. Everyone there was shocked beyond belief at what happened at the hands of Zayika. Eunoia's rage could not be contained. The air was filled with mourning. The anglerfish wept and wailed on the sand, desperate to return to the waters but unable to swim after the loss of the only person it allowed to come near it. Its whale-like cries shook the core of Eunoia. The grains of sand bounced at the frequency and low pitch of each sound. Hippo saw her broken tooth used as a weapon against Amira — the guardian of peace and inspiration.

Anon held her in his trembling arms as his hopes for the future were literally dying in front of him. He managed to speak, "You were the best part of my life, Amira, the most beautiful part."

Zayika's fist tightened more and more with each tear that fell from Anon's helpless eyes.

"You were the only good that came from this planet. You were the start of it all," he continued. "Hope wasn't here until you arrived."

Untrue, all untrue! Zayika felt like she was going to explode. *He has everything wrong! He always does! He wouldn't even be here if it wasn't for me saving him! What was so special about Amira, anyways? She deserved to die!*

Nero couldn't hide his disappointment and distaste in Zayika's choices as his eyes met hers.

"What Nero?" she shouted and stepped over the tip of Hippo's large, bloody tooth that she had rammed into Amira's chest with disturbing strength and almost tripped over it. "Are you really going to judge me? You, of all people? The man here who has no morals?"

Her words are so exhausting. There's no point in trying to explain myself. "That's not true! I do. This is not what I want to be a part of. I don't like this, Zayika."

As Anon sobbed, Zekiel felt regretful of how he had judged him so harshly in the past. *He doesn't deserve this. Not Amira… This is a loss you cannot come back from.* He flipped his long blonde hair down to, again, obstruct his vision from seeing Anon losing the woman he truly loved. *Rest in peace, Amira. I should've been a better friend to you. I always had respect for you. Even when I failed to show it.*

Jameson could hardly believe what he was seeing as his palms grew sweaty. *I didn't think Zayika would really kill her.* He watched Amira's blood drip off Zayika's white dress as she rapidly lost control of her emotions and wore them shamelessly on her sleeve. *She's dead, Amira… What reason could possibly justify this?* He chewed on the side of his mouth nervously as he remembered what Merrick's blood looked like splattered all over the convenience store's floor. *What is going on in Zayika's mind? What could she be thinking?*

"Give me a break! You've been playing along this entire time! You killed Saige and couldn't care less! Plus, you've said it yourself that you think we are alike!" Zayika's voice quivered as she tried her hardest to not cry in front of the men.

An unrecognizable part of her morbidly enjoyed the chaos and destruction unfolding in a confusing way. *You deserve this Zayika, you are doing a great job. Keep ruining everything because that is what you are good at. Say more, come on, ruin more. Keep burning bridges. Push them away. They never loved you… you know that, right?*

She could hardly stand as the weight of the consequences pulled down on her conscience. She fed all of her emotional attention to the intrusive thoughts she was unable to withhold. They were not passing, but instead festering and multiplying at an alarming rate, sometimes so loud that she couldn't hear the meaning behind what others were saying to her—not even what she wanted to tell herself.

Nero jumped in again to defend himself, something he was never fearful of doing, "You were the one who made that assumption. I am not like you."

He hates you, Zayika. So does Zekiel. So does Anon and everyone else. "Whatever. You didn't deny it, so who's to say that some part of you isn't on my side?" *Of course, he isn't. You are worthless, Zayika, and you always have been.*

"I know that we are not the same after what you've just done." Nero shook his head. "You've made everything… different."

Zayika looked at Anon who was still crying a few feet away, more heartbroken than she'd ever seen him before. *Now see what you did to Anon? You really deserve to die now, Zayika! Look what you took from him! You took Amira's life — you worthless being! He picked her over you for a reason! The representatives left you behind for a reason! You want to know the reason? You're supposed to give everyone the greatest gift you possibly can and finally kill yourself. Burn every bridge in sight.* "Don't act like some sort of champion. It's too late to redeem yourself now." *Yeah, it is, Zayika. You are past the point of redemption. Everyone now hates you, and that hate? It will follow you forever. Your decisions… they define you. Now you can never escape your past and it is all you will ever be.*

Her attention was forced onto Anon. "It's time to kill you too, Anon. Let me ask you this… are you even going to fight back?"

Anon set Amira down as he dreaded what was to come. He dreaded experiencing the hurt he would never be able to escape after the shock of her death started to wear off. He also dreaded facing Zayika and the horrors of what their fight would entail. "Of course, I will," he replied with contempt for her that he'd never had for another person before, which was heightened greatly because of the care he also had for her — which was unique to them both.

Theia

Four Hours Later

Aadavan and I spent more time together as Lorelai could almost always be found in the water. It was so uncomfortable for her to even so much as entertain the thought of staying out on the shore for as long as she could stand it. We had no idea what would happen if she was to be too far from safety, as the air suffocated her morphed state. *I'm not sure I could spend as much time alone with myself as her. I have no idea how she does it. I would get far too lonely. I need to make sure she knows that I care for her. I appreciate all the effort she's put forth for Aadavan and me.*

He had ridden the platform up to carry out our plans together during one of the coldest nights we'd ever experienced. I was looking forward to seeing something completely new. It was astonishing just how many surprises we had uncovered since arriving together. Some were better than others, but having someone by my side who never failed to be there for me was the best gift that I could've received. Aadavan's care for me was consistent despite everything else.

It was what he always had for me.

"Where did you find that?" I asked him, shocked to see him dressed in a pearl white suit I'd never seen before as he strode up to the gate. *I don't recall anyone being teleported here in that outfit.*

"I shouldn't reveal my secrets to you." He smiled as the doors opened.

"Now I feel underdressed." I pointed to my ragged, brown pants and black, baggy shirt that I tended to wear.

"Don't worry about that." He walked up to me and lightly touched the side of my arm. "You look great."

I gave him an embarrassed face and looked away, changing the subject. "By the way… how is it I've never seen what you are about to show me before? Are you certain that I haven't?"

His smile wouldn't leave his face. "Because you aren't everywhere all at once even though most of the time you would like to be."

"You don't know everything about me Aadavan." I said, playfully stern.

"No, I don't, but I'm pretty spot on with what I do know." He put his hand out. "Do you trust me?"

"Always." *No matter what has or hasn't happened. I will always trust him.*

His hand remained steadily extended towards me. The fabric on his suit shone under the moonlight. "Please know that you can trust me no matter what. I will always have your best interests at heart."

I took his hand and followed him.

"Too bad I don't have wings like the men in your faction." He helped me step over the relatively wide gap between the edge and platform. "If I did then I could, you know, hold you in my arms as we fly off together."

"You're ridiculous," I replied, laughing loudly.

"Sure I am." His smile was still planted on his face as he struggled to contain his excitement.

"Where are we going exactly?"

"To the jungle. We will need Cloudburst to join us momentarily."

"You know he hates you, right?"

"I know, and I don't care."

"Really?"

"Yes, really."

"Why is that?" I was genuinely intrigued. Aadavan's lack of concern for the opinions of others always fascinated me. "How do you not care?"

"Why would I spend energy on caring?" He looked over at me as we began plummeting down. Air rushed past us as we held onto one another, hair flying in all directions.

We hit the ground.

"Why do you truly not care what others think of you?"

"Who says I don't?" he challenged as we ventured towards the vines.

Saylor was heading away from the faction's treehouse and acknowledged us nearby with a friendly wave. "Hi Aadavan and Theia! Hope you're doing we—"

"Go find Cloudburst, wherever he is, and tell him to go to the pond right now!" Aadavan cut her off, and I touched his shoulder.

"We don't have to tell her to do that. I can take care of it."

"Okay, of course!" she replied happily and skipped off to find him for us.

"She's always been odd," he said as we continued walking.

"In what way?"

"I'm not sure how to describe it, something about her, it's unnatural."

"Many say that about you too," I teased, and he snickered.

"I care what others think," Aadavan revisited our previous conversation. "Just not everyone. It takes too much energy to try to please everyone, especially when they don't care what you think of them."

I took his words into consideration. "What do you feel will be the biggest mental challenge for those surviving here?"

"Getting over themselves."

I inhaled deeply.

"And communicating with one another." He stared ahead as we pushed past his treehouse and through the vines. He continued to lead the way. "If they have those two bases covered, those two sides to the coin of strategizing and prioritizing, then they will survive."

"You know who shows some promise?"

"Who?"

"Nero."

A hint of what could only be described as jealousy flashed over Aadavan's eyes as he replied, "Oh, yes, he's been training. He seems like he will put up a strong fight — that's what Cloudburst was saying at least."

"He will, so will others in my group too."

Aadavan's grip on my hand tensed. "Like who?"

"I have a feeling that they haven't arrived yet, but my final three. I think they will be special."

"Well, I wish your fighters the best."

"I would say it's not a competition but…" I started laughing again. "It literally is."

"Well, one of yours won last time. Maybe this time someone from my group will."

We were nearing the pond, the vegetation thinning out as we walked. My heart raced a bit faster at the sight of it, but I kept my breath steady and tried to not show it too much. The sky was filled with glowing white stars on a deep navy-blue canvas, hints of green speckled throughout.

"The one with the cloud companions seems promising. Or the one with the green wings. I'm sure you have some winners."

"Varid and Gebu. They are very helpful actually," I defended them.

"Of course," he retorted sarcastically while his attention shifted over to the vines. "I bet they're both shining stars."

"I'm needed here?" Cloudburst stepped through the vines at our left. "I was… demanded to 'get over there right now' by Saylor. She made it sound important and time sensitive, but since it involves you both, I doubt it really is. What's going on?"

"You have to go to the waterfall right now," Aadavan told him.

"What? Why?" he groaned. "I have plans with some of the others tonight."

His patience was running low. "What 'plans' could you possibly have? We need you there right now. Find something to do while you wait." He turned to face me. "Theia, please send him there right now."

"Are you s—" I paused. *I said I would trust him, didn't I? Just trust him and see what happens.* "Uh, um, alright." I went over to Cloudburst and put my hand in the air, eyes closed, and within an instant I sent him away. "So are we going to watch what he does next?"

"No." Aadavan's smile was radiant as he took both my hands in his.

The ground began shaking as I tried to remain calm. "What's going on? Are you causing this?"

As I looked at our feet, he softly put a finger under my chin to lift my face up. "Look."

"At what?" I glanced at the sky, and it looked the same as before, the light I'd cast around Cloudburst slowly dissipating away. Rocks and dirt rumbled and bounced.

Trees swayed in the disruption, and a warm wind blew in calmly around us. "I don't understand."

"Don't look at the ground, look at what's in front of you. If you don't..." he pointed to the pond. "You will miss very, very special moments."

The crocodile was rising out of the water, and it seemed larger than the last time I saw it. His eyes shone brighter than all the stars in the sky combined, the purple hue covering each leaf, branch, and rock. The water was the same color and seemed as if it was sparkling. The creature let out a hum as Aadavan redirected my attention up, this time directly towards the sky as the crocodile moved its eyes up too. Everything I saw was vibrant and stunning. Something happened that I'd never seen before...

The clouds turned orange.

"Isn't that the most gorgeous thing you've ever seen?" he asked as I stepped in front of him. "Aside from yourself, of course."

While keeping my eyes on the sky, we embraced each other and watched together. The purple waters shone below orange clouds as blue lightning joined in the beautiful madness. I held onto him, and he wrapped both arms around my waist, his face gently resting on my right shoulder as we swayed back and forth. We were far away enough from the fighters to focus on the silence and peace that surrounded us. I turned my face to meet his, and he moved in closer to mine as we shared a kiss.

"Thank you for showing me this. I'd never noticed it before."

"Because you get very wrapped up in everything that's going on. Plus, you haven't been here while this has happened before," he said with calm understanding. "Theia, that is okay. But I needed you to see this at least once."

Normally after sending Cloudburst to the waterfall, I would dissociate from reality, fighting off the feeling of regret of what I was doing and even trying to hide from questioning my own motives and decisions. I would detach so far from what was really happening that sometimes I barely knew what was taking place… or was able to see the beauty within it.

"Your eyes…" Aadavan said.

"What?"

I had never heard him speak in so much awe before, "There are stars in them."

CHAPTER SEVENTEEN: THE BLUE TRANCE

Aadavan

Present

Theia's eyes looked magnificent as I was captivated in their beauty. Orange and blue stars shone predominately amongst a sea of others in them at me. I showed her the special orange clouds and how strikingly they stood out amongst the ones we were used to seeing. Unlike the clouds, I could never get quite used to seeing her. Theia had the most calming presence. Our disagreements wouldn't take the shape of toxic conflict, but instead that of healthy competition. She inspired me to sharpen myself as a person and my involvement in the grand scheme of uncovering and embracing the unknown. It felt as though anything was possible with her by my side.

"I'm looking forward to the next test," I told her. "We are getting closer to reaching the number of people we need."

"We don't have to assign ten people to each of us, you know. We could have fewer competitors this time around."

"We should prioritize consistency. I would say that it went very well before, so why change anything? We have to keep the stakes high."

Theia's eyes returned to normal as the extra saturation in the clouds lost their intensity. "We are making people fight for their lives either way. The stakes will be high no matter what. Why not do it diff—"

"Because it works the way it is," I cut her off. *Why did one of her members have to win? Now she thinks she can call all of the shots.* I'd battled with mood swings often ever since I drank from that bottle at the waterfall. "I was the one who oversaw most of that game. Why are you not thanking me for that, anyway? I made sure everything was evenly planned and paced."

"Please relax, Aadavan. I just think this time around we shouldn't intervene. We need to have faith in those we chose. We should see where their thoughts take them because it would be fascinating. Their abilities correlate with their personalities; some are simply more equipped to survive than others."

"Fate exists, but it can also be altered," I replied.

"I'm not sure about that." Theia tried to remain calm with her next words, "Do you also feel watched by the planet?"

I felt my skin go cold. "What do you mean?"

The colors of the sky continued to be drained of life as our conversation carried on, I couldn't shake an ominous feeling.

"I feel as though it is watching our every move. What we say and do is not only our own. I'm unsure that there is even any privacy here at all."

Her thoughts seemed alarmingly sudden. *How much does she know about the stone? I don't want her to worry about it. In fact, I don't want to talk about it at all.*

"It's Cloudburst," she said.

"What?" I wasn't surprised at the mention of his name. "What about him?"

"H-his thoughts… this is what I wanted to tell you about earlier." Theia nervously tapped her thumbs on each other as she stumbled again on her next sentence, "I can h-hear them."

"Excuse me?"

"Only him. His thoughts are exposed in my mind."

I didn't know what to say. "What does this mean? What has he been thinking? Is he plotting against us?"

"I believe in privacy. I'm unsure how I've been granted this ability, and why specifically with him, but I've decided to not question too much."

"Alright then." *Why do I feel like this?* The thought of Theia sharing an intimate bond with Cloudburst grated at me the wrong way. "Well hopefully it stops soon." *Geez, I would've rather talked about the unnecessary stone had I known this is what she was going to say. Why is she experiencing some sort of higher connection with him that she isn't with me?*

"At least we'll know if he's telling us the truth or not, or if he will potentially put us in danger," she told me.

"Do you hear his thoughts all the time?"

"When we are close enough to each other, his mix with my own."

"There has to be some sort of explanation for this." I was extremely uncomfortable. "I haven't had that with anyone else here, nor has Lorelai that I know of."

"I know. That's why I'm sharing it with you. I wanted you to know."

"Fine." I crossed my arms. "As long as he can't hear your thoughts then I don't care."

"He never told me that he can."

"Great," I huffed.

"Don't worry, Aadavan," she attempted to reassure me. "This won't change or impact anything negatively. If anything, this is a win for us. Getting an upper hand in any way is something that should be celebrated—not discouraged."

"I'm just not okay with how much is out of our reach. There is, dare I say, too much we do not understand."

Theia gave a small grin. "Would you say you are worried? Will you actually admit that you are?"

I grinned back. "Now don't act as if I don't show genuine emotion. Of course I am worried to an extent, but don't tell anyone else that."

She paused for a few moments to think about what to say next. "What has worried you the most so far about all of this?"

That's easy to answer. My response flew out of my mouth without a second thought, "When the planet fought me over the stone. I was terrified." I kept my voice low enough for only her to hear.

"I could tell. I would have been too. I'm sorry you had to go through that."

"Don't be. We will be alright. This place may try to retaliate and punish us, but those who truly should be concerned are those who are next in line to fight here. Not us." I almost doubted my own words but tried to not let Theia see that.

"What if, because of what we're doing, we have our own type of sentence that we now have to face?" she asked. "What if we are not exempt from karma? From law and order? Aadavan… what if we truly are in grave danger now? What will we do?"

I tilted my head side to side to stretch my strained and inflamed neck muscles. "You, Lorelai, and I will band together and protect ourselves."

"With our… abilities?" She also showed a moment of doubt, like we were not as powerful as we thought.

"Yes. With our minds. With what capabilities we hold in ourselves. We will be alright. This place, whatever is coming after us, will regret trying to strike us down."

"I swear it seems like it's up to something." She stared at the sky, her lovely brown eyes just as captivating to look at.

"Like what?"

"I feel as though it's going to force us into some type of a trance."

Aadavan refused to respond as he felt that something seemed cursed behind her words.

Flashforward to CHP. 12 of CARRIERS OF EUNOIA

In a matter of only a few minutes, an earthquake rumbled beneath everyone; they fled to the best hiding spaces they could find. Some were not fortunate to have gotten to a place of protection in time. Omar, who was painting on a ledge, had fallen off and those who saw him in a dangerous situation didn't have enough time to react and help him reach safety. Anon was utterly devastated at what happened and went to hold him in his arms, thankful that at least he wasn't going to die alone.

Right as Anon's hands touched Omar's disfigured head, his whole body to his core went numb. It was exactly then that the sky became completely blue along with everything else. The usual white cliffs turned blue, blood pouring out of Omar, the clouds, and everything in between. *What is happening?* He called out after Amira, but she wasn't there. In fact, no one else actually was besides him and, to his ultimate surprise... Zayika.

Everything was bizarrely quiet and yet somehow the silence was so loud. Then the wind started to rush around and all those who died on Eunoia when getting morphed started to talk to Anon from within the air. They were asking him what they did wrong, trying to have him explain to them if they deserved to die the way they did with so much pain and unfair suffering. He felt the pull and disruption of their misery tearing at the emotions he wore on his own ripped half-sleeves.

Others were, at the same time, asking if he could free their souls and made it clear that their consciousness' were very much intact and unmistakably begging for help. They spoke through the gusts of wind. He wanted so badly to silence them. Blue lightning was sent down to get his full attention.

Hippo wailed out ferociously in the waters from a toothache, and Ghoul remained quiet and withdrawn in the pond. Anon started hallucinating as his friend talked to him cryptically. "This isn't okay. What you did is not okay. This will follow you for forever Anon," Omar said in a disappointed tone, his eyes rolling backwards and blue tears escaping them. Anon panicked and dropped him hastily. *This can't be happening!* He told himself at the realization of just how out of control everything in his life had become as a result of his past choices. The planet's appearance shifted around him, and once every single inch of it turned blue… that's when she appeared. *I have to get out of here!*

"Hello Anon," Zayika said enchantingly in a wicked tone. "I learned that not only can I heal with stars, but I can do a lot of damage with them too."

Her hair was completely silver and much shorter. The purple half had been cleanly cut off above her shoulders. She was naked and only partially covered with glistening stars. He couldn't take his eyes off of her. Each sparkle bounced around and off of her skin in a hypnotizing way. He felt paralyzed as she captured his undivided attention in his exposed state of mind.

"What is going on?" he asked as her new self started to show, leaving her almost unrecognizable.

The stars formed a glimmering dress around her and decided to show Anon a glimpse of what she would be clothed in next—an outfit he wouldn't be able to forget.

"You will learn what I am capable of because of what you've done to me." She exuded the energy of fatal attraction. "Actions should have consequences. Negligence needs to be reprimanded, especially against those who are being mindfully inconsiderate."

He was confused and repressed his mutual interest in her. "What? I don't know what you're talking about!"

Lightning shot down again as the planet wanted to make a point at his words. The sound was deafening. The color blue had eaten into everything.

"Are you okay?" an unknown voice asked him suddenly, and in a way that was able to pull him out of the blue trance.

Zayika and the distorted reality around Anon disappeared at once, but the feeling he had in that moment never went away. It began to grow and fester in his brain, heart, and the lightning that traveled through the intricate pathways of his veins. She always felt close, no matter how far away he got from her.

Present

Theia and Aadavan stood only feet apart but felt worlds of distance between them. He shifted on the heels of his feet while searching for how to confront her about their future plans.

Ignore what she's said about a trance. We can't give attention to what may overcome our efforts, he thought. *Theia needs to be careful on what is spoken into existence.*

"I would like to take over the leadership," he said abruptly. "I think we need to be involved more than ever in seeing that our vision is fulfilled with what happens on the grounds. I fear that certain information we reveal during the ceremony will be misinterpreted, over-analyzed, or at worst—ignored."

"I think you're worrying too much."

"You must've mistaken me for Lorelai," Aadavan tried to joke. "But I'm being serious."

"So am I when I say that I would like a fair shot at leading just like you got. Since Cloudburst won, I feel like that designates me as the next in line to determine how we handle technicalities and what guidance is given."

"You know what?" *I'm growing tired of trying to back up my points so often.* "Let's see how you run things. I'm sure Lorelai will go along with whatever we choose anyways. We'll see what you do with this round, Theia, but if I may truly suggest—"

"Enough suggesting." She stepped closer to him. "Just watch and see. Sometimes things won't develop in life if they can't naturally grow on their own. You can't force and control everything, especially not the minds of these fighters."

"I'm not trying to control them, I'm trying to influence them." Defensiveness coated each word. "Do you even know how balanced and prepared Saylor is, for instance?

Albeit odd… she is very strong and level-minded when it comes to being present in the moment; meditating and preparing for what's to come. You know why I'm so confident in her abilities?"

Theia smiled. "Let me guess. Because she reminds you of yourself in some way?"

He was quick to shoot down her answer. "No. Because she is already trying her best at focusing her energy on training and inspiring others. The ones like her? They are the ones who make it the farthest. They are the ones who make it home."

"Well none of your own seemed to in the previous game." Theia cleared her throat as he rolled his eyes. "Sorry to be so blunt, but it's a factual statement. Those in the Over Grounds are also going to make it far. I can see amazing capabilities in all of them, and not just because of their superpowers."

Some of them were lurking nearby, unbeknownst to the two representatives. Varid was in the front of the rest, Mae mostly covered in her cloak, Kason and Lyra side by side, and Nero leading the way for Gebu. They hushed one another as they stayed concealed by the leaves.

"Stay quiet. This has to go without a hitch," Gebu said a bit too loudly.

"Take your own advice, none of us were even saying anything." Nero shot back in barely a whisper. "Wait, why is Aadavan here? Varid! You said that cloud showed you that she was alone!"

"I-I don't know!" Varid shrugged as he watched the orange cloud that was floating closest to him. "Why did you not show me both of them?" he asked it.

The cloud flickered in yellow tones as he sighed. *Should've been more careful. I need to practice working with these companions more than I have so far.*

"Dude, are you serious? How are you so unprepared?" Nero asked and muttered under his breath, "Whatever. Stupid clouds. Let's improvise." He stepped forwards past everyone else and quickly strategized, "Send the purple one over to Aadavan."

"What exactly does it do?" Mae asked, unable to get a clear answer from Gebu earlier.

"It causes distortion, emotional angst, and frustration," Varid replied.

"Yeah, it's unpleasant, to say the least, and it lasts for a few minutes," Gebu exaggerated and shivered at the memory.

"Send it over to him," Mae agreed. "It will work. Then you can send the green one over to Theia."

"What does that one do?" Gebu asked.

Varid nervously bit at his nails. "It causes temporary amnesia."

"Alright. Send them. Push Aadavan off course and mentally stun Theia. Once she has no idea what's going on, I will, um, I'll..." Nero's attention wandered to the pond. "I'll figure something out. I just want to get this over with."

"This doesn't seem well thought out," Varid said.

"Well, I don't care. Your clouds are bright enough as they are, they'll catch unwanted attention if we don't get a move on. Maybe Kason will surprise us all with a hidden ability."

"Oh come on, Nero, you know Gebu and I were only given wings," Kason responded quickly.

"How would you even know? You never train," Nero told him. "I'll go over to speak with her and you can sneak up to knock her out. Once she's awake, we will make sure she's restrained and get her to teleport us all back. One by one. Send them out, Varid, let's go."

Varid rolled his shoulders. "Here goes nothing." He commanded the purple cloud to go over to Aadavan, and it carried out his command correctly.

They hardly registered the clouds before their effects were set into motion.

"I hate those hills, that stone, and the attacks that we've had to endure," he told Theia angrily.

"Let's not think about that right now," she replied softly as the green cloud came up behind her and hovered over the top of her head.

"I can think about whatever I want to! Don't tell me what I can talk about!"

"What do you mean?" She forgot what was just said.

"I mean that you can't discern what concerns me or not!" Aadavan's posture tensed further.

"Who are you?" Theia forgot her name, who and where she was, with no idea who the man standing right in front of her was.

"Forget this! I'm not playing these games with you!" He abandoned their conversation without a second thought as his turned violent.

To their luck, he stormed off in the opposite direction from the Over Grounds group.

"It's working!" Varid got excited. "The plan is working!"

"Don't celebrate too soon." Nero kept his expression stern.

"Alright, Kason. Head in."

Kason followed his orders and approached Theia.

"Who are you?" she asked Nero, who was heading her way.

"I'm not going to bother answering you. All of this will be over soon."

"What do you mean?"

Nero's eyes looked past her at his teammate. "Go on."

Kason's hands shook as he held onto a particularly large rock. "I can't do it."

"What?"

"I-I can't!"

Theia looked to see who was speaking behind her, and Nero reached past to take the rock from Kason.

"If you won't do what needs to be done, then I'll just do it myself!"

Before she could see what he was talking about, Theia was struck in the head, knocked unconscious, and she hit the ground with a very loud thud.

"What was that?" they heard Aadavan call out, circling back towards them.

"The cloud's effects are wearing off!" Varid tried to warn from the sidelines. "He's heading this way!"

Nero threw the rock as far as he could before the dweller representative approached in the blink of an eye.

"What in the world have you done to Theia? Why is she unconscious?" he asked with a sweaty face, clearly in panic at the sight before him.

"We don't know," Kason lied.

"Yeah, we just came across her like this," Nero continued the facade. "She must've been coming over here to see you. We were out here practicing fighting and came across her like this."

"You already said that," Aadavan responded suspiciously. "I don't know what your intentions are, or why it seems that Theia has been attacked, but each of you need to leave my sight within the next five seconds or else you will be fed to the crocodile so fast that your life won't even have enough time to flash before your eyes."

"We'll get out of here." Nero replied and tightened his fists.

He and Kason walked back to the others as fast as they could and kept their voices low.

"Our idea failed." Kason's voice was unsteady.

Nero's wasn't as he responded, "That's why I thought of a backup one."

CHAPTER EIGHTEEN: THE PHANTOM LIGHTHOUSE

Lorelai

Present

Let's hope this doesn't go wrong, I thought to myself as Zavier and I swam beside each other. He had been successfully morphed with a tail like the rest of us, besides Enya, and given the ability to push seaweed out of his palms like she was able to. Though the two of them had a lot in common, I sensed that he was lacking some of the tenacity and fighting spirit that she displayed. *Maybe the fish is intended to fight alongside him?* I knew the anglerfish in our waters was important and had been capable of taking orders, but similarly to the planet's atmosphere, it wouldn't budge most times without resorting to violence when I'd try to get it to do something.

"Why are you taking him further out there with you?" Enya asked as she noticed us leaving my underwater structure and getting closer to the unnamed fish. "You told us we didn't have to do anything for a little while still, so what are you forcing him to do?"

"These matters don't concern you," I told her, looking back at Zavier. "You'll be okay. This is something that you have to do; we have to try and see what happens. This creature may be proven to be very useful in self-defense. You may speak to Enya later, but for now you have to follow my orders," I said to him as he swam behind me, venturing deeper into the ocean than he'd ever been before.

"Are you sure it won't hurt me?" he asked.

The fish's light illuminated everything in front of us, including the bite mark in my arm that I tried to cover from his view. She made everything clearer to see in the waters—unfortunately, even the parts that should've remained concealed.

"I'm sure. Just go towards her, please. See what she does." I was growing nervous as he did what I asked.

Zavier began to swim over to her, hardly able to take his eyes off of the orb and jagged teeth around it. The luminescence she emitted was piercingly bright, and the color of it complimented several of the coral clusters she usually gravitated to. "I would rather fight alone." He turned to face me, having second thoughts. A small school of fish rushed behind him and in the opposite direction, away from the large beast.

She let out a faint squeaking sound that reverberated in the waters around us, alerting anything, or anyone, nearby of our presence. Her squeaks started to sound deeper as she grew, deep and gravely unpredictable like the waters she explored.

She's doing it again, she's panicking… why?

The fish began opening her ginormous jaw — reacting to him the same way she did to me. Each eye on either side of her head looked overly cautious and on the verge of showing us how angry we were making her at any moment, dark black and gleaming with ill-intentioned radiance. Although anglerfish were known for eating dead fish that would sink to the floor, she had no issue with consuming those who were still alive, hunting and ravenously thrashing them apart with her teeth, similar to a shark. I knew that she would not have a challenging time killing a human, but I was unsure why she seemed aggressive and untrusting of us Oceanic Guardians, who inhabited the ocean for the purpose of protecting our own.

Why does she not want to be near us? Why is she making things difficult? Something tells me she is here to accompany one of my fighters. I just know it. If not Zavier… then who?

Her fear was quickly turning into anger as she couldn't understand why we were swimming and breathing in the same waters with her. The squeaking grew into one long continuous and contentious squeak, rising in volume as her orb seemed to glow brighter the longer she dragged it out. The anglerfish, who ate practically anything in sight, made it a distinct point to attack any of us that tried to come near her. Despite this, I made the careless mistake of still trying to have her help us in some way.

"I don't want to go any closer!" Zavier kept his eyes ahead of him but told me with great seriousness in his words how unsettled he was becoming, "Please don't make me do this! She doesn't want us here!"

Aadavan's crocodile has a purpose, I told myself. *There has to be one for this fish too. I need him to try. I'm sure she can sense his fear. He should exude confidence, even if it's fake. Soon it will become real.*

"Just swim a bit closer. Put a hand out in front of you. She is probably sensing your fear and misinterpreting it as hostility," I replied to him.

He shook his head at me and looked down below at the pitch-black ocean. We both were unable to see the floor at all, even with how deep we already were, completely unsure of just how much farther the true lengths of it went and what else was lurking and living below our tails. "No… no way. She's going to kill me! That fish will eat me alive! Please don't make me go closer to it!"

The anglerfish's eyes were as dark as the seemingly bottomless abyss. Her green, bumpy skin shimmered in her light. I could see the cuts, scrapes, and scars she'd suffered from fighting other whales, jellyfish, sharks, and mutated schools of fish. Small white specks floated in the water. Her mouth remained wide open and in a fixed position. Each fin rolled with every flap she took, generating strong underwater current pulls that began to reel him in closer than he was comfortable with. I kept a safe enough distance away.

"She's moving me!" He tried to swim with enough force to fight against the fish's attack. "She'll lunge! Lorelai, help! All I can do is shoot out seaweed! I have no chance!"

For some reason, I began to understand the unfair gravity of the situation and finally decided to intervene. Seeing him so hopeless and terrified reminded me of my own self in a way, similarly to when I was told to retrieve the stone for Theia and Aadavan. It made me question why I was forcing him to put himself in so much danger when I wouldn't want the same done to me.

I'm able to tell these aquatic creatures what to do. I can move water. I'll save him. I cannot lose one of my own to this fish. Am I allowing Theia and Aadavan's opinions and influence to get the best of my judgment?

"Go away!" I yelled to the anglerfish. "Leave at once!"

She didn't take to my command, unlike all of the other creatures who would normally listen. I put my palms out in front of me and controlled the water around her to move and push her away. The water did its job and ushered her from us in the opposite direction. This distracted and bothered her just enough to save his, and probably my own, life. Not wanting to spend her energy fighting against the current, she gave up on Zavier and swam off, away from us.

He stared me down with a scornful look as the waters grew darker with her exit. He took a few moments to speak as I moved some of my hair away from my eyes. The currents returned to normal. I felt ashamed. I got too carried away.

"Why did you bring me here to this thing?" His voice shook.

Maybe we are not supposed to choose who her fighting companion is… maybe she is the one who has to choose.

Zavier looked as though his head was spinning as we ventured back over to the castle together. He swam frantically and refused to look me directly in the eyes.

"I'm going to be sick."

We eventually swam up high enough that the natural light allowed us to see one another properly, gently bouncing off the beams and statues. Zavier went to rest near a cluster of salmon-colored seaweed at a coral reef off the edge of our faction's main terrain. He led the way, and I followed after him but maintained a far enough distance so as to not make him too uncomfortable all over again. I'd already crossed a boundary that shattered an irreplaceable layer of trust.

"May we speak to each other about what happened?" I asked nicely.

"I'm not sure I want to." He stared down at his forest green tail and tried to steady his breath, propping himself up with a shaky hand on the nearest rock. "What was that horrifying thing? What kind of shark? Whale? What even wa—"

"It is a female anglerfish. Traditionally, they only grow to between eight to forty inches, but as you saw, she is not at all what is usually found in the species. The males are much smaller, and I have yet to see one down here. What we have is some sort of a deep-sea angler, I presume. They lure in prey with their hanging light and swallow them whole."

"What? Are you serious? Why did you bring me down there with you? It could've killed me!"

"It wasn't going to." But I didn't know that, not for sure anyways, and I wasn't going to pretend to have the type of certainty I didn't possess. "I mean, I'm not certain if it would've attacked you or not, seeing as though you are morphed and are an important part of this oceanic environment and symbiosis."

Zavier's expression changed to somehow reflect even more surprise at my words and actions.

"Really?" he chuckled brokenly. "Pretty messed up to risk my life down there like that, and for what? To fight in some messed up bloodbath you're forcing us to be in? You know my brother is here too, right? You are tearing families apart. Why did you do this to us? Can you even answer that?"

"I'm..." I paused.

Aadavan wouldn't want me to admit mistake, to admit error, to be weak in the fighters' eyes.

"You're what? You're actually sorry? That's hard to believe! It's extremely difficult to believe even one word that any of you representatives say." He buried his face into his scale-covered hands and stayed seated on part of his tail as I turned to leave him alone.

"I actually am." It felt as though an anchor with a thick rope knotted to it was attached to my waist, dragging me down in what I could only describe as regret. It was heart wrenching to look at him sitting there, panting with great fear after he truly believed his life was going to end. He brought my attention to his brother who I'd seen a few times before, suffering so badly that he could hardly breath at all, and I wrestled away thoughts about my own siblings and what it would be like to see them in that state of distress.

I remembered what it was like to be tugged into the ocean without a way of escaping. How hard the sand felt as I fell and the air was knocked out of my tightening lungs. The bruises my fall left behind on my skin. I touched the tender scar on my arm and kept it concealed from his view as I swam away from him.

"I really am sorry…" I said so quietly that I was unsure if he could hear me. "Whether you believe me or not."

Flashforward to CHP. 9 of CARRIERS OF EUNOIA

Omar watched Zayika heal Anon's leg in the bedroom after he was struck by an Oceanic Guardian. He endured a near fatal wound with torn open skin and significant blood loss as the aftermath of many stinging and potentially venomous tentacles destroyed it. *How is she able to do that?* He saw her hands light up as they latched onto the life-threatening gash. It was repaired in just a few astonishing moments. Anon's discomfort eventually subsided as he let out a deep sigh at the overwhelming relief. The shock hadn't fully worn off yet after being attacked by an ocean fighter not too long before. Gritting his teeth at the pain, he and his friend hurried to the castle as fast as they possibly could and were thankful for the rising platform.

They caught Zayika fast enough before the injury was out of their own hands. She got wrapped up in what she was doing to the point of her two friends being taken aback by her interest. She had a hard time backing off from using her ability after the healing process was initiated. It was as if she couldn't let go of her hold, that something else had a hold on her.

I don't get to be a part of anything, do I? Omar thought to himself in the corner of the room when he first saw the stars being released from her fingers. *I wonder what it feels like? To be able to do something so effortlessly? To be handed that sort of importance?* He felt a rise of envy while being reminded of his lack of personal ability.

"Okay. I think we're done here," Anon chuckled and pulled back away from her.

She didn't stop even after he was fully cured.

"Alright, knock it off, Zayika." Omar went over to them. "Seems like you're getting a bit… carried away?"

Zayika returned to normal and pushed Anon aside. "Both of you now owe me favors for fixing that."

Omar reached out and caught Anon in his arms as he lost his footing. "Thanks man," he told him and went to put his damaged pants back on.

"No problem."

"Get out of here," Zayika told them coldly. "Don't forget about the favors you owe me."

As they left her alone, Omar decided he wanted space too and parted ways with Anon for a couple hours. The night felt longer to him than others had, he was restless and yearning to escape the feeling of inferiority that followed him around in his mind everywhere he went. *I'm so unprepared for whatever is coming next.* He left and ventured closer to the Land Dweller's territory to take a walk alone. *Everyone will be falling asleep soon anyways; I won't be in their way. Besides, if something happens to me then so be it. Would anyone care if I'm gone?*

"You really shouldn't be out here Omar," a familiar voice told him.

The moonlight covered the narrow path of dirt he followed closely. *Who was that? Should I say something back?*

"Please be careful. The fight has already started, remember?"

"Who's talking to me?" He grew afraid. "Show yourself!"

It was as if the leaves at his sides were laughing at him as the sound carried into the night. *What is going on? Am I about to die?* His heart thumped loudly as he stood still.

"It's just me." Saige was before him in the blink of an eye.

She was dressed in all black, her hair blending in perfectly. She smiled and tapped on his upper chest playfully.

"Where did you come from? How did you even do that?" Omar looked behind her. "Is it just you out here?"

"Yeah, it's just me. Why? Who were you expecting to see with me? Ze—"

"Of course Zekiel." He laughed under his breath. "It's sort of challenging to even imagine you both not by each other's side."

"Why is that?" She shivered as goosebumps covered her arms in between the vines and leaves that had become one with her skin.

"Oh, here, take my jacket." Omar unzipped and pulled it off quickly to lay over her. "You guys don't have any? You'd be surprised with what they conveniently have at the castle in my faction. I'm not sure why they have extra clothes here for us. You also find that odd, right?"

"I have a theory about that."

"What is it?" His interest grew.

"I think the clothes they offer us belong to all of those who came before us and were killed."

He then felt the urge to take off the shoes he was wearing and shuddered at the memory of Kason handing them to him. "You're probably right."

"Don't worry about it, though. If I was to pass away here, I'd want those who come next to get something useful from me. It's what I'd hope for. Pass on some help, hope or something, you know? Sorry. I'm rambling." Saige tucked some hair behind her ear and looked at her feet.

There was a brief silence between the two before Omar broke it. "Anon got hurt. Did you know about that?"

Her eyes widened. "I didn't. Is he okay?"

"Yeah, he's alright, you know him. He manages to get himself out of any trouble he seeks out. It's sort of… annoying? I think annoying is the right word. Do you know what I'm talking about?" He crossed his arms.

"Hm. I know what you mean." She crossed hers too. "He honestly is. Like, swimming out to find that random light in the ocean? The phantom lighthouse?"

"Terrible idea." He chuckled slightly with a pursed lip.

"Pretending everyone's ideas are his own?"

"Making the worst decisions and then blaming everyone else when things don't go his way?" Omar couldn't hold back his laughter. *I'm so glad someone else agrees with me.* "He tries to act like he's some sort of daredevil, but he really isn't. He just makes last second decisions that put himself into danger, and with dumb luck, he manages to always survive."

"He just wants attention."

"And everyone gives it to him for some reason." Omar inhaled sharply. "Sorry for ranting."

"You don't have to apologize for having feelings or an honest opinion on someone else. Those are two things we all have the complete freedom to exercise and not shame ourselves about."

"Yeah…" He fumbled with his words and tried to ignore the thought of his life being saved on the hills. *I'm tired of him just being treated like a hero because he did like, one, important thing.* "I'm not sure how to say this about him because it's like—I don't want to seem like a bad friend. I mean, look at you and Zekiel; you guys have a perfect friendship."

Saige winced and shifted her gaze up at the moon. "Oh. That's how you see it?"

"What? That you two are friends? Of course," Omar replied. "I can also see that you want to be more than that with him."

"What?"

"I mean, to be frank, we all can see that you're in love with him. You would do anything for Zekiel, wouldn't you?"

Her cheeks flushed red, and she put a hand to her mouth to hide her smile. "It's not like tha—of course I would want—I would do anything to help him."

"Why are you out here talking to me anyways? I'm surprised you're not with him right now."

"He wanted some alone time," Saige replied. *As he always does.* "With my ability, I figured it best to get some alone time myself. I figured it wouldn't hurt."

"So how are things going with you guys?" Omar asked. "Are you going to tell him how you feel?"

"Oh, no, it's not really like that."

"For you? Or for… him?" *He is distant with her; seems partly platonic.*

"I'm not sure. I mean, for me… I know my love and where I'm coming from. I've known for the entirety of our friendship. You know?"

Omar smiled. "Not really. Not like that," he lowered his voice softly. "How would you feel if he doesn't feel the same way?"

Saige looked up at him curiously. *Why would he even ask me that?* "Um… I would of course…" *I'm not sure, but I don't want to sound desperate. I don't need to tell him about this.* "Of course, I would feel fine? Yes, fine."

"Would you be okay?" He was truly invested.

"Y-yes. I'd be okay. What makes you ask?"

"I've just been hurt by others a lot of times. Be careful who you let into your heart. I feel like telling you because it's obvious that you have a caring one," Omar said. *I hope he doesn't break it. It's a privilege to have one in such an honest and loyal way.*

She gave him a kind smile and tried to keep the diminishing hope she fought off acknowledging when it came to Zekiel concealed. She lied to herself and others some more, "I'd be totally fine staying friends with him."

"If that's even true to a certain degree, you know, there are other options out there you can be more than friends with."

I'm not sure I could ever see someone else and distance myself like that. What would Zekiel do without me? Her feelings never felt more conflicted as she pulled the jacket tighter around herself. Omar stepped a little closer to her, and his eyes slowly met hers.

"Thanks for spending some time talking with me tonight, especially since we apparently shouldn't be." White hues bounced off his dark hair as a deep blue washed over them, stars swirling in the sky as almost everyone else was asleep or in quiet hiding. "I don't really care what they tell us — I refuse to resort to violence."

"That's an admirable trait."

I wonder what Zekiel has said to her about the Wish Carriers? She is very special, and I'm not sure she knows it. "Do you think it's okay for us to be talking to each other? Will we get in trouble?"

"We met on the hills before they even forced us into these groups. Of course, there's nothing wrong with us talking. Don't worry so much. We can make our own rules." Saige smiled and studied his expression closely. "We're going to be okay. Maybe the six of us can find a loophole out of here without killing. Maybe that could be possible. We just have to keep our focus on what matters."

Omar nodded. "Definitely."

"Well, we should go to bed." She gently touched the side of his arm. "Thanks for talking with me."

"Anytime, Saige." He quickly remembered Zekiel's temperament and territorial tendencies. "You aren't going to tell Zekiel about us spending time together, right?"

"No. I wasn't planning on it. Why?" She smiled. "We're just talking."

"Yeah, I know, but…" *I don't want to be on his hit list. Screw that.* "Just, let's keep it between us?"

She dug her hands into the cotton-lined pockets. "Okay, yeah, I get how he can come across to people."

Omar laughed. *His fist really came across Anon's face not too long ago.* "Thanks. I appreciate the privacy."

"You want this jacket back?"

"No, you should keep it," Omar replied. "Sweet dreams, Saige."

"Sweet dreams, Omar."

He watched as she walked back to the treehouse, practicing making use of her powers, and he involuntarily felt a flutter of excitement in his chest at the thought of talking to her again as she literally faded away.

Present

Aadavan was leaving the jungle, on his way to confront Lorelai about the lack of visions she was having. He wrestled with his thoughts about what he'd discussed with Theia, his mind on what he would say next as he saw one of the guardian fighters walking nearby the ocean—Enya. He watched as she traveled on the sand, noticing how she was able to walk quicker than the average human. She had very long hair that covered most of her outfit made of seaweed strands, though she mainly kept it tied up to not obscure her vision.

She must be slower than the rest under water with those legs. My fighters need to target the grounds first and then hit the guardians. I have no idea what sort of capabilities they have, if they have any fighting companions, what they are able to do. They'll have to be drawn out of the waters for a fairer fight. Either way, Theia most likely has the strongest fighters out of us three, even though I hate to admit it. What I will admit, though, is that Lorelai is taking way too long to tell us who is to be brought here next. We need more visions! Why is she taking forever?

"Hey, you!" Aadavan shouted at her as he escaped his own tirade of exhausting thoughts. "I need to speak to Lorelai!"

She stopped in her tracks, leaving behind a long trail of sandy footsteps, and threw her arms up at him. "What do you expect me to do? I don't answer to you! She's your friend, after all!" *For some unknown reason,* she thought.

"Well, go get her for me!" he continued yelling instead of going over to her, slightly fearful of getting attacked. "Don't just stand there! It's not like you have anything else to be doing right now!" *I won't even bring attention to her lack of practice. In no way will I willingly give advice to make the others stronger.*

"You can get her yourself." Enya pointed to the ocean. "Why don't you go for a swim? I'm sure that anglerfish would love to see you."

He pushed his glasses up. "How are you able to stay out of the waters for so long? You really don't have a tail? How odd. How long have you been out here?"

"I'm not sure. I guess I'm different from the rest."

Aadavan dropped a bit of his guarded demeanor and stepped over to her. "I refuse to go down there. Can you just tell Lorelai that I said she needs to have another vision? The next competition is fast approaching, and there is more morphing that needs to be done."

"'Vision'?"

"It's not your business. I just need you to relay a message." He pointed at her.

"Sounds like something you can't force."

"Well, you wouldn't know anything about our matters, and it will remain that way. Just tell her that we need to move along. Time is being wasted."

"You're a terrible person." Her voice quivered.

"Excuse me?"

"You're a terrible person for doing this to me and everyone else here," she elaborated. "I wanted to tell you that at least once to your face before I die, because I'm pretty sure that I will lose my life on this wretched planet, unfortunately and unfairly."

A rocking canoe on the calm waters caught Aadavan's eye. Softly it went left and right. *Thinking that way will get you killed. But why would I tell you that? I don't need to bring your attention to how your thoughts obviously shape your reality.* "You speak to me as if I'm the only representative here. Why is that? Do you carry the same tone with Lorelai? Theia?"

"I've never really spoken much to Theia," Enya told him. "But Lorelai? No, I don't speak to her this way. I don't think she is as much of a terrible person as you are."

"Oh really?" Aadavan clutched onto his stomach and tried to hold down a nervous chuckle. "You speak to me with shocking confidence. I'm worse than her in your eyes, huh? Why exactly is that?"

"She actually feels bad about the wrong she has done."

CHAPTER NINETEEN: A BLUE MOON
Flashback to CHP. 9

Nathaniel went completely into hiding to keep himself concealed from the representative's view while in the bunker. He would only leave at random times, mostly during the night, in order to spend more time outdoors. Every night he thanked his lucky stars that the three of them still hadn't discovered him tucked and hidden away within the plants. The lack of socialization, though, was becoming hard to deal with—even for someone as introverted as him.

It feels like I have lived on this planet for over twenty years, even though hardly any time has passed. I'm aging more and more with every second, each ounce of any energy stripped from my spirit.

A man from the Over Ground's faction crossed paths with him in the jungle. Nathaniel, in that brief moment, wasn't invisible as they ran into one another. He was surprised to come across someone that survived being morphed so soon after the next people arrived. At first, he was startled with a wave of anxiety, fearful that his presence would be revealed against his own wishes, but he still decided to converse with him since he had already been seen. He couldn't tell at first that the other man had even been morphed in any way—which was far from common.

I hope he doesn't mention this to Aadavan, Lorelai, or Theia. I don't know what they'll do to me if they find out I'm here. They'll either have me compete again or kill me on sight. Neither can happen.

"Whoa, there! Sorry!" the stranger exclaimed as they bumped into each other. "Wait, who are you? I've never seen you before!"

"That's sort of the point," Nathaniel replied under his breath.

"What?"

He cleared his throat. "Um, nothing, you just can't let anyone else know that I'm here, that you've ever seen me. Got it?"

"Sure thing. I won't tell anyone."

"Promise me?"

"Yes. I promise."

Nathaniel looked him up and down suspiciously. "What faction do you belong to?"

"The Over Grounds."

"Have you been morphed already?"

"Yes, unfortunately." He frowned. "Worst experience of my life. I'm looking for help, and for a friend."

"Well, I cannot help you with the latter, but I may be able to provide you with some useful information." Nathaniel kept a comfortable distance between them. "What are your abilities?"

"I have wings, so I can fly around. I tend to float instead though. Much more comfortable that way. I'm scared of heights. Ironic, right?"

"I'm a bit confused," Nathaniel replied to him. "You have… wings? Where are they?"

"Can you see them now?" He turned around.

"Oh, so you do have them. I was honestly surprised to see you floating. I wasn't too sure if they were really back there or not." *They look like tree leaves.* "I now see proof of what leader you belong to."

"How many more of you are there?"

"There's only one of me. I once fought for the Land Dwellers not too long ago. My story is a long one, though, and I'm unable to go over all of the details of it with you. I cannot overstay my welcome, even during this conversation. The stakes are far too high." Nathaniel's brown eyes shot around to survey their surroundings.

"What are you allowed to tell me about this place?"

"As long as you keep your mouth shut about me… then I will tell you anything you want to know."

"Stop worrying about that. I won't mention anything to anyone about you ever. There's actually something specific I want to ask you, in that case." Gebu made dodgy eye contact. "What happens if one of us from the Over Grounds loses our wings?"

I can still hear his screams like it happened yesterday. Moments from the past flashed in Nathaniel's head as he tried to not pay attention to them. Unable to escape the miserable moments, he relived them at least once every day. *There was nothing I could do. It wasn't my fault. I couldn't have stopped that portal from sweeping him in. I couldn't save him from such an act of barbarous cruelty. Hopefully, he is somehow in a better place, perhaps the place I should be.*

"Um, hello?" the stranger interrupted his thoughts. "Are you okay? It looks like you are going to faint."

"Ahem. Yes, I'm alright. If both wings are lost, you get consumed… by darkness." Nathaniel let out a shaky breath, visible in the chilly air before him.

Gebu was silent for almost a complete minute before responding, "What does that mean?"

"We aren't very sure." The hairs on his arms stood up under his hefty jacket at the memories he couldn't forget. *I shouldn't have left my sword in the bunker. I need it with me at all times, just in case.*

"What else should I know?"

"It's hard to say. I only have bits and pieces of information. Some of it may truly not pertain to anything you may encounter, like a teleportation command reversal."

"What is that?"

Maybe I should tell him. I wished someone else had provided me with some of the knowledge I know now. I should pass it down.

"Once someone wins the game and goes back home, or even gets sucked into darkness, which strips them of whatever valuable 'keys' they have, I'm quite sure they can be brought back here right out of thin air."

His jaw dropped. "Are you serious?"

"Of course I am." *I'm particular about who I talk to and the information I share from what I read in the books I found in the bunker.*

"When could that happen? So we are never safe?"

"From what I've gathered, it doesn't happen often. Don't worry about it. Based on my previous readings, it's only once in a blue moon that a teleportation command would even happen in the first place."

Gebu let out an obvious sigh of relief and put a hand to his forehead.

"One of the representatives is able to teleport people to and from this place. I know that for a fact. All it takes is lifting her magical finger up into the air."

"Well, I hope she never uses it to try to bring someone back here after they've been crazy enough to survive through all of this. You would need to actually lose your mind somehow to think that's a good idea."

"You can say that again." Nathaniel replied.

Flashforward to 15 days before CHP. 1 of ECHOES OF EUNOIA

It was day fifteen of Zayika being left on Eunoia, almost completely alone, with no idea where the three representatives were hiding from her. Anon and Amira went back to Earth without taking her, and the shock still hadn't worn off even after the second week of absolute solitude. It was just the beginning of a long journey of uncomfortable self-reflection. The nights felt even longer than the days because of the dreams she had. In the daytime, dark, twisted fantasies would tempt her mind in the form of intrusive thoughts—but they were out of her control and she didn't know how to claim her individuality and sanity back. The only escape she had from the influence was her dreams.

That night, she slept the best she ever had with a dream she never wanted to wake up from. Zayika tended to sleep in the jungle when she was able to get any rest at all. The air was chilling, and fog surrounded her as she found the best place to lie down. She laid against a tree and produced some warmth for herself from her hands, small fizzling stars sparking at her fingertips as she smiled.

It won't stay cold forever.

Sometimes she felt as though her thoughts weren't her own anymore, that the intrusive ones were like a brain eating amoeba taking her over from within. Even physically, it felt to her that something was growing inside of her head and was eventually going to run out of room to expand. She rested her back on the tree bark and tried to not pay attention to the searing tension headache in her sinuses that was especially pressurized behind her eyes.

It's okay to rest, get some rest, she tried to tell herself. *They will come back for you. There must be some valid reason they left you behind, okay? They didn't mean to…* The pain in her head worsened… *Anon and Amira didn't mean to hurt you.*

She couldn't hold back several cold tears as they bounced off her freckled skin.

Zayika put her face down into her hands and began to sob. With each huff of tears she saw another person's face from the past in her mind, along with a mental list of every single way she felt she failed all of them.

They will never love me.

When she tried to look around, she couldn't see as her vision was too cloudy.

They'll never understand how much I care.

She was then reminded of when she first dyed her hair, of the violent and irreversible actions she carried out not too long when going after Myles.

I cannot believe I did that to him. What really has come over me?

Everything started to spin around her.

They think I'm an awful person who deserves to be left behind.

Her skull felt like it was going to crack as she hummed in pain.

Well, maybe I should've been left behind. Maybe I am supposed to be alone.

With that last thought she drifted off into a peaceful sleep that was free from the sharp headache and her emotionally draining thoughts.

In her dream, she wore a black dress with long sleeves. The bottom of it sat at the base of her thighs and matched her tall, shiny boots. The dress flowed in the wind just like her hair did, and it was its natural color, dark brown. She wore it down and allowed it to fall wherever it wanted. It went from straight to curly as the rain hit it. Everything was moving in slow motion.

Zayika walked in the rain in a straight line on a barren land that cut directly between Anon and Amira, who had been staring at one another, holding hands, and maintaining perfectly leveled eye contact. She pushed them away to either side, and they looked at her in shock as she strode forward, not turning back to see them.

The scenery began to fade and change around her into one giant, grassy, green hill. It was raining even harder as her steps became faster, turning into a full blown sprint as she didn't feel the weight of any emotion holding her down.

She put her hands into the air and genuinely smiled up at the sky as the raindrops lightly made contact with every inch of her beaming face, soaking wet and feeling freer than ever before. No one was around to doubt, judge, misinterpret, or try to control anything about her. Not even her own self. Her mind in her dreams was free from the reality of abandonment, abuse, and self-destruction.

She lived in that specific and simply magnificent moment in her dreams for as long as she could before being coldly awoken by the planet speaking harshly to her, its voice bellowing loudly amongst the stars.

SPEAKER: Zayika

Did you forget your promise? A booming voice taunted me in my thoughts. My heart raced in my chest. I felt all of my peace being ripped away once again as Eunoia's words echoed around in my crumbling mind.

Someone has to deal out the consequences that are due, and you are the only one who can do that. My eyes flew open. I was on the verge of crying and smiling at the same time as discomfort controlled and manipulated my behavior and reasoning.

You have to bring him back soon. It felt like bugs were crawling up each strand of my hair. *Zayika, you have to bring Anon back to Eunoia.* I cried out loud as the sensation of brain freeze overtook my head. *You have to make him finally pay for what he's done.* Blue lightning struck down in the direction of the ocean. *Stop wasting valuable hours and get back to work.* Groupings of white eyes were watching me from the clouds up above. *It's time for the teleportation command to be reversed for the very first time ever.*

Cloudburst

Present

I was given a short break before Theia teleported me again, as she and Aadavan were distracted and arguing about other, somehow more pressing, matters. Varid and his friends proposed an idea to me to trick the representatives into letting us leave. I didn't want to let their hopes down, but I also couldn't lie to them about what we could accomplish. I figured almost anything was worth a try in order to escape the ordeal we had all been forced into.

No plan we devise will work. We were given supernatural strengths and capabilities, but we can't supersede the forces that brought and changed us here. Only in our wildest dreams.

Hope was so hard to find at that point, despite many attempts from those in my faction. I interacted as little with them as possible. I couldn't promise safety. I couldn't promise a happy ending. There was no way for me to get Theia to give us what we wanted besides using force. Unless I threatened her, used the electricity within my arms to hold it against her, our plans would never become a reality. I wasn't going to threaten to kill her, though. There were certain levels I refused to stoop to even if my life depended on it. Just as words couldn't be unspoken... some boundaries couldn't be uncrossed. Regret could never be fully forgotten.

It may be tempting to retaliate in a vengeful way... but I can't live with that on my conscience for the rest of my life.

The only other person who I'd truly gotten close to walked near to me as I debated with myself in my mind far enough away from Theia, creating a pro and con list of what each outcome could be for possible escape.

No options looked good.

There were no pros.

Present

"Cloudburst," Nathaniel's voice approached. "Funny to run into you here again. Seems that everyone comes to the dweller's jungle when they need to get their thoughts straightened out."

The privacy of their interaction was short-lived.

"That's an understatement," Cloudburst responded and noticed two other fighters passing by unexpectedly.

Nathaniel quickly went invisible.

Cloudburst felt prompted to distract one of them, "Do you have something I could throw, by any chance?"

One crafted a small knife for him and handed it over with, surprisingly, no questions asked. "Here you go."

"Be careful who you craft for, Draydon," Saylor warned. "You're a bit too... generous."

"Do you really want to discuss this right now?" he asked.

Cloudburst let out a small sigh. *Can't have them hanging around here with Nathaniel so close.* "Can you two please go somewhere else? I sort of need some space right now. No offense."

"Gladly." Draydon saluted as he walked away with Saylor right by his side.

"Thanks, by the way! I wish you both luck in the upcoming fight!" Cloudburst called out and threw the knife as fast and hard as he could at the nearest target once they were out of view.

He hit the middle bullseye perfectly.

"Okay, then. Good aim." Nathaniel gave him a half smile as he reappeared once the other two were gone. "Maybe I didn't need to save your life at the end of the first challenge after all? Your precision under pressure is quite impressive. Many here are fantastic at making our weapons, but aiming? Not as much. Not like that. Seems like you could've handled yourself back there in the field without me intervening."

"Nah. Please don't say that. I can never thank you enough for saving my life. I wish I was able to save yours in return. I hope I'll be able to, seriously man."

"What's on your mind? Are the representatives going to force you to participate in the next, you know, killing spree?"

"I hope not."

"I can tell you're thinking about a lot."

Cloudburst shook off the memory of Theia's voice in his head, too embarrassed to let Nathaniel know how violated he felt. "It's like I have no privacy here."

"That's one of the worst feelings."

"You know what's somehow even worse?" He paused as he held back a shaking lip.

Nathaniel silently nodded for him to continue when he was ready, keeping eye contact to a minimum to not pressure him. Wind whistled past the trees as the night was coming to a close.

"I have no way of getting my life back without taking someone else's. What should I do? I can't threaten Theia like the others are saying I should. They tell me to just carry out their commands like at the waterfall. It's not that simple! I'm not going to do something like that! They don't understand!" Cloudburst fell to his knees in pure exhaustion. "I cannot win. I am so sorry, Nathaniel."

"Why are you apologizing to me? You've done nothing wrong."

"But I feel like I have! My hands are not my own, my voice is not my own, where I step, even what I think is not my own! I'm trapped forever now! I must have done something to deserve this! For that I am sorry!"

Not too far in the distance, Theia was making her way to the ocean to visit Lorelai, anticipating news of her mystically twisted visions. She caught Cloudburst's voice in her head once she was close enough to him. *What do you think you've done wrong? Why do you feel so guilty? Is it because you secretly enjoy what we are making you do?*

"Stop! For the love of everything, stop!" he screamed out, still on his knees, tears welling up in his eyes at her intrusive and private response. "You do not know me or my true thoughts! Get out of my head!"

Nathaniel slightly shook at the sight in front of him, seeing no one else but Cloudburst breaking down. He crouched to face him eye to eye and spoke thoughtfully, "I have no idea what is going on with you, but I'm dearly sorry you are in this much distress."

More visions are approaching. You will be back at the falls soon. People are waiting on you, Cloudburst, Theia told him.

"No, please! I don't want to ruin anyone else's life! Please! I can't go back to the waterfall, why are you making me do this?"

Nathaniel listened intently to his words. *They will send him back soon to get the final participants. What if he doesn't return? What if they hurt him for speaking out against them in this way?* "Can you please promise me one thing?"

"Of course, Nathaniel."

Their eyes met.

"Promise me that no matter what happens, how terrible this all gets, that you will never hurt yourself. They've unfairly taken away all of this freedom from you. The representatives have stolen the most valuable thing that we are given in our lives—time—but stay strong, nevertheless.

Another fight will be here soon. Can you promise me that you will continue fighting for your life? That you will never harm yourself in this turmoil?"

Cloudburst paid close attention to each word spoken to him. Each syllable was in rhythm with his pounding heartbeat. The moon was blue, and the clouds had turned back into their eye form to watch what was taking place.

"Why are you talking to me like we will never see each other again?"

Nathaniel swallowed what felt like multiple scratchy lumps in his throat as he reached his hand out. "Please just promise me what I asked from you."

Cloudburst took his hand to stand up off the ground. "I promise."

"I hope you make it home. In fact, I wish that you will." With Nathaniel's words, a small string of light passed from his hand to Cloudburst's.

CHAPTER TWENTY: SNOWGLOBE
Present

There were six remaining slots to be filled. One for the guardians, two dwellers, three grounds. Those in Theia's group were feeling the most prepared out of the three. Despite their first failed attempt at subduing their representative, they were making other progress in their thoughts and gathering themselves in preparation for what was becoming an inevitable fight. Mae had become accustomed to her role as a healer, gaining confidence in her abilities and willing to help those in need – especially those she favored. Gebu could almost always be found outside practicing and coaching Nero as he stayed focused on the main task at hand at their training corner.

Kason was too afraid to fly with his dark grey wings, similarly to Varid who hadn't used his and spent more time trying to understand the trio of clouds over his shoulders instead.

On a particularly stormy day, Lyra discovered what her ability was as she stared at the rain through her bedroom window. It wasn't until she kept watching the drops roll down the glass that her thoughts became heightened and began to pick up speed, as if they were racing one another in a similar way to the water that was sliding in front of her.

"I think I'm making it hail!" Lyra called out to Varid and Kason as she noticed the drops getting harder. "Come look! Look at what I'm doing right now!"

The two ran out from a different room to see what she was so excited about, focusing intently on everything that was happening outside.

"What's going on?" Varid asked. "Is this your ability? Are you causing this?" He had to raise his voice as he entered the room, practically drowned out by the sound of the hail tapping sharply against the glass.

Kason was impressed as the amount of hail tripled in number right before their eyes. The three lined up along the window and rested their arms on the dusty wooden frame.

"That's incredible. I've never seen anything like this before." Kason's face lit up. "I wonder if they can do anything special, you know? Like how Mae can boost abilities?"

Varid looked up at his clouds and remembered something he'd learnt from his first training session. *How will she find out what she is fully capable of without testing the rain? What if they do something else once she's outside?* "Would be cool to go outside and—"

"Not sure if that's a good, or safe, idea." Just then, Lyra's instincts fired off; "Where is Mae?"

"She's outside getting some fresh air near that arch by the benches. You know the one covered in vines?"

Lyra promptly spun around and jogged out of the bedroom over to the courtyard doors.

"Where are you going?" Varid asked as Kason trailed behind him. "Are you going to head out there?"

"I'm not sure it's safe!" Lyra replied and yanked both doors open, feet firmly planted on the ground inside as she looked around for Mae, spotting her nearby. "Hey, you need to be careful!"

"Are you seeing this hail?" her teammate replied, standing up off one of the benches.

Lyra's worry increased with each second. "Please watch out, I'm not sure what's going on! I think this is my pow—"

Mae didn't listen and stepped down from the archway area and out from under its protective cover.

"No! Wait!" the other three cried out, but it was too late.

She was pummeled with razor sharp pieces of hail, cutting and tearing at her fragile skin. Mae cried out in agony as she sprinted forward, despite the excruciating pain. She fled into Lyra's arms as fast as she could, and the two fell backwards into Varid and Kason, who were directly behind her.

Lyra sprang up and continued to hold onto Mae as she bled. "Close the doors!" she told Varid.

"Already on it!" He jumped up and pulled each shut without asking questions.

"What's going on?" Kason had his hands on his head as he stared down at Mae, covered in so much of her own blood that she was practically unrecognizable.

"It's going to be okay," Lyra told everyone as she softly put her hand on Mae.

Kason and Varid moved out of the way and watched to see what would happen next.

"What can we do to help?" Varid asked.

"Don't get too close. This bleeding needs to stop, and none of us can make that happen. Only..." Lyra didn't look back at them and kept her eyes on Mae. "I know you're in a lot of pain right now, okay? I need you to please listen to me."

"W-what?" She could barely speak.

"You have to heal yourself. I know you can do it. It's time for you to use your ability, alright? Please, Mae, you need to heal yourself."

Mae closed her eyes as she rocked back and forth in her torn clothes, her shaking fingertips trying to hold parts of her skin together. She let out a deep breath, the room completely silent. With the sound of her breath filling the room like the gusts of wind outside, the thick hail heavily bouncing off the castle's walls, she began to glow, brighter and brighter. The other three covered their eyes as they could momentarily no longer see her.

She's doing it, Lyra thought to herself. *She is going to be okay.*

As her light eventually dimmed, Nero stormed into the room, Gebu — who had just talked him down from attempting to kill Theia while she was stuck inside due to the weather — following after him.

"What's going on?" Nero asked quickly, putting a handful of his knives into his favorite pocket to pull them from.

"Are you all practicing your abilities too? Is everyone okay?" Gebu asked beside him, noticing Mae lying on the ground in destroyed clothing, several traces of fresh blood around her.

"It was an accident." Lyra helped her off the floor.

"That hail out there." Nero stepped forward. "Was that… you?" he asked Lyra.

She kept her eyes downcast as she answered, "I think so."

Nero nodded. "Alright then. How about you never do that again while any of us are outside?"

"I second that." Gebu stated.

She shrugged and felt weighed down by guilt as she looked at Mae. "Don't worry, I'll try to make sure it never happens again."

"How about we get back to practicing?" Gebu asked Nero and looked at Kason and Varid. "You two should join us if you're feeling up to it. Our battle is coming soon. We need to be ready."

"You're one to talk, Gebu." Nero scoffed. "I can't even get you to hold a knife in your hand, let alone face the threat of our representative when she's least expecting an attack."

"That sounds good. I guess? More practice couldn't hurt," Varid replied. "As long as I don't have to fly, I really don't care."

Mae stepped away from Lyra. "I think I've practiced my ability enough. I'm going to lay down for a moment."

Everyone began filing out of the room and down one of the corridors while Nero hung back for a moment to speak with Lyra. "You all go on. I'll be there in a second."

"I'd rather be alone right now," Lyra told him gently, trying to gather herself.

"We don't have to talk long, but I wanted to tell you..." Her eyes met his as he spoke quietly, "Your power is awesome. Use that out there on the grounds, alright? If we aren't able to get home before the fight starts? Just make sure we're all out of the way. If you practice enough, you may be able to call the hail down a specific area. Even if you practice while we're inside and end up taking out a few others before it all really goes downhill—there's nothing truly wrong with lowering our numbers ahead of time. Get what I'm saying?"

She was taken aback by his comment and wrestled with her conflicting emotions. "Um… okay. I'll try."

"Would be really helpful if what Gebu's been telling me is true." Nero bit on his tongue softly as he thought about what he learned through his advice from Nathaniel. "Just put yourself out there. We'll figure this out."

Lyra nodded, and he left the room with those words. Her heart rate was beginning to settle as she looked back outside at the gunmetal grey rain clouds. *I have to be ready to lend a helping hand… no matter what happens to me for doing so.*

The Land Dwellers, on the contrary, were trying their best to rest and mentally prepare in silence. Aadavan remained in his room during almost all of his downtime, stirring around anxiously as he thought about the advice he wanted to give to those under his watch. *Don't act rash. Communicate with each other. Try to outsmart the other teams; know their weaknesses like the back of your hand.* Saylor and Draydon began to spend the most time together. After the rest had hid in their quarters after the damaging hail stopped falling, they took turns designing different tools and weapons and testing them out at their target practice area.

"I hope the knives I sent off work well," Draydon thought out loud while crafting a boning knife from his palm.

"What? You 'sent off' weapons?" Saylor asked. "What does that mean?"

Did I just say that out loud? Ugh, better just be honest now, I suppose. "To someone from the other faction, he needed something to fight with."

Saylor dropped the stack of wooden sticks she was holding. "Are you serious?"

"What?"

"Why would you help the enemy?"

"Oh, come on, Saylor, the real enemies are the representatives—not the others who were forced to be here too. They didn't ask for their lives to be taken away either."

"Aadavan has been trying to help us, actually. Can't you see that?"

"He forced us to be here."

"Why would you say that?" she asked preemptively. "We woke up on those hills." Her finger shot over to the grassy lumps in the distance. "Sure, he played into our emotions and misled us when we first met, but maybe in a peculiar way he was trying to look out for us from something that we can't even see yet?"

"You might want to think about your words for a bit longer before you say them, respectively. Clearly those three are in control here. We need to be looking out for each other as much as we can in order to get home."

"Whatever. I just think that arming those who will be hunting us down soon is a bad decision. A terrible one, in fact."

"Well, guess what, Saylor?" Draydon sighed. "Forget it. I didn't ask you for your opinion."

"So what I think doesn't matter?"

"It doesn't affect you," he replied. "At least it shouldn't. Why don't you focus on your own problems?"

"I just don't want us to do anything we will regret," she said.

"I'm not going to regret helping out someone else who needs it."

"Glad that horrifying storm stopped." Fabian approached the two as they stood off tensely. "Is everything okay?"

"We're just practicing." Draydon kept his eyes fixed on Saylor.

"Right…" he said. "Seems a bit rough out here. Why don't you guys watch my aim with these grenades? I'm hoping they will come in handy. Just wish my smoke had a special effect. Would be nicer."

The Oceanic Guardians stayed underwater, swimming around aimlessly. Orson carried his hammer, Marcellus his bow and arrow, while Elena kept her spear securely by her side. Each found their weapons scattered around what looked to be a wrecked ship deep down near the ocean floor. They passed the group of mossy statues, past the boundary Lorelai had told them to stay behind. They were all desperate to find answers to the corrupted changes they underwent. Each of them became a part of the ocean life as they breathed the murky waters in. Patches, sometimes all, of their skin completely changed into fish-like scales. As they ventured further into the unknown, they came across the nameless anglerfish. They kept far enough away to not aggravate her, though her beacon of light was bright enough for them to stumble across useful weapons and uncover parts of the ocean no one else had ever seen before.

Enya would typically stay closer to the shores, swimming in the shallow waters or completely out of them as she walked along the sand. Zavier would hang around the canoe and speak with her, the rest of the guardians hardly ever seen. The others either remained in their bedrooms trying to talk to representative Lorelai or practicing whatever ability they were given.

Minutes felt like hours.

Hours like days.

The worst for all of them to confront was fast approaching.

Flashforward to CHP. 12 of CARRIERS OF EUNOIA

Omar looked over the supplies he'd gathered from Nathaniel's bunker and debated over which brush to use first to paint with. *The sun will be setting soon. I'll go outside to find a reference.* The castle's window was wide and tall. Golden rays from outside seeped into his room as he sat in deep contemplation on messy sheets. He took his canvas, brushes, and paint bottles outdoors where it was silent in an uneasy way. Many of those on the planet who were still alive had gone into hiding for as long as they could until they were forced to fight for their lives; occasionally walking around or making small talk amidst the fear. For a little while, it was quiet, which made it easy for Omar to hear Amira and Anon's voices carrying to where he went to sit on a ledge.

He sat down and began painting, listening to the waves and the couple's conversation below filled with subtle flirtatious hints, emotional vulnerability, and mutual understanding of important information.

They make a good pair, he thought to himself as he dipped his brush in the pigmented orange paint. *They're good for each other; balance is created between them.* He smiled at the thought of Anon, someone who quickly became one of his closest friends, happy with a woman who had mutual love for him. *He really cherishes her, doesn't he? And she has always defended him. Even at the start, even when I tried to tear him down. I hope I find love one day. It doesn't have to be perfect.*

Omar added details to the yellow rays of sunlight bouncing off the greenish-blue waves of his painting, including a simple purple and pink gradient that blended out from the distinct orange hue of the sunset. He thought about those he'd met and the lessons he already learned in such a short amount of time.

Maybe this love is something I can provide to myself? I could defend myself. Maybe then others' words won't get to me as much?

Then Omar remembered again.

I miss Saige, talking with her was the best.

His chest started to ache.

Off and on he would see glimpses flash in his mind of the jungle covered in blood. He tried to forget, wishing to unsee what happened.

His stomach turned at the thought of what Nero did.

Why did it have to be her? he thought with tears welling in his big and innocent eyes. *I'm not sure if I can make my wish before I die, but if I can, I'll do it right now.*

Some paint dripped down onto his pants while he struggled to fill in the waves. He shuddered while trying to keep painting, the scarring sight of Saige losing all life and falling limp to the ground, replaying in his head. Lonely and traumatized he sat in front of the sunset, trying to capture the beauty in front of him before all shock fully wore off.

"I wish to have my life taken next instead of whoever else's it will be." Omar spoke out loud with genuine emotion and intent behind every word.

A small glow escaped his fingertips as he outlined the ship in his painting with a shaking hand.

What was that?

It trailed off in front of him, and seemed to fly in the direction of Amira before fading away. Omar then continued glancing down at her and Anon who were still admiring one another at the shore.

I'm glad Anon has been a good friend to me, even when others maliciously eavesdropped in the hallway, he was able to play along with lies if it meant protecting those he loves. The lives he took on the beach, Nathaniel… he did what he thought was best. For that, I only want the best for him.

Omar set his brush down momentarily to cross his arms and think, *I also want the best for myself.*

Finally.

Present

Lorelai was restless waiting for her next vision, feeling the pressure from Aadavan and, subsequently, Theia. She wrestled with an inner voice that tried to tell her that she was taking too long and becoming less important. *I'm failing to see what is in this for me.* She was alone in the castle, drowning in thoughts that became dissected beyond comprehension. *They'd hardly notice I was gone if I left this place, wouldn't they?* She thought back to her previous visions. *Am I as useful here as they say I am?* A pain thumped in her chest at the thought of what she could be missing in her life back home.

She had been instructed by Theia to lay low for the second game and to give her fighters enough space to fight without her involvement.

Aadavan was frustrated by the hands-off laissez-faire approach that Theia favored in the midst of such a treacherous and intensely brutal death match. *Why can't she just let me oversee this?* His palms grew sweatier as each hour they waited to hear about another vision passed. He dismissively pushed his members away, one by one, withholding his advice as a means of attempting to preserve what delicate connection he had with Theia, wanting her to know that he did respect her in his own way.

Theia felt positively about those who had been assigned to fight under her. She only needed three more people before the opening ceremony. *I hope those who arrive next will survive being morphed.* She stared out of the castle's tall mosaic window from up high in the sky and looked down to oversee the quarters of Aadavan's quiet earthy treehouse. She tried to keep their thoughts off of their recent conflict and emotions. *I already have many great fighters. Nero is finally getting his emotions under control. His aim is extraordinary. Lyra's hail is amazing; if used correctly, she can shave down the number of opponents exponentially. Mae will do a good job healing and guarding them. Everyone needs to watch their backs, but more importantly, where their head is at.* She shifted her gaze up at the sky and sighed. *If only it snowed here like it does back home.*

Her group decided to take a chance at a second attempt of catching her off guard, wanting to strike her from the sidelines when she was least expecting it. This time, she was already alone and withdrawn in her sleeping quarters of the castle. Aadavan was nowhere to be found, and they didn't have to worry much about Lorelai showing up unannounced.

Nero directed Kason to take the lead.

"Why?" he asked.

"So you can redeem yourself after last time," Nero responded. "That was pretty embarrassing back there."

Kason looked at the others and then down at his feet, feeling their stares and expectations—especially from Nero. "Um…" *I need to figure something out.* His heart thumped loud enough for almost all of them to hear as anxiety filled his body. *If I can pull this off then I will be a hero, respected. I can save everyone's lives here. I've always wanted to be remembered for something, right? This is probably my one and only chance.* Both of his palms were soon covered in sweat as he shook his head. "I'll figure s-something out."

"That's what I thought." Nero urged him to head towards Theia's room. "Let's speed this along. You know it's only a matter of time before that Aadavan guy is rambling at her side again. I'm sure he'll invite himself back over here again soon."

Kason succumbed to the peer pressure, hastily making his way to confront their representative without thinking anything else through, not questioning any of them as to why they weren't planning on helping. Nero, Lyra, Mae, and Gebu waited in the hall for him as he knocked on the door.

She opened it and looked him up and down. "Kason? What is the matter? Do you need something?"

"I-I… I need to talk to you about something, yes," he replied as he saw her through the sliver of the open door.

"Come on in." She let him inside, and everyone who watched held their breaths in anticipation to see if he'd find a way to outsmart her.

Right as he stepped inside of her room for the first time, his stomach plummeted as he and Cloudburst made eye contact.

"We were just talking about some of you, in fact," she said while taking a seat in her favorite raggedy chair. "What is it you need to discuss?"

"U-um… I…" he kept his eyes on Theia as his nerves got the best of him. Everything that he had prepared to say fled from his mind as tensions were at an all-time high.

"Are you looking for some advice or something?" Cloudburst asked, aware that Kason was there to carry out some type of plan.

"I'm actually…" Kason wiped the fresh beads of sweat off his forehead with the back of his sleeve.

Theia smiled at Cloudburst. "Nervousness can completely hinder all train of thought, can't it? I'm so glad you didn't allow yourself to be distracted by fear when you fought. I'm so proud of you."

Kason's worry turned to irritation as he felt a rising bout of embarrassment within him. *I look so stupid right now,* he told himself. *I can't even get my words out properly. What a complete joke.* As he insulted himself more intensely in his mind, snow began to fall with the same intensity outside the window.

"Oh my goodness." Theia stood up from her seat at once to fully pull her red blinds open. "It's snowing. It's snowing! Do you see this?"

"Never seen it here before." Cloudburst looked at Kason. "How long have you known that you can make it snow?"

The two stared at him as he seemed beside himself. "I don't know. I've never done this before. I had no idea."

The snow began turning into a storm in a matter of seconds as his heart pounded harder. Sweat dripped off him.

"I have to go investigate it. I wonder what Aadavan will think? Lorelai will never believe this either." She went to leave the room, stopping to speak before promptly ushering both outside, "You two need to get out of here. I'm going to lock the door. But before you go, what is it you needed to tell me Kason? You seemed to have something on your mind."

He was at a loss for words as he watched the snow falling and whirling outside the worn glass. "I forgot what I was going to say." *I cannot believe what I am capable of.*

Cloudburst let out a sigh as he left the room after him. "Keep your eye on the prize, Kason. You can make yourself valuable in some way here."

"I hope so. I really, really do hope so."

CHAPTER TWENTY-ONE: #BB4B89

Theia

Present

After my conversation with Kason and Cloudburst, I went down to the ocean to speak with Lorelai, hoping for any valuable updates about people joining our forces. I was curious about what she'd seen in the waters when Aadavan and I sent her to swim down deeper, feeling that it was unlikely she didn't find more than she reported when I spoke to her with Cloudburst at my side. I didn't want to force her out of her comfort zone in our conversation, though, and wanted to grant her enough room to share with me what she felt led to. I could sense she had something of great meaning to speak about.

Lorelai spoke to me as we sat on the sand together, "Thank you for telling me about the snow. I otherwise would have had no idea of it."

Everything was silent around us as everyone had been anxiously awaiting the upcoming ceremony. *We'll have to keep it brief. We can't overwhelm them any more than they already are.* Aadavan was presumably trying to train the others again as much as he was able to. *We would benefit greatly from a leadership approach that allows them to have more freedom, encourages them to think for themselves, strategize and communicate together in order to be more aware of their true selves.*

"Are you listening to me?"

I redirected my attention to her. "I'm sorry. Yes, I'm listening, I just have a lot on my mind."

"Don't we all?" she replied solemnly, holding tightly onto her arms.

"What were you saying again?"

"I was telling you that my instincts are kicking in again."

I felt my chest rise with adrenaline. "You mean...?"

"Exactly what you're probably thinking." Lorelai stared at the waves as they glistened in the sunlight, the members of her faction below them.

"You had another vision?"

"Yes."

"That's fantastic news! We're so close to commencing the second game."

My friend refrained from looking over her shoulder at me. I could feel how anxious she was. "Is it really 'fantastic news', though? Are you sure that what we're doing here is positive?" She trembled.

"What's got you feeling this way? I thought you were on board with all of this?"

"I was, I am, it's just..."

"You can be honest," I reassured her. "What's going on?"

She watched the ocean. "I didn't find the stone down on the ocean floor like you and Aadavan wanted... but I discovered something else."

"Did you find it near the castle?"

"No, it was off past the statues and closer to where the anglerfish likes to swim."

"What was it?"

"A rock shard with a sequence of letters and numbers. I tried to grab it, but I felt the absolute worst pain behind both eyes when my fingers touched it. Theia, I'm afraid we may not be as sure of what we're doing here as we think we are." She covered her face as tears began escaping her. "I'm very scared of what's to come. There was something on that rock. Something about it was cryptic. We are not the only ones making overarching decisions here."

I forced a jittery laugh. "Well, of course we aren't, we have the fight—"

"Theia, no!" She turned to finally face me. Her eyes were terror-stricken. "You don't know what I've seen, what I've read. You and Aadavan do not understand, the powers that exist here are far beyond our involvement!"

"Like what?"

"Are you familiar with the color hex..." she inhaled deeply, "#BB4B89?"

"What?" *Where is she going with this?* "No, I'm not, why?"

"There were engravings on some stones down there. My intuition tells me that they do not mean anything good. Something is coming for us, Theia, past anything we could ever dream up or create on our own."

I felt chills trickle down my skin as my blood went cold. The wind was picking up, and it was as if the clouds moved slower to keep a steadier eye on us. "What makes you say that?"

"We are not the most powerful force on this planet."

Flashforward to CHP. 12 of ECHOES OF EUNOIA

Only a few contenders remained alive at the finish line. The round had been reversed right at the end and devolved from the main purpose of survival into something further rooted in a curse of self-destruction and unprecedented chaos. Needlessly violent and shockingly cruel, Zayika stood and panted tiredly as her white dress was freshly splattered with Amira's blood. As she let go of the hold she had around the anglerfish's tooth, the realization of what happened had already begun setting in.

"No, no, no!" Anon screamed out as he grabbed onto Amira's body. "Amira, no Amira!"

Wait… what have I done? Can I ever come back from this? Maybe I should heal her? Zayika thought to herself as her heart ached. *No, don't think like that, no! I'm doing what I have to do! I have to ruin everything in sight! Ruin everything else!* "How does it feel, Anon?"

"Why would you do this? I never took away someone you loved!"

That's not true. "You might as well say goodbye soon, she's about to bleed out."

"Heal her! Come on!" Anon cried out. "Zayika! Don't do this! Why do you have to take everything so far?"

She battled with the planet's hold on her mind as her true thoughts were suffocated, unable to come to the surface of her attention. This led to more damaging and hasty decision making, spewing out toxic words to match each destructive action she took next.

The planet wanted to see the two turn against one another, testing the limits of their trauma bond and ultimately discovering who would survive to become the next victor of the mental torture they endured. Anon and Zayika exchanged their last words with one another.

"You aren't just angry, are you? You are upset. I can tell." Anon sensed that a part of the real her was buried somewhere deep underneath the spiteful outward shell she'd developed while roaming alone. "You are hurt… aren't you Zayika?"

Anon! You see me! I'm here! I'm right here! Her one tear soon turned into many as they eventually outnumbered her thoughts. *Anon! It may not be too late to save Amira! Help me, please help me! I'm begging — I want to live! I want to live!* But Eunoia chose her words. "You still don't understand who I am? I am crying because I'm happy. Ending you, Amira, and everything else is like having a torturous itch finally scratched. I will finally be able to breathe. This is over now."

She wiped her tears as Anon cried too. "Amira…" he began his sentence out loud and finished the rest quietly as a thought right before he lost his life… *I'm on my way.*

Zayika and Anon killed one another at the ocean. Everything was coming to an end as there were only two others alive by that point, Nero and Jameson, who were shaken to their cores at the turn of events in the last hour.

Zekiel had willingly stepped off into the void to further isolate himself away from everyone else and the problems in his mind he thought he could never be free from. To him, there was no solution to what felt like a never-ending issue. He could find no escape from what haunted him besides the void, and he was too fearful of what death on the other side of life would be. He pushed others away as a means to protect himself, trying to maintain a hardened social exterior which was layered from years of dissociation, unfair loss, and emotional abuse. All Zekiel wanted was peace and solitude, and he knew he wouldn't be able to experience it until he put only himself first, saying whatever he needed to in order to have his desired outcome—or completely pushing others away and leaving those who cared about him in the dark for days, weeks, and even months at a time. The void was where he wanted to be, to aimlessly exist in a sea of plentiful stars.

The other three, Amira, Anon, and Zayika, turned against themselves out of desperation, confusion, and lost hope, which left them subconsciously turning against each other.

Nero and Jameson had no other choice but to work together or part ways as one final wish was held by Jameson, and neither could see from the other's perspective on what words to believe and which to use as ammunition against the other. Nero felt he had no choice but to kill him, jamming a knife into his neck, securing the wish for himself, and ultimately ending the game. He used what little energy he had left to find Theia and ask to be sent back to Earth. She was found residing in Nathaniel's bunker, hiding from Zayika and the curse after the tragic deaths of Lorelai and Aadavan. They both felt as though they were dreaming as the teleportation wish was cast and the planet destroyed, and more importantly, its purpose had been revealed.

Each person was brought to Eunoia to have the strength of their mind tested and put to the ultimate challenge of truly uncovering their destiny and facing whatever their fate might be; coming to terms with the pieces of themselves that they didn't know how to address; utilizing their strengths and finding how to confront their weaknesses in a place where their minds seemed to be actively working against them. A misconception was that those with the strongest minds were the ones who survived the game—but that wasn't true, as the stone stated alongside the color-code engraved at the bottom, hidden from most of the others.

ON PLANET EUNOIA

THOSE WHO CONFRONT THEIR FATE

AND SUCCUMB TO THEIR DESTINY

HAVE TRULY WON

THE MIND'S TEST

Present

Lorelai and Theia tried to figure out what the writing on the shards meant as the others prepared for their fast-approaching battle. They could hear them training off in the distance, some preparing more compared to others.

Nero specifically practiced throwing his knives, aiming them as accurately as he could and discovering tricks he could play with the wind in order to move them and himself faster with his wings. He channeled his initially anger-fueled fear into a sharpened and determined mindset towards surviving. For as many hours as he could in the day, he trained. Then he would train again. And again. He also worked on being aware and mindful of his thoughts and how they affected his perception of reality. His muscles became stronger. Discipline was his main motive. His thoughts were intentionally productive.

He was ready to win.

Flashforward to CHP. 8 of CARRIERS OF EUNOIA

Enya was at the ocean, and with strained eyes, she looked at the aftermath of the fight that took place earlier that day. Many lives were lost. She spoke directly to each of them, wishing for them to rest in peace, and noticed the dead bodies of others from rivals who were there too. *Of course this had to happen one of the rare times I'm down trying to explore the ocean. I wish I had been on the shore. I would've helped them fight.* Regret ached in her mind as she was shocked at the turn of events. *Oh, Elena, what have they done to you? I can tell that you at least went out fighting.* She noticed pieces of flesh on her sharp shark-like teeth and how she had a harpoon gun wound that ultimately took her life. *If I could go back in time to help you out here, don't believe for a second that I wouldn't.*

"What do we have here?" Nero asked as he approached from the direction of the platform. *I'm totally going to win this*, he thought to himself. *With how naive and reckless these other members are, they stand no chance against someone as insightful and strategic as me.*

Although the night was growing darker by each passing minute, she was able to see him clear enough as only one wing was behind him, each hand holding onto three throwing knives. Stars covered the sky above them as he stepped on the bloody sand. He was shirtless, and she could see several fresh cuts on his chest, arms, and back.

"You're from the Over Grounds faction." Enya stood up and away from her deceased friend to fully face him.

"Are we stating the obvious?" He looked over her body. "Odd how you're staying out of the water this long for a mermaid. You must not have a real tail like everyone else."

She didn't take her eyes off of Nero. "I sure don't."

"Interesting, so you're defected?" He laughed. "Don't take offense to that. We also have people in our group that aren't very special too, if you could even believe it. One guy has no abilities at all. He's a very sad case."

"Do you usually talk this much to others who you're about to attack?" she asked him as he stepped over another dead body.

"Depends." *Keep running my mouth. She's hardly noticed how much closer I'm getting to her. How unobservant.* "I'm just surprised to see you walking around out here on the sand this late in the evening. You like to take risks?"

She put her palms outward in front of her. "Those I need to take, yes."

Nero stopped walking and discreetly slid five knives into his pockets, keeping one in his right palm and concealed from her view. No one else was to be seen near them as the two faced one another off, each hand ready to counterattack the other's ability.

"You have giant holes in your hands," he stated as he was taken aback by the sight of them. "Wait a minute, I think I've heard about you already; you are the fish freak that captured Anon's girlfriend at the start of their journey, aren't you? He ran his mouth about you for like an entire hour after arriving. Was so annoying. You're just as he described."

"That was me."

"Why would you force someone into a faction for one of the representatives like that?" *Keep distracting her with these questions. I couldn't care less, but at least she's thinking about something else rather than getting the upper hand on me.*

"My leader had me do it."

"So you agreed to help her?" Nero smirked. "You're a sick person."

"There's more to it than that." Enya was bothered by his choice in words and lowered her hands slightly at the sound of them. "Don't call me that. You have no idea what us guardians have endured down in the ocean."

"I'm sure I don't—but you don't know what I've endured either."

She fake-laughed. "Like what?"

"Well, similarly to your hands, most of my body has holes that have dug and opened through each layer of skin. I was put into a box that destroyed me." Nero faked a strained voice as she got emotionally invested in what he was saying.

"Must be uncomfortable."

He took a small step forward. "It really is. To be honest? I say some of the insults that I do because… well… I'm trying to cope with the defect that I am."

She completely dropped her guard with each hand at her side. "Really? In what way?"

"Don't pretend you didn't notice." Nero made his eyes look solemn as he pointed to his missing wing. "They only gave me one."

He took another small step forward.

"What? Really?" Enya was genuinely confused for a moment. "That seems unlikely. I feel like I've already seen you around with both of them? Are you lying to m—"

Before she could finish her question, he lept towards her and commanded the wind to pull him faster in her direction. He grabbed her right arm and flew past her with a firm grip, yanking her down to her back.

"Ow! Let go of me!" she yelled out.

Nero flipped around and stomped down onto her face. "Not a chance! You're a gullible idiot!"

Her nose broke and bled as she flipped a hand upward in his direction and commanded seaweed to get a hold of his neck, pulling him down roughly beside her.

"Screw you!" he said after the impact.

She used her left elbow to pin him down. "How dare you lie to trick me!"

"Oh, come on," he replied and made sure to keep his eyes staring ahead sternly. "Those are the survival basics. Get a clue."

Their hands wrestled one another until she got cut deeply in the wrist with the knife hidden in his right palm. She winced in pain and lost her hold on him with her other hand to tend to the injured one. He had used that window of time as an opportunity to flip her down onto the brown, freezing cold sand instead. Her green salty hair was sprawled out in different directions. The moon was bright above them, and the clouds watched as the two fought to survive.

"Nice try," Nero told her. "But I'm going to win."

She sent seaweed out from both her hands, but he grabbed at it quickly and began tying it around her arms, using her own power against her. Once she was caught off guard, he dug into his pocket and pulled out another throwing knife. "I can't believe you're doing this," she told him once she realized she had no other way of fighting back against him.

"Doing what? Playing fairly by the rules? Surviving?" Nero roughly stabbed her in the heart. "I'm never going to apologize for any of that."

Present

Theia parted ways with Lorelai to clear her mind and think about what she'd learnt. The color hex sequence kept repeating in her thoughts. *#BB4B89. What could it mean?*

Why that specific color? She was thankful that Cloudburst could not hear what she was pondering.

After she rode the platform up to reach her castle, she emptied both shoes of the scratchy sand that had collected in them. As she tipped and patted them softly, Nero approached her with three throwing knives in each of his hands.

"When is the ceremony?" He stood shirtless, clutching his knives with a sturdy hold on the blades' handles. "Tell me more about it."

She put her shoes back on before answering, "Soon. It will be here before you know it."

"Will you be answering our questions?"

"Yes, some of them, of course."

"Like which ones?"

"We'll see when we get there, Nero." She tried to walk away from him to head back to her room, but he grabbed her arm. His knives were pressed up against her skin, leaving tiny cuts in their wake. "Please take your hand off of me."

"I'm not letting you go until you stop being so vague. All of us here deserve and demand answers. We're tired of sitting around and watching you psychopaths bring more innocent people here to be destroyed too. Tell me what I want to know."

Theia caught sight of a few others from their faction watching timidly behind him. "I see Lyra, Gebu, and a few others over there. Why are they watching us?"

"Why would I answer your questions when you can't even answer mine?" Nero shot back as he began to walk over towards the foundation's edge, yanking Theia along with him. "Unlike me, you cannot fly. To my knowledge, you can't do much besides bring people to and from here, right?"

"I-I'm not telling you what I can do."

"Fine. I'm observant enough to already know what I just stated is true. You're going to send me and the rest of us home now, got it? And Aadavan isn't here to stop me."

"'Stop' you from what?" She began to tremble, peering over at the rocks down by the ocean. "What are you going to do?"

"You're getting thrown over if you don't do what I say," he replied angrily. "I've had enough of my time wasted here. Tell me when we are getting sent home! Now!"

"I can't do that! Get your hand off of me!" Theia panicked as the others came closer.

"Nero!" Kason yelled out. "This wasn't the plan!"

"Why are you escalating things?" Lyra asked next to him.

Gebu tried to support the other two, "Come back and we will talk!"

"It's too late for that now!" Nero responded.

"No, it's not." Cloudburst walked front and center past the rest as he confronted Nero, "This isn't who we are, and I think you know that."

"Oh, really?"

"And if you knew her a little better..." He stepped right next to Nero to only whisper in his ear, "You would know that she isn't really that way too. Do you get what I'm saying?"

There was silence. Big, fluffy, white clouds raced above them and just barely began to fill up with cold silver hues of grey, another storm ready to emerge from the sky.

Nero looked down at Theia and then back at Cloudburst. *I better not regret stepping away from this opportunity.* "Fine." *I will win. I'm only backing down for the others. I don't care about any of these representatives, and I will make it a point to not even remember their pathetic names.*

Cloudburst let out the breath he was holding as Theia stepped quickly to safety. *I'm glad she's alright. I hope she repays me for helping her out.*

Then he heard Theia respond in his head only seconds later as she sprinted away, *don't worry, I will.*

CHAPTER TWENTY-TWO: DÉJÀ VU

Aadavan

Present

I had two very strong feelings. One was that more people would be waking up on the hills soon—I could sense it. Second, I needed even more alone time with Theia. The next game was drawing nearer by the minute. I tried to conceal my boiling frustration towards her for how she tried to diminish the power us representatives had, feeling as though she was advocating for silencing our voices in a game where leaders needed to be ever present in order for the correct lessons to get across. *I swear this may all fall apart under her leadership style. Things are going to get out of hand. Miscommunication, selfishness, acting on emotion instead of reason. She doesn't understand. These fighters will not have the emotional capacity to face what we are putting them through without guidance on what our purpose is in the first place.* I loved her too much to turn against her, but at the same time, I couldn't deny when she was wrong. Even though we still needed to get on the same page, larger problems arose for us to handle.

"You trust me, right? My reasoning?" she asked for reassurance. "Some of my own have tried devising various plans to get rid of me or force me to send them home early, as you've now heard, but I've been standing my ground. You think I'm doing what is correct, right? Is this justified?"

"I can't say I see entirely where you are coming from with your judgment, though I'll sit back and see how all of this plays out," I replied.

"Do you think I deserve the death threats? The extra hostility?"

"Not at all. It's only because of your very special ability that you are targeted the way you are. What would make you worse in the eyes of others compared to me or Lorelai? Please be honest with yourself, Theia. Can't you see what everyone else does? With just your finger you are able to bring life into this planet. Is that not the most powerful ability imaginable? You are a masterpiece."

Theia didn't know how to respond.

"Don't overthink what they've said and done to you. You don't deserve for one minute to be put into that sort of danger. In time, they will all understand the purpose of what is really going on here. They will come to see their faults and what truly is at stake."

Theia finally replied, "But if things go wrong here, the death and loss of structure could be greatly unfathomable."

"In what way?"

"The type that we cannot come back from."

Flashforward to Two Months after CHP. 12 of ECHOES OF EUNOIA

Nero was having a surreal time trying to merge back into society on Earth with everyone else. Even with his own family, it took a great deal of time for him. He created distance between himself and those who he knew before everything took place. He told himself that no one would trust any of the stories he had to share, and that if he tried to tell them, it would only backfire in his face for trying to be honest. He was unemployed for a long time and became a drifter who would visit countless new cities, landmarks, and do anything he could to get his mind off of all the people he experienced unfathomable tragedies with; trying to escape memories of the problems and horrific deaths he caused.

Sleeping at night was almost entirely impossible for him because of the regret. Not a day went by that he wasn't reminded in some way of the people he murdered and those who almost took his own life. He told himself whatever he needed to in his head in order to find a moment of solitude. For the first time in many months, he was finally free to do whatever he wanted, but he was hardly able to move on as he felt like a prisoner to the past.

It wasn't until he experienced a moment of sheer panic that Nero was able to finally lift the lingering haze that followed him everywhere he went.

At a dimly lit and cozy shop, he stood in line, waiting to place his order. He was bundled up securely with his dark hood up. He didn't make eye contact with others unless it was absolutely necessary. The smell of drinks and freshly made bakery items filled the air. He felt calm. For just a moment, he was able to get his mind off of the memories that normally haunted it.

"I'm sorry about that," he heard a woman who was walking over to someone else in the line ahead of him say. "I wasn't sure where to go! I forgot where I was for a minute there. Thanks for waiting for me."

His heart skipped a beat when he looked up and saw that the woman's hair was the same colors as Zayika's.

No, it can't be.

He rubbed his eyes and stood fully upright.

She died. That can't be Zayika.

Even their voices were too similar for comfort, and his heartrate didn't return to normal until she finally turned her head enough for him to see her face. He let out the breath he was holding in and lost his desire to order anything, quietly leaving the shop.

Present

Three dwellers were on the outskirts of the jungle, practicing their abilities. Saylor and Draydon were crafting a large variety of weapons, making each weapon quicker than the last. Fabian was partly disappointed with his smoke grenades as he formed and threw them near his two allies.

"Hey!" Draydon called out. "Watch where you're throwing those! We are trying to see over here!"

Fabian sighed. "Whatever."

"Seriously, Fabian." Saylor coughed and stepped away from a cloud of smoke. "If you hinder our vision too much, we may hurt one another by accident! I can hardly see anything right now."

"The positive here is at least the smoke seems to be thicker the more upset you are." Draydon waved off a gust passing by his face. "They can come in handy for catching the others off guard."

"The Over Ground members are like really, really powerful." Fabian's eyes shot up to the blue castle in the sky.

Saylor shrugged. "So are we."

"Have you even seen any of them training? Especially that Nero guy. He's insanely threatening and can be quite cruel. He has an entire set of throwing knives. His aim is way too good with them... I wonder where he even got those."

Draydon looked down at the ground as Saylor's attention went to him and then back to Fabian. "It's actually a really funny story. I'm sure he's the same one I heard about not too long ago."

Fabian was confused. "What?" Then he realized, "No way. Seriously, Draydon? Please tell me that you didn't help that dude out and make those knives for him? Was the person you helped named Nero? Oh, come on. Your generosity is seriously going to get us killed!"

"That's what I tried to tell him earlier," Saylor said.

"How about you both don't gang up on me?" Draydon finally lifted his eyes up from the dirt to look at them and replied shamefully, "and y-yes, that was his name."

"Us telling you the truth is better than the enemy ganging up on us…" Fabian sighed heavily before finishing his sentence, "with the weapons you made for them! How screwed up is that?"

Draydon's arms were crossed as he responded defeatedly, "Alright, I get the point. You both don't see where I'm coming from."

Fabian looked at a stack of grenades he created near his feet. "I definitely don't. Is there anyone else that you made weapons for?"

"Only him."

"One is too many for me," Saylor interjected.

"Don't worry about it so much!" Draydon raised his voice. "Who's to even say that we will fight him in the first place? That may not even happen! To go back and forth and argue about it has no point! Just lay off me, will you?"

Fabian's eyes exuded distaste as he watched him. "You better not regret it. That's all I will say."

"Let's just go for a walk and blow off some steam," Saylor told them. "We should all calm down. I see Aadavan up ahead, why don't we find out if there's any new information we can get from him?"

"Sounds epic," Fabian said sarcastically as he followed them.

Draydon kept his thoughts to himself. *They're being too hard on me. They just don't understand. If the roles were reversed, I'm sure they would be begging the other group to help us out in some way. I'm paying forward a good deed. Securing positive karma… right?*

Flashforward to CHP. 6 of CARRIERS OF EUNOIA

Saige and Zekiel ran as fast as they could into the forest after Nero killed Saylor in the Land Dweller's jungle. A conversation that escalated too quickly ended in tragedy; three dweller lives were already lost before the official opening ceremony. He stood in shock at what he just did and panted to catch his breath. Blood dripped from him; his face and hands, and mainly his back where one of his invaluable wings had just been cut off by Saylor right before he angrily retaliated. Nero was unsure if he was going to live or die from the amount of blood loss he endured and made his way back to the Over Grounds faction where he spoke with Gebu and got healed by Mae.

Saylor laid lifeless on the soil in a pool of her own blood. Small, blown up remains of two other dwellers surrounded her on the trees and rocks; the innocent fighters who'd been suffocated in the grip of Nero's strong wind right before she passed away too. Her eyes were stuck upwards in the direction of the moving clouds. Her hair was more red than blonde. Some time had passed before anyone discovered her body.

It wasn't until Draydon and Fabian left the greenhouse to talk and practice outside that she was found. Fabian noticed her first and stopped walking as he did, unable to move or speak at the sight.

"What is it?" Draydon looked over his shoulder to ask. "Why are you making that expression?"

He couldn't answer, but instead waited for him to turn his head back around. It was in the next ten seconds that everything changed for Draydon as he realized who was dead not too far from him.

"Saylor?" His heart began racing as his feet did too. He fell to the ground by her side and pulled her body into his arms. "Saylor? No! What happened?"

Fabian noticed the guts and other body parts of their teammates around them and put his face into his hands.

"Saylor!" Draydon saw the very large cut across her neck where she was attacked. *Someone cut her, someone attacked her before the ceremony. What sort of monster would do this sort of thing?* "Don't tell me..."

"What?" Fabian was finally able to speak as he realized another layer of panic overcame one of his closest friends. "What is it, Draydon?"

He watched as he grabbed a hold of a blood-covered knife that was in the dirt next to her and began sobbing. "This is because of me! All of this! It's my fault!"

Don't tell me that's one of the knives that he made for Nero. Fabian shook his head. *Nero did this, didn't he? He must've.*

"Someone from the Over Grounds faction did this! This is a dweller knife!" Tears poured over his face. "No one of our own would have done this! I-I made knives for Nero, why did I do that? Saylor was right! I should have listened to her!"

Fabian could feel regret radiating off of Draydon's body as he fell completely over hers in despair. "Come on, you need to get up." He tried to pull him off of her.

"No!" he cried out. "Leave me here to die with her, I deserve it! I helped the enemy, this is my fault," his voice broke as it trailed off.

Fabian knelt down and took the knife out of his hand before he did something rash with it. He was about to throw it off into the distance before he paused, noticing through the dripping blood a crafting symbol that only belonged to Saylor—not Draydon. "Wait just a moment." He sprinted off and dunked it into the pond to clean the weapon. "Draydon!" He ran back to him.

"What?" His face and the upper half of his body was covered in blood as he looked up to see what Fabian needed. "What could it possibly be?"

"Look." He put the knife in front of his eyes and pointed directly towards the sun and moon symbol on the handle. "Saylor made this."

There was silence.

Draydon began crying harder and took her face into his hands as he spoke, "I'm proud of you for fighting. May you rest in everlasting peace, Saylor."

Present

They traveled in silence for a few minutes, the air still tense around them. As they got closer to Theia, they overheard the last thing she said to Aadavan, prompting a new flood of questions in Saylor's mind as she approached first.

"What will we not be able to come back from?" she asked the two representatives as they conversed by the castle after Cloudburst had already vanished.

"Oh, come on, Saylor, why even ask?" Draydon said. "I'm not sure how you keep thinking we even have a chance at getting the truth out of these two. Aadavan doesn't really want what's best for us."

"Do you both really have to have this conversation all over again?" Fabian added as he ventured behind them.

Aadavan put his glasses on top of his head to rub his eyes in disbelief. "Why in the world are you three even this close to Theia's faction anyway? And more importantly, why are you speaking about me as though I am not right here? What makes you think any of this is acceptable?"

"Didn't realize that we were required to stay at the treehouse," Fabian told him.

"I never said that, but it's better practice to remain on your grounds until it is time to fight the others." Aadavan put his glasses back on.

"Are you going to answer my question?" Saylor circled back. "By the way, hi Theia, you look nice today."

"Thank you." Theia looked at Aadavan with confusion.

"Oh, stop trying to kiss up to them!" Draydon threw his hands in the air. "Are you serious right now?"

Theia nodded. "The flattery is welcomed, Saylor, but I'm afraid your companion Draydon is correct here. We are not who you need to get on the good side of. It's best for you to collaborate and come to terms with where you stand alongside those of Lorelai's and my factions."

"On the contrary," Aadavan cleared his throat. "You all should look out for fellow dwellers only. Protect your own."

"When does all of this start? I want to get it over with," Fabian said.

"Soon. Now let us continue our conversation while we are still able to have a peaceful time together," Aadavan replied and ushered them away.

"Do you think peace still exists?" Theia asked once it was only the two of them again.

He took her hand in his. "No matter what, no matter who wins, if something ever happens to either of us… we know some things will always be true. You are my love."

"You are mine as well. Everything will work out. We will be safe," Theia said with as much air of confidence as she could muster up. "Cloudburst will be back soon, and we will see for ourselves how everything will play out."

"Speaking of things working out, I have a few items that might help. Earlier, I created something that may be of great use," Aadavan told her. "As it now turns out, I have extra abilities aside from what you're already aware of. I've been excited to show you. It's been hard keeping it a secret."

"Is that so?" she asked.

"Yes." He swiftly reached into his pocket and pulled out two handmade walkie talkies designed from various pieces of nature. "Speaking devices. I've already tested them out, and they seem to work well. I'm not entirely sure how I did it, but they might be useful."

"We shouldn't be wasting time making things like this," Theia shot him down. "Leave the tinkering up to the fighters. Many of your people already seem to have taken an interest in such activities to pass the time. Draydon, for instance, has even helped out one of my own."

"I wouldn't be too sure about that," Aadavan tucked them back into his jacket. "Doesn't sound like him."

Theia struck a nerve with her next words, "Maybe you don't know some of them as well as you think you do."

"Why are you telling me to not create new things anyway?"

"What would their purpose be?"

"For my fighters to speak with me directly. They can help streamline our communication when it comes to future member retrievals."

"We need to focus our attention on the ceremony instead."

"Why so?"

"We need to keep it brief. To the point. Try to avoid as many questions as possible."

Aadavan dropped his shoulders in defeat. "I won't fight you on this, Theia. Lorelai and I will follow your lead and see how things turn out. I'll trust your judgment."

"I actually want Lorelai to present at the opening ceremony this time around."

"Really? Why?"

"She has no choice but to keep it short and concise. She's good at condensing information into valuable, bite-sized pieces."

"Ironic word choice, you know, considering her arm."

Theia rolled her eyes. "Not the time for jokes, Aadavan. She was in a lot of pain."

"Forgive me, but jokes help take some of the stress off of reality."

"Thank you for trying to lighten the mood. It's about to become very, very heavy."

"Are you ready? To see your next participants in action? To find out who wins?"

"Of course I am, though I'll admit I'm a bit nervous for them. I'm not looking forward to discovering how many lives will be lost this time around. Hopefully not many."

"If they communicate and strategize well, then it could be a very clean and effective game." Aadavan lit up. "One of my own may stand out this time around."

"That would be nice for you," Theia responded truthfully. *But at what expense?*

"Oh! I almost forgot!" Aadavan reached into his other pocket. "I also made these for you. Grappling hooks and strings. For the platform. The gap to get over is a bit too wide, with time it seems to be getting wider, so they could be the difference between life and death."

"Really?" She took them from him. "Thank you. I haven't needed anything like this, though. You know that. Maybe there is a small part of you that wants to help my fighters? Dare you ever admit it?"

He fought off a smile and changed the subject. "There's a small cave I found not too far from here. I'm fairly certain that it's entirely empty, but before the next wave fully begins, I'm going to bring a torch in there and ensure there's no writing on the walls, symbols, or anything else important we may have missed. That stone was bad enough."

"Thank you for being so thorough, Aadavan. You've been an amazing better half to have throughout this journey."

He stepped forwards and gently placed his hand on her face, peering at Theia over his glasses. "I love you."

"I love you too."

"May the best fighters win."

CHAPTER TWENTY-THREE: WISH CARRIERS

Lorelai

Present

One night down in the ocean I experienced a haunting and unforgettable vision about the waterfall. Never before had I seen it in such a sinister light. Everything about the location was chilling as I closed my eyes and saw it clearly. The waters hummed in my ears as loud, overwhelming swooshing noises occasionally passed, the creatures outside my structure's unstable walls searching for their next meal or rivals to push away from their own resting places. I felt as if I could never feel truly alone, not even for a moment, as my dreams had been turned into visions of individuals who were called to a higher purpose.

I swam to the closest pillar I could find with my eyes closed, trusting that my hand would brace me for the practically blind impact against it.

I can no longer sit. I need to swim. I feel like I'm going to lose my mind down here.

Those appointed to my faction didn't want much to do with me as their discomfort couldn't be mitigated, no matter what words I used or how much I tried to show them that they could be the strongest elemental group.

In my visions, I would see all different types of people who were, most notably, at such different walks of their unique lives. Ever since first seeing the woman with the colorful hair at the start of it all… I never felt the same. I also never saw her again until the night I experienced one of the biggest epiphanies I'd ever had.

I flipped my tail to push myself in a burst forward to touch the pillar.

Be mindful of my surroundings. Stay calm. Everything will be okay.

Though when my finger touched something in front of me, I knew in an instant that it wasn't a part of my underwater remains — it was a human. My eyes sprang open, and the vision seemed so real in front of me.

The woman with the silver and purple hair turned around slowly and looked at me. She had several freckles on her tan skin and green eyes. She was wearing a white dress with long sleeves, a short turtleneck, tall black boots, and a smile as she noticed me. Her hair was very long, tousled by the currents. Light escaped both of her hands. She was clearly morphed and a product of the planet—*but how? She's never been here before?* I was unsure if she was truly before me or if my hallucinations were actually becoming tangible and part of reality.

Who is this? Why does she seem so familiar?

"Who are you?" I asked.

"Your worst nightmare," she answered. "But I could also be your greatest dream come true."

"What?"

She glanced down at my tail with an unsatisfied look and rolled her eyes. "You representatives think you have all of the power here, and that's admirable, but it's important you understand that you don't. The Wish Carriers do."

Wish Carriers? My body felt like ice, and not because of the waters we were in, but because of her voice, as it didn't sound like it belonged to a human.

How is she breathing, speaking, existing under the water like I am right now?

I reached to touch her again.

"They truly hold the power, not the illusion and false narrative you three have written for yourselves."

All of a sudden, as I blinked, her wavy hair turned completely brown, and she fell down to her knees on the ocean's floor. The woman choked for air, clawing at her own throat.

"The planet. That's…" A cluster of bubbles messily flew out from her mouth as she began to suffocate and fade away into the sand below her. "It's cursed here. All who kill. Cursed."

Before I could try to save her or ask any questions, she was gone.

The vision was over, and the pillar where she disappeared came back into view. The oddest part of that particular vision wasn't seeing her, but how hard it was to remember her right after it ended.

"'All who kill'? 'Cursed'? Cursed to what?" I heard a creature wailing off in the distance as I felt my blood rushing again, "To death?"

Flashforward to CHP. 10 of ECHOES OF EUNOIA
SPEAKER: Amira

The worst was about to come as our fate was going to be revealed soon. For some reason, Anon chose to distance himself from me. In the dire turn of events, I couldn't understand why it didn't make him want to work together as a team more than ever. Instead, he seemed to be running away from Zayika, me, and all of our problems. Being brought back was a nightmare come to life for the both of us.

I deeply regretted the times I doubted him when we were back on Earth, unfairly putting pressure on him that he did not ever deserve. I wanted to look out after Anon, support him, and make sure he always knew he was loved.

We will not have a chance at surviving if we don't talk this through. We cannot let fear control us. Everything is beginning to fall apart.

I felt hopeless trailing behind him as he geared up to head in a different direction than me. He apparently had his own plan for how to handle the threat of our opponent, but I couldn't see from his perspective how running was making anything better.

"We're going to part ways for just a little while. There is something I need to do," Anon told me as I followed after him.

"Can I go with you?" I asked.

"Not right now. I'm sorry."

I was nauseous with anxiety as my mind couldn't comprehend why he wouldn't be taking me with him.

"Why not? What is it you're doing? Are you trying to take on Zayika alone? What about the plan?"

He took my hand in his as he responded, "I will be back. I will see you again. I just need answers."

Why can't we get them answered together? Why can't he feel confident enough in our capabilities as a team? "Why can't I go with you?"

"Because I don't know what's going to happen. I want you close to your fighting companion since I'm heading away from the ocean."

"But… you are my fighting companion." *Can Anon not fully accept my love?*

"I want you near Hippo just in case. Stay with the other two for now, please, and when I come back, we will face Zayika and finish this once and for all. There isn't much time left."

We looked into each other's eyes for what felt like a lifetime. I just desired for him to be completely honest about what was going on his mind.

I wish I could read his thoughts. Why can't he trust me? Why does he want to go after Zayika by himself?

He leaned in slowly and embraced me lovingly in his arms, small flickers of lightning sparking against my trembling skin. I was able to ignore the pain. I had so much adrenaline that it was hard to feel at all.

We both kissed one another and found peace in the cold silence.

I want him to trust me.

Anon glanced over his shoulder at the hills we both woke up on when the nightmare began.

I want to spend the rest of my life with this man.

I will never, ever take our time for granted.

Present

Lorelai attempted to shake off the bitter feeling that the most recent vision created as she soon experienced the next one. It helped get her mind off the words that Zayika spoke up until the next vision which showed her a crime scene at the town's waterfall. There were two women taking notes and conversing with one another there. It was instantaneously shown to her who from the duo was destined to be brought to the planet.

A crime scene? Investigators? There's been too much suspicious activity there. Are we in some way going to get caught?

She met up with Theia at the waters' edge as soon as she could once it was over, keeping in mind the most important details that she could relay to Cloudburst. Lorelai remained partly in the water, as usual, to reduce the discomfort the air caused her as she mentally prepared herself for the conversation. For some reason, she knew instinctively that there was something different about her final vision in particular, the woman in it, that she was destined for great things. That she carried power.

I'll share all the vision's details later when we meet with Aadavan; hopefully hearing this information from me directly will make him ease off.

"I'm excited for these visions to stop," Lorelai said hesitantly, unsure of what her friend's reaction would be.

Theia sat down in the sand with her shoes off, toes occasionally greeted by the chilly small tips of rushing waves. "Why is that?"

"They're pretty exhausting. I feel as though I'm looking into someone else's life in a way that I shouldn't be. It feels… inappropriate?"

Aadavan's mindset influenced Theia's response, "You were appointed to a higher calling. It's best that you accept and embrace it. You have to remember why we are doing any of this at all."

"I know how we justify things. It's just, it's lonely down here in the water, if I'm being honest. It's challenging being so alone. To be transparent, if I may be, I feel that I'm losing my mind."

"You isolated yourself, Lorelai. You went into that ocean. We didn't force you," Theia told her.

"That's not entirely true, and you were not here to see the full truth. The ocean took me in by itself. It chose me. I didn't decide to be yanked to the depths of the most horrifying terrain. When I stepped in, I didn't realize what would happen to me. I was screaming out for help, you and Aadavan saw."

"I don't remember it that way. Try to see the positive in this."

"I know, Theia, it's just difficult sometimes. Maybe you don't relate because you and Aadavan have it bett–" Lorelai stopped herself from continuing to prioritize Theia's comfort over her own, afraid of confrontation. "Forget it. Everything will be fine. I'm just ready to see what the future holds now."

"Aadavan and I want you to present the rules at the next ceremony. We trust that you will keep private what needs to be private, be mindful of everyone's time, and be cautious of how long you can stay out of the water. Please host it well. We can't answer too many questions or else it will all get out of hand. Let me know if you need help with what you have to say. Word choice is crucial."

"I'm glad you both trust me enough to delegate such an important task to my discretion." Her eyes shone with wonder. "What if there's a way I could stay out of the ocean longer? What if we could change my body in some way? Like, what if I laid down on one of Aadavan's stone beds? What if it could alter me in a more human way?"

"I'm not sure about that," Theia responded.

"It would be incredible if we were able to try." Lorelai sighed as she heard some of the mermaids rise out of the water behind her. *Why right now? No distractions while I'm discussing this with Theia, please.*

"Is it time yet?" Orson asked from the waves. "Are we finally going to get off this planet?"

Marcellus, who was swimming beside him, added, "We see you both are talking again! How do you talk so much, yet still nothing happens? How many empty words do you share with one another?"

"Are you going to sound the trumpets now?" Elena and Enya behind them asked in unison, moving wet hair off their faces to see the expressions of the representatives better.

"Not yet!" Lorelai, for the first time ever, raised her voice at them. "Just keep practicing your abilities until you are told to fight! Train more!"

"That's all we have been doing down here!" Zavier shouted, the farthest behind. "This is getting ridiculous how you're making us wait while we narrowly dodge the attacks of all of these frightening things in the ocean! Have you even seen what's down here? They're going to eat us at any moment! Come on already! The suspense is literally unbearable!"

Lorelai sighed, and Theia took over, stepping partly into the ocean to get closer to them. "Please be patient for just a little while longer. The wait will be over soon, and I'm certain that you all will be wishing to return back to this moment, the calm before the storm, once it all begins."

They each went back under the water with glares of discomfort to continue training. Elena, Enya, Marcellus, Orson, and Zavier were the group of five that remained closest to one another in the depths. Each grew used to how freezing cold the water was as they almost always stayed in it, only going onto the shore every once in a while for as long as their scaly skin would allow them to temporarily escape the hidden aquatic terrors.

Enya was the slowest swimmer because of her legs, but she made great use of shooting seaweed out of either palm with precision, similar to Zavier. Her lengthy hair grew quickly and was the same green as his tail. Their similarity in abilities drew them closer together from the rest at times, bonding over their unique experience and the care she often showed for his brother who became ill after being morphed. He kept his name a secret from everyone else, so Zavier was careful to never accidentally mention it, and he would hardly venture out from a specific part of Lorelai's faction by the concrete statues that they used for target practice.

As Marcellus, Orson, and Elena trailed nearby to practice the use of their hand-held weapons while maneuvering the waters, Zavier and Enya checked in on his brother nearby. Her maroon-colored eyes watched as he led the way and swam slower than normal so that she was able to keep up with him. His brother was sitting on a big mossy box on the ocean floor, holding onto his tail in distress as he watched them draw nearer.

"How are you both doing?" he asked. "What did Lorelai say up there? Is she talking with Theia again? I really hope Aadavan hasn't gathered too much information. He will use it against us… and to his advantage."

"No new information. We were only told that we have to wait longer for the fight to begin." Enya slowly approached the side of the metal fixture he was resting on.

"More importantly…" Zavier added. "How are you doing? Feeling any better yet?"

"No, unfortunately, the nausea comes in waves. No pun intended." He coughed up green bubbles as they stared at him worriedly.

"I wish Lorelai would take our health more seriously." Zavier looked up at the tops of the waves. "I can't believe they've done this to us."

"I'm not sure what else can be done. I wouldn't even want them to try to help heal this infection with what's already happened to me." His tail looked like it was rotting, several scales flaking off and floating in the waters. The rest of his body was also drained of most of his color and life. With tired and hopeless eyes, he searched around. "You both didn't see anything nearby while on your way back down, right? Only the anglerfish has been passing by from time to time. At least she provides enough light to see what we need to. Her green bulb is way more effective compared to the purple bioluminescence of the other fish. When she's near… I just stay as quiet as possible."

"She seems to not go out of her way to attack anyone unless she feels threatened," Enya tried to reassure him. "But no, don't worry, we didn't see anything swimming around."

"I want to find a cure for you. I'll try everything in my power to search for answers, okay? But you have to stay strong. Don't lose faith down here. We will be okay." Zavier swam close to his brother and leaned on the crate's empty space next to him, his tail blending in with the swaying moss. "We'll see Mom and Dad again. Every uncle and aunt. And…"

"Please don't say her name," his brother groaned as he tried to not think about his wife and kids back on Earth. "Please don't say their names. I can't imagine how they're doing right now. They must be so worried about me. I wish I could return and tell them everything will be fine. I want them to know I love them." He coughed again, but this time some blood came out.

"They know that you do. I'm sorry, brother. I hate seeing you in pain and suffering like this. We will return to our family." Zavier pulled him into a hug. "I will try my best to fight in good health for you once the trumpets ring."

Enya's voice rippled to them as she began to distance herself away, "I'm going to go train with the others to give you both some space. I hope you feel better soon. See you later, Zavier."

"Be safe over there," he replied. "We'll be on the lookout and warn you if any dangers approach."

"I appreciate it," she responded while slowly swimming away. "Don't forget to call the other fighters if needed. The ones with the jellyfish tentacle arms will be particularly helpful in combat."

Elena was the first to notice her coming their way, her pale scales shining brightly. "How is he doing? Symptoms improving?"

"They're worse now. He's started coughing up blood."

Marcellus and Orson let out sighs in unison.

"Very sorry to hear that." Elena held her spear in one hand and was playing with the water with the other, making small spinning tunnels from her fingertips as she anxiously spun it around. "All we can do is get better at fighting so we are able to return home. We have to have enough drive in us to do it for ourselves and one another."

"How's the bow and arrow going?" Enya asked Marcellus.

"It's good."

Orson laughed as he held onto his weighty hammer. "Don't downplay yourself, man. He's great at long-range attacks and dodging. Will come in handy when we face the others."

"He's got incredible reflexes," Elena added.

"Glad to hear it." Enya held her hands that were filled with layers of open holes together as she responded, "We're going to need all the help we can get."

Flashforward to CHP. 12 of CARRIERS OF EUNOIA

"I just cannot believe that Zavier and his brother were killed," Orson broke the tension in the air with the remaining guardians as they awaited to find out their fate with who was to be faced next. "That man with the lightning, the one Amira's always wasting time flirting with, how devastating. I'm pretty sure his name is Anon. I cannot believe he electrocuted them like that. It was terrible."

"Please, Orson, you have to stop thinking about it. We cannot keep discussing those of ours we've already lost. I know they are missed and it's tragic that they died, but we have to keep ourselves focused on self-defense," Marcellus replied as he prepared arrows to fight with. "There will be more attacks before we know it. Many of the others are very well trained. We need to be mentally prepared to survive, so let's try our best for those who can no longer join us. There are hardly any Land Dwellers alive to my knowledge, so we will be facing off the rest of the Over Grounds on shore."

It was in that moment of desperation that the true significance of events hit Orson harder than ever before. "Marcellus… it's only us two now. I mean, Amira is also alive, but we have to be honest that she isn't going to help us. Even though she has Hippo, she isn't going to fight by our side. She's chosen to help Anon instead. We have to team up together now more than ever. It would've been amazing if we had whatever it was that rock was talking about, but we aren't so lucky."

"Please, Orson, stop worrying about what that stone said. I've told you this many times now. The representatives probably placed it down here to play with our heads, to distract us from the overall picture. It's probably a manipulation tactic from the other groups. We won't fall for lies. We also shouldn't worry about Amira as she has no loyalty to us. Our efforts until now haven't gotten through to her. Why keep thinking about her disinterest?" Marcellus took in a deep breath of water.

"Because she told us earlier she would help us fight. Why would she go back and forth between telling us one thing and then doing the opposite whenever someone else gets involved? It's just not fair. It's not right that she chooses the enemy over her own."

"She made her choice. Actions tell us all we need to know, so who honestly cares what words she's uttered that have not come from her heart?" Marcellus replied. "Alright. Enough about that. Let's get this over with, shall we? Are you ready with your hammer?"

"As ready as I'm ever going to be. I wish they would come into the waters to fight us. I'm far more comfortable here."

"Well, we can't swim around just waiting for them. We need to go out where they are to get this done."

The two swam up from the depths of the ocean to face those on land who were also prepared and armed to fight for their lives.

"Here come the last two," they heard Mae announce as they reached the shallowest part of the waters. She pointed at them as their human legs returned.

Orson saw Amira with those who were their greatest threat and felt a rise in his chest to speak before thinking. "Amira, stop talking to them! We have to fight them!" He tripped on his adjusting feet as he ran forwards, hammer in hand, and targeted Gebu. The heavy weapon flew from his fingers and knocked all air, and life, out of him bluntly.

No! Gebu thought as his hands clung to his throat in excruciating pain. *I can't die! I was supposed to get back home! No!*

Mae saw Gebu die right next to her and went into complete defense mode. "You shouldn't have done that!" she yelled at Orson, and for the first time sent out a glowing string around his neck with her boosting ability, forcing him to suffocate just as her friend did. "Suffer the fate you have casted."

Marcellus watched in horror as he died, only him and Amira remaining from their faction. *Not Orson! They will pay for this! A life for a life! I don't care whose it is!* He began shooting arrows with his bow at Mae and Anon, who dodged them efficiently.

"He's gone," Amira announced Gebu's death and went back over to the other two who her ally was trying to take down.

"So is he." Mae made it clear that Orson was gone too, worsening Marcellus' level of concentration as loss panged at his heart.

Why Orson? We were supposed to make it out of this! The grip Marcellus had on his bow loosened as he saw him lifeless and purple on the ground, all of the oxygen stripped from him in only a few harsh moments. *Why him and not me?* As he was thinking, he didn't notice that Anon was at the sidelines near him, flying up into the air with his black wings and flickering blue arms, ready to send lightning his way. A few shots flew downwards and sent off electrifying shocks near his feet. *Oh my goodness! No! I have no chance!* Marcellus realized Anon was after him and dodged as many electric hits as his stamina offered. *They will all gang up on me!* He shot an arrow at Mae who was closest to him on land and killed her in an instant. Life fled too fast for her to heal herself as she'd learned when enough time was offered. Right as she was killed, he was sent a particularly hot bolt of lightning down from Anon that electrocuted him to his core.

With that attack, only Anon, Zayika, and Amira were left at the ocean's shore; all three of them were desperate for a conclusive ending that was fair and necessary, but they were instead left with serious conflicting emotions as to who from the trio was going to live or die and be the first to ever make it back to Earth.

Present

Back at the ocean, Theia and Lorelai continued their previous conversation and faced one another with concern. There was no escaping the impending tragedy, hints of it already lingering in the air they breathed in unsteadily. All guardians retreated back underwater as they continued talking. With each conversation, they were unsure if it would be their last—but never outrightly acknowledged that.

"How well do you think your fighters will compete based on what you've seen?" Theia asked her.

"I'm not sure. It will be hard for me to not help them. Sitting back and watching is agonizing. Feels… wrong. More wrong with each passing minute," Lorelai replied. "It seems that they tend to drift away from one another a bit too often, I think if they group together, they will be stronger in numbers."

"Sometimes I feel the same way about those who are already under my supervision. It's imperative that they try to see from each other's perspectives as much as possible. Speaking of which… how was the last vision? I'm sure

Aadavan will be ecstatic to hear all of the details. What can you tell me?"

"It was unsettling." Lorelai watched a grouping of small crabs dig their way into the sand as she didn't hold back how she really felt, "I would like us to discuss it with one another and effectively prepare Cloudburst for it. He needs to know what he's getting himself into. This one is different from the rest."

"In what way?"

"He will have to conduct an extraction in the middle of a crime scene in order to get who he needs to."

"Really? A crime scene? Oh…" Theia's voice trailed off. *This cannot be good.*

"I'm concerned, though, that this could go very wrong. What if the investigators discover something about the portal at the water? What if there is a trace of the liquid we drank? That glass bottle? What if they find something that will reveal our presence to them? What if he tries to tell them what is happening? What could they even do if they found out?"

Theia was a bit taken aback by the situation and points Lorelai was making. "Everything will work itself out. Try to not worry so much."

"I try all the time, but worry always finds and consumes me."

"I know it does. You've always been that way. But you don't need to be stressed out so often, you are doing a great job down there. We couldn't have made it this far without you. Everything that's taken place is for a reason, and you've made it possible with your remarkable opportunity to see who is destined to contribute."

Lorelai felt a bit of warmth at Theia's words and the first true compliment she'd ever received. "Thank you. That means a lot to me." *I feel seen.*

"It's time for me to go get Cloudburst and tell Aadavan to meet us at the castle," Theia said, preparing to head out as she dusted sand off her pants and arms.

"Do you think we will ever get back to Earth? You, Aadavan, and me?" Lorelai asked, staring at Theia's pointer finger, before retreating under the waters.

She waited a few seconds before responding, looking down at it, "To be honest, between only us? I hope so."

Flashforward to CHP. 8 of CARRIERS OF EUNOIA

"Two women and two men from our group are under attack!" Anon announced as he, Gebu, and Omar got closer to them at the ocean. One of the men was Kason who he quickly interacted with and tried to plan how to fight those of the guardians who were prepared to strike against them. They took on those they could while Varid tried to get the other two to help, irritated and overly stressed out by that point at himself for not making greater use of the clouds he was given.

"Why are you both not fighting? What is wrong with you?" Varid asked frustratedly, speaking to them but also asking himself the same questions.

"W-we don't have powers. I mean, I can f-fly, but I can't do much more than that. I'm so-sorry," Gebu told him.

He gave him one of his weapons. "Well, you could still at least make yourselves useful. These are the only two I have. You know how to use this, right?"

"Of course," Gebu lied and thought, *what is wrong with Varid? Why is he not using his clouds? Why does he seem so… angry with us? What happened when he trained? Did he realize something he shouldn't have? Is it what Kason said about us?*

"What about you? How do you not have any weapons on you?" he asked Omar next.

"I have one right here." Omar took out a boning knife.

"Stop standing around and go help then! Why is Anon the only one pulling any weight around here?" he shouted in distress before sending a harpoon shot at the guardian who attacked Anon with a quick hit. She didn't die immediately from his efforts and rose out of the water with vigor. She slowly began to bleed out as she became fixated on Varid for striking her.

I cannot believe this, Varid thought as he looked over at his clouds and shook from the cold, his thoughts racing faster than ever before. *I should've never casted that amnesia effect on myself! I've had no true peace since. I should have been more careful in training!* He recalled the attempts he'd made with the cloud trio, neglecting to keep his focus on what would benefit him the most. The woman from the ocean was headed right towards him. *This is my chance to survive! I have to make it out alive, to prove my worth! To finally find my purpose!* He closed his eyes and tried to muster enough emotional strength to command his green cloud over to the guardian, but he accidentally sent it over his own head, then the pink one, followed by the orange one. All three struck down their bolts into his brain. Varid drowned in his own subconscious turmoil of conflicting emotions as the guardian, Elena, quickly came out from the ocean and drove her spear into his chest.

Present

Theia passed by some of her fighters as they were the most nervous she'd ever seen them. Varid stood out to her the most as he was trying to cast commands with the clouds he was given.

"Not again!" He was getting angry with them, as they weren't doing what he wanted them to.

Her plan was to walk past and ignore him, but that became difficult after hearing all of Aadavan's passion and enthusiasm about offering words of encouragement to their own participants.

Maybe I should say something to him? Maybe he will be able to learn something from me? Theia thought but quickly talked herself out of it. *Nevermind. I'm sure he'll be okay. I don't need to hold the hands of those who can help themselves.*

Varid was on the verge of tears as he told all three of his clouds to leave him alone, giving up on trying to train further with them. *Forget it. I'll just fight with a handmade weapon instead of my thoughts — they're too much of a mess. If I lose my life out there then so be it. Maybe I'm supposed to pass away here. Besides, who will even notice if I'm gone? Not like I will ever have the life I've always wanted. I'm better off lying to myself or not living in this lie at all. I cannot love my true self.*

Those on Eunoia inadvertently helped seal their fate with the thoughts they had, completely unaware of the power they held.

CHAPTER TWENTY-FOUR: THE CRIME SCENE
Cloudburst

Present

I was going to be sent to the waterfall again. My terrible curse of an existence had been reduced to the task of forcing other people into this nightmare with me. The representatives were getting close to reaching the maximum number of people they wanted to morph. Lorelai gave me a sad look for some reason as she approached. Theia and Aadavan were sitting close by at the nearest table as we waited for her to arrive. The other two met with her in one of the corners to speak before involving me in the conversation, but they almost always spoke loud enough for me to hear. Lorelai had a vision of the next person to be brought to them, a woman who was at what she saw to be a crime scene at the falls.

She told Theia every detail she could recall and made it very clear how it was important that I took one in particular back. Two women were investigating the town's problems together. Theia, Aadavan, and Lorelai hoped they wouldn't see anything suspicious there, like the drink they found or the gateway they stepped into. They wanted it all to remain their secret, without involvement from others who would expose their mind games and control.

I paced around while listening to them discuss instructions for the next capture out loud. I tried the best I could to take in the planet's views while they spoke to one another.

"Apparently there is a large crowd of bystanders watching the investigation," I heard Lorelai say as I waited nearby. "He'll, as always, need to waste no time."

"Understand? Do not draw any attention to yourself. We cannot risk anyone seeing what is truly taking place." Aadavan called me over.

I was on the brink of completely breaking down. "I cannot keep doing this for you all. I can't, I can't…"

"Pull it together!" he demanded. "This is urgent! We need her here so the remaining five can hurry up and get this started! You cannot somehow be this unreliable! You have completed how many retrievals already? Why is it that you are giving up now?"

"Aadavan, stay calm," Theia comforted him.

"Don't tell me what to do."

"I would completely give up if I really had the option to," I responded. "I would've stopped helping a very long time ago."

All three representatives ignored me.

Lorelai uncomfortably went back to discussing what she saw. "There were two beautiful women in my vision."

Aadavan was nodding with each syllable she spoke, his expression silently screaming at her to continue faster.

"One is to come here."

"Only one?" He threw his hands up in irritation. "Really? We only need six more people, but you are not having enough visions, we need to get thi—"

"Please, Aadavan, relax," Theia tried to settle him down. "It's not Lorelai's fault she isn't having many visions."

"It's those hills! That stone! This planet is ruining its own destiny!" he ranted. "Ever since it started bringing others here on its own! Ever since that group arrived on those stupid hills!" He shook his head and went to step out of the room.

I can't believe this is how they, especially Aadavan, are acting about what is going on. I cannot handle living with this anymore. If only the planet would actually fight back for good and end all of the wrongdoing taking place here.

Theia gently took a hold of one of Lorelai's hands. "It's alright. We will get this one and wait for the others."

"Well, those others better not spawn on the hills!" Aadavan interjected, unable to stop himself from joining in as usual. "I swear the ones who wake up there do not morph as well as those that we bring here ourselves! They have defects! Their personalities, well, they… they only cause trouble!" he spoke with a pointer finger in the air as he lost track of what he was saying in the first place.

"Aadavan, at least two of your people who spawned on the hills have been proven to be very sane and useful already," Theia informed him.

He gave her a blank stare as he embarrassedly scrambled through his brain, trying to remember their names. "Um, yes, I remember of course. How could I forget?"

"Mhm. Name them, maybe?"

"There's no way I could forget, uh, Damien and… uh… T-Taylor?" He looked at Lorelai as she facepalmed.

"Draydon and Saylor," Theia corrected him. "Come on, Aadavan. You're better than this. Don't allow stress to get to your head this badly."

"Ugh! Whatever!"

He finally walked out of the room and shouted as he spoke his parting words, "Hopefully the others don't take long to get here either."

I was provided with a detailed description of the next victim to look for, and Theia prepared herself to teleport me. Lorelai accidentally awoke everyone as she hastily told us about the vision. There was more emphasis and excitement in her voice compared to normal as she tried to calm herself down.

"What is going on?" Nero asked from around the corner, practically pushing Mae out of his way with some of the others close by him also listening in.

Varid stepped forwards past the rest as his clouds remained by his side. "Is it time? Are we finally starting? We're ready Theia. We've been ready for a little while now."

"Many of you are hardly ready if you're being honest with yourselves." Nero rolled his eyes. "But I am. I've actually been getting ready for this moment for what feels like way too long now. We've been hearing you all muttering nonsense to one another from the halls. What you owe us is now far past overdue. So… what is it?"

"Not yet. It still is not time for the opening ceremony. You will have no doubt in your mind once it begins," Theia replied. "All of you need to go back to getting as much rest as you can. We will let you know when you're needed."

"None of this feels right," Kason said. "We're sitting ducks waiting to be shot."

"Who else is joining us?" Lyra asked, addressing the elephant in the room. "We don't need many more people, right? Like, three?"

"Cloudburst is about to be on his way right now to get another woman. We aren't sure what faction she will be assigned to, possibly ours, it depends on what her calling will be more inclined towards. Same as it was with all of you; placement won't be determined and carried out until she is here. All of you return to sleep. You need your rest," Theia announced and put her arm out towards me. "But before you go, Cloudburst, please follow me. We need to step outside for me to teleport you to her."

Why would she ask me to exit the castle? She never has before. Don't tell me this is some sort of trick.

I was surprised when she didn't answer me silently in my thoughts but instead waited until we were completely away from the others to resume our conversation.

There must be something important she is about to share.

Flashforward to CHP. 12 of ECHOES OF EUNOIA

The color-coded curse was coming to an end. Zayika had completed almost every harsh and devastatingly dire command, nearing final moments of experiencing the polar opposite of sobriety. Her dress became stained with blood. Her hair was forever changed by the dye and hex that devoured free thought, peace of mind, and ultimately solace. She tore Amira's life away, prompting the ultimate downward spiral of tragic events in the mind of Eunoia as the point of no return was officially crossed. There was no coming back from what was done. Right as Amira let out her last breath of air, her life over, it had become final.

It was time for the end.

Zekiel was overwhelmed with grief. Sorrow panged at his insides. He could no longer withstand enduring the pain of loss and regret of previous choices he made and those he didn't. He stared deeply into the eyes of the clouds, confronting the type of person who he truly saw himself to be. He believed there was no way out. Once he took off Anon's wings, he felt as though his fate was officially sealed, that he had come full circle to the moment he almost took his own life at his apartment complex. The portal to the unknown opened up once more, and there was nowhere else he could possibly think of wanting to be but in absolute silence; to swim amongst stars for the rest of eternity. Free from his reputation. Free from remembering the faces of those he loved and believed should still be alive instead of himself. Free from pain. Nero tried to talk him out of stepping inside, but Zekiel's choice was already made even before he woke up on the hills next to Saige. After sharing final words with his opponent, he thought to himself while stepping into nothingness, *take me to the void.*

Once he disappeared, only four fighters remained: Zayika, Anon, Jameson, and Nero. The storm was in full effect as they grew accustomed to the freezing cold. Grains of sand swept past them quickly and stung like the cuts of several small razor blades. Thunder boomed to the beat of a rhythmic drum, and the lightning striking down sounded like riffs from an electric guitar. The purple sky cast down a distorted layer of color over each of them as the ultimate rug of stability was tugged out from under their feet. The ground shook at the words Zayika and Anon exchanged with one another. Eunoia was ready for the mess of events to finally be over, so disappointed in all that the representatives corrupted and controlled.

"You know who was supposed to lead us, the starting six, from the beginning?" Zayika asked as she ran in circles around Anon, unable at all to stand still. "I was. You never led any of us."

"Neither of you did," Nero interjected, speaking on what he felt and partially observed. "It seems that you both were so busy focusing on your own priorities that you didn't look at the bigger picture here."

"That doesn't matter now," she responded. *It's too late to undo what has been set in stone.*

"So…" Anon found enough courage to speak out loud as he sweated nervously. He felt tightness in his throat and a pit of despair growing in his stomach at facing the consequences of his actions; of leaving her behind. "Is this really the end?"

"Yes. So, do you have any last words?" Zayika asked after marching over to him, feeling the urge to prolong their exchange for as long as possible before it was revealed who was going to lose their life next.

Anon listened to the waves and wind moving around them. *Please tell me there's some sort of good that can come out of this; I truly doubt I can defeat her with myself still intact.* "I guess not. I don't know what to say."

"Oh, come on. You're always running your mouth faster than you can think. You can muster up something."

Anon bit his lip and delivered pure honesty with his next choice of words, detailing the hopes he had for every person they each got close to and sharing memories with the original starting six in their journey. Then, he closed with a bold and brash sentiment, "I have no regrets." *I can't regret anything up until now,* he told himself, *there's no use in regretting anything. I can't waste what emotions I have left by giving even more undeserving power to the past mistakes I cannot change. I have to be strong in the face of adversity, no matter the cost. I'd want Amira to be proud of me.*

Zayika began to cry. A single warm tear fell over her skin, blending in with the drops of rain. "Alright then."

"You aren't just angry, are you? You are upset. I can tell. You are hurt… aren't you Zayika?"

"You still don't understand who I am? I am crying because I'm happy. Ending you, Amira, and everything else is like having a torturous itch finally scratched. I will finally be able to breathe." She wiped an outpour of tears she couldn't hold in away and tried to silence Eunoia's thoughts that were dominating her mind and senses. "This is over now."

Anon finally spoke, "Amira…"

Both became charged with emotional energy and filled with frustrated desperation for their suffering to end, to take it out on one another. Zayika strode towards him with stars pouring out from her hands, swirling around each finger, as her hair blended in with the stormy scenery around them. Anon was terrified as he tried to hide his emotions and charge towards her. His lightning stung through his veins and shocked his skin as he kept one hand raised higher than the other. Neither spoke another word out loud as their eyes met. They suppressed reliving the flashes of several memories in their minds of their tarnished journey together that had led them to the point of no return.

Zayika's boots were covered in sand as she traveled faster over to him. Wind blowing through her wet hair, she told her stars to form into a vibrant lasso that she shot out towards Anon. She tugged on his torso to yank him forwards. The gap between them was closed quickly as he had no choice but to trip and be pulled practically off his feet at her command. He tried to fight against her strength, but he was unable to set himself free. He took his trembling hand and reached for her neck as her eyes were focused on the stars she encompassed him in. Anon's eyes were almost lifeless as he could hardly hold his head high enough to look up at her. He charged up a lightning strike to command over her throat, and with the stinging heat, he dug through her melting flesh to attack it, tearing it out so quickly that she didn't realize what had happened at first.

It was in that same second she used her stars to eat into his flesh, stripping it away layer by layer until he was completely disemboweled, with no way to heal himself or ask for any help. Their abilities shone brightly together in a messily devastating confrontation. Lightning shot down from the sky. The clouds watched as Anon's insides fell out onto the shore, some of the waves coming in far enough to take his blood with them back into the ocean.

Anon knew that Zayika wouldn't heal him. There was no chance because he also knew that there was no possibility she would heal herself.

The anglerfish Hippo wailed out in misery as it laid near Amira's body, needing to go back into the waters but also needing her companion to wake up and fight by her side as they used to. Her cries filled the air as yellow stars and blue lightning collided in a mix unlike anything else seen before on the planet.

As Anon realized his time was up, he looked at Amira so that she would be the last person he saw before dying.

Zayika looked past them, over in the distance at the green hills, and smiled as she saw herself dressed in all black dancing on them in the rain; her hair was brown and flowing in the wind.

The two fell to the ground lifelessly next to one another.

Cloudburst

Present

Right as we went through the doors, I was desperate for an explanation. "You could've just taken me back to the waterfall from inside. Why are you —"

"Shh." Theia spoke in a hushed manner even though we were already out of hearing range from everyone else, "Cloudburst… I'm sending you back to Earth, okay?"

"I know that," I replied helplessly.

"You don't get it." A glimmer of happiness shone in her eyes, accompanied by a tear. "You don't have to come back."

"What?" *What is she saying?* "Are you kidding right now?"

"No. I would never play with another's emotions like that. Don't come back. We shouldn't have kept you here this long. You deserve to be set free. You deserved to be free a long time ago."

"What? Really?" I was skeptical, still guarding my emotions. "You're really being serious right now? What's made you decide this? I have so many questions if you are speaking the truth."

"Of course I'm being truthful. You are going home."

My heart felt as though it was going to beat out of my chest. My eyes welled with tears as I pulled her into a tight hug.

"Theia, I don't know how to thank you."

"Thank me by not taking your life for granted and be careful what you put into your mind." She hugged me back and held on, our embrace drawn out for a few moments, something that I never thought would happen.

My body tensed as I pulled away from her. "But I'm not sure I can completely forgive you for what you've done to me so far too, though. You aren't blameless. I can't forgive what you've put me through and what you enabled the others, especially Aadavan, to do to me."

"I know that. I honestly don't expect you to forgive me. I'm not sending you back to be redeemed. I think I'm too far gone for that to be a valid option." She looked through the window uneasily as tears streamed down her cheeks. She wiped them away with the back of her hand. "You need to go before the others catch onto our conversation and see us out here like this. For all we know, they could be watching from the windows. This isn't any of their business."

I didn't know what to say. I nodded. Eventually, I was able to reply, "Okay."

Theia redirected the subject back to our previous one. "Bring the woman to the hills as far away from us as you can. Once I know you are back, you will be sent to Earth, and you will never see any of this afterwards. You will never see any of us again. Your body, and life, will return to normal as much as possible."

"Okay," I repeated as my muscles began to relax for the first time in weeks. I took a step backward. *I have to try to reach out to the families of those who've died; I wish I could provide them all with an explanation.* "Theia. Despite everything that's happened... I hope one day you can be sent back to Earth and escape the control of this planet. I hope you are able to cleanse your past in whatever way possible."

"I'm not sure about that."

"Just because you made bad choices doesn't mean they have to define you for the rest of your life. Mistakes are not a life sentence. Regret isn't either. Even with several bad choices made in a row. Move on Theia. You have the power to. They don't make you a bad person. No matter how lost you are, you can always find your way back to where you came from. People can change." I gave her a serious nod. "You can even leave them here and get a fresh start... if you know what I'm saying?"

"I could never do that, not after all Aadavan has done for me. I love him with all my heart. Also, what about Lorelai? She is one of my closest friends. I will remain by their sides until death. I will never value anything more than loyalty."

"Why is that?" I asked.

"It's the truest thing we can offer one another. It doesn't rely on only faith alone of the unseen, but it can be seen and felt through actions. We can provide loyal stability to those we love. It's time for you to return to those you love the most. I'm sorry for taking your life away from you." Theia put her hand up once more. "Goodbye Cloudburst. Thank you, dearly, for all the time and energy you have sacrificed. I know how valuable all of it was."

"Goodbye, Theia."

With her finger lighting up in the air, she carried out her task again, and with that simple, powerful gesture, I was sent back at once.

Faster than the blink of an eye, as she wasted no time, I was back at the waterfall. The air gave me goosebumps, and I watched my breath waft into it as I tried to adjust to the stark temperature change. I was hardly given a heads up before being sent back.

I saw two women at the crime scene when I arrived. The one that Lorelai described to me from her vision was nearby, trying to get her camera steady enough to take photos of the victim on the ground. The other woman had red hair and was shaking her head and looked agitated. There were several bystanders nearby which made it particularly difficult to remain unseen while going after her. I tried to navigate through the buildings and between the trees to stay hidden. She was catching on to me following.

Even though the others around me also stared at them, I didn't blend in enough for attention to not be drawn to me. One pointed up to the windows of the building where I tried to hide to get closer. I tuned out their conversation and instead focused on closing the extra distance in an unsuspicious way, well aware of the fact that the three representatives were watching me and I didn't want them to think that I was wasting any time.

Her eyes locked with mine through the window while I was on the third story. Neither of us broke eye contact, and I was unable to keep myself from smiling.

What's coming over me? I'd noticed small, but unhinged, changes taking place within me ever since I was morphed with something from Theia; involuntary reactions that I was looking forward to finally being free from.

Get out of her view and go over to the waterfall. The light will pull her in. Just like the anglerfish attracts its prey. I have to make the capture fast.

As she became preoccupied with taking photos and talking to her partner again, I left the room I was in, headed down the stairs, and traveled on foot over to the waterfall. Each step felt weighed down by regret as I went along, ready to discover if Theia was being truthful in our last conversation, if I would really escape them after this.

I went behind the waters and waited patiently for her to be lured in by the light. As soft droplets hit my skin, I got chills. My heart rate climbed as each second drew me closer to freedom, yet another victim to captivity and suffering. I accidentally stepped on a tree branch, snapping it under my foot.

Stay quiet. Don't mess this up. My entire life is at stake.

The wind grew stronger. The speed of it seemed to pick up with every breath I took. I waited in the shadows patiently as the two continued talking.

Please don't take much longer. I want to speed this along.

I waited for the waterfall's light to draw the woman over to me. One was speaking with such a shaky voice that it was difficult to make out what she said while scribbling notes down messily on a notepad.

As more time passed, I grew impatient and anxious.

Flashforward to Four Months after CHP. 12 of
ECHOES OF EUNOIA

Almost half a year had passed since the destruction of Eunoia, the final wish spoken into existence after Nero won the last challenge and decided to send Theia back to Earth with him. Once they returned to their normal human state with all their abilities and otherworldly traits stripped away from them, they didn't utter a word to one another. They each hoped to never cross paths again, knowing all of the terrible torment they put others through to survive until the end.

They arrived where they first left to the unknown: the waterfall. It was an eerie sight. The sound of rushing water was no more, and there was almost always a storm lingering up above that carried down below to whoever visited. The trees seemed fragile as they withered. Hardly any leaves remained, and everything felt hollow. Empty.

Nero ran in a different direction once he got there, silent and desperate to find and speak to his family again.

Theia didn't run at all. She instead stayed at the broken falls for many hours. She had no family to return to; those she was closest to she had already lost. Lorelai passed away, and so did the love of her life — Aadavan. She stood in pure silence as she reminisced about both of them; the first time they saw the portal open together; Aadavan holding her lovingly in his arms as they swayed back and forth; Lorelai carefully checking around each corner to ensure safety for each of them. *Oh, how I miss their presence. I'd give anything to see and speak with them again about our dreams.*

She found herself living in the same small town she had once hoped to escape from, returning to the empty falls while clinging to memories from a past she couldn't get out of her head. It was an experience that no one else on Earth would believe she went through. She felt that a piece of her heart had been left on Eunoia, along with her mind, two things she knew she couldn't ever fully get back. Theia thought about what she could remember of the past, back when many feelings previously made up the majority of her being.

One day as she rested near the falls with a blank stare ahead at the rubble of rocks, dirt, and branches where the water used to magically flow… she could not believe who she saw as footsteps approached from off in the distance.

Theia hardly had any energy left when she turned to see who was there. She hadn't spoken out loud or seen any other human up close in weeks, but her mouth fell open at the sight of him. She was reminded of when she first meditated on Eunoia near the blue castle and he appeared right in front of her.

"Cloudburst," she said, giving him a very small smile.

"Theia." He kept his face expressionless.

She was shocked as he took a seat beside her on the dirt and stared up ahead at the nature that was destroyed before them and thought, *I can't believe he is here right now. That he is even beside me… after all the wrong I did to him. After everything he has been put through. How can he even look at me right now?*

"You can't hear my thoughts anymore?" *Right? Like right now?* He tested them out.

She smiled larger. "No, no I can't. I'm speaking the truth."

"What a relief," he sighed and nervously laughed on the inside. *I really hope that she's not still able to.* His life was finally returning as close to normal as possible.

"Why are you here right now? Why would you ever return to this place?" She didn't take her attention off of him.

"Been keeping an eye on it. I noticed you came here and needed to know that my life is truly my own again, that I wasn't somehow dreaming," Cloudburst told her while still looking up ahead and refusing to make eye contact. "Thank you for bringing me back here and keeping your word."

"Of course." Theia inhaled deeply. "Do you want to know what happened in the second fight to the woman you brought before you left? Amira?"

"No. Please don't tell me. I don't want whatever happened on my conscience along with everything else."

"Okay."

He began to stand up to leave without saying anything else before Theia asked one last question, "What is your name? Your real one?"

He sighed deeply while pondering his reply. "I'm not going to tell you that. Learning someone's name, who they are, carries a great deal of importance. I believe that it's shared amongst those who are deserving of vulnerability and respect. Our names carry the power of our individual living entities."

Theia looked back at the waterfall wreckage with a quivering lip and silently nodded with crossed arms.

"I don't want you to ever know my real name." Cloudburst said while starting to leave, "It is the one thing that I will rightfully keep as my own. I will protect it for as long as I live."

As his voice trailed off, the only sounds that could be heard were from the wind. A colorful storm was emerging from the sky, displaying itself in an array of green, pink, and orange in the clouds.

The power of the mind was revealed.

Present

The waterfall was surrounded by handfuls of onlookers who couldn't take their eyes off of the aftermath of an awful crime. That evening, a fight between two men broke out that quickly got out of hand. There were hardly any eyewitnesses who saw the true events which ultimately led to the death of one of them, who was rigid on the ground. Only four people who were visiting the falls and about to head home heard and observed the final moments of the confrontation and fight that turned gruesomely physical.

They recalled what they saw to Arcadia as Amira kept close by. Each detailed the argument they heard, not completely sure of what they were speaking about. They could only recall the mention of a drink both men had drank not too long before things escalated.

Arcadia inhaled sharply at their words. Her hand swayed unsteadily as she dragged the ballpoint pen over the bright yellow notepad.

"D-did they mention what it was that they drank?" she asked timidly, accidentally tripping over her words.

"No. Not exactly," an eyewitness responded. "They only said that they found it nearby, I guess. Sounded like they shouldn't have been messing around with it at all in the first place."

More curious passersby started to fill in along the caution tape that enclosed the area.

"You can say that again," Arcadia replied breathily and then raised her voice to add, "Anything after that? Did you hear anything that they were talking about?"

Another observer jumped in, "They just sounded really drunk to me."

"Well, they did mention some sort of hole, with stars, like an opening I think? Near the falls?" the third person added.

Arcadia dropped her dark magenta-colored pen.

"Are you okay?" Amira asked, picking it up for her. "Do you need to step away for a moment? Need some fresh air?"

"I've been doing this work longer than you. Of course, I am okay," Arcadia snapped back and tucked the notepad under her right arm. "We will ask you more questions later, though. A break wouldn't hurt, I suppose," she told the witnesses.

As they walked off to a corner, Amira kept her focus on her partner. "This is a lot to take in."

"Yes, it is." Arcadia's attention was caught by the huge influx of people trying to hear and see what was going on near the trees. "There are way too many people here. Do they not have anything else better to do? Instead of watching a trainwreck, they should mind their own business enough to ensure they don't get in one of their own."

Amira stayed silent in response and sensed another layer to Arcadia's rising anxiety.

"I mean, seriously, why are they just standing around?" The sound of the rushing falls and crowd chatter was so loud that she raised her voice with a strained throat to be heard over it, "You all need to step back! Can't you see that this is a crime scene?" she shook her head. "Get away from the area!"

As the two continued their conversation and investigation, Cloudburst followed them closely, his focus set on Amira. The lingering effects of the Eunoia still had an impact on his body as he traveled from the buildings, trees, and by the waterfall itself to complete his final mission. He wanted so badly to finish this so he could be on his way to freedom, which was unfortunately at the expense of many. After so many restless days, sleepless nights, and terrifying encounters with other victims, he was finally able to escape the pull of the planet he wished to never see again.

He glided over as quickly as he could and grabbed Amira by the neck after she spotted him. He used the extra power he was given to speed everything along at an exponential rate, accidentally sending a shockwave through her.

I hope she's okay. I hope that didn't hurt too bad. This will never happen again.

Cloudburst didn't know and couldn't fully grasp the amount of power his own double-edged ability could conjure. He kept Amira from alerting Arcadia by pulling her down onto her back, trying to ignore the flashes of panic inducing memories. For every second, he thought about all the other lives ruined at the hands of Theia, Aadavan, and Lorelai.

Desperate to return to his previous life, but knowing it would never be the same, he carried out their final orders so he could finally escape to Earth for good.

Arcadia hadn't caught sight of what was happening at all to her colleague after wandering off. Instead of looking into her sudden disappearance, she instead remained more focused on the deceased victim at the crime scene, scribbling down more disturbing notes as she inspected the victim's body closely. She tried to stop mentally scolding herself for the mistakes she made, the regret she could hardly fight off, and ultimately the memory of when she visited the falls and left her cursed bottle and past behind at the water. She didn't want Amira to know the truth.

I'm glad she isn't looking over here. I don't want her to somehow get mixed up in this mess too, Cloudburst thought before refocusing his attention back on Amira, one of the names he would never, ever forget.

"Good luck getting back here," he grumbled quietly, forcing her to enter Eunoia with him.

Once he had a hold of her as she fell unconscious, Theia brought them both to the hills right away, as he was told they would be. He walked with her quietly in his arms. His terrible task was almost finished. His life was almost his own again. He'd be free to exercise his own train of thought, beliefs, and individuality without the suffocating hold of someone else's power-hungry grip.

Yet another storm was heading their way, the sky filled with green, purple, and orange. Clouds moved slowly in the sky, blue lightning bolts shooting down harshly and accompanied by deep echoes of thunder.

Cloudburst laid Amira down on one of the hills farthest from the wheat field, ocean, and faction grounds. He knew what was in store for her. He knew who she would soon be meeting, the terrors that she would face, and the horrors she would eventually have to overcome. His shoulders ached, and his muscles were so tight that he'd gotten used to the feelings of pins and needles in them.

Regret ate away at him as he questioned what he should have done differently. As he turned away from her, he let out a deep breath and slowly, but surely, started to finally let it go right as Theia began sending him back to Earth.

He realized then that the terrors of the mind could be escaped, the best parts of the mind could be preserved, and that the mind was ultimately powerful enough to be able to overcome regret.

Cloudburst gave Amira one last final look as he thought, *let's hope your mind survives this challenge.*

THE END

THEIA
Bright Light
Within the brightness of the light,
there is a greyness.
Pleasing others with all my might,
sight lost in the darkness.
A love that burns brighter than the sun,
the beauty of manifestation when two become one.

AADAVAN
Competitive Love
Stars in the only eyes I can drown in.
Challenged to be better in the midst of chaos.
Desperate to impress her elegance and strength.
Embracing the moments of unconditional love,
when dazzling orange clouds fill the sky above.

LORELAI
Thalassophobia
Insecurity
runs deeper than the ocean.
Unfathomable.

CLOUDBURST
Promise
A slave to the mind,
unfairly robbed of time.
Several lessons learned,

many people lost in return.
Freedom finally in my grasp,
my future fully mine at last.
No matter what will come my way,
I'll protect my mind until life fades away.